THE BANE

MARANDA
BAUTSCH

Copyright © 2023 by Maranda Bautsch

All rights reserved.

No part of this publication may be reproduced, distributed, or transmitted in any form or by any means, including photocopying, recording, or other electronic or mechanical methods, without the prior written permission of the publisher, except as permitted by U.S. copyright law.

The story, all names, characters, and incidents portrayed in this production are fictitious. No identification with actual persons (living or deceased), places, buildings, and products is intended or should be inferred.

Book Cover by @oliviaprodesigns

Paperback ISBN: 9798218957506

eBook ISBN: 9798395959980

*To my mirrored soul, my twin sister, my light in dark valleys.
Without you, Mal, this story would not exist.*

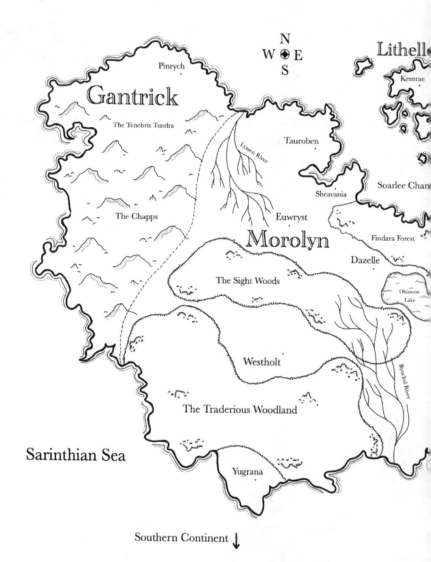

THE BANE

MARANDA
BAUTSCH

Chapter I

Adresia Bellum was running from death.

That's what she told herself, over and over. She would not fail.

This time was better than before. Or was she just exposing the true extent of her skill? She didn't entirely care, not as adrenaline sparked in her veins like wildfire, autumn air whistled in her ears, and sweat trickled down her skin, tanned after an entire summer in the blazing heat.

Light footsteps approached behind. She willed herself faster, swifter. At least until she lurched forward quicker than she could react and slammed into the ground.

"That *tree*," she growled, her grumble of frustration echoing through the forest. And while she wanted to unjustifiably blame her mistakes on that ridiculously inconvenient oak tree, it was really because of her arrogance—because years of training had taught her balance in unstable conditions or unknown territory, and those lessons only ever failed her when she twisted confidence into pride. She pushed herself onto her hands and knees, her sight dancing with stars, and touched her head. The subsequent sharpness and crimson-stained fingers revealed she'd been cut.

Leaves crunched faintly, distantly, and she tightened the grip on her fallen dagger and pressed her back against a thick oak. With a deep inhale, she prepared to confront the tracker. But then the steps halted. Hush consumed the forest.

She carefully peered left, around the tree. No one awaited her. That was what she was supposed to think. But Adresia knew this trick. She sensed what would come next in her bones—because, thank the Goddess, this wasn't death.

This was just a boy.

She whirled to her right, her blade instantly under his chin. He inhaled sharply as if sensing how easily she could slice his flesh with the flick of her wrist. "Why are you attacking Westholt?" she demanded. She didn't need to raise her voice; the soft lethality in her tone had aided her for years. He didn't answer, so she went to repeat her question, but hands were suddenly on her shoulders, shoving her away.

Her weapon flew out of her grasp, but she found her balance just as the boy seethed, "This doesn't concern you." The words were just as irritating as the first time she'd heard them four weeks ago. He couldn't be more than fifteen. What did he think he was fighting for?

Irritated and overconfident, she swung. To her surprise, the boy dodged her strike, and, in half a movement, he caught her foot and sent her crashing into the soil. Before he could back away more than three feet, she wiped the dirt from her face and *lunged*, stomach dropping as they collided. They landed precisely where she'd wanted them to. Before he could take a full breath, she snatched her dagger, pinned him against the soil, and pressed her blade against his neck. Her hair grazed his face as she ordered, "Stop attacking us."

He blew her chocolate strands from his eyes. "Your efforts are wasted."

She pressed harder against the column of his neck. "Are they?"

The look in his eyes was the same as the others—falsified fright in an attempt to survive the warranted retribution of the most neglected province in Morolyn. "Are you going to kill me?" he asked.

She remembered being his age. She remembered feeling strong. She also remembered being brutally reminded that life is unreliable and unpredictable. He'd probably been fed the useless lies that he could somehow pull their kingdom from the wretched state that it was. But he would spill what he knew with a little effort; most of the raiders she'd encountered were harmless. She exhaled and stood. "The more you return, the more compelling that option becomes."

His eyes widened again—with real alarm—and she was debating whether she'd actually sounded that threatening when she realized he wasn't looking at her. She glanced over her shoulder. A cloaked individual was approaching, two curved blades hanging from both hands. When Adresia looked back, the boy was already sprinting away. She spun with a groan. "*Great*, Cota. You scared away my only hostage." Stopping before her, Cota sheathed his blades and pulled back his hood to reveal golden hair glowing in the evening sunbeams, emerald green eyes, and a handsomely sun-kissed face. She strapped her dagger back to her belt before noticing her best friend's frown. "What?" she asked.

"You're bleeding," he said.

She crossed her arms. "I tripped."

"It should be cleaned."

"It's *fine*, Cota."

Ignoring her response, he flipped open the pack under his cloak and grabbed a cloth and leather skin—prepared as always. She had a tendency to hurt herself. Accidentally, of course. "That didn't look like a hostage situation," he remarked with half a smile. "You could've gone after him."

She waved a hand. "It's not worth it."

Water spilled onto the cloth. "They'll be back. We'll find out something then."

"You didn't catch anyone either?"

He rose and turned her head to clean the dried blood that had dripped down her face. "We never do."

She huffed even though it was exactly what she'd expected, and, in her irritation and despite knowing her protests were useless, she muttered, "I can do it myself."

He glanced at her face before stuffing the bloody cloth into the bag. "I know."

He grabbed a second clean cloth and gingerly swept her hair behind her ear. The heat of his fingers lingering on her jaw were like tiny flames against her skin. Her concerns seemed to drift away like ashes in the wind. "You're always so…warm," she said.

"We *do* live in the second warmest province in the kingdom."

She bit back her smile. "*Of course*. I wasn't insinuating anything else."

"And here I was, thinking you were complimenting me."

"What would I have been complimenting, may I ask?"

"My alluring personality, perhaps." His eyes twinkled with the sort of mischief that had resulted in them chopping wood for a week as children.

"Well, you *do* know how to charm someone with your hands." Heat instantly rushed up her neck. By the Goddess, had she said that out loud?

She shifted on her toes to break the silence. As if snapping from a trance, Cota cleared his throat and lifted his attention from wherever it had dropped back to her wound. "This might sting," he said.

The warning barely registered, and when he didn't move, she urged, "Just do it already—"

She hissed as the cloth met her skin and pain shot through her head. "I warned you," he purred with his ridiculously infectious smile.

"You took forever." She hoped her face was no longer flushed. "Lady Jessanite could have done it faster."

"Lady Jessanite is probably older than the village," he refuted, pulling away to grab a silver tin. When he opened it, they both peered inside; the salve was running dangerously low.

"We shouldn't waste that," she said.

"You need it."

"It's just a scratch."

"We'll get more. Just—let me—" She blocked his advances twice before he dropped his hand in defeat. "Why won't you let me help you?"

"I don't *need* it," she said.

There was no way to explain it—how, recently, every time she got a slash or scrape, it healed thrice as fast as it should. A small cut like the one on her head would be completely gone by morning, if not in a few hours. It was practically hidden on her hairline, so she only hoped Cota wouldn't notice tomorrow. Perhaps her body had somehow adapted to two decades of consistent injuries...or perhaps it was something else. Something like the stories her parents had recited to her as a child.

"Besides," she added, "we can't afford more right now." Cota clenched his jaw, but calmly put the supplies back into the bag. When he finished, she said sheepishly, "Thank you for always caring for me."

He couldn't hide the smile that bloomed on his lips; he was never one to brood. "Well, when I'm old and wrinkly, I'll call in all of your debts."

She rolled her eyes before sighing. "That was a good run. It's reassuring to know they aren't attacking with the intent to harm anyone, at least."

He pulled his bag back over his shoulder. "You don't need reassurance, Adresia. You're a better defender than everyone in Westholt—*especially* Brazen."

Brazen, the village boy who'd gotten her into more trouble than all of the other villagers combined, despised her just as much as she did him. She mimicked the high pitched squeals of every young Lady at the recent announcement, fanning her face with her hands. "Don't you know? He's going to be a *knight*! Can you believe it? Morolyn will finally be safe!" Cota grinned, but Adresia's delight scattered like a shadow in the sun as she retorted, "Sure it will. Everything will go back to normal now that one person from Westholt has been accepted into the Shield for the first time in a decade." She kicked a stray rock and watched it skid away. "No one cares what we're doing—that the two of us come out here week after week instead of Harley." The Duchess of Westholt had done close to nothing to stop the raids; she hadn't even seemed *bothered* by them. It was so unlike the woman. "Everyone looks at me and sees what they always have—all of the mistakes I've spent the past five years trying to correct. They think they know who I am, but they don't." Her voice quieted. "Maybe I never should have changed."

"That girl was lost," Cota began, "and broken, and *terrified*. But you did change; we both did. And that's not a bad thing. With everything we've been through...these people *never* could have handled who you might have become if you hadn't—if you had let that darkness overtake you. They don't know; they don't understand. And maybe they never will. You just have to do the best you can to show them."

She exhaled loudly and dragged her hands through her hair. "I just...I hate that we don't know what the Queen is doing. I hate that whatever it is, it's causing these riots to arouse so much panic. To create chaos over who knows what. I don't know what to do anymore."

Cota grabbed her hands, forcing her to meet his solemn stare. "I see that you're trying. Despite being beyond our responsibilities, you still do everything you can to retain the peace. I see how you can't stand these threats and what they might mean—because just like me, I know you don't want another night like that to happen again."

Another like the one five years ago.

Vivid images and memories flashed in her mind: her parents screaming for her to run; Cota clutching her, begging her to leave with him; his parents' corpses on the floor after failing to help their closest friends.

Adresia had been fifteen, Cota a year older, when royal guards had stormed her house and attacked her family. The night had ended with both of them as orphans.

She hardened her gaze on the ground. Just the thought of Queen Narissa's crimes made her furious. Rageful.

"I'm here." Cota's voice brought her back from thinking about the other part of that night, the part that had made her hate Morolyn's ruler almost as much as the brutal murdering of her parents. "I've never stopped preparing for the next time those guards come."

Because after what she did, they would come back. They had to.

"I'm sorry," she said. She always did this; blamed herself for their deaths even though neither of them knew the truth behind the assassination.

"It wasn't your fault. What happened, happened to both of us, and if everyone in this sorry excuse of a province wants to judge you for your actions afterwards, then they must not be paying enough attention." His gaze was soft and fierce. "We've both done things we regret. We've both gone through the aftershocks. But I told you I'd never leave you, and I don't plan on it anytime soon. So don't listen to anything those fools think they know. *I* know you, and that's all that matters."

Her lips tugged at the corners the same time village bells echoed in the distance. They glanced toward it, then each other, and, with nothing but matching grins, they raced toward Westholt, jumping over fallen logs and averting hanging branches in the narrow path.

When they reached the edge of the market square, they slowed to a swift walk, breathing hard. Adresia swerved around a hasty couple that nearly knocked her over and met Cota in the center of the bustling area. "I beat you," she sang cheerily.

He breathed a laugh, and they watched a group of workers return from the Traderious Woodland. Wagons wove in and out of the busy area, carting around all sorts of oak wood: chopped, stripped, carved, rotted. Full loads headed toward the South Road where they would be transported to Yugrana, the closest—and only—province in present contact with Westholt; emptied loads headed back to the sites where they would refill after another laborious day of chopping, cutting, and exporting. Lumber: it was the livelihood of Westholt.

Despite their lack of trade with the rest of the kingdom, this year had been extremely busy. No one had received a break in months. But dependence on the southern province to combat their solitude from the crown didn't bother anyone. Westholt offered something few other places could provide: a chance at a simple, fulfilled life. Most days that ideal was the only thing that kept Adresia from going straight to the Queen and getting retribution for what had happened to her parents. She wouldn't ruin this chance. She wouldn't give up everything her family had fought and died for her to have.

Whatever that might be.

"I bet you're overjoyed to return tomorrow," Cota quipped.

She looked at him sideways. "I'm just glad autumn is finally here. The summer heat I can handle. The incessant babbling of Frey-guess-where-my-parents-are-now-Holsen? I don't think I can stand another day. At least the *trees* don't talk."

A smirk. "It's only another month. You'll survive."

The thought of being replaced during the colder months—or rather, the mildly warm months with an occasional cool breeze—made her want to dance. She would relax with her best friend during the entirety of winter until someone requested his tutoring services or she resumed working in the spring.

Cota gestured toward the shops and booths. "Care to join?" She peered past him, and although she didn't care about the villagers' stares...the thought of interacting with any of them right now seemed more than daunting. She shook her head. "I'll meet you at home," he added with a smile before parting.

Avoiding the dozen workers carrying an enormous log atop their shoulders, Adresia crossed the square and swept into an alley, taking her usual shortcut across the province. Unsheathing the dagger from her belt, she carefully observed it.

It had been harder to hold back this time. Since the day her father had placed a sword in her hands and taught her to defend herself, he had always emphasized her incredible skill. Cota believed it *was* because her father—one of the most renowned Generals in the war—had instructed her during her youth. But what her best friend didn't know was that she was suppressing her strength. She had been for years. It wasn't just a result of her upbringing. It was a constant restlessness in her that never stopped, never depleted.

For four years, she didn't train with Cota. The activity itself hadn't deterred her, although the memories that the weapons and dented trees brought with them were sometimes so difficult to bear that she couldn't breathe. After that night, after her parents, something had awakened in her. And stepping into the woods with Cota, feeling it roiling in her veins and fusing within her bones...she'd walked away, if only to protect him from herself. But she hadn't been able to remain idle and inactive and still. She never could. That thing within her soul wasn't so easily stifled. So for four years, she'd honed her body in private—in a way neither Cota nor her father had ever known about.

A year ago, when she'd approached the edge of the woods and had spotted those familiar paths and training glens, her chest had finally felt like it wouldn't cave in. So she'd found Cota, asked him if she could resume training with him, and he'd agreed. He hadn't commented on her unaltered prowess, but she knew he'd noticed; observing was in his nature. He studied people and settings as easily as she predicted where someone would strike next in combat. But if he didn't want to call her out, she would let the memory fade—for his sake if not hers. He couldn't know how powerful she truly was. No one could.

Not yet.

Adresia skidded to a halt, realizing she'd passed her street long ago. The Sight Woods were a wall of outrageously tall redwoods before her—the defined northern border of Westholt. A border that no one passed.

White flashed somewhere ahead, then disappeared. She didn't notice anything odd as she peered through the trees, but when a chill spider-walked down her spine, something in her told her to run, to hide, to do anything but *be* here.

They had never been assigned to this forest. Only south, in the Traderious Woodland. Why they avoided the north, she didn't know. There were stories about things in it; things across the continent, too. But who believed the lunatics who recited such tales? They were soft bedtime fables, uttered around fires in hushed voices. Narrations of magical creatures and otherworldly abilities; faeries and nymphs and more beings than they could count.

Legends claimed there was a battle eons ago that dawned the current era of magic: The Fallen War. The Creators of the world—the God and Goddess—had gone head to head. Very few know what truly happened, if anyone at all, but as the story goes, there was great darkness before. Evil plagued good, and it was that imbalance that sparked the cataclysmic event. When the War ended, the imbalance still remained—and the God and Goddess were never heard of again. They were still worshipped along with the minor gods, but no one knew if they were still there; if the Creators even existed at all. And then, fifty years ago, every mystical being and trace of magic—it all disappeared.

As if everything had gone into hiding.

Five decades had passed and it continued to be talked about as if it prevailed. There hadn't been a single presentation of power over the years, but many wanted to believe they remained: those with control over the elements, with powers of healing, strength, and shapeshifting; beings who had the hearts to aid ordinary humans, to use their gifts for mundane tasks of farming and building and defending. People say it was pure magic: good. Something Morolyn could possess one day, when mages and pixies and all of the creatures returned. But not while Narissa ruled. Because if she ever obtained something like that...there would be no surviving the damage she could wage. Morolyn was lucky magic disappeared when it did. Only the gods knew what the Queen would have molded their kingdom into if it had remained.

The trees swayed again. It was nothing; probably just a bird or leaf. The woods were safe. Adresia kept telling herself that, even as she sped back to her house, a ball of dread in her stomach. The woods were safe. The blade in her hand was a comforting weight.

The woods were safe.

Adresia opened the front door and headed straight for Cota's room, sheathing her dagger at her waist. He'd be back by now, and with all the reading he did, he had to know something. Her voice echoed through the house. "Cota, do you know what...?" She was three steps down the hall when she halted, took three steps back, and spun into the kitchen, its door already wide open.

Cota sat at the underused, round table with crossed arms. His gaze was set on the man across from him, who beheld her with a pleasant smile. "You have a visitor," Cota stated. Her. Not them. She took a hesitant step into the room.

The stranger, who looked to be only a few years older than them whilst somehow giving the impression he was substantially more experienced than any young Lord she had ever met, provided no doubt of his nobility despite forfeiting such luxuries to travel here. Unsullied clothes, immaculate posture, dark brown hair that looked like it was trimmed often; he was royalty—or as close to royalty as one could be. But the Queen had no family besides her sister, the Princess. So who was he?

The man clasped his hands atop the table. "You must be Lady Darbania."

Her stomach tightened at the name as she slid into the seat beside Cota. There was no comment on her unladylike appearance: pants instead of a dress, unbrushed hair, skin covered in dirt. "I am," she said.

The man's sapphire eyes glinted with a luring curiosity as he looked between them. "My name is Caspian Harvryd. I'm the Hand of Queen Narissa—and currently at your service."

Cota's hands dropped to his lap, but she ignored the sudden pressure in her chest and yielded to her curiosity, a distracting habit. "Aren't you quite...*young* to be the Queen's Hand?" Out of the corner of her eye, Cota gave a subtle look of warning.

The Hand smiled again, his stubbled cheeks crinkling with the movement. "I'm younger than most accustomed nobles, yes, but I've been in Court since I was a boy. It's all I know. I'm more than fit for my position."

She pressed her lips together. "What exactly is your purpose here, Lord Hand?" The title sounded foreign in her mouth. She hoped she'd remembered correctly after so many years.

He reached into his jacket. When he retracted it, grasping a folded parchment, Adresia relaxed the hand that had drifted toward her weapon. "The Queen has tasked me with delivering this letter to you—" He placed it before her— "as well as ensuring the safety of your travels."

"Travels?" Cota asked.

The Hand gestured toward the letter. "Most of your questions will be answered once you read that."

Adresia knew exactly what it said. But knowing waiting would only prolong the inevitable, she swallowed the lump in her throat and grabbed the parchment from the unworn, wooden table. The snap of the red seal—the Queen's signet—resounded in the quiet room. Adresia quickly scanned the contents. Once. Twice. The words couldn't seem to leave her head, stunning her into silence as they rattled in her skull. She'd expected it, yes, but a part of her had hoped...

Concerned, emerald eyes scanned her face. "What does it say?" Cota asked.

One breath wasn't long enough to prepare herself. "To Lady Darbania," Adresia read aloud. "You have been summoned to Dazelle by the sovereign leader of Morolyn, Her Majesty, Queen Narissa Vander. The laws are resolute. Refusal equates to a death sentence." She wasn't sure if Cota was breathing. Her own bones seemed locked in place. "I have entrusted my Hand to retrieve and accompany you back to the castle. Further instruction will be given upon your arrival. Prayers for safe travels. Signed by Her Majesty."

Adresia had nothing to offer the Queen. Both her and Cota had rejected their inherited earldom five years ago, those commitments burned alongside their homes. And yet, Narissa wanted her. Why not Cota, though? He was Earl of Darbania. Adresia loosed a long breath. Wondering why she was special didn't matter. There was nothing she could do; nothing that didn't end in punishment and death. Avoiding the Queen's call was the first step to losing everything she loved—and Adresia would risk nothing if it meant losing Cota. She couldn't lose anyone else.

"Do you know why the Queen requires my presence?" she asked.

"You are one of the few Countesses residing in Westholt," the Hand replied. "Although contact between our provinces have been sparse, I thought you would have expected such a visit sooner or later. I suppose I was mistaken."

"Certainly not," she refuted. "I'm just...surprised at the timing."

"Because of your reluctance to embrace your noble obligations?" he asked. Her brows rose, but the Hand just smiled. "I don't hold your past against you. There is no reason to fear retaliation."

After the more-than-tiring day she'd had, she didn't have the energy to ask what that meant. "So you don't know what the Queen wants?"

That smile dwindled, but didn't fade entirely. "I'm afraid not."

A moment of silence passed in which her heart was beating so loud she swore both men could hear it. "I desire Lord Darbania to accompany me," she suddenly blurted.

Understanding the words as agreement, the Hand said, "That can be arranged."

She hid her relief, aware that any hint of further disinclination, of weakness, could—*would*—be used against her, and firmly replied, "Thank you."

The Hand rose and stepped toward the door. "Pack your things, Lord and Lady Darbania. The guards are staying outside the province so as to not cause any disruption to the activities."

Or, Adresia thought, *because they want my departure to remain discreet.*

"They'll meet us at the front gates at dawn to escort us back to Dazelle," the Hand continued. "It's quite the journey through the Sight Woods." He grabbed the latch. "Be prepared for anything. You never know what's out there."

Adresia didn't know if he meant in the woods or Dazelle.

Chapter 2

That evening arrived all too quick. Everything seemed to be happening before it could be processed. Time seemed to be stealing the precious comforts Cota Bowyer had come to realize had never been his to claim.

From the door frame of her room, Cota watched Adresia fill a satchel with the few personal items she owned at her bed. How she was faring, he didn't know. He still felt...stunned. Like he was in a daze. And when she glanced at the desk across the room a third time, a pile of ink and parchment atop it, he prompted, "Is there something on your mind?"

She set down the tunic she was folding. "Do you think this is really such an awful thing?" His responding approach was almost involuntary, and he stopped at her bed as she finished, "We don't know what she wants. We shouldn't assume the worst."

"We abandoned our noble duties five years ago, Adresia. Regardless of the crown's absence here, we're lucky to have gone undisturbed for as long as we have."

"So that's it?" She looked at him. "You honestly believe she just wants to punish me for my desertion?"

He *hoped* not, but where the Queen was involved...

"If that's her intention," she continued, "then why not finish what she started? Why not send another assassin? And why just me?"

He didn't know. He'd gone through every possibility, every reason, and he hadn't the slightest *clue* as to why the Queen would want Adresia—*just* Adresia. "We're walking into this blind," he said.

"She gave us *nothing* in that letter." Nothing except the threatening extent of her authority when it came to her citizens' obedience.

Adresia squeezed his shoulder. "I haven't seen you uneasy in a long time. It's making me nervous."

With a mumbled, "Sorry," he dragged a hand over his face and didn't bother correcting her claim: *she* didn't get nervous. Not anymore. She made sure there wasn't a threat to be nervous about. He wasn't blind; there were things he didn't know, things she wouldn't talk about. But she had more than enough reason not to share, and he wasn't going to make her. His parents' death had scarred him, but *her*...something had broken that night. It was precisely why he made sure she wasn't around on the nights when *his* grief was still too much, when the nightmares dragged him from sleep and it took everything in him to keep from bursting into her room to make sure she was alive.

She had never seen him break. Never.

Adresia's voice sliced through his thoughts. She was standing at the messy desk. "I think we should look at it in another light. The opportunities this summoning presents... We've never had a chance like this."

He crossed his arms. "That is, if she doesn't take away everything we care about."

"Yes, if we survive the encounter," she said wryly.

"I'm serious. What future awaits us?"

"*I'm* serious. We've both heard the rumors. These raiders claim they simply want to stir panic in Westholt, but there *is* something going on. The atrocities we've witnessed are horrific and unjustifiable."

Very few could claim Narissa was an admired ruler. Admittedly, she'd kept Morolyn out of foreign wars while retaining respect from the other kingdoms of Felbourne: Gantrick, Tethoris, and Lithelle. But inside these borders, the Queen did naught to win the people's favor. While the wealthy, privileged citizens were captivated by the fortunes of Dazelle, her name was feared across their land. Even in their detached province, they heard stories. And the two of them knew what she was capable of on a level no other person in Westholt could understand. She was a monster and a murderer and nothing more.

"One day," Adresia continued, eyeing the papers atop the desk once more, "she will *slip*, and when that day comes, there won't be enough soldiers in her castle to protect her from that repercussion."

Cota looked at the desk again. "You've been busy."

"I've been scouring our history. It isn't unusual for nobles to be summoned, but the Queen hasn't communicated with Westholt for years, and now she suddenly decides to summon *me*?"

"So...you've been looking for correlating factors between the nobles at Court?"

Adresia nodded.

"But you haven't found anything, so you want to go find out why?"

Another slow nod.

He crossed his arms. "That has Narissa's corrupted agenda written all over it."

"So?"

"So give me a compelling reason to be okay with this summoning."

The lantern on the desk illuminated Adresia's tattoo as she shifted on her toes. Wrapping around the outside of her upper left arm, staggered peaks were drawn on either side of an uninked strip, created a mesmerizing pattern: her family crest. Her mother used to draw it on spare bits of parchment when she was bored. She'd even stitched a dress with it too, but, like everything else, it had burned with the rest of their homes. Adresia had gotten it four years ago so she'd never forget; it meant her family lived on, that their legacy was still evident in this world. They would always be with her. Her father had had it tattooed on his chest too, and that's who Cota thought of as Adresia squared her shoulders, face set with that same unyielding courage that had been continuously evident in one of Morolyn's most renowned and respected Generals. "I think we can find out why our parents were killed."

He didn't know why he was surprised. This was *just* like her—to devise a scheme completely insane and act like it was obvious all along. "What, exactly, is your plan? We meet Narissa, and then...what? Ask, 'Excuse me, Your Majesty, sorry if this is a bit odd, but why did you murder our parents?' If securing your demise is your goal, then that's a great strategy."

"We're going whether we like it or not, Cota, and if I can somehow uncover the truth, then I'll do whatever it takes. I want answers—and I'm going to get them."

Whatever it takes.

He almost didn't catch the falter in her features. But the tightness in her jaw, eyes barely narrowed...he'd seen her hide her emotions often enough to know she was keeping something from him, like she tended to do. Something big.

"There's more," he said. He watched her grab a book atop the dresser—a book she'd claimed to hate—and shove it into her bag. And he wouldn't have cared, he would follow her anywhere—except they didn't keep secrets. And whatever this was...it sure felt like one. "Why are you *so* convinced you shouldn't take the first chance you have and run far, far away from here?"

Something like fire flashed in her stormy eyes when she faced him. "Because as much as you say otherwise, what happened five years ago had something to do with me. With Narissa. I just—I *know* it's where I'm meant to be. And I know that doesn't make any sense, but you have to trust me. You have to trust that I know what I'm doing." She grabbed his hand. "Please, Cota. I can't do this without you."

They'd rolled their dice with fate and this was the only move left. So she would take it, no matter the consequences. And that scared him—her willingness to use and risk herself in whatever ways necessary if it meant getting what she wanted; what she needed. It scared him more than he would ever admit. But he trusted her with his life, and he'd made a promise to remain by her side. He wouldn't break that promise.

"We'll go," he consented at last, "to get the answers we deserve."

And despite his apprehension, he marveled at her grin and the flames dancing in her eyes.

Chapter 3

The sun hadn't entirely risen when Adresia ripped the covers away and darted behind her bed, the wooden floor cold under her toes. She sucked in a breath when the door creaked open...and grabbed something to chuck at Cota when his head poked in.

"Good morn—" His eyes went wide as a pillow slammed beside him.

"I thought you were coming to murder me!" she cried, throwing herself back onto the mattress. Not really. She knew she was safe; everyone in Westholt had witnessed her ease with weapons since she was a child. They knew who her father was and who that made her. But her nightmares hadn't relented last night, and she was more than jumpy this morning. "It's too *early*," she groaned through the sheets. Cota snickered, and a moment later, the warm quilts were yanked away. She glared at him. "You're so annoying."

"That's why you like me."

She stuck out her tongue, then scrambled away with a squeal when he managed to pinch her. "You *know* I hate that!" There was a laugh in her voice despite the claim.

Cota chucked the covers back atop her and turned. "Let's take a walk before we go."

"A *walk*?"

"There's something I want you to see."

She groaned. "Can't it wait ten more minutes?"

He was already halfway through the door when he chirped over his shoulder, "It's not long until dawn."

THE BANE

Adresia changed into the only gown she owned. It was as green as the meadows she'd frequently escaped to as a child. Her father had bought it for her five years ago, when all the village girls had bought gowns intended for their twentieth nameday celebration. She hadn't mustered up the courage to put it on three months ago, but now was better than never, she supposed. When she glanced in the tarnished mirror, she felt different, somehow. Comfortable. Beautiful.

It was her mother, she realized. She looked like her mother.

Adresia looped a brown belt around her waist, threw her satchel over her shoulder, and grabbed the dagger at her bedside. As she slipped it into the undetectable pockets her mother had wisely suggested adding, she recalled when Cota had gifted her the weapon a few years prior. He'd made her promise to protect herself, even if she hadn't wanted to train. He couldn't lose her, he'd said. They only had each other.

The blade had aided her more times than Cota would be comfortable knowing.

Adresia didn't look at the house as she left. If her predictions were right, they wouldn't be back anyway. So she descended the last few steps down the porch and found Cota leaning against the wall of a near-collapsing shack down the road, grasping a half-eaten apple. His gaze swept her up and down as she approached, a chill wind scattering dirt and leaves past her feet. He didn't comment; he simply chucked the fruit to her. She easily caught it and took a bite before remarking, "Go on! Lead me to this intriguing matter you won't speak about!"

His voice deepened playfully. "Right this way, m'lady."

Gravel crunched underfoot as he turned. With one last bite, she tossed the fruit onto the ground and trudged after him. As the minutes passed, she attempted to count every tree, but after multiple failures, she conceded defeat and continued ignoring

Cota's frequent backward glances that were nothing but confusing. She loved surprises, but what was he up to?

When the path veered, an unwelcome familiarity crept into her mind. She was so busy trying to figure out what it was that she didn't realize Cota had halted and crashed into him. With a mumbled apology, she backed away. But her lingering amusement sputtered into hollow tension as she beheld the place she hadn't been to in five years.

It was where their parents had died; where their houses had burned to the ground; where their lives had been ruined and stolen from their grasp in mere moments. All that remained was a pile of chipped stone, cracked glass, and permanently scorched ground.

"I know you haven't returned," Cota began, "but I come here sometimes. A few weeks after it happened, I was in a rough state. We both were. It was probably the hardest day for both of us."

She remembered. Brazen had been unveiled as a knight-in-training, and being the heartless individual that he was, he had thanked—*thanked*—the Queen for her contribution. He'd rejoiced in that announcement, finally seizing avid dominance over Adresia after years of taunting. He'd thought it meant he could control her—that he was powerful. Later that day, she'd done something so insanely stupid and impulsive to prove him wrong that even a week later, she hadn't been able to breathe without wincing. It still made her smile, though; Brazen had looked worse when Cota and six other men broke them apart.

"I had this feeling," Cota went on, "like someone was telling me to stay." Her best friend faced her. "So I did. For five years, I've kept coming here. Looking. Watching. Listening."

"For what?"

"To remind myself what our parents believed in."

She swallowed. "Why are you telling me this?"

"Because…sometimes you get this *look*—and I think you forget that they would be proud of us. Of you. I hoped this would remind you."

She blinked away the burning in her eyes, and before she knew it, he was hugging her. Somehow, he always knew what she needed before she did. "Thank you," she breathed, soaking in the comfort that came with his embrace. When she pulled away, his familiar warmth-invoking smile had returned.

"Of course, Res."

Her brows rose in delighted surprise. "You haven't called me that in years!"

With an arm around her shoulder, he pulled her back to the trail. "Better get used to it."

◆

The Hand was already at the gates when Adresia arrived. She parted from her best friend and approached the man, curtsying when she stopped at his side. He inclined his head with a small smile. "You look lovely, Lady Darbania."

She tugged on the flowy skirts of her gown as if to exemplify that she wasn't as uninformed about her nobility as he might expect her to be after years of ignoring it. "Well, as most people don't approve of my usual attire, I thought it wise to wear something more *befitting* of my title."

His eyes twinkled. "How did you sleep?"

"Wonderfully." Terribly.

"Will this be your first time on horseback?"

"No. My father used to take me riding frequently as a child."

"Are you nervous?"

She met his gaze with narrowed eyes. He asked a lot of questions. "Should I be?"

A shrug. "I'd be surprised if you weren't."

Of course he would. "You didn't answer my question."

His smile turned into a smirk as he leaned toward her. "You didn't answer mine."

She kept her mouth closed, letting him watch her in that curious way he did. *Be prepared for anything*, he'd said yesterday. *You never know what's out there.* What did that mean? His expressions were calculated, as if he decided exactly what to show before showing it, although there *was* something in his eyes: amusement and mirth, sparkling like the calm waters of Niamth Bay. She couldn't figure out what *that* meant, either. So, to return the confusion, she grinned.

Surprise flickered in his features—but that calm, controlled expression slipped back into place before she could blink, exactly as she expected. With a smug smile, she retreated back to Cota's side. He didn't comment despite how intensely he'd been watching.

A part of Adresia didn't want to look back, didn't want to think about this place and what it meant to her; what part of her soul it harbored while saving it at the same time. A miniscule part of her, a part that she almost detested but couldn't help but agree with, hoped they wouldn't be back. The possibility of what that future meant was a future she'd spent the majority of the night pondering about. And then there was another part. A part that wanted to look—that *needed* to. Because if she didn't...

The Countess peered over her shoulder, across the empty square, past the buildings and houses, as if she could see all the way to the vacant mansion miles behind them, abandoned in that beautiful glade in the depths of the Traderious Woodland. Darbania Manor. Cota and Adresia's parents had joined all their savings to buy the massive estate, planning to have both families live together under the same roof once they could move from their original homes.

They never moved in.

THE BANE

Two weeks after becoming orphans, Adresia and Cota had relocated to the least populated, most-underdeveloped sector of the province where they were left unbothered. It was the farthest they could get from the manor without leaving Westholt. *That* was why Cota had told her what he had this morning—because she hadn't fulfilled her parents' dreams of moving in, and because she didn't believe she was still worth everything her parents had fought for.

When she at last turned back around, forcing the heavy thoughts from her mind, she heard it. Like clashes of lightning, the sound of hooves struck the air, growing louder with every passing second. A dozen guards appeared at the front gate atop horses of all sizes and colors and breeds. They brought spare ones to the three of them. After a brief introduction, they left Westholt and entered the Sight Woods. She had almost forgotten they would be venturing through this ancient expanse.

The morning sunlight bounced off silver chest plates. The guards' behaviors were alarming, to say the least: unsettled, wide eyes, tense frowns, uncomfortable mumbles, and brooding silence. A glance at Cota told her he was thinking the same thing: they weren't nearly as intimidating as she'd expected them to be. They weren't as she remembered them five years ago.

One guard *did* glare at them a few times before eventually snapping, "Queen Narissa expects us in a week and the journey is arduous. Quicken your pace and *move*." He guided his horse to the head of the group, and Adresia obediently clicked her heels to get her mare moving faster, if only to lighten his undue demands.

"Captain Hadrian Aeron," Cota muttered at her side.

That was the Captain of the Shield?

"How do *you* know?" she asked. "You've never met him."

Cota smirked. "The sigil on his uniform."

A defeated laugh. "Of course."

"Harley would be having a fit right now if she knew you weren't paying attention," he teased. The Duchess of Westholt had guided them along their newfound earldoms after their parents' deaths. She was the sole reason Adresia wasn't completely shaken by the idea of Court: weeks of advice turned into months of lessons, from Court etiquette to anything and everything that the woman had learned as Duchess. Harley hadn't been surprised to see them go, though. To her, this was just another obstacle that they had to face. Whether they wanted it or not, this was their life.

Adresia scrunched her nose. "There are *other* details I'm gathering that might prove far more valuable." She observed the Captain. Likely in his late-twenties, he had dull blond hair, muscles that protruded under the bulk of his cloak, and faint scars on his ivory face. He was also scowling, but that wasn't what bothered her. It was the way he kept watching her out of the corner of his eye like she was a criminal in need of perpetual oversight.

Her gaze traveled to the Hand, who was two horses away. His rich, dark hair shimmered in the autumn sunlight. He wasn't like the Captain, if their interactions so far proved anything. But who *was* he? Why did he warn them? What did he stand to gain from being friendly? She blinked, realizing his gaze now fell on her too. Had he been staring the entire time? The Hand faced the front once more, but not before grinning widely—precisely the way she'd done earlier.

Yes, she was sure he had been staring long before she took notice.

The sun hadn't entirely fallen under the treetops when they stopped for the night. The men set up camp, which was smaller than she'd expected it to be. Every few yards there was a fire, some used for cooking and some for light. Adresia was in the middle of preparing for an *extremely* comfortable night's rest with their thin, slightly itchy bedrolls—tents would take too much time to disassemble every morning, supposedly—when the Hand approached them. Cota mumbled a quick hello and goodbye before turning to finish setting up, leaving Adresia and the man to converse.

"You're quite far away from the rest of camp," the Hand said by greeting. "Are you sure you don't want to move closer?"

They *were* far, but she'd been watched all day, and she'd rather not have eyes on her while she was sleeping too. "Thank you, but I prefer the privacy."

The Hand tilted his head. "How did you fare today?"

An honest huff. "I wish we didn't have to spend the *entire* journey on an uncomfortable horseback, but the woods are captivating, nonetheless."

"My apologies, we couldn't acquire a carriage—"

Her laugh wasn't entirely forced. "I'll survive. I've never even been in one anyway, and I love horses. By the time we arrive, though, I'm sure I'll never want to ride one again."

A sigh that told her he agreed. "This isn't the longest excursion I've ever participated in, but it's still draining. Have you ever traveled, Lady Dar—"

"Can you please not call me that?"

"Sorry?"

"Lady Darbania."

"Oh." His brows furrowed. "I'm sorry if I offended you."

"You didn't."

She guessed his question before he voiced it. "Why not?"

"I don't use that name. It's just what's written in the records."

His gaze wandered behind her. "So you're not...?"

She held up her ringless hand. "Cota and I share the name because our parents bought Darbania Manor together before they died." *Died*—as if they had peacefully drifted into the afterlife and hadn't been brutally murdered. But words were a tricky thing in Court, and he *was* the Hand of the Queen; for all she knew, he was the one who executed their death sentence. Her throat tightened at the thought. "When we inherited the earldom, we inherited the property and the name—but we're not married." She couldn't tell if the darkness was betraying her vision, but she swore something like relief flashed across his face, if only for a moment.

"What would you have me call you, then?" he asked.

"Lady Bellum." She jabbed her thumb toward Cota. "He prefers Lord Bowyer."

"I'll be sure to correct the records, then."

The corners of her lips lifted slightly. "How long until we reach the Ryncled River? I've been told it's quite a sight to behold."

"Three days. Dazelle is three after that."

"Have you ever been to the river before?"

"Once or twice."

So he *had* been in the Sight Woods before. She wondered what occasion would call for such a risk—and why they were daring to travel through it now.

Suddenly, Cota yawned behind them—loud enough that the Hand cleared his throat. "Well, we have an *exciting* journey ahead of us, Lady Bellum. I suggest you get some rest. I'll see you in the morning."

"At dawn, no doubt?"

A small smile. "At dawn."

And she didn't know if it was the conversation or his company, but she didn't want him to leave just yet. He was Hand, yes, and perhaps he'd been ordered to make conversation, to find out as much information about her to relay to the Queen when they arrived...but he was easy to talk to and seemed relatively interested in *her*. Maybe she could use it to her advantage. So before he could take a step away, she quipped, half-joking, "Does the Shield have a mandatory policy to wake up that early every day or is it just out of choice?"

He turned around slow enough that she knew he was trying to conjure up an answer. "When it comes to these woods, we generally don't want to spend too much time in one spot. It's more productive to keep moving."

"More productive—or safer?"

And she honestly expected a forced laugh or prepared response meant to falsely console her, but the Hand surprised her when he quietly replied, "I think you already know the answer."

From the moment they'd entered, the men had been on edge. Nothing had happened so far, but they'd had the advantage of daylight on their side. Now, encompassed by a blanket of darkness with nothing but moonlight to illuminate the branches above, the guards continued to check over their shoulders, hands not straying too far from their blades as they sat with their backs to the fires. She suspected it was the reason she'd been asked to move closer, too.

"My advice?" the Hand continued. "Watch your back. And as for your other question: we don't get a choice—in anything. You do what you're told and do it without complaint or comment. Which is why," he added, taking a step closer, "it's so important that you have a friend at Court. And if that friend is me, then I'd be happy to oblige."

Well *this* was interesting.

"A friend would be nice," she said.

He dipped his chin and stepped back. "Prayers for good rest, Lady Bellum. May the gods guide you through your dreams and be an anchor to the light. May you remember the beauty of creation and...and..."

She hadn't uttered the prayer in years, not after everything that had happened. But she was pleasantly surprised that she remembered, and finished for him, "And thank the gods above for every breath."

They shared a soft smile. It was strange how easily they conversed, like they *were* friends. She turned away the same moment he did—and immediately met Cota's piercing stare. She sat across from him on the bedroll he had so thoughtfully laid out, but he didn't speak until the Hand's steps faded. "What was that?"

She grabbed her bag, aimlessly ruffling through it. "What?"

"I saw how you looked at him." She stilled. "How he looked at *you*."

"We were just talking," she said.

"That's not what it seemed like." Her head whipped toward him the same time he blurted, "Do you trust him?"

"We met yesterday, Cota."

"And?"

"And *nothing*." She locked eyes with him, daring him to say more. He broke first, and with a sigh, fell onto his back. "I don't trust *anyone*," she said. "You know that."

He pressed his palms against his eyes. "So you're toying with him." Was that amusement in his voice, or...relief?

"We're nobles, remember? A little manipulation should be expected from a *Lady of the Court*."

Cota actually sputtered a laugh, then, and pulled his hands from his face. "I'm sorry. I just...I need *something* to think about. Otherwise I'll spend every moment believing we're falling right into a perfectly planned trap set in motion the night our lives were miraculously spared."

Almost, she wanted to say. *Almost spared.*

She sprawled atop her bedroll, folding her arms across her stomach. "It doesn't matter if we are. We keep going, Cota. We keep fighting, everyday. And if *anyone* tries to take away what little I have left..."

He caught her words; caught who she meant. "It'd be us against a kingdom." Us—because he would never leave her. Because if that's what she wanted, he would stand at her side no matter who opposed them.

She would do it, if she had to. She would *destroy* anyone who tried to take him away. And maybe that made her a monster. Maybe that made her as bad as Narissa. But she didn't die when she should have five years ago. *They* didn't. And that meant something.

Chapter 4

Caspian Harvryd watched Corvina Vander stalk along the bookshelves of her room, each step a graceful movement of her body. She dragged a manicured finger across the spines of the weathered volumes, her most prized possessions. If the Queen knew what forbidden information they held, if she merely suspected her sister's true identity...the Princess would've been beheaded years ago. Caspian had spent his entire life making sure Narissa didn't end the lives of those he loved.

Corvina faced him, blonde strands flying over her shoulders. "Do you notice the tension as I sense it?" She tilted her head, honey eyes capturing him in a stare he still hadn't grown accustomed to even after two decades.

"Whose unease are we speaking of?" he asked.

"My sister's, Caspian."

He slouched onto the wooden bench at the foot of the bed. "You know I refrain from additional engagements with Narissa outside of our meetings. And you're aware of her actions more than I am; you *always* know." He perked a brow. "You haven't recently discovered how to mind-read and chose to keep it from me, have you?"

Her lips tugged up in the slightest. "No. That, unfortunately, is beyond my abilities."

Corvina had always been different—unique. Magic had been nothing but a story he'd known as a boy until he and Corvina discovered her power in their youth. They'd searched the most abandoned parts of their small, unused library until they'd found what Corvina was and how to control her magic. He asked, "Then *what* have you discovered, Cor?"

THE BANE

She crossed the undecorated room and plopped herself at his side with a clenched jaw—the only hint of dismay she would show. The Princess' perpetual calmness would've frustrated him had he not also learned how to conceal his own emotions long ago. Although, he expected she could hear his quickening heartbeat, with her abilities. "We've watched my sister for years," *she said.* "When she's alone, you can hear her whispering to herself. To...something else."

"Our Queen has a dark past."

A shake of her head. "It's not that."

He refrained from grabbing the sword at his side, as if there was some sort of threat in the room he had to protect her from. Narissa wasn't afraid of anyone or anything. The fact that Corvina was implying otherwise... His voice was edged with a lethal calm. "What is it?"

"I'm not the only mage," *she stated carefully.*

"That's—that's impossible. They're gone. You said so yourself."

"I was mistaken."

"Then who...?" *A cold, bitter feeling crept up his throat.* "Narissa?"

At her responding nod, he swore. "There's always been this strain," *the Princess explained.* "I thought it just came with my power, but recently...it's changed. I can feel it: all of her incidents and outbursrts and otherness. Her magic. It's getting stronger everyday."

"Can she sense you?"

"No. I've never possessed that much magic."

Mages could sense other mages, but the less powerful ones like Corvina weren't so easily felt. They'd avoided detection for centuries when wars had broken out among the beings—when the strongest ones had hunted the weak. "What kind of mage is she?" *he asked.* "A Mundane barely has powers—"

"She's not a Mundane."

"Well, you can handle another Mystik."

Corvina shook her head. "She's not a Mystik."

He went still as death. If Narissa was a Bane...she would tear the world apart with that kind of power. "Are you sure?"

"I know it."

He swore again as he rose and paced the chamber. The room was thrice as large as his, but it suddenly felt cramped. What was he going to do? What could he do? He'd been trapped under the service of a tyrannical ruler his entire life and now... "I'm leaving for Westholt. Today." He crouched before the Princess and grabbed her hands. "I don't want to leave you, but you know I can't disobey orders."

"I've come this far," Corvina reassured. "I can protect myself just fine. But...there's something else." The Princess patted the spot next to her, waiting for him to sit before continuing. "The nobles Narissa summons are quickly disposed of once consulted with. There is no gain. She doesn't need these people."

He knew that already. "Why summon them, then?"

"She's searching for someone."

"And?"

Something like quivering reverence flickered on Corvina's face. It was so faint that he could have made it up, but evident enough that his stomach dropped. Because perhaps it wasn't what the most powerful being on the continent had to fear—but who.

"I think she may have found her," the Princess breathed.

It suddenly became hard to swallow. "Who is she?"

"Someone threatening enough that Narissa will stop at nothing to find her."

"Does that mean—"

"That she's a Bane?" Corvina shook her head. "I don't know. When she arrives, I'll be able to tell—but so will Narissa."

He loosed a long breath. "Gods."

"You've always had a flair for the dramatics. I'm sure you can handle it." He bumped her shoulder with his own. "If I remember correctly, you're the one who had the entirety of Dazelle celebrate your nameday two months after because it had been raining for half the year."

"I was fourteen!"

THE BANE

Their laughter echoed across the expanse of the chamber, bouncing off the dusty corners in which darkness absorbed sunlight. "My invitation still stands," he said. "You might be confined to this castle, but you shouldn't be miserable in a room far too large for only yourself. My chamber is always open. I know you enjoy my company," he added with a smirk.

Her smile held a sadness he hadn't seen in a long time. She always tried to be joyful, even when everything around her screamed not to. "I'll keep it in mind." He rose, but before he could step away, she grabbed his hand. He looked at her once more. "Thank you, Caspian."

He squeezed her fingers. "Anything for my family."

That evening, Corvina wished him safe travels as he departed to retrieve the woman Narissa was waiting for—a woman strong enough to stop their Queen; strong enough to oppose the most powerful being on the continent.

Caspian hoped she knew what she was doing.

Chapter 5

Birdsong accompanied the herd of horses stomping lavish, green blades of grass into the soil as a cloudless, azure sky shone above magnificent redwoods and various conversations were heard from either end of the company. This was what Adresia had experienced for three days. Three days of unending, tiresome travel, hour after hour after hour of doing nothing but unpleasantly sitting on horseback. It had felt like three weeks.

She *had* been granted time to ponder countless matters: the Queen's motives for wanting her, interactions with the Court and the inevitable events they would attend, not to mention enduring horrid, arrogant nobility. And while it'd kept her from dying of boredom...she was ready to get off of her mare and do *something*.

The sun was high in the sky when it was finally announced they had reached the Ryncled River and would remain here for the day. She practically threw herself off of her horse before handing the reins to a guard and prowling toward the river, grimacing at the sticky sweat on her skin. When she was twenty steps into the trees, a voice sounded behind her. "Lady Bellum!"

The Hand.

He appeared at her side with a smile. "Running away already?"

She had every intention to abandon her friendship with him the moment she got the answers she wanted. But...he was charming. And amusing. Enough so that her lips tugged up. "I spend most of the year in the boiling heat for a living," she said. "I'd rather not prolong that misfortune more than necessary, but seeing as that's not an option...a refreshing dip in the river will have to do."

"Do you know where you're going?" he asked.

She opened her mouth before closing it. She knew a *general* direction.

With a smirk he said, "Then I'll just have to escort you." She shook her head in silent amusement, but didn't stop him. When they'd wandered deep into the forest and the sounds of the company had completely vanished, he asked, "Have you always worked? The Duchess informed me I was taking quite the committed laborer from the province."

Of course Harley had. Adresia explained, "I joined the lumberers shortly after my parents died." She paused, unsure if she should go on. Talking meant sharing, and sharing meant letting him in. She *wanted* to—because he seemed so genuine, like he actually cared what she said. But what had Narissa told him about her? What did Narissa *know*? The Countess glanced at the Hand. He watched her expectantly, lips drawn together, primed to listen. A friend; that's what he'd said he was. Even if she wasn't. For some reason, the lie sent a pang through her chest, but—answers. The plan. "Being so small, Westholt has limited opportunities. I began woodworking, and, fortunately for Cota, who was raised surrounded by knowledge and books, the province was always looking for a tutor. So we managed, despite the modest incomes. That's how it's been for years."

"That must have been hard at such a young age." No questions about her parents. No further remarks about her earldom.

"It was," she said. It'd taken her a long time to realize that grief wasn't what her parents would want. The pain would always remain, but she knew the best way to move on was to try to be better; to fight for those who deserved it and for those who couldn't. It was what her parents had always done and it was what she would do until she couldn't any longer—even if she didn't believe she was worth being fought for herself.

Caspian was watching her softly, tenderly. The shock of it hit her hard enough that she wracked her brain for something to say, if only to get the image out of her mind. "Have you always served the Queen?"

His responding smile didn't reach his eyes. "I was dropped at the gates of the castle when I was six years old. I have no recollection of who my parents are or where I came from, but all throughout my childhood, I would get these...dreams." As if distracted by the thought, he gazed longingly ahead. "Snow-veiled plains that went on forever, white-capped mountains that stretched into the sky, swirling streams of frozen water. I don't know if they're real, or just that—a dream—but they've always returned. They still do, sometimes." Seeming to realize he was rambling, he gave a pointed, timid cough before continuing. "Narissa took me in and the royal household raised me until I was old enough to care for myself; until I understood how the kingdom worked and found my place in Court. I once requested who I had been before—if the Queen knew. All I received was that she had looked into it once and found nothing. She declared my full name as Caspian Harvryd on my seventh nameday and has never spoken of it since. At least I have my—" A pause, followed by a heavy sigh. "The memory of my home," he finished. "At least I have the memory of my home, if that's what it is. I'll find it someday."

"Are you and the Queen close, then?" She hoped the question sounded nothing more than innocent.

"I was made Second in the Shield when I turned fifteen and, eight years later, named Hand, so I've learned and served alongside her, but she's been ruling for so long that sometimes it feels like I'm still an outsider."

"Do you enjoy what you do?"

He tried to hide his hesitation, but she caught it. "The more difficult obligations can be hard to face, but they're something I've long since committed to. I'll do whatever it takes to help this kingdom prosper."

She wanted to believe him. Desperately. Because he was just like her, and if he *actually* was who he said he was...

"We all do things in order to live," she said. "To survive. Things we don't like. I won't judge you for your actions as long as you don't judge me for mine."

"Is that an invitation to share more about yourself?"

"What are friends for?"

"If we're really friends—" He held out his hand— "call me Caspian."

She glanced at it, still unsure why he was so interested. Save for Cota, no one had ever liked her so easily. But...things were changing.

And this was a game, after all.

She took his hand. "Adresia. Although I'm sure people would *love* to hear us address each other as such."

A wink. "We'll have to reserve the informality for when it's just us, then."

They arrived at the bank of the Ryncled River. Roughly sixty feet across, both sides met deeply in the middle where a menacing current surged, a mess of slapping waves and rugged, half submerged boulders. She'd heard it could drag you under so unexpectedly that you wouldn't know what was happening until you were drowning beneath the waves. The translucent shore was calm, thankfully. At least enough to where someone could step in without risking their life. Adresia was going to do just that, already slipping off her boots, when she noticed Caspian leaning against a tree, smirking. She gave him a pointed look. "Are you just going to stand there and watch?"

His playful visage deepened. "Did you think I walked all this way just to turn back once we arrived?"

Her cheeks bloomed, something that *rarely* occurred, and she quickly hid her fluster by remarking, "I expect you to be a *gentleman* at least."

"A *gentleman* would make sure you didn't die in this savage stream." He pivoted away, dramatically swinging his head as he added, "I suppose I'll just have to trust you."

"I'm more than capable," she muttered as she unbound her hair, expecting him to be gone. But, for some reason, he'd glanced back over his shoulder, eyes shimmering with something she couldn't read.

"Don't die," he reiterated.

"I thought you trusted me."

"It's the water I don't trust."

She tossed her boot at him. "*Goodbye,* Caspian."

He lunged out of the way, chuckling as he left.

An hour later, Adresia strolled back toward camp, her damp, braided hair still dripping. She'd have to steer Cota toward the river, although her lips perked as she imagined his outright refusal, insisting it was useless when he would be just as filthy by the time they reached Dazelle.

The leaves had already begun to fade from a wild green to a soft orange. Westholt was too hot to be even remotely appealing in the colder seasons; the oak leaves simply withered into an unexciting brown and left the forest empty and bland. But here, in the Sight Woods, where the summer-plagued forest was shifting into a glorious, warm-toned autumn...it would feel like a new world. Enchanted by the majestic redwoods and beams of golden light shining around her, Adresia began to softly sing.

The spirits, they come, to a land of poems;
the elves run around their glowing domes.

THE BANE

The nymphs, they bring life, of water and earth;
the witch tells the tale of your unsullied worth.

It was her mother's favorite hymn, something she had sung to lull her daughter into blissful rest. Even now, Adresia could remember the magic in her dreams, vivid enough that as she glanced around, she felt an odd familiarity. It was in the cleverly carved alcoves in the trees, just out of reach from human touch; the fallen branches and limbs that were coincidentally out of her path; the way the wind swayed the leaves in tune with her gentle singing.

Bring me to the king and queen,
my fair love, o'er land and ravine.
Keep my secret, our sacred oath,
then will our lives have meaningful growth.
Let me stay in this kingdom of—

A twig snapped. The sound echoed from tree to tree, disrupting any reference to the source. Adresia's fingers closed around the dagger in her pocket, but when the Captain appeared between two thin redwoods, she subtly withdrew her hand. "Captain. I wasn't expecting to see you."

It was his approach that made her pause: slow and prowling and unsettlingly observant. "What are you doing out here?" he asked. His rough voice made the hair on her arms stand up. How had she not heard him long before?

"The Lord Hand accompanied me to the river. I sent him away when we arrived. I'm on my way back now."

The Captain stopped before her—*very* close before her. "You shouldn't be in these woods all by yourself."

Something inside her roared in fear. Roared...and died. This wasn't the first time she'd faced a menacing man. "I'm not alone anymore."

As if amused, the corner of his mouth tugged up. "Why does the Queen want you? You're nobody to her."

"I'm nobody to you," she countered, tucking his words away. "Why are *you* so interested?"

He began circling her, the sword at his side thumping against his leg with each step. "Morolyn is an ancient kingdom, filled with ancient things. But monsters don't just lurk in these woods."

"Where else, then?"

"In the shadows of the city; in the grand ballroom of our Majesty's Court."

Adresia crossed her arms. "Isn't that the Shield's duty—to oversee the welfare of Dazelle and stop such foes from entering the castle?"

"I think you know just as well as I do..." His voice lowered as he appeared in front of her again. "Not all of those people can be denied entry."

She met his stare with a sharp one of her own, unflinching and full of bitter resentment. "No. Not all, it seems."

"I'll be watching you, Lady Bellum."

Her confidence faltered. "How do you know my name?" she breathed.

A chilling grin. "I know a lot of things. Like your troubling lack of service to the Queen. Like your peculiar closeness to Lord Bowyer. Like your intentions to use the poor *Lord Hand*." Something like ice ran down her back. "What would he think if he found out you don't actually want to be friends?"

She struggled to formulate a response. "I—You—"

"Enjoy your stay at Dazelle," he said. And then he sauntered away as if nothing had happened.

She put a hand over her mouth and watched him depart back into the trees. He knew. He'd overheard her and Cota and he knew about her plan and would use it against her and—

She stopped. Worrying would do nothing. Either he would tell someone, or he wouldn't. This was a lesson: to remain alert at all times; to not let herself fall unaware; to not take for granted the false security that the luxuries of nobility would try to instill in her. She was Adresia Bellum. She didn't make the same mistakes twice. And as her mother would say: *What is done is done. It's the yearnings of your heart that control you. If you don't like the results, capture your thoughts. Change what you say. Act differently. Only you can rewrite your story.*

Chapter 6

The little girl with stormy eyes and long, chocolate hair had only met the unusual, old man a few weeks prior, but trusted him completely. He was a mentor of sorts, but she preferred to call him a friend. "Kovare," she said one afternoon, "Father says I am only a week away from finishing my lessons. If I do well, he'll end my schooling and teach me the rest himself! I'll be able to visit you more!"

The man's eyes crinkled at the corners. "Indeed little Lady, you possess wisdom far greater than many I have crossed paths with. I have no doubt you will surpass even the wisest citizens in Morolyn. Your smile holds a warmth I have not experienced before." His voice was gravelly, like he had spent his entire life talking. She'd never met someone so gentle and prudent and wise—besides her father, of course. "You will do great wonders in this realm, sweet Adresia."

Their encounters always took place in a small glade not too far into the Traderious Woodland, and while she never whispered a word to anyone about Kovare, it seemed that no one even knew such a man existed. Adresia didn't mind; she was able to have him all to herself. He was no ordinary man. Because although the only magic she was aware of was in recollections from her parents, something in her could not get over the idea that he possessed an inkling of those unearthly powers.

"Do it again, sir, please!" she begged, plopping atop a fallen log, eyes wide in anticipation. Kovare chuckled deeply, his long staff stomping on the ground as he widened the distance between them. Ten feet away, he faced her, his lengthy gray hair falling over his shoulders and a beard spilling down his front.

THE BANE

Without warning, he swung his staff fascinatingly through the air: around his waist, behind his back, over and under his arms. Adresia was as mesmerized as the first time she'd seen him do it. She doubted a soul would dare oppose someone with such skills. Which was why, when he finished, she pleaded, "Please teach me! I want to know how to defend myself like you can. I want to protect the people I love!"

Kovare tilted his head. "And what about the people who will come after you—the ones threatened by your might?"

"I'll fight. And if I can't, I'll go in the Sight Woods. No one goes in there." She shrugged. "It seems like a good place to hide."

"The Goddess was said to have spawned all sorts of creatures across this kingdom; for protection, yes, but for punishment too. Some believe that they still remain, even after the War. Why is it that you are not afraid? Most wouldn't dare upset what wanders in the uninhabited depths of this land."

The young girl bit her lip before answering, "Why should I fear what the Goddess provides? Father says that 'fear is a tool to be shaped and molded'. It can cause men to do good things or bad things. If She intended to protect, then we have nothing to fear but ourselves."

"A smart one, you are. As is your father."

She smiled at him through lowered lashes. "Will you teach me now?"

Resting his staff on the ground, Kovare crouched in front of her. "Now, my dear, you are very young—"

"I'm only nine!" she countered.

"Hear me, Adresia." His wild, brown eyes latched onto hers, and she was instantly transfixed. "You have an entire life ahead of you. And what you will endure in years to come, whatever it may be, I know you can handle. You are strong enough. But..." She didn't hide her blooming grin, and Kovare sighed in defeat. "I would have no greater pleasure than to aid you in becoming the finest Lady to have ever lifted a weapon." He shook her nimble fingers and gave an encouraging smile. "On my honor, I will teach you how to fight."

So he taught her. For five years, Adresia secretly received lessons from Kovare, until she was as good as him, until she was as good as her father—a warrior who had seen war time and time again and had never let the horrors ruin him. It was that courage that continued to inspire her.

One day, Kovare met her late in the afternoon.

"Where have you been? It's been hours," she exclaimed, halting her pacing.

"My sincerest apologies," he said.

She noticed his slow stride, the hands limp by his side, the dark circles under his eyes. "Kovare, what has you so exhausted?"

"No matter, my dear. All is well."

"It is not," she countered. "I see the weariness in your posture. You cannot hide it from me—nor can you try to suppress the dreadful news you are surely going to speak of. Go on, then. What do you know?"

He peered at her under his brows, too jaded to fully lift his head. "Before I do, you must promise me one thing: you cannot reveal yourself. What I have taught you, the true extent of your skill...you must tell no one. Not until the time is right. Not until it is all that you have left. You will know the moment. You will know when you are ready. But not now. Not yet. I beg you—swear this."

"I swear," she breathed.

A heavy exhale. "The current state of the Queen has forced my hand. I must remove myself from Felbourne."

Her stomach plummeted. "You—you're leaving? And what does the Queen have to do with it? Our realm is at peace."

There was a hint of a grim smile on his wrinkled face. "My girl, peace is, at this time in Morolyn, completely and utterly a fool's hope."

She receded a step. "But you must leave the continent? Why?"

"There is so much you do not know. But we will meet again and I will tell you—one day. You are destined for great things, my dear friend." He began to retreat, step after step, word after word. "When you hold a shattered world in your hands and have the strength to crush it completely with the *might of who you are...that is when you will truly understand all that has been and all that will be."*

Her throat burned and voice shook as she asked, "What does that mean? How am I meant to know? Why can't you just stay?" The man had been a comfort and close companion since the moment they met all those years ago, and now he was just...leaving. Leaving as if her entire life—her future—depended on it.

She twisted as he pointed behind her to Westholt, to the family who was surely waiting for her, to Cota and her parents.

Kovare stated, "You already know how it ends."

When she turned back, he was gone.

Adresia's eyes shot open. She breathed deeply, unevenly, the memory provoking an emotion she wished to never feel again. She rose and slipped on her boots with slightly trembling fingers before walking from the camp, needing to clear her head, to calm down. She eventually stopped at the base of a large trunk and took long, calculated breaths. In and out. Out and in. The memory had been so vivid, so extremely real, that, for a moment, she'd almost forgotten she was no longer a little girl.

You already know how it ends.

Six years later, she still didn't know what Kovare had meant. She didn't know why he had left either. Perhaps he had foreseen the calamity that would take place a year after his departure. Or perhaps he was just a normal man with a tragic past he hadn't wanted to face.

Adresia peered into the dark sky above. She'd never learned the names of the constellations—the ones that many prayed to dusk after dusk; to the glorious Goddess above, who relentlessly adored Her creations, and to the Almighty God, whose attention never strayed from Felbourne.

The God and Goddess are always there, her father used to say, *always awaiting those who need them.*

Adresia had long since stopped hoping for her prayers to be answered. For all the tales of their good works, of how they never failed to produce miracles when circumstances called for one, of their unfailing affection...the Countess had yet to witness any sort of guidance. Her father might have been right about their Holy Creators, if the breath that flowed from Adresia's lungs was any indication. But maybe his conviction that the otherworldly beings who created them could do no wrong had been sorely misplaced. Or maybe her lack of trust was exactly why she felt so forgotten.

Branches snapped, and she knew it was only because he wanted her to hear his approach. A trickle of moonlight danced across Cota's face as he approached her and said, "I wondered where you slipped off to every night."

"Rest has not come easy this journey," she said.

He leaned against a tree. "No, it hasn't."

She gazed in the direction of the sleeping camp. "Do you think any of those guards aided in the murder of our parents?" The men couldn't have been there—Adresia had made sure of that—but they could've helped. Information had to have trickled in from somewhere.

"I don't know," Cota admitted. "Uncovering people's secrets has always been your gift, not mine. You'll figure it out. You always know who to trust—even if you know nothing about them."

"You can tell who to trust if you know where to look."

"And what of the Hand?"

She looked at him. "What about him?"

"You seem...closer."

Gray-blue eyes narrowed. "*I'm* the one lying to *him*, remember? He's not manipulating me." Even if she was starting to like him more. Maybe she *was* being tricked.

"I'm just making sure you aren't falling for anything. He's Hand for a reason."

She shook her head, smiling in irritation.

"You can't be right about everyone, all of the time," he added.

"No, I can't. But his intentions will be revealed in time."

"And if you find them not in your favor?"

"I'll do what I need to do."

"Don't do that."

At his tone, at the strange inflection in his voice, she looked at him. "What?"

"Don't—don't *use* yourself like that." He stepped closer. "I *know* you, Res; I know the things you're willing to do to keep us out of poverty and debt and trouble. But you don't have to. Not anymore."

"It's not that simple—"

"Yes, it *is*. You are worth so much more than you think. Manipulate him; befriend him; do what you can to get the information you want. But you *don't* have to cross that line. Because if you do and something goes wrong…" He let out a strangled breath. "I can't lose the only person I love."

Her throat burned as if she was forcing a lie out. "You won't lose me, Cota."

Gray eyes met glimmering green ones and, with a sudden inhale, he leaned closer, as if preparing to—

Adresia's ears perked at a nonexistent breeze, an unuttered noise. Something different; something…*off*. She'd always been able to sense things others couldn't. To her surprise, Cota seemed to pick up what she had as well. There was only silence as they waited in the dark.

Until there wasn't.

Like thunder rolling across the land, a deep purring thrummed through her veins. It didn't get louder, but *deepened*, as unnatural as the frigid breeze on her skin. She sucked in a breath as invisible claws raked down her spine, and when a sickening odor poisoned the air, her blood ran cold. She knew that smell. It haunted her nightmares.

Death.

Cota instinctively laced their fingers together, pulling her along as he took several urgent steps toward camp.

"*Run,*" a voice said in the darkness.

They did.

Only their instincts and years of training kept them from stumbling into a tree or falling into the clutches of whatever chased them. She hadn't realized how far she'd wandered. And while she couldn't *see* anything—she felt it. It was weaving through her hair, snaking along her arms, curling around her ankles. It was everywhere and nowhere all at once. Real, yet...not.

They were fifty feet away when Cota began shouting.

The woods. There's something in the woods.

Men scrambled awake, instantly grabbing their weapons. Cota and Adresia stumbled into the clearing, their breaths ragged in their throats, and while they now appeared safe in this lighted glen...she had a feeling that whatever was out there had let them make it back.

Caspian was before them in an instant. "What happened? What did you see?"

"We didn't *see* anything," Cota sputtered, gulping down night air.

As if explanation enough, the Hand waved over a bearded, broad shouldered sentry and ordered, "I want half the men stationed at the edge of the clearing, the other half searching the woods. The moment you come back, you report your findings to me." The man nodded, but Caspian added, "Remember—use fire. Steel will do no good against what's out there." Perhaps less confident than before, the sentry retreated, passing on the order. When Caspian faced them again, Adresia realized his hair wasn't a mangled mess like the others. Why had he been awake?

"We're staying here?" Cota asked.

"We can't leave," the Hand stated.

"The Captain doesn't give orders?" Adresia asked.

Caspian's gaze drifted across the glade to where the Captain mutely watched them. "When I'm acting on behalf of the Queen, these men answer to me."

"And you had to remind them of that?"

"You'll find that not every man's loyalty lies where it should. Some believe in promises that do not have the right to be made."

Still keeping an eye on where they'd come from, Cota asked her, "Do you have any idea what that was?"

"I was hoping you would know," she said.

He looked at Caspian. "Do *you* know what's out there?"

"If I did, we wouldn't be out here right now."

"But you *do* have an idea...don't you?"

Adresia stilled at the bite in Cota's words.

Caspian's eyes narrowed. "Have you ever heard of what the gods created to roam the very redwoods that surround us? Of the creatures that watch us between thick trunks?"

Yes. Kovare and her parents had told her all about them. Profusely.

A nearby guard argued, "Those stories are meant to frighten children and keep 'em out of the woods."

"So what chased us?" Adresia retorted.

The man shook his head. "There's nothin' out there." But she noticed his cautious glance toward the dark edge of their clearing. It was only then that she realized Caspian probably hadn't accompanied her out of pure friendliness to the Ryncled River—but as a guard.

"You don't trust me," Caspian told Cota, "and that's understandable; that's *smart*. But you don't know what I know. You wonder why there is no one else here? Why there is no sign of civilization besides our own? Want to know the truth?"

And despite how the past few days had played out, how smooth the first part of their journey had been so far, when Cota said,

"Enlighten me," in a dangerously low voice that she hadn't heard in a *very* long time, her hand drifted toward her dagger.

"There aren't any *to* stop at," Caspian said. "No one lives here. No one *can*. And contrary to the belief that the people of Morolyn like to travel the vast expanse of this kingdom, not everyone who enters these woods are here out of choice."

Cota dropped his snarl—because perhaps he'd realized the same thing Adresia had: that the grief in Caspian's eyes might not be because he'd lost people to whatever creatures were out here...but because he'd sent many here himself. As punishment.

Cota was right to fear what the Queen had in store for them.

"Didn't you already travel through here to reach Westholt?" she asked.

Caspian's hardened gaze found hers. "Yes."

"And?"

"And the guards currently escorting you are three men fewer than they were when they left Dazelle."

It took everything in her not to balk. "Why did that guard say there was nothing out here?"

"The men were taken in the night without a sign or trace. He believes they fled."

"And what do you believe?"

"I believe the three heads I found in my path a day later."

Adresia's insides folded in on themselves. "Why risk returning?" she practically whispered. *Why had people been willing to die in an effort to retrieve me?* she wanted to add.

"The Queen wanted to waste no time on a journey thrice as long if we were to go around. You're too valuable."

She didn't know what to make of the information. She simply advised, "I don't think your men should leave camp." Cota nodded his agreement. Caspian observed them. She could almost see his mind analyzing what they'd revealed about themselves: their intellect of the kingdom, their skill of surviving whatever monsters wandered these feared woods, their keen sense of awareness that was continuously on alert.

He turned to the waiting huddle of guards readying their blades, the air thick with tension and fear. They knew what awaited them if they went. So it didn't surprise her when the men bowed their heads in respect and gratitude as Caspian announced, "Disregard your previous order, men. We head out at first light and make haste to Dazelle. There will be no monsters to catch tonight."

Caspian was true to his word; they reached Dazelle the following afternoon. As they emerged from the forest, Adresia tried—and failed—to hold in her astonishment. By far the most populated and prosperous province in Morolyn, Dazelle had a proclivity for luxury and flamboyant architecture. The dwellings were of great extravagance, their intricate exteriors stunning Adresia into mute fascination as they rode through the city. The streets were more than active: ladies in opulent dresses, couples with armfuls of goods bustling in and out of shops, children running about, crowding the already dense main road.

The stone wall encircling the castle came into focus at the end of the street. The world darkened for a moment as they passed through the gates and entered the courtyard. At the sight of the castle, her stomach dropped. It was massive; there had to be a hundred servants just to manage it. Complementing a blue-gray roof, pale stone walls and dozens of windows aligned the first and second floors. Each corner was a three-story tower, open arches allowing guards to peer over the defensive wall protecting the castle.

Leaving their steeds in the care of the stableboys, the guards headed toward the opposite gated entry. A servant boy approached Caspian and mumbled something, to which the Hand gave a grateful nod and beckoned for Adresia and Cota to follow. In front of what she assumed was the barracks, Adresia spotted another group of guards. The grassy area was worn to pale dirt, and metal struck metal as the men followed different drills of combat. Despite her soiled appearance, she noticed the many stares her way as she passed. A satisfied smile found her lips; she couldn't remember the last time she'd been looked at in that way. But as they entered through the castle's arched front doors, already open for them, her smile slipped. Would she be a coward to only *now* admit that this might actually be a ploy to get her into the Queen's grasp? The idea had seemed so ridiculous before. But seeing this place—*being* here... It felt like an all too real possibility.

As Caspian led them up the grandest staircase she'd ever seen, he glanced over his shoulder. "I'm afraid there isn't enough time to give you a tour before tonight's ceremony, but the layout is easy enough to figure out."

She shared a glance with Cota. "Ceremony?"

"You'll be introduced to the Court at one of Her Majesty's marvelous balls." The Hand gave a reassuring smile. "If it makes you feel any better, I was informed when we arrived as well." They walked through a covered hallway that was opened on both sides to the elements and then took three turns before stopping at a door. Like he'd claimed, the castle wasn't as complex as she'd expected it to be. "Your personal chambers aren't ready yet, but this guest room will be fine for now." With a gentle push of his hand, the door opened.

Directly across the chamber were french doors that led to a balcony. In the middle was a single bed, bigger than any she'd ever seen before. There were two doors on either side: bathing chambers and closets. Combined, it was bigger than Cota and Adresia's entire house at Westholt.

When several servants strode in and curtsied, the Hand added with a smile, "I'll retrieve you before the ceremony begins." He shut the door behind him, leaving them with the six awaiting individuals. Cota only gave Adresia an amused grin before they were swept away in a blur of soap and fabric.

Chapter 7

Caspian Harvryd turned down the main corridor of the Suites. The halls were busier than when he left. Even outside, the Inner Gardens bustled with familiar faces trimming and pruning the hedges. The Queen hadn't shown this much effort since the King of Gantrick had visited a quarter of a century ago when Morolyn had been briefly involved in the war. Why Narissa was doing so much for Adresia—someone who could likely be her greatest enemy—Caspian couldn't guess.

He eyed Corvina's chambers down the length of the hall. She'd be waiting to hear how the excursion had unfolded. He hoped she hadn't risked snooping around while he was gone like she so often did. She knew what she was doing, but still...he couldn't help worrying. He'd been caught more than enough times in his life. Punished, too. The Queen wouldn't withhold her wrath from anyone, her sister included.

Three doors separated them when, unsurprisingly, Hadrian Aeron stepped in Caspian's path. The Hand halted so as not to run into the man, but it wouldn't have bothered him if he did. He'd been wondering when the Captain would show himself. "You never could last long without frequenting a visit to the Princess," Hadrian sneered.

"I just brought our new arrivals to their chambers to prepare for the ceremony."

Brown eyes slid past him, flashing in wicked delight. "Enjoying the company of the new Countess already?"

"Adresia isn't like—" He realized his mistake the moment it came out of his mouth.

"*Adresia?*" That perverse smile widened. "Already calling her by her first name, are you? Maybe more happened on the journey than we noticed."

"That's a lie and you know it," Caspian snarled. The bastard knew he wasn't like that. Not anymore.

"And what if your past misdeeds *accidentally* slipped out to Lady Bellum? What would she think of you then?"

Caspian cooled his glare. Hadrian had always gotten under his skin; this wasn't new. The man rarely committed to his threats. He merely enjoyed watching people squirm. "That was years ago, before I had any common sense and responsibility."

"Before you became Hand, you mean." Hadrian crossed his arms. "I never understood how our Queen saw you adequate for the position."

"Those reckless years haunt the both of us." The Captain was only a year older, so they'd grown up, trained, and, as much as Caspian hated to admit it, had sought out the pleasures of Dazelle together. "The only difference," the Hand continued, "is that *I* decided to leave those habits behind while you remained. You had every chance to secure this position." Especially when Narissa favored Hadrian over himself. "It's not my fault you aren't enough for our Queen."

The man leaned close to his old friend. "Don't forget who I am—what I can do. You may have beaten me to our Queen's side, but I command the full force of Morolyn's troops. My resources are unlimited, my soldiers steadfast, and my power immeasurable. I have eyes *everywhere*." Caspian just stared into Hadrian's unflinching gaze. "You haven't anything to say now, *Lord Hand?*" A cruel smile. "I'll see you and our new company at the ceremony. Until then..." He bowed at the waist, deep and mocking.

Caspian's resentment didn't pass until he'd taken a long breath and Hadrian had vanished around the corner. When he finally entered Corvina's chambers, she didn't look up from the book she was reading before saying, "You took your time."

"You can thank Hadrian for that," he said, throwing himself onto the bed beside her.

"One of these days he'll be put in his place."

That was unlikely. "Have you missed me terribly?"

Corvina rolled her eyes, but smiled. "Of course." She gestured around the room. "You'll be pleased to hear that I finally opened the windows. The servants squealed with delight when the sunlight warmed the room." Servants—not Ladies. She'd never had Ladies, thanks to her sister. "But you don't want to hear about me." She carefully closed her novel, looking at him expectantly. "Well?"

He cracked a smile, because she wanted to know exactly what he couldn't stop thinking about. "She's not what I expected."

Her brows rose, but when he didn't go on, she exclaimed, "That's all you're giving me? *She's not what I expected*?" The book in her hands smashed into his arm.

"I don't know what to say!" he sputtered with a laugh.

"What is she *like*? How does she act? Have you noticed her powers? Does she even *know*?"

"No signs of her powers, but I don't think anything has happened yet anyway. As for what she's like…" He wracked his brain for the right words. "She's far more intelligent than I was at her age—"

"Mature, you mean."

"And she's witty—"

"Probably funnier than you."

"And she's keen and confident and peaceful. Both instinctive and rational; impulsive, I suppose, if I gathered anything from our conversations—but in a good way. Like she's willing to do what's right even if it means breaking the rules."

"Well, we wouldn't want a submissive noble as the deliverer of our people."

A crooked smile. "I think submission is the last thing she would tolerate." It wouldn't surprise him if Adresia somehow managed to work around whatever chores Narissa wanted done. The Countess didn't seem so easily tamed. He'd seen Hadrian leaving the forest after she'd emerged; how the Captain hadn't stopped watching her. Something had happened, but it hadn't rifled her. And she hadn't shown a hint of fear at the creature that had chased her and Lord Bowyer. She'd gathered as much information as she could before sleeping again, and all morning, even since they'd arrived, she'd remained calm. Alert, but calm. Composed. She was more adept than most of the men he'd trained in the Shield, and that was saying something. She *wasn't* what he'd expected.

She was remarkable.

When Corvina's lips tugged into a knowing smile, Caspian rolled off the bed to hide the heat that colored his ears. "I have a meeting." He took two rushed steps toward the door.

"Wait."

He stopped, and with an impatient and slightly embarrassed groan, spun.

Corvina jumped from the bed, her gown spilling after her. "You'll want to hear the news from me."

"News?"

"I know why Adresia is here."

Dread pooled in his gut. "Why?"

"Narissa wants to make her an Ambassador: someone to do the dirty deeds that my sister doesn't have time for because she's already busy destroying someone else's life."

"I thought that was my job," he muttered.

"You assist in the demands and shortcomings presented directly here. Adresia, however, will be sent wherever Narissa desires. Across Dazelle, across Morolyn—to another continent, if she so wished. Whatever my sister wants, Adresia must do. I suspect she's still slightly upset that the Countess abandoned her duties five years ago, but it's easier to keep the only threat to her rule under her direct command, distracting Adresia with meaningless tasks."

There was a grain of relief in his stomach. She wasn't in immediate danger—not from Narissa, at least. "She won't be happy about that."

"She doesn't have a choice."

The humor in Corvina's eyes had vanished, but he couldn't help his confidence as he patted the Princess' arm. "Neither do we."

Chapter 8

Adresia had never worn anything as magnificent as this gown. The servants claimed the light blue brightened her eyes, and while the top was tight enough to accentuate the curves she'd never exploited before, the silky material was as comfortable as water on her skin. Half of her chocolate hair had been braided and pinned to the back of her head. The servants had spoken little, their movements swift and never offsetting another, and she'd seen the subtle smiles on their faces as they'd dressed her; their joy had startled her enough that the nerves the Countess had felt upon her arrival were now diminished into a distant flame—flickering at her fingertips, but no longer able to burn.

Leaning against the stone ledge of the balcony with closed eyes, Adresia thought of the descending sun behind her that melted the sky into whirls of pink and orange. It was strange how the home of such a wicked ruler could possess so much light and life. She hummed a song from her childhood as a sweet scent drifted through her hair from the gardens below.

"I miss that."

She opened her eyes. Cota was leaning against the doorframe, watching her in a strange way. "I'd forgotten how much I love to sing," she said. "It's been so long."

"You could start again."

"And what—sing to myself? That's a bit *too* arrogant for me."

He smiled, his emerald eyes brighter than usual against the dark fabric he wore. "You can sing to me," he said.

"Only if you don't mock my unpracticed attempts."

"You could be silent for a thousand years and I would still be in awe of your voice the day you sang again."

Something in her fluttered and twisted.

"Save me a dance tonight, will you?" he asked.

She mocked a swoon to hide her fluster. "Anything for you, Lord Bowyer." He grinned, and she instinctively smoothed the lapels on his chest before resting her hands on the sleek material. "You're far more handsome when you don't have dirt all over you."

"And *you* look..."

"Having trouble thinking of good things to call me?"

He rolled his eyes. "I was *going* to say beautiful. But now I'm leaning toward—"

"Magnificent? Ravishing? *Exquisite*?" She sighed dramatically before turning and resting her arms against the banister. "I know; the options are limitless."

When he didn't speak, she glanced over her shoulder. His gaze had snagged on her exposed back—where her dress dipped lower than any piece of clothing she owned. There was such sorrow in Cota's eyes as he beheld her scars. They were two jagged, uneven lines that reached from the nape of her neck down to her waist. He reached out a hand before pausing, but, perceiving her silence as permission, he touched her back. It was barely a brush of his fingers before he pulled away. "I've never seen them fully healed," he practically whispered.

"I thought it was time I stopped hiding my past," she said, "along with everything that reminds me of the tragedy of it."

"And am I a part of this new beginning?"

She faced him. "If you want to be."

He was inches away. "I do."

She didn't realize Caspian had arrived until he cleared his throat. They whirled toward him. She felt like she'd just been caught. Her heart was racing. His expression was blank, though, which meant whatever he had seen, whatever his reaction, he didn't want it revealed. And she barely knew him, but...she had a feeling he hadn't wanted to see what he had.

"The ceremony awaits," he stated.

Their arrival had been so rushed that Adresia hadn't been able to fully take in her surroundings. But now, as Caspian led them to the Throne Room, she couldn't absorb everything fast enough. The main corridor of the Suites, the chambers designated for nobles, had windows overlooking the Inner Gardens. Tall hedges lined gravel paths and flowers of all kinds sprouted in the shrubs, resisting autumn's chill.

Noting the Princess's chambers at the end of the hall, they turned right at the intersection and exited the Suites. Benches crafted of stone sat under windows; vases of daisies and ferns sat atop tables; elaborate paintings of varying images hung along the walls, giving life to the spacious area. Caspian pointed to the wide corridor ahead. "The lesson hall and spare studies are down there, along with my chambers—second door on the left. Past that, the library, and beyond that, the common folk quarters. "We're going this way." He beckoned them left, through the covered walkway. A cool breeze fluttered across her skin as they passed.

Adresia actually beheld the foyer this time: a thick, gilded banister lined the spectacular main staircase and from the ceiling hung a magnificent chandelier adorned with dozens of candles. Caspian led them down the steps, through the first floor's covered walkway, and entered an area almost identical to the second floor, with branching hallways and a wall of windows overlooking the Inner Gardens. To their right was a gated entrance guarded by two men. Downward steps led into darkness. There was nothing except empty silence, as if all the noise had been sucked away down there.

Caspian's grimace matched her own. "The dungeons. That way—" He pointed left, where two open doors beckoned with life and light— "is the Throne Room. Beyond that, the Queen's chambers. And that door right there," he added with a smirk, pointing to a small door to their left, "is a servant's passage that goes straight to the kitchens. Idyllia, the head cook, always has extra pastries."

They entered the Throne Room. Nobles were cramped on either side of the vast chamber, leaving a path directly in the middle as if the Court dared not to be in the Queen's way when she arrived. Two thrones sat atop the dais straight ahead: the left slightly taller with intricate whirls of silver and black; the right a simple, elegant mixture of white and gold. Adresia could guess which one belonged to the Queen.

As they wove through the sea of nobles, she prayed no one paid her too much attention. She already hated being singled out in Westholt, and here...everyone knew everyone. They halted by a table with varying drinks. Caspian faced them the same time a strong pounding surfaced in her head. "The Royal Court," he began, "consists of the many nobles presently living at the castle under the Queen's protection and command, awaiting orders to engage with their various authorized obligations as our Queen sees fit. On the other hand, there is the Queen's Council, consisting of hand-picked advisors that aid in instructing the Royal Court and handling other pivotal matters of the Queen's. These selective nobles will be watching your every move—so if you have any secrets, I'd suggest keeping them to yourself," he added with a twinge of humor, although she didn't find it very funny. "As of tonight, Lady Bellum, you are part of the Queen's Council."

Adresia let out a surprised noise as Cota blurted, "*What?*"

"It is a surprise to many, but Her Majesty sees potential in you." The Hand glanced toward the doors. "I cannot say more than that. Just trust that all will be revealed in time. We'll talk later."

Before he could turn away, she quipped, "Why is there an entire celebration for me? I don't understand why I'm so important."

There was a flicker of a smile on Caspian's face. "You *are* important," he said, "but it's just a ball. Any excuse for festivities and the Queen takes it." He whizzed away a moment later.

She believed him...but she also knew there was more to that truth. This was no normal ball, just like this was no normal summoning. *Trust*, he'd said. But who could she trust?

✧

The throbbing in Adresia's head had grown obnoxiously irritating. She pressed a palm to her temple as if it would help and grumbled, "We've been waiting forever."

"It's been half an hour," Cota countered. "Have some patience."

She crossed her arms. "I hate waiting."

But perhaps the gods truly pitied her, because the room suddenly quieted. A servant announced, "Her Royal Majesty, Queen Narissa Vander of Morolyn!"

The man had barely finished speaking before Adresia felt...something. It was a presence you couldn't run from; a darkness you couldn't hide from. It radiated everywhere and nowhere, filling her veins, provoking needles behind her eyes. Nausea washed over her. No—she couldn't be ill. Not now. She would *not* vomit in front of the Queen.

And then Narissa entered.

She was exactly as Adresia had always imagined. Despite being over fifty years old, she looked half that age. Raven hair spilled over slender shoulders, blending with a beaded, onyx dress that hugged full curves and trailed along the floor. Her face was of astounding beauty: full, rosy lips, distinct cheekbones, and eyes... Many might confuse them with black, but even from where Adresia stood at the back edge of the crowd, she knew what color they were: violet. One of the rare shades that had been lost when magic disappeared.

It wasn't so lost anymore.

The Court bowed low, barely a loud breath sounding as footsteps grew closer, then passed. The Queen ascended one, two, three steps before sitting upon her dark throne and watching them. Finally, her chin dipped, and they rose. If the Court wasn't intimidated by her sharp stare, the jeweled, regal crown atop her head would do the trick. Narissa scanned the crowd impassively, but Adresia swore the woman's gaze landed on her for an instant. A chill swept down the Countess's spine. It wasn't that she was being watched; it was the *way* the Queen watched, as a hunter watched its prey. Because that's what they were to her.

Prey.

The servant's voice sounded again. "Her Royal Highness, Princess Corvina Vander of Morolyn!"

The Princess was as far from her sister as a sibling could be. She was stunning and graceful and light. She had bright, honey eyes that matched the tiara sitting atop her glistening, blonde hair. Her cream gown had a laced high neck, long sleeves that billowed at the wrist, and an intricately layered skirt. With a polite smile, she sat beside her sister and nodded to Caspian, who had appeared at the Queen's side.

Narissa stood. "I thank you for attending such a wondrous event." Her words, while modulated and clear, held an undertone of demand and authority. "While I don't want to keep you from the festivities any longer, I would first like to introduce a new member of my Council who will be staying with us indefinitely: Lady Bellum, a Countess from Westholt."

Defeaning applause sounded. "She changed your name?" Cota muttered.

The Countess met Caspian's gaze. He shrugged, but his lips were pulled into the smallest smile. "She was forewarned," Adresia replied.

"For too long has Westholt been withdrawn," the Queen continued. Adresia suppressed her scowl. *Withdrawn*—as if Dazelle hadn't completely abandoned the province for years. As if it was *their* fault it had become the independent, laborious place it was. "But no longer. This collaboration—"

"An inescapable alliance, she means," Adresia muttered.

"—signifies the broken boundary of our provinces now fastened together once more! Lady Bellum, an extraordinary future lies ahead of you and your province. May you receive all that you merit," the Queen proclaimed, eyes glowing in the torchlight. And whether the woman remembered who Adresia was or what had happened five years ago, the unspoken challenge was too tempting. So much that Adresia made to step forward—

Cota's fingers wrapped around her wrist, tugging her to a stop. "Don't," he warned. "That's exactly the reaction she wants from you."

Indeed, when Adresia looked back, a faint smile had found the Queen's lips. She knew *exactly* who she'd summoned to her castle and how Adresia would react. The Countess clenched her jaw, but stepped back to Cota's side.

"What would you have done anyway?" he asked. "Spat at her feet?"

"In her face," she corrected.

"You'd earn yourself a cell in the dungeons instead of a chamber in the Suites and what good would that do you?"

"It'd be worth the punishment."

"Tell me afterwards if that sentiment remains."

By the time Narissa rested back on her throne and an upbeat melody filled the air, Adresia's headache had almost subsided. The crowd broke into a dance around them. "If you let your anger control you," Cota said, quiet enough for only them to hear, "if you make even *one* mistake that you can't take back—there's no chance we'll find out the truth. She's going to test you like she did tonight. Are you prepared for that?"

Adresia just crossed her arms.

"Not answering is an answer too." He leaned close and added proudly, "I'm right."

"You always manage to be," she said.

"Is that confirmation?"

The excitement around her was too endearing to not smile at. "Take the pride while you can, Lord Bowyer. Soon enough *I'll* have it when I meet all of the Queen's advisors and am given personal invitations to parties that even Harley would envy."

"Will do. And are there, perhaps, a plus-one to all of these fancy occasions?" He puffed out his chest. "Maybe if I dress up enough they'll mistake me for one of these famed Lords."

Adresia let out an unbridled laugh, running her hand messily through his hair. "*Definitely* not. I like you much better the way you are now. And it seems someone else does too." She pointed to the Lady who gave Cota a bashful smile and held out her hand. He glanced at Adresia before accepting it.

A part of her had wanted to keep him back, to make him stay with her instead of dancing with the other Ladies eyeing him around the room. Honestly, she'd forgotten all about them. But when she, too, was whisked away by a handsome suitor, she let the thoughts fade as a night of dancing began.

✧

Adresia lost track of how many hours passed. By now, it was well into the night, and she abandoned her latest partner when the music slowed, snatching one of the golden goblets from a table before pouring herself some water and popping a berry in her mouth. A minute later she'd made herself a full plate and cleared it instantly; she hadn't realized how hungry she was. Gulping down the last bit of water, she faced the floor again, her feet rubbing mercilessly against the ridiculous shoes she'd been forced to wear.

Caspian appeared at her side, a goblet of merlot liquid in hand. "Enjoying yourself?" he asked.

"Immensely," she replied. "But tell me: when is this supposed to end?"

"The night is young."

She gaped at him.

He smiled before adding, "I always sneak out just past midnight. The Queen has yet to notice and I doubt she'd detect your absence."

The Queen definitely would, but Adresia didn't argue. She took a steadying breath, watching the Court in a daze. Balls and dancing, she loved deeply. But she didn't know how much longer she would last after a week-long journey across the kingdom. Definitely not through the entire night.

Caspian tipped the rest of the wine in his mouth, set the goblet on the table behind him, and held out a hand. "Care for a dance?"

With a defeated laugh, Adresia took it.

As they circled the floor, he asked, "Can I ask you a question?"

"Of course."

"What happened to your back?"

She kept her face blank. Was this his attempt at procuring the confession out of her? "I was attacked when I was younger."

"By who?"

"I—I didn't know them," she answered a little breathlessly. Did he really not know?

"And they hurt you?"

Her gaze hardened. "In more ways than one."

He tensed, his concern only confusing her more. "Why?"

"Why do you care?" It came out harsher than she intended.

"Because people don't deserve to be hurt like that. You don't."

"You barely know me."

"Well, not just *anyone* would let a stranger escort them to a river in the middle of the woods only three days after meeting. I think that says something about our friendship."

"Maybe."

"I'm sorry I brought it up."

She shrugged. "Questions were bound to arise. It was my choice to show my scars."

"That's very brave." His fingers tightened at her waist. "Remind me to not ruin our conversations by asking any more personal questions."

"You didn't ruin anything."

"Thank the gods. I wouldn't want to scare you away after a mere nine days of knowing each other. That'd be embarrassing."

She couldn't help but smile.

He grinned. "I like this Adresia *much* better."

"And which Adresia would that be?"

"The happy one." Her chest strained at the truth of his words. There had always been two sides of her. "Well," he said, "while I would love to claim my dancing partner for the rest of the night..."

The last thing she saw was his sparkling, blue gaze before she spun out of his grasp and slammed into another. Her eyes widened. "I am *so* sorry—" She looked up to find her best friend beaming at her. "*Gods*, Cota, you scared me!"

He echoed her laugh. "I remember you promising me a dance."

"Care to lead, Lord Bowyer?"

His responding grin was impish.

The strange looks they earned weren't enough to compel them to stop being the rowdiest pair on the floor, performing the most folksy dances they could recall from the few celebrations they'd attended during their childhood. Whilst most of the Court regarded them with discomfort, they also gained a few spirited supporters from the crowd. Their excitement broke the unease that had begun to creep into Adresia's mind; she didn't remember the last time she had felt so childlike.

After one or three or ten hours later, they stepped off to the side, unable to continue any longer. "There's no way I'm getting back to my chambers," she said, leaning against the wall beside Cota. "You're going to have to carry me." Her best friend's responding chuckle faded when a woman stopped before them. She stared blankly ahead, her brown eyes unmoving. Adresia pushed from the wall. "Can I help—"

"I have a message," the woman said monotonously.

Adresia hadn't even blinked before a wrinkled parchment was pressed into her hand. Confused, she couldn't do much else but scan the faded ink.

The greetings of many faces are one in the same.

Greetings of many...what? "I don't know what this means," Adresia said. "Who are you?"

The woman smirked, as if it was precisely what she'd wanted Adresia to ask. "A shadow." And then she disappeared into the crowd.

Shadow indeed.

Adresia shared a look with Cota before they pushed through the bustling Court, searching and scanning. Everyone looked the same. And just when she was ready to give up—

There. The woman glanced over her shoulder before slipping through an obscured side door. Adresia sped after her, hoping she wasn't gone. They paused in the dim passageway as the door clicked shut behind them. The woman was ten feet ahead, her back to them.

"Who do you work for?" Adresia demanded.

The woman turned around, but said nothing.

"She asked you a question," Cota said.

Again, no answer. Only that slim, ambiguous smile.

They whirled as the hallway brightened and chatter drifted into the space. Caspian watched them from the doorway, brows contorted in confusion. "Are you alright?"

"I—" Adresia glanced back to explain, but the woman, along with any chance of answers, was gone. "I thought I saw something," she finished.

Caspian opened the door wider for them. Before they were fully through the door, she shoved the note into Cota's hand, who slipped it into his pocket. But as they emerged back into the room, Adresia's mind wasn't on the celebration. It was on the Queen's pulsing stare. And although the Countess hadn't found out anything even remotely useful, she was sure this was only the beginning.

Chapter 9

Adresia relished in the luxuries of day-to-day castle life over the next week: warm baths whenever she wanted, appetizing meals at her command, an endless wardrobe full of the most extravagant gowns she'd ever seen. At least, she *had* enjoyed it—until two days ago, when she'd repeated the same routine for the fifth time in a row and had grown desperately bored and irritated. Being a noble hadn't been at all what she'd expected.

Her chambers were remarkably spacious. Against the back wall sat her bed, adjacent to the wide windows overviewing the Findara Forest; to her right, the bathing chambers; and opposite her bed was a lounge and fireplace. One of her favorite things was the bookshelf to her left. There was a limited supply of dust covered volumes, but if it was any indication of the types of novels she'd find in the library, it was a good sign—not only because she loved having a supply of stories to remedy her passion for worlds unlike her own, but so she could scour any and all information regarding the puzzling riddle that strange woman had left her a week ago. She couldn't get it out of her head.

The Countess sat up in her four poster canopy bed, the transparent drapes hooked to the front columns. A faint smile bloomed on her lips as fractured rays of sunlight spilled into the space. Maybe she wasn't all *that* tired of the lavish reality that was now her life.

Kicking off the heavy linens, she glided into the bathing chamber, her bare feet padding against the floor. She was finishing tugging the sleeves of her lavender daygown over her shoulders when Cota remarked outside the door, "You take forever to get dressed."

"Try putting this on yourself and then reconsider the difficulties of being female." She emerged. "And *why* are you in my chambers so early, may I ask?"

"If I recall, you have something to tell me."

Right. They'd celebrated his twenty-first nameday four days ago, and *somehow* he'd managed to convince her to reveal her plan to him. It was good. Blunt, if not easy. Perhaps a *bit* skeptical...but she disregarded the specifics. Especially when Cota voiced his concern.

"*That* is your plan?" he asked. "Really?"

"I know what I'm doing," she said with as much conviction as she could, just as she'd rehearsed.

"It's practically a death wish."

She rolled her eyes. "The Queen won't behead me for having a few questions."

"Confronting her about what we're doing here, why she killed our parents, and if she plans to kill us too sounds like a *plan* to you?"

She waved a hand. "I told you, I'm leaving those little details out. I'm not stupid." He gave her a look that said otherwise. "I know what I'm doing," she repeated sharply.

"What are you going to say?"

"Oh, you know...'Your Majesty, I was wondering what malicious schemes you're hiding—'"

"You don't know, do you?" Her feigned smile vanished, and she crossed her arms. He stared at her, waiting. She didn't budge. "Fine," he groaned at last. She looked at him doubtfully, but he sighed. "If you believe discussing arrangements with Narissa rather than letting her come to you is best, then I trust that you can handle it. You *will* handle it. It's not like I can tell you what to do anyway."

"Even though you would lock me in this room if you could just to keep me from my *rash* decisions?"

An unapologetic smile. "*Yes*."

She patted his chest and strolled past him. "Good to know."

"You would've gone with or without my support—so why did you go through the headache of this argument just for me to give it to you?"

She plopped atop the sofa, not looking back as she said, "I don't need your support. Just your trust, and the assurance that you won't stop me."

She heard him walk across the room and open the door. "I couldn't stop you even if I tried."

"No," she said. "You couldn't."

"You better be alive the next time I see you," was all he said before he left.

When the door opened again, Adresia groaned. "I don't need a lecture, Cota—"

The words died on her lips. It wasn't her best friend, but two young women, beaming excitedly. "That's the fourth time we've caught him leaving this week!" one remarked.

Adresia's cheeks heated. "We were just talking, Gillian." But despite continuously reminding the women that Cota and her had been best friends their entire lives, the more comments the servants made, the more Adresia couldn't help but start thinking them too; the more she realized she'd been thinking them long before she'd left Westholt.

Gillian laughed, her ginger curls bouncing around her face. She laid a tray brimming with fruits, porridge, and several beverages on the short-legged table by the hearth. Kasya routinely unlatched the window to let the outside air in, her blonde locks billowing in the breeze. While Adresia ate, Gillian wove the Countess's hair into an intricate plait over her shoulder. The sound of Kasya stitching a new dress filled the silence between one of Gillian's glorious stories about her seven siblings and the next, and the trio broke into squeals of laughter when the woman recalled the time her brothers started throwing mud at her and the rest of her family had rescued her by retaliating until a full-out mud war erupted.

A knock unexpectedly sounded. Adresia called to enter, and the three of them rose, curtsying when Caspian walked in, an unfamiliar man at his side. "Lord Hand," Adresia greeted.

"You have quite the marvelous room," he said.

"I wouldn't be that kind with *my* description."

"Not to your liking?"

"Oh, it's more than enough—but even jewels grow dull if you stare at them for too long."

There was a surprised cough from the second individual. Seeming to remember his companion, Caspian gripped the man's shoulder and said, "This is Sir Fox Atlas. He joined the Shield when I was made Second—and was the only fifteen year old recruit that has ever impressed me."

The knight's dark hair was just past his shoulders, the upper half bound behind his head. Everything about him screamed warrior, from his towering posture to his burly arms. A terrific sword hung at his side, but what really caught her attention was his face: amber eyes pierced her like a knife and a prominent scar ran down his right side, from his brow to his cheek. Fortunately, the incident had left his eye undamaged, whatever had happened.

"It's a pleasure to meet you, Sir Atlas," Adresia said.

His gaze slipped from somewhere behind her to her face. A dip of his chin followed; bowing—to her. This was normal, she realized. Respectful. She *was* a noble. And she outranked him. It shocked her enough that she didn't hear anyone speak until Caspian cleared his throat.

"I'm sorry, what?" she asked.

"I was just wondering what your daily routine tends to look like," the knight said. "Do you leave the castle often?"

"No. My servants have been more than enough company this past week."

Fox's gaze drifted to the women, and while his face didn't change, his eyes twinkled in awe.

"Would you like an escort around the grounds?" Caspian prompted. "Perhaps you two could become more acquainted."

Adresia peeled her eyes from the man. "And why is that necessary?"

"The Queen has assigned him to personally escort you and protect you from any tribulations."

What tribulations? she wanted to ask. *Why a guard?* But this was fine. A pestering knight was the last thing she wanted, but her plan could still work. She just needed the opportunity to leave his sight. "A walk sounds delightful," she said. She strolled into her bathing chamber and snatched a cloak from her closet before pausing at the door.

"Does she think I'm her guard?" she heard Fox ask. "Because you know we aren't the same thing. I'm a *knight—*"

"Technically, you *are* her guard," Caspian replied. "But, yes, I know how you're stingy about the titles." There was a noise, like Caspian clapping Fox's shoulder. Heavy footsteps sounded. Fox was walking away.

When the knight spoke again, it wasn't to Caspian. "Do you make all of your own clothing?"

Adresia wouldn't have thought he'd been able to speak that soft had she not just heard it herself. It was intriguing enough that she peeked through the cracked door.

Fox's relaxed shoulders were sagging compared to his rigid posture before, although his hands still remained behind his back, fingers white from how tightly they wove together.

Kasya smiled. "Yes." Her voice was a pipsqueak compared to his.

"You're beautiful. Your—your clothes, I mean."

"Thank you. You're very kind, Sir Atlas."

Adresia stopped listening and hastily tucked a blade in the pocket of her gown before entering the bedchamber again. Fox had returned to Caspian's side, just as stiff and tense as he'd been before. Because of her?

She glanced at her servants. Gillian had a massive smirk on her face and Kasya's cheeks were flushed as she continued sewing the garment in her hands.

"Shall we?" Adresia asked the men. Caspian gave her a wide berth in answer.

As she led them into the hall, the women chirped a farewell in sync. Adresia wiggled her fingers, grinning as Fox and Caspian followed.

✧

Adresia didn't need to escape Fox's clutches that evening. Caspian had left almost immediately for a meeting, and halfway into their walk around the castle, the knight had mumbled something about meeting him back at her chambers and disappeared. Fortunately, Adresia had ran into Cota. They'd spent the rest of the evening in the gardens, discussing the dull ongoings he'd been forced to endure before he'd left for yet another. When Fox hadn't returned looking for her, she'd decided to test the lengths the Queen had instilled upon him to guard her—and to see his reaction when she returned two hours later than they'd agreed. She found him waiting outside her chambers at dusk, arms crossed.

"Where have you been?" he asked.

"The gardens," she stated.

"It's late."

She wondered if he knew he was this little pawn of the Queen's. "And that matters because...?"

"It's just an observation."

"Well, thank you for that observation." She walked past him.

"You should be careful," he warned.

She hid her smile before facing him. "Are you threatening me? Or is that just another *observation*?"

"It's not me you should be threatened by."

"Then who?"

"There are things you shouldn't do; people you shouldn't associate with. *People*," he added pointedly, "that you might be close to."

"What are you—"

"You know precisely what I'm talking about."

She straightened at his tone. Why would she need to be careful around her best friend?

"I'm just trying to help," he said. "Nobles *watch* here. Nothing goes unseen. And if you want to hide something...you won't."

"What makes you think I have secrets I want to keep hidden?"

"Everyone has secrets, Lady Bellum." And seeming to know every question in her head, he stated, "I don't know what the Queen wants with you, I don't know why you're here, and I don't know who you are. But I've been tasked with your protection, and I will do everything I can to ensure that my duty is not frowned upon. The next time I tell you to return to your chambers, don't act like a child and stay out late."

She narrowed her eyes. "If you couldn't find me, maybe you're just not as good at your job as you thought you were."

"I've been here for eleven years; I know this castle like the back of my hand. I'm *more* than adept at my job. I knew where you were the moment I left and where you've been every moment after that—and it's obvious you don't want a guard. Your efforts to evade my vision were more than pitiful."

She contained her grin once more; he'd told her exactly what she'd been wondering all day. Although it *was* slightly unsettling to know just how much he was aware of. Perhaps he was feeling her out as much as she was him. "And what were *you* doing?" she asked.

"That isn't your concern."

"You may be my guard, but I outrank you. You can't tell me what to do, nor when to return to my chambers."

"Next time, I won't let you leave my sight."

"Will there even *be* a next time? Or will you just run off again to do whatever you were doing today?"

A muscle flickered in his jaw. "Just do what I say and stay where I tell you."

"Because you're in *the Shield*?"

He sighed hard as if he was holding back his temper. "I intend to protect you. Your safety isn't an idea to be tossed around with clumsy hands."

"You hardly know me."

"That doesn't mean I can't do my job to the best of my ability."

"Fine." She faced her door and grabbed the latch. "What's so wrong with a relationship, Sir Atlas?" She hadn't pointed out his flirtation with her servant, but he seemed to remember anyway.

"Lower class relations are treated differently. But you, a noble, and with a direct connection to Her Majesty... Just *be careful*, Lady Bellum. For your own good."

Why tell her these things? They'd met that morning, and he had no incentive to like her, to help her. Maybe he didn't care. Not about her, anyway. But why say anything at all? Why risk her suspicion instead of scoping her out undetected? Was he warning her for her sake—or his?

She turned back. "Why are you—"

But he was already down the hall.

Friend or spy—that was the question. She didn't know which one was worse.

✧

A curious lady wondering where her Queen was—that's how Adresia presented herself to the sentry posted outside the Throne

Room the next day. She remembered Caspian mentioning a general direction, but she wasn't willing to wander off on her own just yet. She hadn't forgotten the Captain's warning during their journey here: *I'll be watching you, Lady Bellum.* She had a feeling an encounter with him—and only him—wouldn't go in her favor.

The sentry readily directed her: the Queen's chambers were just past the kitchens, through the main corridor of the servant's quarters. It was an odd place for a ruler to have royal chambers, but at least Narissa was unlikely to traverse across the entirety of the castle to keep an eye on the Countess. Spies were easier to deal with.

Her heart skipped a beat when she exited the servant's passage and stopped before the extravagant, arched entry. Before she could take a step closer, a petite voice sounded behind her. "Her Majesty awaits your presence, Lady Bellum." The Countess was deciding whether to strangle the servant for sneaking up on her or ask how the Queen knew she was coming when the girl beckoned her forward.

Adresia was mistaken. Spies were so much worse.

After a hesitant moment, the Countess entered the most luxurious chamber she'd ever laid eyes on. Numerous carpets lined the floor and countless furnishings adorned the walls. Bookshelves and tables and chairs were cluttered with candles and jewelry and tomes. Three rooms branched from the lounge: a study with stray parchments atop a desk, a bedchamber with the largest bed she'd ever seen, and bathing chambers with a large tub built into the floor, greenery lining the edge of the steaming water. The Countess had no idea where the servant had gone, whether it be back through the entrance or some hidden doorway.

Adresia's gaze finally landed on the Queen, who lay atop a velvet chaise sofa, so engrossed in observing the vase of foreign flowers before her that the Countess nearly jumped out of her skin when the woman spoke. "Do you enjoy the taste of wine?"

This was a horrible mistake. She should leave. But what would she say? She couldn't very well just walk out on the Queen. After all this time, she didn't have the nerve, the *courage*, to face the woman who had ruined her life.

"I asked you a question, Adresia."

The Countess blinked, only to find Narissa's midnight eyes reading every emotion on her face. Adresia curtsied deeply. Thank the gods, her voice was steady when she responded. "I haven't had the pleasure, Your Majesty."

"The funds, you mean," the woman said. Adresia stiffened. "You haven't had the *funds* to buy wine. There's a difference." Narissa rose, her satin robe spilling to the floor. She sauntered to a tray of beverages, her steps near silent. The Countess wondered where she'd been taught the art of stealth. It wasn't everyday that a Queen knew how to hide her footsteps.

"Your chambers are magnificent," Adresia commented. Narissa picked up the largest decanter and poured a generous amount of dark red wine into two florid chalices. "I wasn't aware there were chambers larger than the King's." Not that she'd ever even been in a castle to *see* such chambers.

"The King had two chambers. This is one, created for greater privacy and separation from the rest of the Court. I took residency here the day I was crowned. The other is upstairs, abandoned and useless." Narissa approached Adresia, answering the unspoken question as she went. "As long as I reign, there will never be a consort on this throne."

Adresia accepted the glass and took a hearty sip, if only to distract herself from the shiver that skittered down her spine.

"You may speak freely," Narissa stated. "I understand there is an earnest matter you wish to address."

How, exactly, she knew these things... "I wish to discuss the purpose of our requested presence here at the castle."

"As in Lord Bowyer and yourself."

Adresia felt like it was the wrong response, but said, "Yes, Your Majesty."

Narissa smiled into her cup, gesturing to the cushioned armchair across from her which the Countess sat in. "*Our*. Such a funny thing, friendship. Best friends usually come as a package. I once had a best friend, too, as surprising as it sounds. We cherished this world together." Adresia couldn't help thinking that the Queen was looking at her throat. "But I summoned *you*—not him. Do not make the mistake of mixing up that little fact again." The Countess refrained from scowling as Narissa smiled again. Whatever was amusing her...it was getting under Adresia's skin. "What do *you* think you've been called here for, Lady Bellum?"

"Well, the land we inherited—"

"Land? No, you have no land. You have an empty manor that rots on a null, negligible property as we speak. And money? As we've already established, you have nothing in your pockets."

Adresia clenched her jaw. She *knew* she was talking to her Queen, and she *knew* she should bite her tongue, but the woman had basically declared her life worthless. "If I am so invaluable, then why am I here?"

"Just because you *own* nothing does not mean you *are* nothing, nor that you cannot provide anything." Narissa ran a finger around the lip of her goblet. "You're young; unwed. An attractive woman of nobility." The wine in Adresia's mouth suddenly tasted like poison, but she forced herself to swallow. "You hold much potential in Court."

Adresia set her goblet on the table in an attempt to distract her irritation. She had one desire: to know what she was doing here. That was all. She hadn't come for a meticulous examination or insults or gossip, whatever it be the woman was doing.

"I told you to speak freely," Narissa stated. "Speak."

Adresia wouldn't give in—she couldn't. "I want to know what I'm doing here."

"I don't think that's the whole truth."

Oh, her temper would be the death of her. "I don't think you ever fully say what you mean either, but who's to judge?"

The Queen tilted her head. "I've called you here because I'm making you my Ambassador. It's already been discussed with the others. I was just waiting on confirmation...and I believe I've just received it." The magnitude of the statement barely hit the Countess before Narissa went on, "You're confused. And perhaps upset that I haven't formally addressed you since your arrival. That's understandable." As if the woman could ever understand. "But it was a simple matter of how much you value your time here. I summon nobles quite often with little to no explication. Not once has any of them done anything except bathe in the wealth and luxury that Dazelle offers—that *I* offer—for weeks without a single inquiry. Much like I expected you to do when I witnessed you so fervently enjoying my ball a week ago. They do not care to serve their Queen or make a life for themselves, and so their futile, rapacious lives spent wasted in my amenities come to a steadfast end and they are sent home, perhaps worse off than before."

Adresia truly had a death wish. "So I've unknowingly passed this test of yours and now you believe I have what it takes to be in your Council?"

Violet eyes narrowed. "And for what reason does this displease you?"

Her stomach tumbled. "I didn't mean—that wasn't worded the right way—"

"On the contrary, it was faultless. But you're an *impeccable* liar. It's precisely why you're ideal for this position."

Adresia was unsure whether to profess gratitude or be offended. "What do my duties as Ambassador consist of?"

Narissa sank back into her chair; so un-queenly. "Earls and Countesses are normally on an estate, collecting taxes and governing a specified area of land, fulfilling their pitiful aspirations of being as close to a ruler as they can be. Instead of governing in Westholt—as you have nothing there—you will visit various villages and towns across Morolyn and handle matters that I am not able to handle as quickly myself, much like you would do as Countess if your royal duties hadn't been forsaken."

"So this is about me abandoning my earldom?"

"It's about whatever you want it to be. All that matters is that you serve me now. Since you'll be on the road quite often and will certainly deal with plenty of unkind folk, you'll begin training as soon as possible—something you're well acquainted with, to my knowledge."

"Training?" She felt nauseous. There was no way the woman knew *that*.

"Yes," Narissa answered slowly, likely analyzing Adresia's reaction. But any hint of momentary skepticism disappeared as she elaborated, "You will train with my Hand alongside the Shield. He mentioned something about your familiarity, which is more than convenient."

Of course Caspian had told Narissa of her skills. At least, what he *assumed* was her skills. He was Hand, after all. She shouldn't have been so naive to have thought he would have kept anything from his Queen.

"And what of Lord Bowyer?" Adresia inquired.

"He won't be joining you as Ambassador, if that's what you're wondering. I'll keep him occupied just like the rest of the Court."

Relief pooled Adresia's gut. He wasn't being sent away, thank the gods.

"Unless you have any further inquiries, you're dismissed," the woman said, strolling toward the bathing chamber. "And Adresia?" The Countess halted mid-curtsy. "The next time you come to me, whether it be to question, confront, *challenge*...remember who it is that keeps that pretty head of yours on your shoulders."

When the Queen disappeared behind the bathing-chamber door, Adresia practically darted from the room. She was halfway across the castle when she overturned the encounter in her head. For some reason, she found it incredibly hysterical. The things she'd said... A soft laugh burst from her lips. She *was* lucky to have her head. But her smile vanished as Fox stepped into her path. "I thought I warned you," he said.

"You and I both know that's not what you meant," she said, stepping around him, "but I'll take 'not willingly talking to Her Majesty ever again' into consideration."

"Lady Bellum." He grabbed her arm, and instead of sending him to the floor, she let him stop her; turn her. A pleasant, surprised Lady, that's who she had to be.

"Can I *help* you, Sir Atlas?"

"Why are you doing this?"

"Doing what?"

"Why are you *here*?"

"Your questions are best addressed to the person responsible for them." She gestured behind her. "Her Majesty is that way."

He gripped her arm tighter as she made to walk away again, but, this time, Adresia spun, no longer containing her glower. "I would advise letting go of me. Immediately."

He did, wisely, and even had enough sense for those amber eyes to appear unsettled. "I'm just trying to do my job," he said.

"Good. Then let me do mine."

"And what is that, exactly?"

"The only thing you should concern yourself with is your duty to guard me. Do you even know where I've been all day? Or was your little speech yesterday simply a bluff?" Silence. "As I thought. So don't tell me you're trying to do your job when you aren't even doing *that*." He stared at her, his features somehow expressionless yet portraying precisely the same irritation she'd felt only moments before. "You don't trust me, do you?"

"I don't trust anyone I've only known for a day."

Not caring to finish the conversation, she took a step away.

"Just remember what I said."

"Are *you* excluded from this list of people I should be wary of? You watch and listen a lot yourself, you know."

"Maybe."

And perhaps it was the fear still coating her tongue from her conversation with the Queen, or the taste of danger had just made her reckless for more, but she leaned toward the knight. His fingers tightened around the handle of his sword, the movement so small he probably didn't realize he was doing it himself. The satisfaction she received from it was far more exciting than she'd expected it to be, and her mouth curled into an innocent smile as she said the exact words she knew he'd been waiting for since they'd met. "Maybe you should watch out for me, too."

Chapter 10

It had been an unusually dull morning—and that was saying something as Hand. The halls were abnormally quiet, days had passed since the Queen had summoned him, and even the servants' gossip was hushed as they went to and fro. Perhaps the change would grant him a break in his tedious duties, but he doubted it; there were still crucial meetings to attend, heavy discussions to have, and pestering nobles to administer to.

Caspian's chair groaned as he propped his boots atop his desk. Sunlight streamed through the wall of glass behind him, warming his back. He held a wooden quill in his hand, the inked point digging into the tip of his finger. Things would be interesting soon enough.

The moment he'd heard the chatter, he knew who they'd spoken of. *A Lady addressed the Queen.* It took two words from him before the whole story emerged—no lies or petty twists that the Court liked to exaggerate. His servants had served him his entire life, and they knew well enough not to report anything but what was confirmed true.

He still felt a slight pang of fear at the thought of it. Gods above, she'd *confronted* Narissa. She was lucky to be alive after some of the things she said. He'd seen the Queen send men to their graves for far less.

A light knock sounded. "Come in."

Clad in a simple lavender gown, Adresia entered, pushing the study door shut behind her.

"How are you?" he asked.

She plopped into one of the armchairs in front of his desk. "Noble life hasn't been as exciting as I expected it to be."

"Is that so?"

She met his gaze with a blank stare, not a care in the world about what she'd done yesterday. If he didn't know better, he would've believed her. "Perhaps, I don't know…having a friendly chat with the Queen sounds familiar?"

He barely caught the flash of panic in her eyes before it vanished. "How many people know about that?"

It was enough of a confession that he grinned. She was completely aware of just how bad things could have gone. That meant he didn't need to lecture her like he'd initially planned. He couldn't—not when he so desperately needed her to agree to what he was going to say. "That's not what I summoned you here for. I have an offer, of sorts, that I'm hoping to trust you with."

"What kind of offer?"

He debated how much to reveal. "There are people here who will do everything they can to find out the truth."

"The truth about what?"

"Anything," he admitted. "There's always information circulating in a mixture of gossip and honesty; that's how Court works. And some are willing to lie and cheat and *kill* to get it." He lowered his feet and set his quill atop his desk. "I haven't the slightest knowledge of why Dazelle has been withdrawn from Westholt for so long." A lie. He knew, now. "I'm willing to bet your summoning is only the beginning of something." He propped his elbows atop the desk and clasped his hands together. She watched him closely, in that way she watched everything. "Things are changing, Adresia. Who you choose to ally yourself with is crucial. Every move you make, every expression on your face…it will shape how you fare during what is coming."

Her expression was unreadable. And it surprised him—how well she knew this game given she'd never been to Court even once in her life. "Why do you really want to be my friend?" she asked. "What do you want?"

That was precisely the question. What could he tell her to convince her he was on her side? How much could he confess without revealing everything he knew?

"There's a substantial number of citizens who hold the belief that our Queen is evil," he stated. No reaction came. "You don't seem bothered by the idea."

"I'm familiar with the haunting depths that people can go to acquire what they want."

He didn't think it was right to ask *what*, exactly, the Queen had done to her. The Queen had done many things to him, too.

She asked, "So you want me to...what? Pray to rid the evil in our land?" Her words were half comical, half soberingly serious.

"I think we can help each other," he said.

"How so?"

"I need your trust. I *want* your trust. I want you to know that we *are* friends, and if you ever need anything, I can help you. If yesterday indicates anything, it's that you aren't the fondest of our Queen. The sentiment isn't foreign to me."

"Because you hold the same belief as the rest of those believers—that she's evil?"

She really knew how to read him. *And* how to get him to reveal more than he'd planned. "In some ways."

"You're quite distrustful of the ruler you've proclaimed allegiance to. I'd expect you to be the Queen's most loyal advisor."

"Very few can be trusted completely."

"Can you?"

"I want to be a man worthy of trust. For now, all I'll say is that I have my own reasons for wanting to help you—and for keeping information from the Queen. I will be your inside man; anything you need, I will do my best to be at your disposal as we unfold the truth of this *evil*."

"What would I do for you in return?"

"You'll be accompanying some assigned groups to various locations to survey targeted matters as the Queen requests. I would ask you to...probe the village; the citizens. Watch who goes where and listen to what is discussed—anything particularly strange. You may not understand what is said, but it is *crucial* that you remember the peculiar events that will indeed transpire. While I am your eyes and ears here, you are mine outside these walls."

She leaned forward, elbows digging into her thighs. She was intrigued, if not wary. "You want me to spy for you?"

"I want you to observe." At her pointed look, he couldn't help but smile. "Yes, I want you to spy."

"Why can't you do it?"

"I'm constantly being monitored. People are suspicious of me—and with good reason."

"Why?"

"Let's just say I've done a few things in the past that went unnoticed. I've learned since then."

"Won't I get caught?"

"While my clothes and sigil give away my status and my face is recognizable among many, you're just another unfamiliar individual to blend into the crowd. I'm willing to bet that's one reason our Queen chose you as Ambassador in the first place: unknown, you're free to act however you wish. And I believe you're more than capable of handling what's out there."

"You might be right." She studied him for an unsettling amount of time. Did she trust him? Suspect him? Had his forwardness deterred her? "If I went and told the Queen about this little conversation, would she honor me for my loyalty or behead you?" When she pushed from the chair, his hand shot out in alarm. Her eyes were wide with interest as she sat back down. "My trust isn't something I readily give away," she said quietly.

His relieved exhale came out shaky. "Nor is mine."

"This is about more than just spying." It wasn't a question.

"Nothing is ever as it seems. Not here."

"Are you ever going to tell me the entire truth?"

"Is that agreement to my offer?"

She opened her mouth, but no words came out.

"You don't have to decide right now," he said.

She leaned back in her chair in response.

He let her think, busying himself with one of the countless documents before him. Ten minutes later, he was about to let her leave when she said, "I accept your offer."

He looked up from the desk. "You do?" He hadn't expected an answer so quickly. Honestly, he hadn't expected an answer at *all*. The fact that she'd agreed...

"I will be your spy outside of Dazelle," she declared, "and in return, I will have your absolute trust and secrecy with whatever I need." He nodded his agreement. "The Queen mentioned training?"

"Be expecting word within the next few days."

She peered behind him as she stood. The elaborate wall of glass panes revealed the courtyard. Beyond that, the Obissean Lake seemed to stretch infinitely into the eastern expanse of Morolyn. "I like the open space," she said. "It's almost like I'm outside." With a sideways glance, she observed the arched entrance that led into his bedchamber. She walked over, parting the floor length curtains to the side. He'd requested the design once he'd become Hand, identical to the one that led into his bathing chamber. "This is the only chamber I've been in that doesn't have doors separating the rooms." She scrunched her nose. "But what about privacy?"

He smirked. "Care for me to show you?"

She shook her head in silent amusement and strolled back to the door.

"Adresia?"

Her fingers grazed the handle as she halted, and the way the sunlight hit her face, making her eyes sparkle and skin glow and hair shimmer...he couldn't rip his gaze away.

"Caspian?"

He blinked, having forgotten what he was going to say. "Despite being my spy," he said smoothly, "I really enjoy being your friend."

The brightness in her face vanished. Did he say the wrong thing? He shouldn't have let himself get tangled in his thoughts. Why had he been thinking those things? He *couldn't* be thinking those things.

But instead of a snide remark, her lips lifted. "No one's ever said that to me before." And with the amount of raw, unshakeable pain he observed in her eyes...he thought it was the saddest smile he'd ever seen.

Chapter II

Sat before her vanity, Gillian brushed Adresia's hair, recounting the servants' gossip from the day before. Through the mirror, the Countess watched Kasya on the sofa, who hummed quietly to herself as she sewed an exquisite burgundy cloak with fox fur trimming. Being named Ambassador meant endless opportunities for new garments. "Of course the lad didn't know what he was doing," Gillian said, "but no one told him how to be a proper steward. He took one look at the stern Lord and fled at the first command!"

Servant duties sounded entirely more interesting than Ambassador's. Adresia had had her first meeting with the Queen's Council, and it'd been painfully dull, to say the least. There hadn't been a *single* mention of the stirrings in the kingdom—just city expansion, province inspections, and a briefing from the Duke of Dazelle.

The Countess preferred spending the evenings with her servants, engrossing herself in their lives and trying to forget about hers; about her new service under the Queen's command; about her confusing feelings for her best friend; about Caspian and his unexpected offer.

She hadn't known how to respond. There he was, the Queen's most loyal servant, professing to be the exact opposite. She'd pored over the contrasting possibilities, however ridiculous or mundane they might be, and had come to two conclusions: either Narissa was exactly who Adresia expected—Caspian's shocking faithlessness proved as much—or it was a trick. Adresia just hoped she'd chosen right. She hoped Caspian wasn't lying. Because despite her initial plan to use him...she hoped they could actually be friends.

Gillian finished Adresia's hair the same moment Kasya strolled toward the bathing chamber, a bucket of dark liquid in hand. "I've just finished dyeing the fabr—" A startled cry left the servant's lips as she tripped, the stained water splashing across the ground. Kasya's face turned the same shade as the rose colored dress Adresia wore. "I'm so sorry—I didn't mean to—I'll clean it up right away."

"That's alright," Adresia said, rising from the vanity. "I can clean it."

"It's my fault, my lady," Kasya countered. The servants hadn't yet gotten used to the idea of calling her by her real name yet. "Besides, you have lessons to get to." The woman opened the bathing chamber door, but, with a laugh, Adresia darted inside first. She emerged a moment later and handed the women several spare linen cloths.

"You didn't have to do that," Gillian said.

"I don't mind." There was no reason for the women to fret over such trivial matters.

When they finished soaking up the liquid, Adresia took the sopping cloths, dumped them into an empty basket beside the tub, and scrubbed her stained fingers clean before returning to the bedchamber.

Fox had arrived, but he wasn't looking at her. She slowed her steps, watching him observe Kasya from across the lounge. Her hands moved in incomprehensible ways as she sewed. When Adresia and Cota had run out of new clothes in Westholt, she had quickly learned to stitch tears and patch holes, but what Kasya did... The young woman never failed to impress Adresia with her masterpieces. Nor Fox, it seemed, as those amber eyes twinkled in adoration. At least, until he noticed her approach and went rigid in awareness. "You're here early," Adresia said by way of greeting.

He glanced behind her, to the faintly stained floor. "Did I miss a murder?"

A pointed look. "I was actually waiting for the victim to show up." Her brows rose in feigned surprise. "And look! You've arrived on time for once."

"I always arrive on time," he countered. "It's *you* who likes to run away and pretend it's my fault."

Adresia was wondering how long the exchange would last when Kasya giggled. It was innocent enough that when Fox dropped the argument, Adresia did too. He beckoned to the door. "Shall we?"

"There isn't anything *else* to do, is there?"

Gillian and Kasya bid them farewell, and Fox glanced at the servant as if wanting to say something more, but decided against it when he spotted Adresia's gaze. Once they were down the hall, he remarked, "You watch too much."

"Aren't you the one who warned me to do exactly that?"

He didn't respond.

She said, "You don't have to keep it a secret, you know."

A sidelong glance. "What?"

"Your feelings."

"Yes, I do."

"But you said lower classes—"

"We *all* do. And if you're smart, you'll hear what I'm saying."

By the time she thought of a retort, they'd arrived.

Lessons were, in her not-so-humble opinion, one of the worst encounters of being a noble. Every highborn child was required to go through several months of unending torture whilst being forced to learn and memorize anything and everything that a noble should know. As a Lady, Adresia wasn't meant to be taught the practices of warfare nor the managerial tasks of maintaining land and commanding an estate. She was expected to submit to an advantageous marriage in which she was worthless if she didn't provide heirs and hold her social status to the highest importance. Her father, Harley, *and* Kovare had taught her differently, but the Queen deemed her short schooling inferior and underdeveloped, and so, Adresia was now being forced to relearn the information in private sessions every morning. The past week had been ridiculous. The woman had made it quite clear she knew Adresia was more competent than the Countess initially let on. This was solely for humiliation and authority-setting purposes.

As always, Fox remained outside while she stepped into the small study. Subtly slipping her hand into her pocket—Kasya had added them to all of her dresses—Adresia made sure her small blade was still there. It was, and she slouched in her usual, old armchair before waiting for her mentor to start. He was merely a scholar, but being alone with a strange man who she knew nothing about...the risk of a blade was worth it.

Her head perked when she was told, as a result of being appointed Ambassador, the subjects of her lessons were shifting. No more reiterations of etiquette and reputational growth. Today, the old man rambled about the provinces of Morolyn, and while she'd rather end the three-hour long lectures altogether, she knew refreshing the information would be helpful when her real duties began.

There were five provinces scattered across the kingdom. Dazelle, the province of riches and nobility, lay inland of Morolyn's northern border. It was comprised of two-faced Lords and Ladies who judged anyone who dared be content with anything less than the wealthy.

Sheavania, the province of harvests and shipping, lay along the coast of the Soarlee Channel. The people lived simple lives in a kind, honorable society. Those who haven't visited deeply yearned to go, if only to experience a sliver of their harmony. It's said to be the most blissful society in all of Morolyn.

Euwyrst, the province of religion and education, was the closest to Dazelle and rested north of the Sight Woods. There dwelt crazed, bothersome fanatics that spit prophecies from the countless gods and vexing scholars who think the best route of schooling is the one that will distinguish the lower class from the highborns even further than they already were.

Yugrana, the province of hunters and merchants, was south of the Traderious Woodland, along the coast of the Sarinthian Sea. It was a place of discipline and rigorous work, but the rewards of being skilled with a bow and blades were celebrated in hearty festivities around roaring fires on the beach as one mighty clan.

And then there was Westholt. The province of timber, stuck between the Sight Woods and the Traderious Woodland. Similar to Sheavania in the sense that the people don't often leave, but different because it wasn't a lifestyle of comfort. Few others dared interact from fear of the northern woods, but merchants occasionally traversed from Yugrana to trade. Westholt was just out of reach from the strict rulings and influence of Court, so they'd established their own traditions and pleasantries; however, because of the remote location, in order to survive, work had to be done. It was their way.

There *was* another place: Abraria. It wasn't a province despite that it lay within Morolyn's northeastern border, and Tethoris had never claimed the isthmus. Whether it was because the Orrycolt Mountains separated the eastern kingdom from the small territory, or that Abraria had somehow proven itself to be both worthy of respect and remain untouched as its own...no one knew.

The Countess was ripped from her daydreaming when her aged tutor appeared before her. "We're done for today," he croaked. "Go fetch yourself something to eat, dear girl."

They'd ended nearly an hour earlier than usual, but Adresia didn't argue. Her stomach rumbled as she closed the door. "I'm going to the..." Fox wasn't in the hall. What a surprise. "Kitchen," she finished to no one. Eyeing the Suites, she realized Cota would still be in his chambers. If she was quick, she could ask Idyllia to make his favorite breakfast tart before lunch preparations began.

Accepting the small bit of excitement as a challenge, she raced to the kitchens. Some of the servants bid her a familiar hello when she entered, and she snagged a few spare sausages, a piece of toast, and two tarts, one of which she ate in three bites, the other she wrapped and put in her pocket. She downed the food with a goblet of water and departed with a cheery "Thanks!" before racing up the familiar flight of stairs—only to slow as an unwelcome face came into view.

"A fine day, is it not, Lady Bellum?" the Captain asked.

"It is."

He stuck out an arm when she made to trek past him. "Where are you off to in such a hurry?"

"That's my business, isn't it?"

He leaned closer. "I've noticed something about you, Lady Bellum."

"What would that be?"

"You never back down from a challenge."

She clenched her jaw. "And?"

"It will be your downfall."

Her features twisted into distaste, and she went to respond, but realized he was right. Any attempt at a rebuttal would only prove his point. Sensing her realization, his mouth curled into a satisfied grin. "Is something amusing, Captain?" she snapped.

His eyes flashed with surprise. But not the beautiful, heartfelt type, like a child receiving a gift. This was dangerous. This was when a spider awakens to find dinner caught in its web. He shifted fully in front of her, making her lean on her heels. She wasn't willing to walk away and let him win this skirmish for dominance that he'd started, but a quick glance over her shoulder told her that if she took a step back, if she so much as misplaced her foot by an inch or tripped on her gown, she'd go toppling down the stairs. And when she met his gaze, she knew they were thinking the same thing: one push. That's all it would take. She gripped the railing at her side.

"What are you trying so hard to hide?" he asked.

"What are you trying so hard to find?" she countered.

He gave an impressed smile. "Now I understand why He wants you. You're something else entirely."

Something flickered in the back of her mind at the word; a memory she hadn't touched in five years. "Who?"

The Captain simply cocked his head and stepped out of her path. Hesitantly, she took one step, then another. She didn't let out her breath until she was long past him and down the hall. *What* in the Goddess's name—

"Lady Bellum!"

She halted, allowing the heavy boots to catch up with her. When the knight appeared at her side, she couldn't help but exclaim, "Where were you? I thought we were past this—" She gestured in the air— "You and whatever it is you're always doing." A part of her felt bad for taking out her unease on him. It wasn't his fault the Captain was a nosy prick. And when she looked again, she realized he was out of breath too, face slightly paler than its usual golden tone. But she was still shaking, and she *was* annoyed at him for never being there.

"I...thought I saw something," he said.

She resumed walking, not waiting for him to follow. "You don't trust *anyone*, do you?"

He matched her pace. His breathing had calmed by the time he replied. "I trust the Shield."

"Because you have to?"

His tone didn't hide his dissent. "I took an oath to serve Morolyn. I won't just disregard my honor—"

"How long did it take you to prepare that excuse?" They both stopped, and she waited for two servants to pass before quietly declaring, "If you really believed in this kingdom, you wouldn't be looking for reasons not to."

"That's not what I'm doing."

"Isn't it? What were you looking for? What did you *think* you saw? If there's nothing wrong, you wouldn't leave my side. But there is," she added quietly. He gripped his sword at the words. "I want to help. So why don't you trust someone other than yourself, Fox?"

He tensed at his name, but didn't reply.

She just glared before twisting away.

"I thought you were a bratty, spoiled Countess before I met you."

She stopped. The words didn't sting; it'd been her intention to instill such misperceptions after all.

"But you know more about Court than I thought you would," he went on. "You know more about a lot of things."

"It's what I've had to do to survive."

He appeared next to her, and, with a wary glance around them, admitted, "I haven't trusted the Queen since the day I joined the Shield."

"Why did you join, then?"

His shoulders sank, even as his features remained emotionless. "So no more innocents would die."

Too quick to judge—that's what she'd been.

"I'm willing to risk everything I believe in for this kingdom," he continued. "Those people are my truth. What's yours?"

She opened her mouth, closed it, and then settled on: "Nice try."

He crossed his arms. "You tell me to trust you, but you don't trust me. Tell me how that makes sense."

"No one gets to know my truth. I can't risk it."

"Why not?" The demand in his words made her lips itch for a smile.

"I think you already know why."

He searched her face. "You're dangerous?"

She *did* smile then, sweetly. "Perhaps."

"*Perhaps* you just want people to think that. If they do, then you have control; you stand a chance."

"Perhaps *you're* lying," she remarked, "and you told me that nonsense so I would reveal my secrets."

"I don't think you're dangerous, Adresia."

"You're wrong." Something inside her demanded destruction, retaliation.

"If I was actually wrong, then you wouldn't tell me I was. You wouldn't give up that foothold; you *need* to appear a threat. But you're not. I know it." He relaxed his grip on his sword. "What happened before I found you? You looked like you'd escaped."

She huffed a sigh. "Even if you don't, someone else thinks I'm dangerous."

"Who?"

"Pay more attention and maybe you'll find out."

"Is that my strategy in this little tussle of ours? To watch everything you do?"

"You're the one who advised me with the tactic, remember? It's time you put it to use."

"I will—if you start letting me ask questions when I find things out."

"Things like...?"

"Like who you were just talking to. Like what motives you have to serve the Queen even though you despise the idea. Like what is going on with you when you aren't here."

"I'm always here."

"Not when you gaze out the window and think about whatever it is you think about."

He paid *that* much attention?

Fine. He trusted her—to an extent. And maybe she should trust him, too. "Use your imagination," she said, backing down the hall.

THE BANE

"It sure gets a lot of other things right." He opened his mouth, but she clicked her tongue. "Don't spoil our fun just yet, Fox."

Chapter 12

"I'm so bored I'm beginning to read these words in another language."

It wasn't until Cota completely lowered the novel he was reading that he beheld Adresia's amused grin. He was sitting on his sofa, Adresia's head on his lap as she lay across the length of the soft cushions. "Another *language*?" he repeated.

"Mhmm."

"And what language might that be?"

"Sanguis."

He chucked his book atop the low-lying table in front of him. "You just made that up."

"No, I didn't! It's from a small tribe in the East that consumes blood to survive—"

His face twisted in revulsion before he cut her off. "I'll just take your word for it." She laughed before returning to her book. Like he'd done so many times before when he was lost in his thoughts, he ran his fingers through her hair. "What do you think it means—the note?" He hadn't been able to get the line out of his head since the ball.

Adresia huffed a sigh through her nose. "I think it means we're supposed to be here."

They'd spent the entirety of the day scouring books he'd borrowed from the library, but had found nothing. They didn't know what to look for, who to look for. And that woman—who was assuredly not a servant—hadn't shown up again anywhere in the castle. It was like she'd completely disappeared.

"Do you remember your parents voices?" Adresia asked.

For a moment, the only noise was the crackling flames in the fire. "Sometimes," he said. "But...we were bound to forget. Time has a twisted way of doing that."

She nodded. "I never realized how happy I was in Westholt. It was hard, and the memories were there, but I knew we were away from worse. I trusted that we had grown up apart from a society that grinded every little flower into dust for its own selfish uses. And now that we're here..." She sat up. "I don't want to forget that: what we had and where we came from."

"You won't forget."

"How?"

"I'll remind you of it, everyday—how special and brilliant and wonderful you are."

"Don't think you aren't any of those things, either," she said. "I know I do a sloppy job of reminding you."

He smiled. "You might not say it in words, but I notice it in your face; your eyes. You always manage to make everyone around you feel seen. It's what I love about you."

She breathed a flustered, "Thanks," before twisting toward the table. Something in his stomach twisted when she plopped a kiss to his cheek. He barely knew what had happened before she quipped, "Goodnight, Cota," and disappeared from the chamber.

Twinkling moonlight greeted him by the time he peeled his gaze from the pages before him a second time. He'd ended up scouring further, if only to distract himself from his own thoughts, but it hadn't worked. Solving the mysteries of this deranged Court was proving impossible.

When a knock sounded at his door, he wasn't surprised. Adresia never gave herself breaks. Knowing her, she would have gone to the library and procured some outrageous theory from an ancient tome that miraculously answered all of their questions. He pulled himself from the couch, tossing the book he hadn't been paying attention to on the sofa and strolled across the chamber. When he opened the door, his mouth went dry. "Your Majesty." He bowed. "I wasn't anticipating your visit."

The Queen swept into the room, an earl gray gown flowing after her. "I wanted to stop by. No one is aware."

He wasn't foolish enough to believe the words were anything except a threat, but he still shut the door. He wouldn't be afraid. Not of her. At least, he *wasn't*—until the woman stopped beside the sofa and turned, her violet eyes ablaze like a dangerous wildfire; waiting, taunting, ready to swallow him whole. "In the short time that you've resided within these walls, Lord Bowyer, rumors have emerged. My Court is expansive, vast, and, if anything, loyal as I expect them to be. You wouldn't know anything about such whisperings, would you?"

He attempted to stand taller, noting the way she'd said *my Court*, as if he weren't a part of it. "What do these rumors suggest, Your Majesty?"

The Queen grabbed his discarded book, opening it with a slender finger and flipping mindlessly through the pages. "I understand you and Lady Bellum are quite close."

"Yes. We've been through a great deal together."

"She is *very* pretty, wouldn't you agree?"

"She is. More so, if I am being completely honest."

"Honest?" Narissa hummed a surprised laugh. The sound was oddly pleasant. "I like honesty. *Especially* from men." She tossed the book back onto the sofa and beheld him once more. "Answer me, then—*honestly*. Are the rumors true?"

He hadn't the slightest clue what his response was meant to be. What did she want from him? "Rumors are tricky things; they can be misinterpreted and misheard. So perhaps they are...or perhaps they aren't."

The Queen approached him with a grin, and he knew it wasn't because she found him amusing. Like a serpent sizing up a mouse, violet eyes followed his every movement. "That *is* unfortunate, seeing as I've taken this gossip into my own council and sought out the truth for myself." His stomach dropped when she stopped uncomfortably close. "I have a strong distaste for such affiliations. Especially ones like you and Lady Bellum so unabashedly exhibit."

"We're best friends, Your Majesty." There wasn't anything going on. Not from Adresia's side, anyway. She didn't feel that way about him. "We've been together our entire lives."

A hand met his chest, and he took three steps back until he hit the wall behind him, his heart pounding relentlessly. "What is it that motivates you, Lord Bowyer? Is it lust? Passion? Children?"

A part of him barked and growled at her predatory, roaming touch, but, suddenly, he didn't feel like moving away. "I don't know what you mean."

She ran her hands up his arms. They tingled with something unfamiliar and unexplainable; something hauntingly desirous. "Lady Bellum has no dowry. She has an abandoned, invaluable property. She can't provide you with *anything*. Is that what you want? A dull, unexciting life, always straining to get by?"

Cota had never noticed the flecks of silver in Narissa's midnight eyes. They were like blazing stars, capturing his attention as if he was seeing the night sky for the first time in his life.

"I can give you everything you want and *more*," the Queen proclaimed.

Her face was a beckoning, a sweet temptation. He didn't want to look away.

"She doesn't need you," the woman whispered. "She doesn't care about you."

Her voice was like a lullaby, soothing him to sleep and waking him up every time she spoke again.

"You don't want her. She doesn't want you. She doesn't *love* you—"

Like waking up from a dream, the word rattled something in him. The chamber came into sudden focus. He beheld the hairsbreadth of a distance between him and the Queen with overwhelming sensitivity. "I'm sorry, Your Majesty," he said, "but I'm going to have to decline…whatever this is."

Dark eyes flashed, but not in offense. Narissa merely cocked her head. "I'll be watching you, Lord Bowyer. You *and* Lady Bellum." She touched his jaw with a lover's gentleness, and he restrained himself from cringing away. "But if I find that your friendship has progressed into something more, the consequences are on your hands. Do not take this warning lightly." She was gone before he could blink. Fresh air filled the room in her absence, soothing his tightened chest. He warily touched his cheek. Where her fingers had been, it was now bitter and cold.

What had she just done to him?

Chapter 13

The last thing Adresia expected was to be brusquely awoken by a bucket of frigid water. With a startled gasp, she flew upright. A rumble of anger lurched from her throat as she beheld Fox at the end of the bed, lowering the empty bucket to his side. She was going to *throttle* him—

"Get up," he said. "Training starts in fifteen minutes."

She glanced out the windows. It was barely dawn.

Fox snapped his fingers. "*Now.*"

"*Someone's* grumpy," she stated before throwing off the chilled, wet sheets and stomping into the bathing chambers. Five minutes later, she was weaving her damp hair into a braid as she trailed the knight. The empty corridors were foreign, their steps the only sound. She stifled her yawn. Why had she not been notified beforehand? She wouldn't have stayed up reading last night. But what peeved her more than her exhaustion was the fact that she hadn't been alert enough to notice Fox's entry. She shot him a glare from behind and asked, "Why are you acting strange?"

Ignoring her, he asked over his shoulder, "Are you really as skilled as Caspian claims?"

"Better, actually."

"We'll see."

"Where are we going?" she demanded. No answer. "*Fox.*" He remained silent. When they neared the front doors, she pulled him to a stop. "What is *wrong* with you? You know what? I don't even care. I don't know what put you in such a pissy attitude, and at this point, your moods are more of an effort to keep up with than the war." His brows rose. "If you're scared of being punished for being my friend and not keeping up with the brooding-guard-facade that you established when we first met, that's fine. But the next time you take it out on *me*, you'll regret it."

For some reason, he didn't look offended. "Is that all?"

Her heart skipped a beat at his lack of rebuke. She crossed her arms and huffed, "Yes."

There was amusement in his eyes. Real and undiluted; the most alive she'd ever seen him. "Your first lesson: don't let everything bother you so much. *But...*" He held out his hand. "I will treat you with only the utmost respect from here until you say otherwise."

It was a test, by the Goddess. And she'd failed. Miserably. She rolled her eyes and swatted away his hand, hoping he didn't notice her reddened neck. "You're an idiot."

"Not as much as the other two you have wrapped around your finger."

Her eyes widened. "I don't know what you're talking about."

"Don't you?"

Her gaze narrowed. And then: "I like being your friend *much* better."

Amber eyes flared with surprise. "Oh gods, I already regret it—"

"You can't take it back! Now let's go. Training starts in two minutes." She faced the entrance and waited for him to lead the way. After a long look, he did; right through the front doors and into the courtyard.

There were several dozen men scattered across the worn dirt expanse. They all eyed her approach, some standing around with weapons while others stretched. Not knowing how to act, she lifted her chin and marched after Fox. Caspian and Cota were already at the barracks. Thankfully, her best friend seemed to have averted his dislike for the Hand this morning, as both of the men had pleasant expressions on their faces. By some miracle, their frequent crossing of paths must have sparked an unexpected commonality.

"Speaking of the two fools," Fox said at her side.

"You just joined the pack," she muttered. His mouth clamped shut.

"Morning," Caspian chirped.

Cota held up the end of her braid. "Did you take a bath before this?"

She waved him off. "Of course not." She smiled at Fox. "Sir Atlas decided to wake me with a refreshing, *cold* bucket of water."

Caspian's eyes went round. "I notified Fox *yesterday* when your training would begin. He was meant to relay the message for the sole purpose of your preparation."

The knight smiled smugly. "I guess I forgot."

"You're going to regret that," Cota warned.

Fox met Adresia's gaze. "So I've been told."

She grinned. "Ready to train?"

Chapter 14

The Hand wasn't entirely unfavorable. Cota had been forced to converse with him that morning before Adresia and Sir Atlas had arrived, and, from the surprised reaction the Count had received, the Hand had evidently expected Cota to snap again like he'd done in the Sight Woods. What was even more surprising had been the Hand's interactions with the guards. They'd joked and smiled and had looked pleased to see each other. The Hand hadn't given a single sign that he thought himself higher than the others. The kindness had struck Cota so much that his dislike for the man fizzled into unexpressed respect.

Training began with an introduction of every weapon the Shield possessed and which ones they used most often. Cota explained which ones he and Adresia were most familiar with, and then they ran through some drills. Cota crossed his arms, Sir Atlas already doing the same on his right as they watched from the entrance of the barracks, a barrel of fresh water at their side. The warm morning sun combated the brisk autumn breeze that fluttered across the courtyard.

Adresia freely swiped at the Hand as she had been for the past fifteen minutes, and while it appeared they were feeling each other out, she'd barely broken a sweat. Cota could see why the man was Second in the Shield: he was incredibly observant, impressively reactive, and seemed to take into account the few flaws in Adresia's movements. But he didn't know what she was really capable of. She'd been trained by a warrior, after all.

The pair paused their sparring and Adresia ambled over to Cota's side. "You're barely trying, aren't you?" he muttered. She smirked. "It's getting boring watching everyone gawk and wait for you to stumble."

A sort of pride glinted in her eyes. "I'm in the mood for some fun." She downed her water and receded back to the dirt square, pointing her shortsword at him. "Only this once, though. Blink and you'll miss it."

He didn't look away, even while the knight at his side indiscreetly watched them, even while the Hand observed them from afar, fingers aimlessly roaming the weapons rack. With a nod, Adresia signaled him back. Cota could hear the man's question as the two circled each other, swords raised. "How much experience do you have, exactly?"

Adresia pursed her lips, eyes wandering around in thought, giving the Hand a perfectly good chance to attack as she let herself fall vulnerable. But he didn't take it, and Adresia answered, "More than you think."

"And you've been trained before?"

"Thoroughly." Her grip tightened on her blade. "My father served in the war. He taught me everything he knew. I was his little soldier from the day I was born."

"Under whose command did he serve?"

"His own."

The Hand's brows rose in surprise. "Your father was a General?"

"General Arrikus Bellum." Adresia cocked her head. "Why don't I just show you what I know? All of this chit-chat is boring."

Unsuspecting, the Hand almost reacted too slowly when Adresia slashed at his undefended side. Luckily, he blocked the blow and, with a bit of effort, drove his sword up and forced her back. She receded with a smirk. He was doing exactly what she wanted and didn't even know it.

At the sudden action, the surrounding guards that had been constantly glancing at them completely halted their training to watch. Cota barely noticed them, too transfixed as the pair erupted into a dance of parries and jabs, the sound of clanking swords bouncing off the courtyard walls. The Hand strenuously hacked to no avail. Adresia deflected every strike. She knew where he would step before he did.

Lined with warning and amusement, Cota muttered her name. She broke from the Hand and gave Cota a look that said, *Really?*

He tilted his head. *Quit playing with him.*

She faced the Hand again and carefully positioned her feet. He eyed her warily, and it was only when she smirked, both in mockery and enjoyment, that he made his move.

They were a storm, almost moving too fast to track each movement. She attacked until the Hand had no choice but to retaliate, even though he couldn't; not when she was forcing him to do nothing but defend himself. He managed to drive her back, but Cota doubted it was anything but allowed on her part. There was a pause, a break in her onslaught, and, knowing he was faltering already, the Hand took his chance.

But it happened too fast for him to counter.

As he thrusted toward her abdomen, Adresia sidestepped and advanced on him close enough to smash his hand with the butt of her sword. Betraying him, his fingers released his sword. She spun, pulling the blade from his grasp and tossing both of their weapons away. She continued twisting until she faced him again, now with the sharpened tip of a dagger pressed against his neck. His arm was still extended where he'd held his sword a breath before.

Half of the men were gawking, the others murmuring incredulously amongst themselves. Even Sir Atlas had taken a step forward, hands slack by his sides in disbelief. Cota just grinned.

"How did you do that?" the Hand asked, breathing hard. Adresia pulled back. "I've been training these men for most of my life and *no one* has ever outmaneuvered me like that." Cota was expecting him to step back, to cringe from the incomparable skill that she'd just hinted at—but, to his surprise, the Hand stepped closer, a sort of awe in his eyes. And although he shouldn't, although he had no right nor claim, Cota's gut twisted.

Adresia just stared at the Hand; stared and stared until, finally, she tucked her blade in her belt and said, more warning than suggestion, "We should do more drills."

Chapter 15

The Queen of Morolyn had grown used to the voices.

They were everything and nothing, light and dark, the beginning and the end. They haunted her nightmares, the only dreams she had if she slept. They never left. And this time, there were so many. Too many. Over and over, they drowned out her thoughts, louder than they'd ever been before.

We feel it too.

You must stop it.

We cannot control it.

It is the greatest threat you have ever faced; the greatest threat you ever will.

"No," she breathed. Uncombed raven hair spilled over slumped shoulders. There was a discarded crown beside her, its ruby jewels shining in the candlelight like blood. Her nails dug into her desk as fear pressed onto her chest. Louder and louder the voices rose, threatening to crush her, suffocate her, drown her. "*Stop.*" She wished, begged, *pleaded* for an end.

It *will be your end.*

It is *your end.*

Once unleashed, it cannot be contained—

Wood groaned beneath her fingers.

"I want to see how far she will go," the Queen rasped, every word a revolt. "I want to know her limits. I *will.*" Her; they could not control her.

THE BANE

A pause. Was it surprise or anger? She didn't care. It was a blessed reprieve. Such soothing, comforting, silence. She hadn't heard it in decades.

Your dread is delightful.

Her head emptied out.

We know you. We know the terrors that haunt you. We know the fear that captivates your attention night after night instead of rest.

It was wrath and rage, comfort and peace. She couldn't tell the difference anymore. Such calmness; their voices too much.

How afraid are you?

Do not lie. Do not lie. Do not lie. She'd learned it the hard way.

"I'm terrified."

What are you afraid of?

"You." Even if she wanted to, she couldn't conceal the workings of her mind. They knew her thoughts. They knew everything.

You do not know us. You have never seen us. You cannot understand us.

"You made me."

You have been made, and you can be unmade.

The realization hit her like that short, sweet silence had. "Not by you, though." A small noise came out of her throat—a chuckle that twisted into a dark laugh. "You cannot touch me."

It can.

"Not yet."

They will forget you.

"They will fear me before that."

They do not know fear, as we do.

What we fear, they will.

You will.

"I will be your reckoning." The words came out before she could stop them.

There was laughing. Laughing and screaming. Roaring cheers, weeping, praying. It was too much noise, too fast, and she just wanted it to *end*—

"Your Majesty?"

The Queen grabbed the servant's throat. "*What?*" she snarled. His fear leaked into her head, swallowing her like an ocean.

"I was told to retrieve you for the ceremony," he wheezed, trembling under her tightened fingers. She released him, and he stumbled back with a hand on his neck. "He's here."

The voices faded into a quiet thrum in the back of her head. They wouldn't admit it, but the power she'd attained, the authority she possessed...it scared them.

Her blood-red lips curled into a grin.

Chapter 16

The steady chatter that filled the Great Hall had entertained Adresia for the duration of the evening. She was seated directly beside Cota at one of the two polished tables extending almost the entirety of the room. Along with a woman she'd never seen before, Caspian, the Captain, and several others in the Queen's Council sat with the Queen and Princess at a third, smaller table in place of the thrones. Narissa could see everyone and everything—including the guarded entrance directly opposite her that she continued to impatiently glance at.

At the end of her table, Adresia found the familiar features of Westholt's Duchess. Not once had the woman ever considered returning to Court. She'd made her distaste blatantly clear five years ago, so the fact that the woman had arrived a month after Adresia had left was more than interesting. Their gazes met, but instead of returning Adresia's warm smile, the Countess only received a tight-lipped expression before the Duchess averted her gaze.

Adresia frowned. "She's acting strange." Cota lifted his head mid-chew, perking a brow in silent inquiry. "Harley," she clarfiied, stuffing warm bread into her mouth. She hadn't yet gotten used to the delicious food.

"Maybe if you stop staring at her like a fox, she won't feel so uncomfortable."

Adresia gave him a pointed looked. "I want to know why she's here."

His eyes flashed with warning. "No."

"But—"

"But *nothing*. It's none of your business, nor should you seek it out."

"I shouldn't have said anything."

"If you hadn't, you would have caused a *scene*—" He poked her arm— "and I would've had to drag you out."

She huffed a resentful sigh through her nose.

His gaze softened. "Don't do anything rash, please."

At her silence, his brows rose. "*Okay*," she grumbled. Maybe it wasn't any of her business. She *should* just listen to him for once.

But maybe it was.

The evening stretched on forever. What had begun as casual, sober musings were now drunken, spirited exchanges that echoed through the hall with bursts of hearty laughter. Half of the Court danced to cheerful tunes in the open space between the tables. Adresia once again noticed that unfamiliar woman beside the Queen: long waves of onyx hair, electric green eyes, an alluring smile. She didn't appear much older than Caspian.

Adresia tapped the man beside her. "Who is that?"

He followed her gaze. "Jadice Wren. The Queen's Warden."

"What does she do?"

A shrug. "She's just returned after being gone for six months."

"From where?"

"Not a clue. But she's mighty close to Her Majesty. They've worked together for as long as I can remember." Adresia could see that in the way Narissa gave the Warden her full attention, as captivated as the nobles around them. Jadice spoke exuberantly, clearly unafraid to speak her thoughts, but somehow still holding the respect of the others. Adresia didn't have to strain to listen; she could easily hear every word from where she sat.

"—were so scared that they pissed themselves! After seeing that I could do far worse than what they'd endured, though, they gathered themselves pretty quickly." The Warden glanced at the Queen with a sort of casualty that Adresia had never witnessed before and lowered her voice in the slightest. "I'll tell you something: I'd rather handle those draygonians again than those whiny men for one more second—"

Adresia swore Narissa's eyes widened before she hissed something at the Warden, who paled in response. A petite, female servant leaned over the Countess' table to refill a goblet, blocking the view, and at a sudden outburst nearby, the girl flinched, spilling wine across the table. She instantly sputtered her apologies, her face reddening. Across the table, a Lord scowled and said, "That is precisely why I haven't bought a female to serve at my estate. Useless women can't take care of anything." The servant looked ready to curl in on herself. "Are you dumb, girl? Clean this up!"

Adresia contained her growl and told the girl, "It's fine. Don't worry about—"

"She's meant to serve us and get out of the way," the Lord snapped. "But, of course, I'd expect nothing more from you. You're the same *breed*."

Adresia opened her mouth to snarl several *very* unladylike words, but Cota's hand was instantly under the table, pinning her fists to her lap. "Don't get yourself into unnecessary trouble," he muttered. She allowed her rage to swell, to be angry with him before it switched back to anger at that terrible man, and with another pleading look from her best friend, she relaxed. The servant was already gone and there was nothing she could've done. Putting the Lord into his place would've been more effort than it was worth. Cota gave one last squeeze before slowly withdrawing his grasp.

Adresia glanced back up. The Warden was gone. Had Narissa dismissed her? She hadn't said anything wrong. Although there *was* a strange word. Dray-something? Draygonians. But what did it have to do with anything?

The Court returned to their seats with a swelling hush as Narissa stood. "As many of you know," she began, "an ascension is in order." A flurry of excited whispers stirred throughout the room. "By tonight's end, the Shield will have yet another Knight, one of the highest honors bestowed by me in this kingdom." With a wave of her hand, the doors opened.

Adresia's heart plummeted as Brazen Voss swaggered in, grinning like a fool. He looked exactly like he did five years ago: dark hair trimmed at the sides with three twisted locks on top pulled into a knot—the same style of the warriors who fought in the war decades ago—and the clearest, ice blue eyes she'd ever seen. He'd be handsome if he wasn't a monster. The only difference from the last time Adresia saw him was a long scar running diagonally across his throat. It disappeared under his tunic, where she knew it continued down his chest along with several other scars she'd given him. The Countess shut her burning eyes, letting the thoughts and memories and emotions fill her head. She thought she'd been free when he left Westholt, after she ruined his life and when he had so nearly ruined hers. She thought he'd be stationed somewhere far, far away, and she would never see or hear from him again. But she wasn't free. Perhaps she never would be.

When Adresia opened her eyes again, people were leaving. Had it already ended? She glanced back to the front of the room. Narissa was already gone—and Harley was in the group making their way to the doors. They'd be past her and gone before she could get another chance. She had to go now. "I have to talk to Harley," Adresia told Cota.

"What? No—"

"I *have* to." The Duchess was almost past.

"I know what you want to know, Res, but you can't talk here."

Adresia just gave him an apologetic look before rising and marching to the group. Before the woman could walk out the doors, the Countess grabbed her arm and said, "I have to talk to you."

Harley moved out of the departing nobles' ways, but wouldn't meet Adresia's eyes. "It's not safe."

"Then where?"

"There's isn't—"

"By the Goddess, Harley, *look at me.*" The Duchess did, nearly flinching in surprise. "Why are you here?"

"For the ascension."

"That's not the whole truth."

Harley stood taller, like the leader Adresia knew her to be. "I can't tell you."

That easily, the woman had dismissed her; like a mother regarding a foolish child, she was keeping secrets.

But Harley was not her mother.

"Did you know about Brazen?" Adresia demanded.

Harley looked away, then back, but didn't reply. She *had* known.

"Why?" Adresia didn't hide the betrayal in her voice. She was *still* withholding the truth, even after the Countess had left Westholt and was unlikely to ever return again. Even now, after what had just happened. Harley opened her mouth to explain, to give some pathetic excuse that meant nothing, but Adresia spoke first, barely keeping her voice from trembling. "You can't just *leave* without telling me anything; without saying goodbye."

The Duchess' gaze softened. "I know you want to try," the woman said, gently touching Adresia's arm, "but there is nothing you can do to stop this. You couldn't then, and you can't now. You have to live with what this cruel world gives you and find a way to make it worth living."

Adresia just stared at her.

Harley glanced at the doors. "I must go."

"The raids," she blurted. "Were they because of me?" The Duchess didn't react, didn't even move—but it was telling enough.

"They were," Adresia breathed in horrified realization. "Weren't they?"

"This is so much bigger than you think, dear girl."

"Please," Adresia begged. "*Please*, don't lie. Not anymore."

Harley's head was shaking as she backed away. "I'm sorry."

"Wait—"

But the woman vanished through the doors, and the rest of the Court flooded after her, eager to return to their chambers.

Adresia doubted she would ever see the Duchess again.

Chapter 17

The library was breathtaking. From the length of the exterior walls, it had to have been at least the size of the Throne Room, but with no windows in sight, the space appeared to stretch infinitely on. Distant torchlight signaled there were books amongst the tenebrous void. Adresia remembered what the Warden had said yesterday, but until she figured out what it was and why the Queen had been so shocked to hear it spoken aloud, it didn't mean anything. And even though she didn't even know what she was looking for, she stepped into the mass of knowledge and ink and began to search.

The hours that passed blurred into an undisturbed silence. From the isolated nook where Adresia quickly lost interest in what she was currently reading, she yawned and stretched her stiff limbs. Gods, she hadn't been here for that long, had she?

The girl tossed the book onto the low-lying table at her feet already laden with stacks of irrelevant knowledge and slouched back into her plush armchair. Not a single word or phrase had clicked. There was *nothing*. And despite her faint hope, she doubted she'd find answers about the Queen, no matter how ancient this library was.

Glancing at the contents before her, Adresia's gaze fell upon a book she must've left open. She went to close it, scanning the page out of habit, but a word caught her eye as she flipped the parchment.

Draygonians.

She threw herself upright, almost toppling the stacks over in an avalanche of parchment and worn spines before eagerly bringing the volume to her lap. Most of the information was written in a strange, foreign language, but there were notes written in the margins: translations. She read them once. Twice.

Several thousand years ago there was a war...violence and bloodshed spread across the continents...many believed it was the end of time... She ran her fingers down the page, skimming the simple excerpts. *Draygonians, referred to as* Death Bringers, *were one of the greatest forces in the Fallen War. The ruinous event was believed to have brought a source of evil unto the world.* "Sounds familiar," the Countess mumbled. *Magical lands were cursed, mages were massacred, and malice was struck into man's heart.* A breeze swept through the nook, sending a shiver down Adresia's spine. *Being the cause of thousands of deaths, terrible beasts were introduced by Roslyn Mendalium.* The girl flipped through the pages. All of the parchments were signed with the same initials: R.M. She hastily reached for another tome, racing through the contents. She *knew* she recognized the faded, yellow parchments. The journal entries were dated weeks and months apart, all written in that same, strange language with those translated notes. *I was able to tame the beasts...I now have a deep fondness for them...They've begun to defend me against others...* Adresia paused, hesitant to continue even though she knew what the journal would reveal, if the twist in her gut was any indication. *I fear they may be too protective now...Not a soul has been allowed near me...I have been unsuccessful in my attempts to calm them...* She inhaled sharply at the final entry. *They have gone wild. My family is dead. My village is gone. Their power has spiraled across the lands. To my utmost regret, I have been forced to stop the beasts. Out of shame, regret, and, above all, fear of revenge for so many deaths, I have changed my name and fled the kingdom.* Adresia pressed her palms against her temples, as if she could force the storm of information she had just read to conform, to make sense as she tried to *remember—*

Draygonians were used as convoys of destruction. And now the Warden had them, and was using them for...for...

It hit her, then, what was happening. Panic built in her chest as the information *did* make sense.

She should have stopped reading.

◆

Adresia hadn't stopped her drills when her hands became sore and cramped—and that had been hours ago. Taking her stance in front of the target, she inhaled deeply and pulled back the string of her bow. A moment later the arrow was flying toward the target...and missed. Her hands slackened at her sides. "What was that?" Caspian asked. "You never miss."

It was true. A dozen arrows protruded from the center circle. They'd already evaluated her skills with longswords, shortswords, daggers, and axes. Everyday was something new and every time she surprised the Hand with her familiarity and experience. Now, her trainings were about stamina, and how long and far she could push herself.

Even if she was still holding back.

Not yet, Kovare had said. She'd pushed, once. Farther than she'd ever pushed herself. And it had scared her—that power within her. She didn't know if Kovare had known, but it explained why he knew she wouldn't need him after he left; why he had had so much faith in her. She *couldn't* lose that skill. It was just a part of her. But it didn't feel right. It didn't feel...needed. So, for now—as she had for nearly ten years—she would still hide it. It wasn't time.

"Adresia."

She met Caspian's stare. "What?"

He watched her for a moment. "You're distracted. Your emotions are diverting your attention, and if the time ever comes to use your skills, that will be your weakness."

A frown. "Sorry."

He sighed, and she prepared for a lecture on how to work harder, be better, control her emotions. But he took her bow and put it on the rack instead. "Why don't we end early today?"

"Why?" she asked carefully.

"Why not? I have a ridiculous stack of documents to review."

"Doing *paperwork* is more interesting than being around me?"

He smiled. "You're more than interesting; it just looks like you need a break."

"Alright. I'll be in the library if you get bored of skimming annual stock measures or whatever it is you do these days." He was still smiling as she slipped through the front doors, wiggling her fingers in farewell.

Her books were where she'd left them: in an underused sitting area in the farthest corner of the library. She fell into a chair with a heavy exhale and rubbed her temples. What she'd concluded yesterday...it was enough to make her stomach drop. But even the horror of that truth hadn't awakened that thing inside of her. Not like it did when Queen Narissa emerged from the shadowed shelves and asked, "Is something wrong?"

"Your Majesty," Adresia sputtered, swiftly getting to her feet. Her heart was pounding as she curtsied.

"I asked you a question."

The Countess tried to stifle the thunder in her head. "No. I'm just...tired."

A humored nod. "I would be tired, too, reading all of this history."

Adresia glanced at the table. It was piled with books and parchments that had seemed interesting and relevant as well as dozens of copied journal entires that had been scribbled and circled on. "My mentor mentioned something about the war during my lessons," the Countess lied. "I thought I would look into it, but my search was duller than I expected." She began closing the books. "I just returned to clean up." Adresia prayed the woman didn't read anything if she hadn't already. If she even *guessed* what dangerous questions were being concocted...

"When I was young," Narissa mused, "I used to spend more time in here than my chambers."

"Doing what, Your Majesty?"

"Concerning myself with things I shouldn't—things that scarcely relied on books. Libraries make for exciting meeting places when one doesn't want to be caught." The suggestion confused Adresia so much that she didn't reply as the woman turned, but before darkness enveloped her completely, the Queen looked over her shoulder. "Your first mission is in four days. No more of this silly reading until you return."

Chapter 18

Adresia's mission was on the opposite side of Dazelle. Her carriage had been directed to depart by midday, which left her rushing to see Cota that morning. They hadn't spoken in days. Narissa was keeping him busy, as promised.

After her second knock, the door opened. "Are you busy?" she asked her best friend.

With a smile, he leaned against the doorframe. "I always have time for you." He eyed the cloak around her shoulders. "Is that new?"

Adresia tugged on the fur lining. "Kasya made it yesterday. Isn't it incredible?"

"Tell her she'll have to make me something sometime."

"She needs something to keep her occupied while I'm gone anyway."

He straightened. "Where's the Queen sending you?"

"The outskirts of Dazelle. My carriage is waiting outside."

"Well...be careful."

"Aren't I always?"

He gave her a look that said, *No. You aren't.* She breathed an amused huff, but he stated, "Really, Res. It's dangerous. We've never been in a city, let alone this one. You have to watch your back."

"I will. I promise."

He seemed to relax a little. "Let's do something when you get back. I miss seeing your face everyday."

"As long as you don't fall for a beautiful Viscountess while I'm gone and abandon our friendship. I need your vast knowledge of the continent's activities to pretend like I know something."

He rolled his eyes. "Don't fall for a mysterious steward and run away from all of your responsibilities. Some of us actually like you."

"That will *not* be happening," she promised. A spontaneous surge of romance? Never again. Not with a random suitor from an alien household. Suddenly feeling oddly exposed at the thought, she took a step back. "Well, I'll see you when I get back." She gave an awkward, little wave. Cota's emerald eyes twinkled as he closed the door with that warm, alluring smile.

She crossed the hall and entered her chambers, intending to snatch her bag on the bed and forget about whatever had just happened inside of her. But, as always, the gods loved to inconvenience her.

"You have quite the selection."

It took everything in the Countess not to flinch. The Queen was standing at the bookshelf. What was with this woman and arriving at the worst times?

"The nobleman you've been tasked with is a difficult man," Narissa stated. He has information regarding a ploy to sabotage the city patrol and create a dangerous disturbance, and has refused to surrender the information to royal guards. Every effort displayed is a waste. Every attempt for him to understand is unheeded. Every guard sent is a life sacrificed to whatever foolish cause he believes he is combating."

A lump formed in Adresia's throat. *Life sacrificed*. This man was killing people.

And because the last thing the Countess wanted to happen always seemed to occur, she wasn't surprised when the Queen pulled a dagger from behind her back. Based solely on the ornate handle and embellished sheath, it had to be worth more than Adresia had ever possessed in her life. The Queen crossed the room and declared, "Under no circumstances are you to return without these documents."

Adresia took the dagger, unsheathing it enough to glance at the silver blade. While her instincts roared at the idea of her using something that belonged to this woman, they also barked with excitement at the marvelous weapon.

Narissa stated, "You are on your own, Ambassador. Do not fail this first task."

Adresia bit down the urge to resist, to fight back, to do anything *but* obey the woman who had ruined so many good things, and nodded. When the Queen left, Adresia let out a long sigh, fastened the dagger on her belt, and threw her satchel over her shoulder. The next few days would be long.

The Countess was nearly at the courtyard, steps lightly echoing against pale stone walls, when the Shield's newest knight turned the corner. His face twisted into vile amusement as Adresia's heartbeat increased in tune with her pace. She grumbled, "I really don't feel like playing this game, Brazen."

He stopped directly in front of her—too close for comfort, as always—and she receded a step, not bothering to hide her displeasure as he replied, "As far as I remember, Adresia, that was your speciality: *the game.*"

She beheld his slightly crooked nose, remembering the day she did that to him. "What do you want?"

"I want to give you a taste of what you did to me." A heinous promise flickered in his eyes.

She knew he would, given the chance. If they remained alone for too long, if someone didn't turn down the hallway, he would do exactly as he claimed. Even with her skills, she'd struggled against him the last time they'd brawled. And maybe it was the years apart, but he looked bigger. Mightier.

She crossed her arms. "If you're still pissed, you have a problem."

Frost-blue eyes narrowed. "Do you remember what your outburst cost me? After three *years* of being shunned, I was finally allowed to resume my training. I was reprimanded and despised by that entire village all because of the rumors you spread—"

"They weren't rumors."

"No? And what about the rest of the information you failed to publicize?"

Her brows lowered. "I know exactly what I did and I know it was wrong. I wouldn't be so stupid as to try it again."

His voice lowered. "Is that not why you're here—to try again?"

Her fingers curled. "I'm not the same person I was back then, unlike you."

"Aren't you?"

"Leave me alone, Brazen." She tried to push past him, but he blocked her path.

"You like playing the victim," he said. "You like people feeling sorry for you." With two fingers, he turned her chin toward him. "Don't deny it. I know you remember what we did together, so you should also recall what we expressed to one another; what we planned. I know you enjoyed it as much as I did, Adresia...while it lasted."

She ripped her face from his grasp. "I did what I did because I was young and in a dark place and a *fool*. But I've changed."

"And I haven't?"

It was her turn to take a step closer. "What are you really doing here? Is this just to get closer to the crown? Or did you actually fall into the Queen's trap—believing being a Knight actually means something?"

Something unreadable flickered on his face before he smiled. "My uses are better utilized this way. With you, I would've been caught. Now, I'll live long enough to see the fruits of my labor."

"You can get all the swords and armor and glory you want, Brazen, but you're still the malicious, vile prick who tried manipulating me into treason."

The amusement in his eyes winked out. "Your lover isn't here to save you this time, so I'd watch your mouth."

"I can do whatever I want."

"Do you see where we are? Do you see how women are supposed to act? You should learn how to follow the rules before something terrible happens."

"That's not what you believed in Westholt."

She tried not to recoil as he tucked a strand of her hair behind her ear. "We're not in Westholt anymore." And the way his breath tickled her ear, how his rough fingers lingered at her jawline and his whisper brushed her face...for a moment, she was back in that room, back with *him*—

And then she was back in the corridor, just a terrified, breathless girl in the presence of a ruthless monster. "I'll never forget what happened," she breathed.

He pulled back. "You act like none of it was your choice. Like I *did* something to you."

"You tried to *force* yourself on me."

"You and I did a lot of things together, Adresia. Things you enjoyed. And if I remember correctly, *you* came to me; *you* made that choice. Until you backed out."

A dangerous chill crept at her fingertips. "Yes, I backed out. And you *hate* that you let yourself be so vulnerable with me. You *hate* that I know your darkest secrets and deepest desires. You *hate* that once I saw the monster you were, I never wanted to look at you again."

"We did those things *together*. You're as much a monster as I am," he snarled. "Afraid of what Cota would think? Or your parents?" A frigid breeze swept down the corridor. "Actually, you couldn't tell them even if you wanted to."

Don't say it. *Don't—*

"They're dead," he finished.

She shoved him away, but even in her haste she couldn't outrun his dreaded voice and that vile, haunting laugh. "Let me know when you're ready to play, Lady Bellum!"

⟡

The house was just like any other noble lodging. On the corner of a busy street, the well-kept front lawn was protected by an iron wrought fence. Thick vines scaled the three story walls. And with the amount of servants entering and exiting the front doors all day long, Adresia assumed there were a *lot* of rooms. She couldn't figure out what, exactly, they were doing, bringing out troves of varying sizes and delivering letters and scrolls, but she would take whatever information she could. The Queen hadn't provided anything except an address, a vague description of the documents she was meant to acquire, and a brief background of her target.

Cota was right. She didn't know this city, and as skilled as she was, she didn't know this man. So as much as Adresia despised the idea, sneaking in to steal the papers seemed like a better alternative than trying to convince the Lord—a proclaimed murderer—to give them up. Well, *hoping* to sneak in; the Countess still had to figure out how to get inside.

The ache in her toes, thanks to crouching in the shadows of the opposite dwelling the entire day before, was unwelcome. She hated this part, the watching and spying; realizing she was intruding in someone's life. Enough damage had been dealt in Westholt when she'd resorted to thievery. She'd been lousy at first, but after a few months of practice—and a few black eyes—she'd been as quiet as a mouse and as quick as a viper.

The brisk night air filtered through the folds of her thin overcoat. She'd wanted to wear Kasya's new cloak, but a bundle of fur and white fabric wouldn't exactly help her blend in. When her gaze drifted back to the house, she groaned. Entering from another level was starting to seem like a *very* real possibility. She'd pondered disguising herself as a servant, but had quickly discarded the idea. She wouldn't get far without being recognized by another, let alone enter without some sort of object or another.

She rolled her shoulders. Climbing was *not* something she'd prepared for. But here she was, on the ground, and there her entrance lay: the third story window into what looked like an abandoned room. It was one of the only places in which no light had come from and no movement had been noticed—although she wouldn't know for certain until she was closer. After waiting for another wave of servants to disappear into the house, Adresia strolled down the street, keeping her hood down both out of caution and to see more of her surroundings. The last thing she needed was to look suspicious. Even if she *was* the Queen's Ambassador, the information would supply no aid if someone intended to harm her.

When she neared the warm entrance of the inn next door, lamp-light illuminating the gravel path, she veered left and strode into the alley. A ways down there were several crates stacked against the exterior wall. Tapping one, a hollow echo informed her they were empty. It wasn't ideal, but it was more than she expected anyway.

The fence rose a few feet above her, but, atop the boxes, she'd be able to leap over. She hoisted herself up, the crates creaking beneath her weight. A glance down the alley told her the noise had gone undetected, but she still shifted as little as she could until she faced the fence. She discarded her cloak on the ground and, not pausing to observe the sharpness of the pointed spikes, she took a deep breath, balanced her weight, and jumped.

Her limbs barked as she rolled, but her legs were steady when she rose. She shook the frigid numbness from her fingers. The chill didn't bother her, but it made sneaking around more difficult. Her body was used to uncomfortable warmth. After inspecting the length of the house, she noticed vines that continued all the way up the stone wall. Finding a particularly thick patch, she tugged on them as hard as she could. They were good enough to climb, at least.

She checked that her dagger was where she'd sheathed it—on the waistband at her back—and found a nook on the wall to place her foot. After a moment of contemplation, she scaled the wall. Chipped stone dug into her fingers. She had to stop every few seconds to rub the debris that fell into her eyes. She gritted her teeth in irritation. Why couldn't Narissa have just sent her to deal with pestering children or something?

Eventually, she reached the third story ledge, exhaling sharply at the tarnished window. It *looked* empty. The speckled scratches on her palms stung as she wiped the glass, wondering *what* in the Goddess's name she would use to unlock it—

The window swung open.

Well then.

Heaving herself up and landing inside without a sound, Adresia shut the window behind her. The room was vacant, just as she expected. But something blocked the light under the door, and she sucked in a breath. After a moment, it passed, and the light returned. With an exhale, she crept across the dust-covered room and so, so quietly cracked the door open enough to peek through. No one was there. She gave herself ten seconds to run through her imagined layout of the house, of the rooms that she was certain of even if there were a dozen more that she didn't know about, before stepping into the hall.

Her steps were undetectable as she snuck through the house, barely breathing as she listened to what lay behind each door. Some doors were unlocked, but most weren't. There was nothing of note. No Lord. How would she ever find the right documents in this maze of a house?

The hair on her neck rose just before light twisted around the corner. Servants. She barreled into the closest room and hastily but carefully shut the door behind her. When she spun towards the space, strands of hair flying wildly around her face, her fingers gripped the blade at her back.

A man watched her, the parchment in his hand pausing mid-air. He set the document on the desk and pulled away his glasses. "Who are you?"

She took half a breath to observe him further: the rolled up sleeves of his tunic revealed strong, scarred arms, the leather pants he wore looked suspiciously similar to the ones the Shield wore, and, to her misfortune, a dagger also hung from his belt. She fully unsheathed her weapon. "Who are *you*?" She didn't recognize the command in her voice.

"As this is my kin's house," the man began, calmer than she expected him to be, "and I asked *you* the question—"

"Adresia," she blurted. There was another door behind him. The light underneath meant it wasn't a closet, so it was her best chance of escape. "My name is Adresia. What's yours?"

"Why are you here, Adresia?"

She rounded the desk. "I'm looking for you."

He receded a step, but not out of fear. "You're looking for my brother." She'd been close; her guess had been based on nothing except that he looked like a Lord.

"And where might I find him?" she asked.

"Not here."

"The Queen sent me to obtain something in his possession."

The man shook his head, strands of gray and chestnut hair slipping over his forehead. "He can't give her what she wants."

"Why not?" She crept closer, raising her blade. He stilled. "Not so talkative anymore," she said. She didn't *want* to fight him, but orders were orders. She couldn't return without those documents. "The Queen told me who your brother was; about the men he's killed."

"He hasn't killed anyone."

"I don't believe you." Why wasn't he grabbing his weapon?

"The Queen has sent many people. We told them the truth and they decided to respond. Faking their deaths was the easiest way."

She halted mid-step. "What?"

Somehow, his blade had ended up in his hand. He raised it with wary eyes before setting it on the desk beside him—an act of compliance. "My brother funds the cause that myself and many others partake in; others who used to work for the Queen, *with* the Queen. Because they believe in the same thing I do, and once they saw that there's a way, they joined us."

"What cause?" Whatever this was... Adresia would make Narissa explain when she returned.

"Do you believe in what she stands for?" he asked. The softness in his voice was betraying her senses. "Are you loyal to the crown?"

"*What. Cause.*"

He held out his hand. "You can join me, Adresia."

This was a trick. A ploy to get her to spill her secrets so the Queen finally had evidence to take her, kill her. It had to be. "There is an attack planned on the Shield," she said. "Just—just give me something, *anything*, and maybe it will be enough."

"Why are you afraid of her?"

She lifted her chin. "I'm not."

"No?" He stepped closer. She stepped back. "I can see that you agree with me. You want to."

"Why are you a threat?"

"The Queen sees anything that doesn't bow down to her as a threat. Are you going to continue bowing down? Or are you willing to do what you need to do to live?"

This...this wasn't real. It *wasn't*. "I can't."

"Can't—or won't? There's a difference between what you want to do and what you should." He glanced at her lethal dagger. "It defines who you are."

Her mouth opened. Then closed. And then she took a deep breath and hardened her gaze. She was Adresia Bellum, by the Goddess. She'd thieved, lied, and manipulated for years. She *didn't* stammer or stumble. And she wouldn't stop now just because she couldn't untangle some strange man's peculiar words in his effort to stay alive. "Why shouldn't I turn you in?" With half a step, she had her blade against his throat. "I could be her most loyal servant and you would never know."

"You could." He watched her with calm, rounded eyes. She couldn't tell if his lack of reaction was because he underestimated her skill or her commitment. "But if you *were*, you would've killed me already and taken my head as a trophy."

"And why would the Queen want your head?"

"Because my brother and I have worked behind the scenes to become two of the most influential nobles in this kingdom. We have almost as much power as the Queen and hardly anyone knows."

The Countess tightened her grip on her blade, infuriatingly confused. "No one needs to get hurt. Just give me what I came here for and—"

"Papa?"

Adresia froze. Behind him was the now open door where a young girl stood in an illuminated threshold. Still staring at the Countess, the man said calmly, "Go back into your room, Juno."

"You said you would tell me a story," the girl slurred tiredly, rubbing her eyes.

"I'll be just a minute, my love. Close the door and get back into bed."

A deep yawn. "Okay, Papa."

Adresia reeled back the instant the door shut, her blade following. What she'd almost done...and there was a *child*.

With a hand on his throat, the man said quietly, fiercely, "Do you want to know who I am? I am a man trying to do what is right for his family. *Who are you?*"

Something like ice settled in her stomach. He wasn't asking for her name. And she wasn't what she'd been told. The Queen hadn't made her an Ambassador, but someone to be controlled. Someone to do the dirty work. A pawn.

"I am someone who is trying to make the world better than what it is now," she breathed. "And if that means destroying those who threaten that future, then I'll do whatever it takes to make sure another innocent family doesn't die."

His eyes glistened with understanding. "My name is Nikohlas Drumwell. My brother is Obryn."

She shook her head. "I can't join you. The less I know the better."

"The Queen already knows who we are. She was just testing our loyalties one last time. And yours, I suspect."

Adresia didn't let herself think about what that meant; the future that they knew was coming and hadn't run from. "Why is she so concerned with an attack on a unit of guards?"

He stepped back to his desk. "Why do you think we're attacking?"

"Riots happen all the time."

"Ones in a spur of passionate anger, yes. But those resulting from continued harassment and brutality...?"

His words hit her like a stone. This wasn't just a riot. People were going to *die* in this attack—intentionally. Sacrificially. But why? What was happening that Narissa had failed to mention in her Council meetings?

Nikohlas opened a drawer, pulled out a stack of parchments, and pushed them towards her. "The documents you're after; identical to the originals, with slight alterations. Whoever she sends won't stop the attack, but they'll make it there in time to find...something.

It'll seem more like a last minute change on our part than falsified information on yours."

The fact that he'd prepared for such an encounter as this—that he'd made replicas because he'd expected someone to come after him—shocked her enough that she didn't know what else to do but take them. "I don't know how to help you." If this attack was detrimental enough for Narissa to want to stop it, that meant the woman knew there would be more. That meant they might succeed. And if there was any chance that they *could*...Narissa would stop at nothing to end them.

Nikohlas smiled grimly. "We're prepared for retaliation, but...we know how this ends. We've been doomed for months."

She thought of Juno, of the daughter whose father would willingly commit treason so they could have a chance at a better life. "Then leave. Tomorrow, while I head back to the castle. That gives you a day to get out of the city before she comes looking."

His lips tugged higher, and he gestured to the door she'd entered from. Several servants strode by, discussing the best way to carry a trunk down the staircase. Nikohlas asked behind her, "What do you think I've been doing?"

◆

Adresia crumpled the documents in her hand as she marched into the Queen's chambers. The door of the study was open like she'd been told, and when she tossed the parchments—and the dagger—onto the desk, Narissa's head snapped up in surprise. "The plans that you so desperately wanted," the Countess stated, words dripping with barely stifled fury.

"Where did you get this?" the Queen asked.

"From the man you proclaimed to be a murderer. He was more compliant than anticipated."

"And how did you convince him to surrender such documents?"

"Sometimes speaking is more effective than force."

"I see." Narissa picked up a parchment, inspecting it with minimal interest. "And you're displeased...why?"

Adresia bit down the truthful retort that would do no good. "You lied."

"I did no such thing."

"That man didn't kill anyone."

"And you would believe someone else's testimony over your Queen's?"

"Should I?"

The paper slipped from Narissa's fingers. "What did you come here to tell me, Lady Bellum?"

The Countess squared her shoulders. "I will not be used as an assassin."

"If you had the inclination to take a life, that was your own doing."

It took everything in Adresia to halt the rage that flooded out of her soul. "I could be growing our political alliances or expanding our foreign presence. *Instead*, you send me to collect documents from an unruly noble. Documents that mention *nothing* about an attack on your men. Why?" She'd read all of them. Twice. The intended damage was to several warehouses under three extremely wealthy noblemen's names—*not* the crown and *not* royal guards.

"I've sent you to collect documents for our kingdom," Narissa said. "The men threatened by this attack supply me with more than just their noble influence. Keeping them protected instills that this castle and this province does not suffer. You have no idea of the sacrifices that keep this kingdom in the prosperous state that it is. You have no idea of what I've had to do. Being Queen isn't as glorious as it's made out to be."

The words tumbled out before Adresia could stop them. "It's a good thing I'm *not* Queen. I don't care about the luxuries of this castle or jewels or royalty. What do you even *want*? Are you just waiting for me to fail? To topple under the pressure of this skewed authority that you think you hold? Because all it seems to me is meaningless busy work."

The Queen slid a finger across the blade on the desk. Adresia realized she'd just insulted the woman to her face a second time. She took a wary step back. Narissa followed the movement before saying, "What I *want* from you is obedience. Obedience to your Queen—" The door suddenly clicked shut— "And obedience to whatever I bid you do."

The Countess went rigid in alarm as someone appeared next to her. "Misbehaving again?" the Captain drawled with a devious smile.

"I don't care what you *think* is right," the Queen continued. "I don't care what you believe, or if you agree with me, or if you feel pity for people who terrorize my subjects and turn them against me. I will not tolerate your defiance any longer. If I want you to gather funds, you will do so. If I want you to bring someone to me, you will bring them to me. And if I want you to kill someone, *you will kill them.*" The Captain's grin turned wolf-like. "Understood?"

"Yes, Your Majesty," Adresia breathed.

"Get out of my sight."

Adresia didn't sleep that night.

She just repeated her and Nikohlas's final conversation, desperately trying to grasp the meaning of his last words before she'd returned to the castle: *Hope is a dangerous thing, but it's what this kingdom has been given. It's what we have survived off of for fifty years. It's what our Queen so regrettably fears. Do not underestimate it.*

It was a hint. It had to be. About what, she didn't know. But Adresia stayed staring at the ceiling until the darkened sky began to lighten, praying that Nikohlas and his family had made it out safely, and begging that, in whatever insane thing he hoped in, this kingdom would soon be set free.

Chapter 19

The old man was one of the many new faces bustling in the Throne Room that night. Adresia was immersed in his story: a soldier who had risked his life to save his troops, facing scorching deserts and waterless expanses. She shared a look with Cota, who smiled at her fascination. It was the first evening in the weeks since they'd arrived that she truly felt like Court wasn't all that bad. People, she'd realized, were actually fun to be around. There were arrogant and rude individuals, sure, but most were just trying to live the best they could, in the only ways they knew how. They each had their own experiences. This storyteller was no different. "And in the end," he continued, "the soldier dropped his blade and spared the friend who had betrayed everyone he loved. When they reunited with his men, the revelry lasted months." The group that had formed around the man smiled and clapped cheerfully.

"It's not as glorious as you make it out to be," someone voiced. A dark-skinned man stepped forward, a large sword swinging at his side.

"I can remember my days of war like they were yesterday, Lord Sallow," the old man concurred. "Would you care to enlighten us on what you experienced that is so different?"

A small chuckle. "No. But I *would* like to say that I'm surprised the Queen allowed us in Morolyn. I've always thought it impolite to deny aid to neighboring kingdoms in times of war."

The surrounding nobles gawked at him, some simply stunned at the remark, some offended. And then the soldier—Lord—grinned, and the storyteller embraced him like an old friend, saying, "You've always been an amusing fellow. I'll give you that, Harkin."

"And you've always been a phenomenal narrator, Wynston."

Wynston faced the crowd. "This here is one of the greatest Lithellian soldiers I've ever known. You'll never meet a more honorable man."

"A Lithellian soldier?" Cota mumbled behind Adresia. "The ones fighting the South?"

She nodded. "Like my father did."

Gantrick had been at war with the Southern Continent long before Adresia had been born. Lithelle had always been an ally, and because Gantrick was known for its mining and blacksmiths and the island kingdom for its surplus of robust men, Lithelle had fought alongside Gantrick while being supplied with the finest weapons on the continent.

In the early days of the war, the Queen had allowed both kingdoms to send their troops across Morolyn to limit travel time. She'd even provided a legion of her own: a tremendous, brutal force. Adresia's father had joined when he was young and rose to be one of the greatest Generals the continent had ever seen. But by the time he and Adresia's mother moved to Westholt to start their lives, Narissa had pulled her forces from the war and warned the kings to never use Morolyn's shores again for a conflict they weren't part of. And although the Queen had long since reassured her people that they were safe from any Southern attacks, it was attempted once.

A fleet had sailed across the Sarinthian Sea and harbored Morolyn's southern plains, looking to use it as an outpost before attacking Gantrick from land and sea. Narissa, however, had refused the troops, and when they'd tried to forcibly take the land...Morolyn had responded with such considerable power that the battle ended an hour after it had begun. The few surviving Southerners hastily retreated and the South had never opposed Morolyn again.

Now, for the first time in two decades, the Queen had reoffered aid to Gantrick and Lithelle.

Adresia faced her best friend. "The soldiers are returning to Lithelle after their replacements relieved them a month ago. Dazelle is their final resting point before they cross the Soarlee Channel."

Cota crossed his arms and raised a brow. "How do you know?"

She scrunched her nose. "The Lord Hand. He says they've been stationed in the South for years."

"Which, in my opinion, was much too long," someone said behind her.

She turned to meet the handsome face of the soldier who'd spoken before. "Lord Harkin Sallow, is it?" she asked.

The man inclined his head, soft curls of chestnut hair swaying. "The one and only."

She curtsied. "Lady Adresia Bellum. It's a pleasure to meet you."

The man looked at Cota. "And you are...?"

A servant, who had appeared at her best friend's side moments ago, finished whispering and disappeared into the crowd. Cota responded with a tight smile, "Lord Cota Bowyer—and leaving, unfortunately."

Adresia frowned. "Now?"

"Lord Whitshend is in desperate need of advisory and Her Majesty will take every opportunity to renew my inexperienced mind."

His departure felt like a hole in her chest. "Find me after. You can tell me all about it."

He breathed a laugh. "As if you *actually* want to hear." At her look, his gaze softened. "I will." He squeezed her hand, and she waited until he slipped out the entrance before turning back to the Lord, who was watching her with interest. After making sure no one was too close by, she muttered, "You were telling the truth earlier—that you're surprised the Queen has let you into Morolyn."

His caramel eyes twinkled. "Don't tell anyone else that. They thought I was joking."

"I wouldn't dare."

"And why is that?"

"Well, like you, I've imparted my fair share of insults. Unfortunately, I've said them to the Queen's face—and *everyone* knows about it."

Amusement twisted in surprise. "Have any scars to prove it?"

She gave a small laugh. "Not yet. How long have you been stationed in the South?" It must have been long; most of his words had an accent.

"Nearly two decades."

Her mouth parted in surprise. Two *decades*? She couldn't imagine being on another continent for that long and away from what she knew. She gestured to the soldiers milling around the room. "And were you on the front lines like most of these men? I've heard the battles are tremendous."

"No, thank the gods. I've worked closely with King Bevon since I was a boy. At eight, he sent me South on his behalf. I was raised in the company of his Council, handling political matters rather than war strategy—although I'm painfully familiar with both."

She could recall being small and hiding under the kitchen table as her father and his men discussed the monarchs in the South; endless piles of papers and conversations elaborating each battle and the intentions of showing power instead of gaining the upper hand in the war.

"What is it like transitioning to the elegant life of a Lord?" she asked. "Being back in your home land?"

"It's...foreign. More foreign than the continent I wasn't born on. But even though the battlefield is all I've ever known, that place isn't my home. Only Lithelle can fill that hole."

"Do you miss it?"

"Very much. It's the most beautiful place I've ever seen."

Something warm bloomed in her chest. "I'd love to see it one day."

Their conversation stretched long into the evening, covering every topic she could possibly think of. She would've been suspicious of his interest if not for his questions being geared toward her favorite game as a child or where she would want to travel if she could go anywhere. More than his genuine inquiries, he made her stomach hurt from laughter every time he snuck behind his fellow soldiers and pretended to rob them. While they were each initially startled, she couldn't help but notice their delight as they realized who it was. They cared for Lord Sallow in a way she had only ever witnessed between her father and his men.

The Lord escorted her to her chambers that night, and she was still giggling from a humorous remark he'd made upon leaving the Throne Room when they stopped outside her door. He unlooped his arm from hers and pointed at her tattoo. He'd been glancing at it all night. "What is that?"

She ran her fingers over the inked triangles. "My family crest."

"What does it mean?"

"I'm not exactly sure. My father had it and my mother loved it. It's always been there. For us, it was the emblem of what our family stood for. Each peak represents something: loving above all else, hoping in the midst of sorrow, enduring all trials with gratitude." She dropped her arm. "I've never been the best at remembering those things, though. It'd probably help me solve a lot of problems."

The Lord tilted his head. "You don't need reminders. Those things are written all over your face."

Her cheeks bloomed. "Other people seem to bring them out of me. People like Lord Bowyer and you."

"Well, thank you for the wonderful welcome—to me and all my men."

"Thank you for not getting bored of my company."

THE BANE

"You're far too interesting to bore me." He held out his hand. "And my friends call me Harkin."

She shook his hand. "It's only fitting you call me Adresia, then."

He bowed, warmth exuding from his caramel eyes. "Until our next adventurous encounter."

"Until then." And as she watched him disappear around the corner, so tired yet so full, she hoped for one thing: that he was who he said he was.

✧

Two days later, Adresia's mind was nowhere near the present as Cota rambled at her side. The Court had been summoned to the Throne Room nearly half an hour ago without explanation, and now were impatiently waiting for the Queen to arrive. The Countess didn't know what to think of it. "It's *painfully* dull," he said. "I've had to sit through chapel and listen to the Lords prattle on about their taxes and disputes and household customs. And when Lord Whitshend is there to rave about the pride of his estate..." Her best friend groaned. "Do you know how little I care about the sum of their harvests and how much they can get away with spending on arms instead of wages?"

"Oh?" Adresia replied absentmindedly, scanning the room. "I thought you liked that," she finished. Cota hit her arm. There were a few perplexed glances their way as she gripped her limb. "*Ow.* What was that for?"

"You weren't listening."

"Yes, I was. You were talking about chapel and Lord Whittle-something..." Realizing she'd been caught, she gave a sheepish smile. "Sorry."

She'd been avoiding public appearance ever since her last conversation with the Queen. Thankfully, the woman hadn't been present when the Lithellian soldiers had arrived, but with her prolonged absence and this unexplained summoning...Adresia wasn't expecting good news. She'd spied Brazen on her way in too. He was now somewhere amongst the crowd, probably watching and waiting to pounce.

Even in her sleep, she couldn't find peace. Her nights were full of horrible images of her parents, triggered by her friendship with Harkin. It wasn't his fault; he just...reminded her of her father. The humor, the build, the kindess—it was the same. Despite the nightmares, she wanted to see him again already. Him and his men brightened the otherwise dull routine of day-to-day castle life.

She tapped her foot, which ached thanks to her new training with Caspian. When she'd recounted her mission, he'd tripled her strengthening and endurance drills, insisting she be prepared in case Narissa *actually* sent her to deal with a madman one day. It was a feasible prospect after Adresia had insulted Narissa yet again. She'd been thoroughly lectured about *that*, too. The Countess glared at Caspian, who stood silently beside the Princess at the thrones, and was about to tell Cota of her plans to throttle the Hand tomorrow morning when the doors flew open.

Narissa entered with two guards, who dragged a thrashing man between them. The Court watched in bewilderment as they stalled at the steps of the dias, waiting until the Queen was seated before mercilessly tossing the man to the floor. From where Adresia stood at the front of the crowd, she could easily identify what had been done to him. In addition to his bloody and swollen face, scratches and bruises and burns splotched his muscled limbs; his clothes were torn and ripped; and his eyes...there was such hollowness that she knew whatever horrors he had endured, he was aware of his fate. That easily, Narissa had destroyed this warrior. Like a bear eats a wolf; predator hunting predator.

"There was an attack on the city less than three hours ago," the Queen bellowed. "Dozens were killed—significant allies to this crown amongst them—and *this* man is responsible: Obryn Drumwell."

Adresia took an involuntary step forward. No.

Narissa's deadly glare fell upon the man, who unsteadily rose to his feet. "He is a prominent supplier of funds and resources to unknown sites across Morolyn. Sites that hold citizens of this city who tried to use this attack as a means of undermining my power; citizens who intend to overthrow me." Whispers erupted around the room. It couldn't—*couldn't* be. Because that meant...

"There will be no such thing as a rebellion in Morolyn," the Queen declared.

It's what Nikohlas had been trying to tell her. *This* was his hope. Adresia hadn't even considered the possibility, or rather, the *impossibility* of such drastic—

"Any and all supporters of this cause will be found and executed," Narissa continued, even though the woman couldn't uphold such promises; not when she had no way of knowing how many rebels there were, who they were, where they were. *Anyone* could be one, even those in this Court. How did she plan on taking care of that?

Obryn struggled to lift his head, but snarled at the Queen, "You. Will. *Burn*—just like the rest of them."

Adresia's knees quaked. There had been people—*burned*.

"No," the Queen countered calmly. "I won't."

The rebel broke into a coughing fit. He wrapped an arm around his front, face contorted in pain. "You have no idea how many of us there are; where we are," he rasped. "Even if you catch every rebel there is..." It was like the entire room was holding its breath. "You won't have enough graves to bury us all."

The Queen jutted out her lip in a fake pout. "Oh. You don't know what I—"

But not even Narissa could hide her shock when a dagger flew through the air and landed in the frame of the throne an inch from her head.

All eyes fell to the rebel, standing straight and unfazed, glaring with burning hatred. He'd been faking the entire time. And Narissa had *fallen* for it. But...he'd been tortured before this. The only opportunity to have received the dagger was on his way from the dungeons to here.

Which meant there were rebels in the castle.

The Queen was staring at the still wobbling weapon when she held up a hand to halt the guards who had darted for Obryn. "Your orders, Majesty?" one asked.

Narissa plucked the blade from the frame, observing it like it was a ridiculous, humorless joke before rising. Caspian started, "Perhaps we should consider the threat of—" But furious, violet eyes met him and he took a wary step back.

"I *have* considered it," the woman snarled.

No, Adresia wanted to say. *Stand up to her! Don't back down!* But she didn't, and Caspian remained submissive, watching as Narissa descended the steps and came face to face with the rebel. Her voice boomed through the room, echoing off the walls. "Let this be a warning and reminder to those of you who have forgotten who is Queen."

Adresia didn't know why Narissa wasn't worried about Obryn having another weapon. His hands were slack by his sides, but he'd concealed one alre—

The room flinched as one as the Queen plunged the dagger into the rebel's abdomen. Adresia stepped forward again, but Cota grabbed her arm. And then there was nothing. Nothing but the sound of the blade being pulled from flesh and crimson dripping from Narissa's fingers onto the pristine floor. Obryn wrapped his hands over his middle, but was unable to stop the fatal flow. He fell to his knees with a harsh thud, the sound striking into the Countess's heart.

Narissa merely stepped around him and nodded at the awaiting guards. "Leave him to the crows once you're finished."

Chapter 20

It was late, but Caspian had forced himself to come. If he didn't, he never would. He was tired of disregarding his questions.

The study door clicked shut behind the Hand. When he turned, something like ice coursed through him. Narissa was in her nightgown, raven hair spilling over dark green satin. "You've never seen me at this time," she said, strangely composed; not at all bothered about what had occurred that very evening. Not at all discomforted by the blood-stained dagger resting atop her papers like a paperweight.

He gripped the edge of the desk and leaned backward as if it would help him feel less cramped in this too-small room. "I need to discuss something with you."

"Do you?" She took a prowling step closer, and his response clogged in his throat. Her midnight eyes weren't looking at his blue ones. "Yes?"

"I..." He *tried* to speak; he really did. But he knew this behavior. He knew it'd only ever been exercised in front of a handful of people. And he knew it had never ended pleasant.

"Do my advances scare you?" She ran her hands up his chest. "Do you not desire a Queen?"

"I—I wouldn't want to insult you, Your Majesty."

A lover's smile. "Do you know why I'm not married?"

He shook his head, heart racing as he begged the God for some sort of rescue.

"Because men are fools." Her hands stopped grazing, and the striking softness of her voice turned sharp. "They question everything a woman claims and think they're *superior*." She pulled back, but not far enough for the warmth of her body to fade. "Is that what you're doing? Did I make the *wrong choice* back there, Caspian?"

Bad—this was *so* bad if she was using his name.

"I would never be stupid enough to think that I'm superior to you," he said.

"Then what were you doing?"

He didn't let himself hesitate. "You made me Hand because you respected my council, so I'm providing it: it would have been wise to consider the rebel's warnings before he was killed. What if he was telling the truth? What will we do if an mob of vengeful citizens suddenly floods Dazelle once they hear of his death?"

"There won't be an mob."

"How do you know?"

"You know better than to doubt my capabilities," she replied irritably.

Yes, he knew better than she realized. But he was sick of simply being ordered around and his opinions discarded. "How are you willing to risk *everything* just because you think you're powerful enough to withstand a possible reb—"

It happened faster than he could anticipate. She grabbed his neck, and pain lashed as her nails dug into his skin. "I will *risk* whatever I want," she snarled, "and if you ever question me again, *especially* in front of our Court..." He felt his toes lift from the floor. "You'll do well to remember this moment."

Helpless to do anything but choke for air, Caspian just nodded.

Chapter 21

The silence was deafening even before Adresia opened her eyes.

It was like everything in the world had gone still.

She peered around her chambers. The fire had died, but she swore Gillian had added fresh logs that evening. Ignoring the wisp of trepid confusion that brushed the edges of her mind, Adresia slipped out of bed. A chill crept from the crack under the door and brushed her toes. She tiptoed across the chamber and opened it. The guard that usually resided outside was gone. With furrowed brows, the Countess crossed the hall, and when Cota didn't answer her knock, she entered anyway.

The room was cold and empty like no one had been here in a long, long while.

She tried to calm her racing heart as she skidded back into the hall. But she began half-walking, half-running as she scoured the rest of the Suites. She couldn't help her panic. It was all the same. No lights. No guards. No sound. Nothing but...whispers. Gentle and haunting, they snaked up her spine, around her bones, through her veins. They were nowhere and everywhere. They tugged at her core, pulling her. She wanted to follow them.

The Countess crossed the castle's second floor and descended the staircase before slowing as she approached the front entrance. It was open as if someone had forgotten to fully close it in their haste. Cool, night air kissed her face as she peered through the break between the wooden doors.

The Court was outside. With torches in hand, they watched something she couldn't see on the opposite side of the courtyard. Those whispers pulled Adresia in the same direction. She bounded through the doorway and across the dewy grass, weaving in and out of the nobles, who regarded her as if she wasn't there. And then there was a frantic shout, breaking the silence so abruptly that Adresia flinched. No one around her moved. She was about to ask a woman if she'd heard it when another shout sounded, the words rippling through the air. "Let—me—go!"

Adresia pushed through a dense patch of courtiers before finding what transfixed them: a platform of wooden logs with the tallest, thickest one in the middle raised to the sky. Four men pressed a thrashing individual against the pyre, binding his hands and feet so tightly that there was no chance of escape. And as they disappeared back into the crowd and the individual came into view, Adresia froze. It wasn't just any man.

It was her father.

Ruthless terror swept up Adresia's spine as the Court raised their torches in the air, flames dancing in eager eyes. She took off in a desperate sprint, pushing and shoving people out of the way, and just when she reached the inner ring of the crowd, several men grabbed her. She tried to kick and thrash and buck free, but she couldn't break from their hold. It was like she didn't know how to fight, her body useless and weak. It was like her entire youth spent training had been a twisted lie.

Her father's eyes were wide in fear as he found her struggling to reach him. "Adresia..."

She began beating the men with pitiful, useless fists, but it didn't matter. Somewhere on the other side of the ring, a torch was tossed onto the awaiting wood. Flames erupted at her father's feet. He pleaded and begged and cried for anyone—for *her*—as the fire singed his skin and clothes. And when the heat grew too much for her face and his terrible screams of pain shattered through the air, she began screaming too.

Adresia woke with a panicked gasp. Grey eyes instinctively scanned the chamber, and, still overwhelmed by the fear that suffocated her like the loathsome heat from her fireplace, her gasps turned into great, billowing sobs.

It wasn't real. She knew that—she *knew* it was just a nightmare. But those whispers were still there, their anguish and terror as wild as what Adresia felt now. They *were* real, to her horror. As real as the tug in her core, pulling her, luring her, begging her to follow. She didn't know where it led. She didn't want to find out. So she ignored it just as she had after every nightmare she'd recently had and scampered into the cool corridor, her thin nightgown blanketed in sweat. "I'm going for a walk," she muttered to the guard outside, trying her best not to sound as distraught as she felt. She didn't know where she was going, but she couldn't stay in her chambers. She strolled down the hall before the man could protest.

The trauma wouldn't plague her forever, she knew. But, for now, it was here, and although it'd gotten easier to handle over time, there were still exceptions like tonight. Those exceptions were never easy.

Forcing herself to do something other than think about what she'd seen, she inhaled through her nostrils, held it for a few seconds, then exhaled slowly. It was an exercise she and Cota had practiced for years, and it worked...sometimes. Her quickened breaths slowed, but her body remained tense, as if ready for a fight—or ready to cry again.

"Adresia?"

Caspian approached her from the covered walkway. He was still in his clothes from the Throne Room, as if he hadn't yet returned to his chambers. The fear she thought she'd smothered inched right back into her chest as he pulled a bloody cloth from his neck with a wince.

"Why are you bleeding?" she blurted.

She must have looked as panicked as she felt, because when he stopped in front of her, he asked, "Are you okay?"

"Are *you*?"

Yes, she'd failed at concealing her emotions—but so had he. Whatever had happened, he wasn't fine either. Before she could formulate an excuse and return to her dreaded room, he stated, "Come with me."

She was still shaking when they entered his chambers. "Narissa did that to you, didn't she?" she breathed. She didn't know why she was so concerned for his well being. She didn't know why him being in danger made her so anxious.

Caspian pressed his forehead against the door and took a deep breath. "If I say yes, what will it matter?"

"Because you tried to warn her about the rebel." It came out as more of a realization than a question.

He turned, watching her carefully for several moments. Then he nodded.

Something prickled in her fingers as she took a stunned step back. "The rebellion is...*real*."

"You sound surprised."

She believed there were people who wanted Narissa gone. She believed in Nikohlas; in Obryn. There *had* been something planned. But she hadn't let herself think about a rebellion. Because more than that hope...she believed in the threat that Narissa posed, in the threat that the people of this kingdom stood against. "You aren't?" she asked.

"That man wasn't the first rebel I've ever encountered."

"There are more?"

"Plenty."

"Do you think they stand a chance?"

"If they have the right weapon."

Her stomach dropped. "What?" she practically whispered.

"Narissa doesn't have Morolyn under control. People are restless. Whatever she's been doing is making things worse."

"What has she been doing?"

Caspian tossed his bloody rag onto the desk. "Do you really think she's going to tell me?"

Adresia felt lightheaded. "How have you survived this long if she doesn't trust you?"

Sapphire eyes darkened. "She has ways of keeping her subjects loyal." A freezing rage crept up Adresia's spine, and she tried to calm herself again, to no avail. "Adresia?" He reached out a hand, but she stepped back, pressing her palms to her eyes. Like a dangerous storm in a box, something wild whirled inside her, growing with nowhere to go.

"I don't know what to *do*," she breathed.

"Everything will be—"

Sensing him reaching again, she turned away. "There is a *rebellion* to overthrow the Queen, and if she wasn't aware of it, she is now, which ruins *any* chance the rebels had of catching her unsuspecting—"

"Adresia."

"—and she just *stabbed* a man a few hours ago without so much as blinking and I could have *helped* him because I should have just asked his brother when I had the chance—"

"Res."

"—and now I don't know what I'm supposed to do next and I don't know whose side anyone is on and I feel like I don't even know *myself* anymore because this was never a part of the *plan* and—"

"*Res.*"

She stopped. Caspian's blue eyes were wild, his breath clouding in front of him. And as she followed his gaze to her feet, it took her a moment to register what it was; what had happened.

Frost crusted the floor around her, numbing her bare toes.

She met Caspian's stare with wide eyes. "Did I do that?"

He held out his hands—not in defense, but...calming her. "Don't be afraid."

A sob worked up her throat. "Why aren't you?"

He bent his fingers, beckoning her closer. "I know someone who can explain."

"What are you talking about?" She looked down again, tensing as the frost grew.

"Just breathe, Res. Don't let your emotions control you."

"You say that like you understand."

"I can take you to someone who does. But only if you calm down. If you don't, any one of my servants can walk through that door, and I don't trust them *that* much."

She breathed through her nose. In and out; out and in. If she didn't control herself, if she didn't control this...this *magic*, she could be caught. People still talked about the last magical creature rumored to have terrorized Morolyn decades ago. About how the Queen destroyed it before it could move against her people.

In. Out. She would not be found. She would not risk Caspian's life. She would *not* be destroyed.

Slowly, frost slithered toward her, receding until there was nothing more than frozen footprints beneath her feet. She took a wary step forward. They melted into nothing. She barely let out her trembling breath before Caspian laced his fingers through hers and pulled her after him.

His lack of fear comforted her as they silently marched down the corridor. When two patrolling guards sounded down the intersection ahead, the Hand hastily pulled Adresia behind a pillar. His eyes latched onto hers, but not in alarm, and he didn't look away as he mutely counted the guards fading footsteps, his head bobbing with every number. It was like he knew precisely how the guards moved and circulated; exactly where to stop and hide—like he'd done it before.

With a glance around the pillar, they began marching down the corridor again, and when they entered the Suites, Caspian turned right instead of left—approaching the only room on this side of the main corridor. Panic coursed through Adresia's body. She dug her heels into the marble floor. "What are you *doing*?" She tried to wrench her hand away.

"We can't stop here," he pleaded. His fingers still gripped hers. "Please."

He must have realized what she'd said in her hysteria; must have heard her intentions of helping Obryn and desire for the rebellion to succeed. "You're turning me in," she breathed.

He instantly released her. "I would *never* do that."

She blinked back her tears. "Why not?"

"Because your secret isn't the only one he's burdened with keeping," said another voice.

Adresia's bones locked in place. Behind him, the arched, wooden door had opened. Princess Corvina was in a modest, white nightgown, her golden curls unbound over her shoulders.

"Come in," the Princess said. At Adresia's hesitation, she added, "Or not, if you want to be questioned by the men coming down the hall."

Caspian only gave another pleading look before Adresia warily followed him inside. She glimpsed two guards walking through the archway of the Suites half a second before the door closed. How had the woman known those men were coming?

Adresia faced the chamber. Numerous candles lit the space, but besides the bed, a sofa, a low-lying table in front of the fireplace, and a single wall lined with dozens of shelves of books, it was completely bare. "It happened," Caspian stated behind her. Adresia spun toward them.

"I know," the Princess said. "I felt it."

"What do you mean you *felt* it?" Adresia blurted. "Why did you say you could explain? *What is going on?*"

When Princess Corvina looked at her and the candles flickered in a breeze that wasn't there, the Countess receded a step, that familiar tingling creeping back into her fingers. And when the Princess flicked her wrist and every candle extinguished, driving them into darkness save for the faint glow of the fireplace that illuminated the woman's striking features, Adresia stopped breathing.

"I think it's time I tell you who you are, Adresia."

Chapter 22

This was a dream. An insane, *impossible* dream, and Adresia would wake up any moment, greeted by the wonderful autumn sunlight and her lovely servants preparing breakfast. But the candles reignited and revealed the bland chamber and Princess Corvina's daunting, breathtaking face. "This might be difficult to grasp," the woman said, "but you have to trust us. At least—trust Caspian."

There was a softness shining in Caspian's eyes that Adresia had only glimpsed in spare moments when he thought no one was looking. "I have no reason to lie to you," he said, "nor any desire to turn you in. I just want to help you—as your friend."

Adresia clenched and unclenched her hands as if she could strangle the trepidation choking her every sense. "What happened in your chambers?"

The pair shared a look that Adresia couldn't decipher, and then the Princess declared, "I am a mage, Adresia. A Mystik. One of the many beings that used to traverse Felbourne, as I'm sure you've been told."

Adresia's breaths came fast as she digested the magnitude of what the Princess had just professed. "Yes, I grew up with tales of magic. It isn't foreign to me."

"Because you know so much about it, or because you have the power flowing through your veins?"

Oh gods. This couldn't be real. "What do you know about it?"

"I can feel it roiling and simmering inside you, ready to snap and explode at any moment. I could feel it the instant you neared the castle—and when you unleashed it just now."

"You knew?" Adresia asked Caspian.

"Yes," he admitted. "Before we met, I knew what you were."

The Countess took a deep breath, grounding herself to this new reality before meeting the Princess's gaze again. "What can you do?"

The woman waved a hand. "Heal wounds, cast light in the darkness; this and that. Mystiks possess simple magic. Nothing like you, though. Banes are rare. Their powers extend far beyond the limit of any other."

"Is that what I am? A...Bane?" She uttered the word like a curse.

"Yes. But they're unpredictable; their power never certain. It could be anything in this world. At their strongest, some can end a life without moving or crumble mountains." The woman narrowed her gaze. "What is your power, Adresia?"

Despite what they'd revealed, Adresia didn't trust the Princess. Not yet. Besides, she *didn't* know what her power was. That frost could mean anything. The Countess stood taller. "You tell me."

There was an impressed glint in the Princess's eyes. "I've never heard of a Bane who possesses *Hiermsall*." The Old Language rolled beautifully off of her tongue. Adresia had never taken the time to learn it, but her father had known a few words from his travels as General. *Hiermsall* was one of the few remaining phrases still used today; it was what the Winter Solstice was referred to in the Orrycolt Mountains. Already a brutal, unforgiving force of ice-storms and frigid power in the summer, it was untamed and destructive in the winter. Yes, *Hiermsall* described precisely whatever frozen storm resided inside her.

"I thought there weren't any mages left on the continent."

"There wasn't," the Princess said. "But by whatever twisted fate the gods like toying with, there are now three in Felbourne: myself, and two Banes."

The world clanged through Adresia. Two. "Who?" she asked cautiously, reluctantly.

The Princess tilted her head. "I think you know."

"No." Adresia said the word like a promise, a wish, as if the truth would somehow conform to her desperate plea. The gods couldn't be that cruel. The *world* couldn't be that cruel.

"Banes had such vast powers," the Princess went on. "There was no stopping them. They did whatever they wanted, whenever they wanted. They spent centuries demolishing kingdoms, bringing rulers to their knees, wiping out a continent with one breath. It's why the Elders—the oldest and wisest mages—made a decree that banned the breeding of Banes, preventing them from overpopulating greater than what they could control.

"But while Banes could wreak havoc and destruction, there were also those who chose a different path; those who chose to use their power for good, who believed they weren't superior. But even they couldn't stifle the fear their ilk had instilled so deeply before. Banes were shunned and outlawed; in many places, trapped, tortured, and killed. They faded out of existence. At least, that was what the Elders believed. Until now. Until you...and my sister."

Adresia tried to stifle the panic in her chest and forced herself to process the words, to accept the information. She'd known the truth, deep down. Being a mage...it made so much sense. It was why she was so much better, why she'd always felt something inside her. It was exactly what Kovare had so subtly hinted about for five years.

"I wouldn't do what they did," Adresia breathed. "I'm not Narissa."

"Which is precisely the reason you can help us destroy her."

A beat of tense, unsure silence. "You—you want your sister dead?"

The Princess was unbothered by the sentiment. "Yes."

"Why?"

"She's evil. She needs to be stopped. And you're the only one who can stop her."

Caspian had been silent so far—waiting for her reaction. And the Princess could be faking her concern to entice Adresia to her side...but his eyes were wide and pleading. And after everything, she trusted him. "I've wanted Narissa gone and dead for years," the Countess admitted. "But I can't *destroy* her."

"I just told you you're one of the most powerful beings in the world, and one of the last. What makes you think you aren't fit to oppose her?"

"You—you can't drop this into my lap and expect me to willingly agree. I found out what I was *minutes* ago."

"That doesn't change who you are and who you've always been."

"Do you realize what you're asking of me?"

Even sorrowful, the Princess was beautiful. "I'm sorry that this is a burden. But it is; it's *your* burden."

"Find someone else."

"Do you think I would've risked the last ten years of my life learning all that there is to know about my kind if there was someone else?"

"I don't *want* this," she said, even though, deep down, a part of her marveled in excitement.

"None of us want this, Adresia, but it's the truth. You are destined for great things."

The Countess practically flinched at the words. "Do you even realize what you're asking of me? I'm meant to risk everything just because you believe I can somehow stop your sister, someone who is practiced and in control of her power—something *I'm* not. How am I meant to do anything while in the same castle as her?"

"We'll tell you if you agree to work with us."

"And if I don't?"

Caspian stepped forward. "I know you've witnessed the horror and pain in this kingdom; I know you hate to stand by and watch. Now, you have a chance to end it. What's stopping you?"

He was right. And she was so *annoyed* that he was, that he knew she wouldn't leave the kingdom helpless. Because of all the preconceived notions she'd considered before coming here, this—a way to end the calamity the Queen wrought—was exactly what she'd always wanted.

She let out a long, heavy exhale. "It's risky."

Realizing what she was saying, what she was agreeing to, they relaxed. Both relief and alarm glimmered in their eyes at the future that now lay before them. "So is living in this castle," Caspian replied.

"It won't be easy."

"Do you really want it to be?"

Her mouth twitched up at the corners, but she said, "Cota can't know. Not yet."

"He won't."

Adresia looked at her hands as if she could see her magic in them. Somehow, something inside of her was strong enough to oppose their Queen. Somehow, she had magic that stood a chance to take down the mightiest being on the continent. Somehow, she had the power to make this kingdom a better place. And because she could, she would stop at nothing to make sure that happened.

✧

Days passed. When Adresia wasn't training, she was studying archives in the library. She'd barely seen Cota in between his countless occupancies and had only spoken to Caspian a few times, their conversations brief. Her only interesting encounters were with Harkin, whom she saw almost daily. With a storm amassing in the Soarlee Channel, the soldiers had been temporarily detained from sailing home. *If we're going to be useless,* Harkin had said, *we're going to be useless together.*

But when none of her friends were to be found and boredom had overcome her—the Queen, it seemed, wasn't ready to send Adresia on another mission just yet—she took to exploring the Findara Forest. The chill of an approaching winter storm awakened her amongst the spruce trees. She stepped under long branches that arched over the faded trail like servants shielding a noble from the heat and discovered a peaceful grove, hundreds of white flowers littering the lush grass. Just like she used to do in Westholt, she sprawled onto her back in the center of the patch. As drops of rain began to sprinkle down, she recalled the last conversation she'd had with Caspian.

"You said the rebels could succeed with the right weapon. *What did you mean?*" she asked him.

"*I meant you,*" he said.

"*Me?*"

"*Corvina's known about the rebellion for years.*" So that's *who gave Obryn the dagger.* "*When she considered who you were...well, why not help the effort by completely taking out the threat?*"

Adresia was still registering that first sliver of truth. "Corvina is in contact with the rebels?"

"*Not in contact. But when you're forced to do nothing but listen to your kingdom all day long, you hear things. She knows where a few of their safehouses are located.*"

"There *are rebels here in the castle?*"

"*Servitude comes with an advantage. Being overlooked provides an easy cover up.*" A slim smile at her surprise. Rebels were disguising themselves as servants. Years worth of thought and effort had been occurring right under the Queen's careful watch. Adresia hadn't guessed; hadn't even suspected. Although, how could she, with Westholt being as removed as it was?

"*You're not a pawn, if that's what you're thinking,*" Caspian stated.

She shook her head. *"I wasn't. I just..."* The danger didn't scare her. It was invigorating, as it had always been. But the hope that she gave the rebels, the chance she offered...the pressure was disconcerting, to say the least. *"Will Narissa know I'm coming?"*

"She can sense what you are. Whether she knows if you're aware of it or not, we don't know. And if you're spending more time with Corvina and I, then, yes, that puts a target on your back. She's grown suspicious. But she can't and won't act without evidence for fear of exposing herself, which as far as she's aware, no one knows about."

"How has she not sensed Corvina? She's a mage too."

"Bane's are the rarest and most powerful. Mundanes and Mystiks? They're embers in a wildfire. You can't feel another unless you've been thoroughly versed in magical presences, or so Corvina claims."

"That's why Narissa and I can feel each other, but not Corvina—because we're both Banes?"

A nod. "The headaches that you randomly get are Narissa's attempts at scoping out your magic."

Of course they were. *"I haven't started practicing my magic yet."* She wanted to, but the thought also rocked her to her core. What if something went wrong? *"Is that what we're waiting for? Me to gain control of my power?"*

"We have time."

"We do?"

"The rebels' plan isn't ready as far as we can discern. Besides, Narissa must contain her kingdom before she can take the continent."

"The...continent," Adresia repeated, as if it would help her grasp the weight of what Caspian was saying. As if this insane ambition could be rationalized.

"You didn't think all that our Queen desires is the stern command of Morolyn, did you? She knows there is no limit to the expansion of her dominion. That's why she summoned you—to keep the only threat to her power under her command while she pursues kingdom-wide supremacy."

Despite the fire, Adresia's arms had grown cold. She rubbed them. "Why do you believe the rebellion has any likelihood of achieving their goal—whatever it is?"

"Their goal is to dethrone Narissa."

Right. She remembered the Queen saying as much. *"Can they even do that?"*

A nod. "The law is like this: after an extended period of time, an abundance of nobles can approach neighboring monarchs with credible evidence reflecting their own monarch's dishonorable deeds. If they can prove that their ruler isn't adequate enough to reign, that ruler can be dethroned. If granted, dethronement usually ensues as a mutual arrangement in which the bordering powers utilize their authority to remove that monarch off the throne in a peaceful transfer of power. However, if they are met with resistance, they are legally obligated to meet that resistance with as much force as necessary until the targeted monarch either gives up their power or is killed—which is why it is extremely rare to convince any ruler to dethrone another in the first place. Once committed, there is no backing out. Not if you want to remain honorable and respected as a law-abiding leader."

Adresia rubbed her temples, focusing on the strand of cool wind that crept through the crack in the window and brushed her face. "So the rebels believe they can convince Gantrick, Tethoris, and *Lithelle to rise against Narissa?"*

Caspian stared thoughtfully at the fire. "King Emlyn might be sympathetic, but he wouldn't risk the prosperity of Gantrick when he has his own war to deal with. King Darnell...he hasn't prompted growth between Morolyn and Tethoris in decades. And while King Bevon has proven to be a formidable force against any potential resistance, he's the youngest king in Felbourne. He hasn't hinted that he would dare rival our Queen. He might be willing, but not without reason. Not without risking his untested reputation."

Adresia digested the unsettling information, the strategies and measures she'd never considered in her life. "Where do I come into this?"

"You're our back up plan for when Narissa undoubtedly resists dethronement."

"Why go through the effort if we know how she'll respond? Why not just kill her first?"

"No one knows about you—either of you. Revealing her power...it might be too much for this kingdom to handle. It might crush all the hope they've spent years building."

"Truth is better than false hope."

"I'd like to see you tell Morolyn the truth and see how they respond."

He was right. If the kingdom found out...people would still fight—and that *was* the problem. They would fight just so they could die. The truth would just incite a tragedy that could otherwise be avoided with strategy, with Adresia's duty, and, as much as it hurt to admit, concealing this. She exhaled loudly.

"Also..." he began, "there was an...incident, a few years ago." He folded his hands tightly, tensely. "I wasn't involved—and I didn't even know it had happened until it was over. I was ordered to dispatch a unit of men to contain two unruly citizens. The men...they never reported back to me. I assumed they were given new orders as they so often do, so I quickly forgot about it. But, after, I heard what happened." He met her gaze. "How the houses had been burned down and two young nobles suddenly inherited their earldoms."

Adresia stopped breathing.

"I found out it was you the day I arrived in Westholt," he added delicately.

He'd known about her past, about her parents. And yet, he hadn't judged her for abandoning her earldom or looked down on her for falling into despair or even pitied her for the past five years. He'd simply treated her as someone with a past; someone worth understanding.

Her voice was soft when she spoke. "Do you know why they died?"

"From what I understand, no one does."

She was starting to think she was never going find out the truth. "Why are you telling me this?"

"Because it's my fault."

She shook her head. "I don't blame you, Caspian."

He didn't hide the shock on his face. "What?"

"It's not your fault that my parents are dead."

" But I sent those men."

"*Narissa* sent those men. *Narissa* killed my parents."

He blew out a loud breath and nodded, but she suspected he still felt guilty. "A part of me wants to ignore all of this and live a quiet, normal life in the shadow of this broken kingdom," he said.

"And what does the other part want?"

He lifted his gaze, those sapphire eyes hard and determined. "It wants to take Narissa off the throne."

Such ambitious words and so little to show for it. What had she gotten herself into?

Adresia raised her hands above her, blocking the drizzle—now a downpour—that had turned her limbs stiff and gown wet. This is what she had to show. Her power. She could feel the magic in her being, weaving through her fingers at every frigid drop that met her skin. It was just there, waiting to be used. Would her hatred of the Queen make her a thing of destruction like the kin in her past, or would she choose a different path? One that was narrower, but better?

She got to her feet even though she wanted to remain out here, to be reckless and enjoy the time in these serene woods, away from the responsibilities of her new life and mutiny for a little while longer. But when a loud snap sounded nearby, loud enough to hear even past the rain, her instincts didn't tell her to stay.

They told her to run.

"Who's there?" she demanded. Through the trees, she could make out the figure of a person enveloped in the shadows. "Who are you?"

A deep rumble of laughter vibrated through the air. "You know who I am."

She squinted, but still couldn't see clearly. "What do you want?"

"What do I *want*?"

"That's what I..." Her snarky retort died on her lips as Brazen emerged from the edge of the grove. Her breath hitched at the baldric of daggers across his front. She stepped back.

He nodded in approval. "Go ahead. Try to run."

Spite almost made her ignore him, but when he inclined his head to the forest behind her, she knew better than to let pride cloud logic. She took off, darting across flooded grass as low-hanging limbs slapped her face, knowing every step mattered, knowing every step was quite possibly life or death.

She wasn't headed toward the castle. That's what he'd be expecting; he'd just cut her off. The only options were to run or fight—and she was in no condition for either. Not with her ridiculously restricting dress. Not when he had an array of weapons she hadn't seen since her father had retired from being a General. And the thought of using her powers—untamed and unpredictable and inexperienced—made her nauseous.

Quicker than she could sense, something barreled into her. She hit the sodden soil so hard a silent yelp came out before she scrambled away, trembling in anger and fear. Brazen prowled before her, an asp waiting to strike. She was panting as she showed him her palms. "Just—just wait a second—"

"You aren't walking away from this."

"We can both walk away. Just go."

"You know I can't do that." No more buffers of mockery. No more empty words and threats. All that remained in him was wrath. She could see it in the way he aimed his dagger at her, in the hostile hatred in his glare. "He wouldn't want me to do it this way. He wanted to do it himself. But I'm sure He'll understand...once He knows how I made you suffer."

The word sent jitters down her spine. "Don't do this."

Brazen didn't listen. And when that feral gleam in his eyes turned lethal, he lunged.

Panic swept up her spine as she slid in the mud, nearly toppling over to evade him. She quickly found her balance and spun, immediately ducking at his swipe. She staggered back in haste as the knight stumbled from the force of his missed blow. It was then, while he was inattentive and unsuspecting, that she struck him: once in his unprotected ribs, once in his jaw. His angered growl tore through the air. But when he straightened—unfazed—her stomach twisted.

Something like a squeal left her lips as he launched toward her, his jabs and dagger swipes brutal and unwavering. Locks of her hair slung in her eyes as she dodged him. She frantically brushed them away, her breath ragged in her throat. He was so much better than she remembered. Inhumanely better.

Reacting purely off of her instincts, she tucked in her arm. His blade sliced through the air so quickly, so close, that the whistle of it rang in her ear. Their eyes met for a moment through the rain and she gaped at him. He would have taken her limb clean off.

"Stop *fighting*," he snarled.

Just to stall long enough to get another breath in, she replied, "You won't get away with this." But they both saw it for what it was: a distraction and a lie. Even if she wanted to fight back with her full strength, that familiar plea rose to the surface: *not yet*.

She darted left, but one wrong move had her receiving a punch to the jaw. She spit blood onto the grass.

"When I'm finished with you," he sniped, "you won't be better off than your parents."

Rage and grief brutally hacked its way through her defenses. Brazen took the opportunity and backhanded her so hard that she stumbled over the muddy folds of her gown, unable to stop his hands from latching around her throat.

No.

She didn't know if she screamed it aloud or just in her head, but it didn't stop the knight. He slammed her into a thick spruce, her back mercilessly scraping against the bark. She gasped for breath as her toes lifted from the ground, and she tried to pry his fingers away, but he didn't budge. Not even when she dug her nails into his skin hard enough to draw blood.

"*Please.*" It was a pitiful rasp, but it was all she could manage.

He just squeezed tighter, watching her struggle with sadistic enjoyment.

She began crying, rain mixing with the salt of her tears. She was so foolish to have thought she could overpower him a second time. She was so foolish to have thought coming to Dazelle would provide her anything other than death.

The word bloomed a terror in her so profound that she began praying for her life, to the God and Goddess who she hadn't trusted in five years. *I'm sorry. I'm sorry for not being better. I'm sorry for wanting to reject this life. But I'll try. Please, just let me try.*

Pain and exhaustion and struggle overwhelmed every muscle and sense and thought. And just when she expected it to end...she crumpled to the ground, desperately choking down air.

They'd heard her. *They'd heard her.*

Consumed with the blessing of her life, she paid no heed to the monster in her presence. Something collided with her head, and she swept into darkness.

Chapter 23

A shortsword hung from Caspian's hand as he wove through the chilled forest, a sort of desperate prayer lingering at the back of his mind. He strained to hear past the downpour. There were no voices. No movement. Nothing beyond the storm.

He'd been at a briefing about an upcoming trip when he'd seen her. Having already made half of the decisions himself, his presence wasn't vital, so he'd relocated to a window, half-listening to the ramblings in an attempt to defuse his boredom.

Adresia had contentedly sauntered into the forest, an unusual smile plastered on her fair face. Someone had entered shortly after, and while Caspian knew she could handle herself, while he knew it could have just been a coincidence, maybe it hadn't been.

He'd immediately excused himself and swiftly followed. The calm rain that had softly tapped on the window had turned heavy by the time he'd passed the first tree. And she might have returned once the storm had begun, but something told him to stay out here. Something told him she hadn't made it back.

That had been half an hour ago.

Now, he stalked through the slowing rainfall with that stealth he'd utilized his entire life. Tracking was useless. Any indication of movement had been washed away. If she was in trouble, he had no way of knowing; no way of finding her. An apprehensive groan left his lips. But then his boot unexpectedly sank into a sloshy muck, and he halted. There was something odd about the mire...

Dread sparked in his gut as he observed the area. It wasn't the mud that alarmed him. It was the way the ground was undoubtedly disturbed, parts of it dug in so deeply that even the rain couldn't alter the sloppy imprints.

There'd been a fight.

He wiped his face and gripped his sword tighter as he trudged deeper into the forest. She had to be close. She *had* to be—

His heart stopped in his chest.

Strung between two trees by ropes around her wrists, Adresia hung limply in her muddy dress, toes barely skimming the ground. She had to be freezing, especially as the rain finally abated, a frigid breeze that strayed through the trees replacing it.

The Hand darted behind a spruce when a rugged, broad-shouldered man appeared in front of her. Watching from his concealed position, Caspian knew she was alive. He could tell by the way the individual lurked before her, waiting. If this man had been able to take *Adresia* down...

Caspian calmed himself, routinely inhaling and exhaling like he'd done a hundred times before. Panicking wouldn't help anyone. Not himself and certainly not Adresia. He had to think.

He couldn't go barging in; the man might hear and hurt her before he could get close. He couldn't try throwing a dagger; the individual was too close to her, and with nothing to dry his wet hands, Caspian didn't trust his aim. He had to wait for an opening. But anticipating her wake felt like watching a sunset that never completely descended past the horizon.

After minutes of dreadful silence, a soft groan sounded. He peered around the tree to find her sluggishly lifting her head from her chest. A cloth tightly gagged her. Her eyes fluttered open in an exhausted haze before settling upon her captor. Even Caspian could see the fury in her gray eyes. But his awe twisted into alarm when the man touched her chest with the point of a blade and sneered, "Not so strong now, are you?" The dagger dragged down her vulnerable ribs. It would only take a bit of pressure to pierce her flesh. "You remember what you did to me, don't you? How we beat each other into oblivion in that square?"

Adresia's jaw tightened.

"No? I know it's in that pretty little head of yours."

She just glared.

"Well, it seems you've forgotten and that just—won't—do." The blade tapped against her cheek in tune with those last three words. "I think a little *demonstration* would suffice."

As Adresia curled her fingers around the rope, Caspian realized in mute horror that whatever was going to happen...she already knew.

"Where should I start?" The man sheathed his blade, but the tightness in Caspian's chest didn't ease entirely. Not as he heard, "How about when you punched me so hard, I couldn't see for four days?"

Caspian flinched as the man struck her stomach. She squeezed the ropes and clenched her eyes shut, but no sound left her; no strangled cry or muffled groan. She simply loosed a strangled breath through her nose and raised her head.

Ready for the next blow.

Seeming to notice her tolerance, the man growled, "How about when you broke my jaw and *then* my nose? Do you remember that?" Caspian's hands trembled in restraint as he forced himself to stay while the man inflicted two more strikes. Adresia didn't give any indication that he afflicted her; didn't give him the satisfaction of knowing he was winning.

The man dropped his hands to his sides. His voice was a deadly calm. "You were really upset about my little *comment* earlier. I'm sure you wouldn't make the same mistake of letting such an incident happen twice...but what if I told you that exact thing was happening to Cota as we speak?" If she was alarmed, her face revealed nothing. "No, you're right. I don't care enough to bother with that pet of yours. It's *you* He wants."

Caspian's stomach fluttered. Who wanted her?

The man casually stepped behind Adresia. In one quick movement, he pulled a hidden blade from somewhere and put it to her throat. "You can come out now!" he bellowed. "I know you're there."

Caspian pressed against the tree. Oh gods.

He didn't know what the man would do to her. He *couldn't* stay hidden; it clearly hadn't worked anyway. So, with a deep breath, he stepped around the tree. Uncontained horror appeared on Adresia's face. Caspian's breathing sped up in tune with the anticipation pounding in his blood. He was mere feet away when the man ordered, "Stop there and drop your blade."

Caspian did. "I'm going to get you out of here."

Adresia shook her head. The man yanked her hair so hard she cried out, but it turned into a dangerous growl. His gaze darted between them, and a following laugh made the hair on Caspian's neck rise. "I was *not* expecting this. The Hand of the Queen...come to save darling Adresia." When Caspian stepped closer, the man's amusement fell. He pressed his blade harder against her throat. "I wouldn't do that if I were you."

"Let her go," Caspian said.

"What importance does she hold to you, Lord Hand?"

"That's between me and the Countess."

A wicked grin. "And here I was, thinking the best friend was the secret lover."

For some reason, his stomach fluttered. "I'm not her lover."

"Then what are you?"

He didn't know. They had their alliance, their friendship, their flirtation...

The man grinned and stepped in front of Adresia. She instantly tried to rip her hands from her bonds, her toes futilely sweeping the ground.

"She nearly ruined my life," the man told Caspian. "I won't let you ruin my revenge."

"You want revenge for something that *nearly* happened?"

Ice-blue eyes narrowed. "She did enough damage."

An idea suddenly appeared in Caspian's mind; dodgy and possibly problematic, but an idea nonetheless. Before he could rethink it, he stated, "I don't think He'll be pleased if you hurt her before He does."

The man halted. "How do you know about Him?"

Caspian shrugged. "I don't." And then he swung.

The man fell face-first to the ground. They both waited for several tense moments, and when he didn't move, Adresia emitted a muffled sob, sagging in relief. The Hand sent out a prayer for him to remain unconscious as long as possible. Pushing past the throbbing in his hand, he removed Adresia's gag and swiftly cut the ropes around her. He caught her as she fell, hoisted her into his arms, and tried not to panic at the red marks around her throat as he strode toward the castle as quickly as he could. What had that man *done* to her?

"I'm sorry," she mumbled, too exhausted to keep her eyes open.

"For what?"

She leaned tiredly against his chest. "The trouble."

"You're not trouble, Adresia."

A noise that sounded like, "No?"

"You're worth the few sore knuckles I'll have tomorrow. Although I might make you pay me back during training next week." He looked down with a smile. She'd already passed out. As Caspian carried Adresia back toward the castle and into safety, he couldn't help but say it again. "You're worth it."

Chapter 24

Adresia awoke to the comfortable stillness of a crackling hearth under dry, cozy sheets.

This wasn't her bed.

It wasn't a struggle to open her eyes, which was a relief, and while finding that her limbs were undoubtedly bruised, it didn't hurt to move as much as it had when the injuries were inflicted. Their origins were not something she'd forgotten, unfortunately. She'd been changed out of her cold, dirty dress and into cotton trousers and a thick sweater. She must've been exhausted if she hadn't awoken even for that. Running her fingers through her brushed hair, she winced at the sudden pain that shot through her wrist. Her skin was raw and rope-burned.

"I see you're as good as new."

Caspian came into focus at the edge of the bed—*his bed*.

"Not completely," she replied.

"Everything is healed besides your wrists and neck."

Noticing the numerous candles dotted around the room, she kicked back the covers and padded to the bathing chamber to peer in the mirror. Like a clouded sky, bruises stained her neck.

Caspian leaned against the arched threshold. "I had healers check on you. They said it could've been worse, but whatever happened...I was lucky I found you when I did."

Yes, he'd been lucky; *she'd* been lucky. Because Brazen had been a better opponent than anyone she'd ever faced. She'd felt the strength of his hands around her throat. He could have killed her if he wanted to. He hadn't though. He'd had other intentions. And she'd known he wanted revenge, but she'd never thought he would go that far. He'd wanted to hurt her. Slowly. Methodically. And when Caspian had walked through those trees... Fearing for him had never been a part of the plan.

"Res?"

She met his gaze in the mirror. She hadn't heard him. "Sorry."

He pushed from the doorway. "Don't say that." Hands reached for her shoulders, and when she didn't tense at his touch, relief pooled in her gut. "You survived. You don't get to apologize."

"I barely stood a chance."

"He had a nasty looking mark on his jaw from what I remember."

"Thanks," she said gravely before strolling back into the bedchamber and falling atop the soft mattress. "But the last time Brazen and I clashed, I had him unconscious in a few moves."

"He's attacked you before?"

"He's from Westholt. We grew up together; brawled together—several times. He ascended as a knight a few weeks ago. You didn't recognize him?"

"I remember the ascension. But I've never seen him in training, nor at any assemblies or weekly progress checks." His brows furrowed. "I've never even met him."

"Is that...normal?"

"No."

"Which means?"

"It means he's not in the Shield."

She straightened. "But he ascended in front of everybody."

"There was an ascension, yes. Just not the one everyone witnessed."

"What?"

The bed shifted with Caspian's weight as he sat beside her. "It was fake; a way to publicly initiate him into his real enlistment."

Her stomach dropped. "Which is what?"

"I've heard things. I thought it was just a rumor, but *now*...now it makes sense. The servants started talking about the Queen possessing a personal infantry a few years ago."

"You haven't checked the rumors for yourself?"

"I have other things to worry about—like keeping my life, for one. I can't sneak around like I used to. If Narissa *does* have a second infantry that she's kept secret, it's secret for a reason."

Fine. It *was* dangerous. "Doesn't she already have the Shield? Why would she need her own forces? And why keep them hidden?"

"I don't know. The servants claimed she would deploy these...soldiers. I've done plenty of unspeakable acts of my own under her command—" Her stomach twisted at that small sliver of truth— "But I haven't the faintest idea what use these men could possibly do that we can't. And Brazen...."

"Brazen didn't attack me under her command." A questioning look. "He might be one of her personal play-things, but there's someone else. Someone who wants me. Brazen kept mentioning a *He*."

"Someone in the castle?"

"I don't know." Brazen had said something: *He wanted to do it himself.* "Whoever it is, I think they're in close contact."

Caspian sighed. Clearly the news was just as disconcerting for him.

"I think..." She swallowed. "I think something was done to him. He was stronger, but not as if he'd been training for years. It was like he'd changed. Physically. *Internally*. There's a part of him that I didn't know in Westholt. Do you think Narissa's doing something—using magic to alter the men?"

"It would explain why the infantry is a secret."

She leaned back and rested her head against the wall. Why was everything so confusing?

"Res?"

"Hmm?"

"What was your plan?"

"What?"

"The other night, when you thought I was turning you in because I'd heard what you'd said when we were in my chambers." He scooted ever so slightly closer. "I did hear you. You said, 'this was never a part of the plan.' What did you mean?"

She loosed a loud breath. "I came here because I wanted to know why my parents were killed," she said. "At least, that's what I told Cota. But...I also wanted answers. I was determined to find out why our kingdom is the way it is, why Narissa does what she does. That was my plan. I guess I know, now. Although, I never imagined *I* would be a part of that truth."

"If it hadn't been about you...were you just going to leave?"

She didn't understand the conflicted look on his face. "I don't know. I've never seen myself as valuable, so I didn't think Narissa would want me for an extended period of time. Honestly, I'd hoped to simply disappear one day with no one to care. I..." A half-smile, half-wince. "I also intended to desert our friendship the minute you stopped being beneficial."

A surprised huff. "So you're just using me?"

"No!" She chucked a pillow at him. He caught it with a soft laugh. "I've always hoped the truth was bigger than me; that what had happened was more than a terrible accident. It was. And now there's a rebellion. But...I didn't stay just because I found what I was looking for. I stayed because we became friends; because I have the power to make a difference; because I can't lose you or anyone else I care about. Not again."

"I'm glad you stayed."

"Me too."

He looked at her so intensely that something in her whirled in excitement, which wasn't bad, but...it wasn't anticipated either. Enough so that a yawn forced itself past her lips. He cleared his throat. "You should probably rest."

"Only if you promise to bathe." She scrunched her nose. "You reek."

He moved away, his laugh skittering across her skin. "Will do."

"Caspian?" He paused on the edge of the mattress and looked at her. She felt unusually timid as she said, "Thank you for saving me."

"You don't need to thank me."

"Yes, I do. I have a terrible habit of overestimating myself and my abilities. I almost died because of it."

"Give yourself some credit. I doubt many people would have lasted as long as you did."

She shook her head. "I don't understand how you continue to see me as some champion. I barely escaped with my life. I do nothing but make mistakes."

He leaned closer. "I don't understand how *you* continue to undermine your value. Why can't you see how extraordinary you are?"

"I'm not as perfect as you believe."

"Who is?"

She hummed a laugh, and although she probably should have, she didn't look away as their eyes met.

Brazen was right. There *was* something between them. And, like Caspian, she didn't know what. She'd noticed his hesitation when Brazen had asked. But when something fluttered in her core, something unexpected and partly unwanted, she whispered, "Goodnight."

"I'll just...be on the sofa," he stated.

She lifted the warm covers to her chin, but she didn't feel tired. She felt bothered. Bothered, because sleeping in Caspian's bed felt like a betrayal to the feelings she knew deep down were true and real for Cota and had been that way for a long, long time. And bothered because she was afraid what she had with Caspian was something else entirely.

The weathered, castle parapets split dawn's golden beams as Adresia gripped the stone railing of the castle wall. She'd recently discovered the unused stairwell that led to the upper wall-walk in the shadowed, vine-covered area behind the chapel and had spent many evenings up here since, basking in the autumn sunlight before it descended below the horizon. She lifted her chin to a cool breeze that floated from the Findara Forest when a voice behind her, feeble and dismayed, broke the serene silence. "Help me."

Her heart stumbled as she beheld Cota. He pressed his palms against his abdomen where a dark stain was spreading alarmingly fast. His lips parted in an effort to combat his shallow breaths. She took a panicked step before halting and looking down in horrified realization. The bloody dagger toppled out of her sticky palms. When she looked back up to explain, Cota was gone—and someone else stood before her.

The hooded figure resembled a husky man, but where his face should've been beneath his hood, shadows poured out like a poisonous, invisible vapor. It felt like darkness and death and terror. She receded from him, colliding with the balustrade at her back. "Please," she said. "I didn't—I don't know what hap—" A scream tore from her throat. She clamped her hands over her ears, doubling over in agony as she tried to explain, to say it hadn't been her, that she hadn't *done* anything, but the pain wouldn't end, wouldn't stop, even as she wondered why no one had yet come and where Cota had gone. And then the pain lessened. It was still there, excruciating and relentless, but it was bearable enough that she lifted her head, cheeks damp with salty tears.

It was magic, she realized. This horror, this devastation and distress—it was *magic*.

The man lifted his hand, and a roaring panic filled her head as she rose into the air, drifting up and over the balcony. She was only on the second level of the castle, but, somehow, the grassy-soil was hundreds of feet below. "Please." She didn't even know what she was pleading for.

For a moment, his hand stalled. Hesitating. When his voice filled the air, a shiver snaked down her spine. "You are scared, child."

A frantic nod. She wasn't stupid enough to lie.

The man dropped his hand. She exhaled in suppressed relief. "*Good.*"

Her eyes went round. "Wait—"

She vainly reached out a hand, plummeting too fast to scream.

"*Res.*"

Caspian was gripping her shoulders with wide eyes. Only the reassurance of his touch indicated that this was reality, but her anguish, her fear...they were vivid enough to convince her that that had been no normal dream. If she thought about it for too long, she could almost feel those shadows. "I'm fine," she said despite her shudder.

He dragged his hands through his disheveled hair. "You wouldn't wake up."

"I know."

"This has happened before?"

She nodded. "For years. I thought they went away, but...then I came here."

"I'm sorry."

"It's not your fault."

He shook his head. "Everything that's happened to you wouldn't have happened if I hadn't brought you here."

"You didn't force me to be here, Caspian."

"No, it was the death sentence that awaited you had you ignored the summoning."

She huffed a half-amused breath. "You're not wrong."

"Still." He squeezed her hand. "I'm sorry."

The touch sent sparks to her toes, and only because she didn't know what that meant, what *any* of it meant, she rose and strode to a table lining the wall. The papers atop it were unorganized and scattered. When Caspian cleared his throat behind her, she held her breath. "Have you tried any teas or tonics to help the nightmares?" he asked. "Corvina used to take some when her powers first showed up. She barely slept those days."

"There are teas that can help you sleep?" She'd never heard of them before, not even as a child constantly around Cota's mother, a woman fluent in herbalism.

"A few."

"What tea could combat magical dreams?"

There was a smile in his voice. "Magical ones."

She spun to find that he was, in fact, smiling. "Really?" The question was lined with awe.

"No. But Corvina says if they're powerful enough to quell even the worst magical ailments, then that's pretty close."

She strolled back to the bed and sat down. "You'll have to ask her to make me one of these teas sometime."

"Anything you need."

The unspoken promise behind his words riled her enough that she leaned over and ruffled his hair. "You must sleep like a maniac if that's what you look like when you wake up."

A surprised laugh. "Try looking at yourself!"

"I look *marvelous*."

"You should befriend Lord Whitshend. You'd get along well with the pompous man."

"Yes, Cota's told me *all* about him."

"Has he, now?"

"Mhmm. And he *also* told me about your…" She put a hand over her mouth. "He told me not to say anything."

His eyes went round. "About my what?"

She shook her head.

"Res!"

She barked a laugh. "I'm joking. I know more secrets about you than he does, anyway."

Their amusement drifted in a peaceful calm before Caspian asked, "Do you want to tell him? About us, I mean, and the rebellion?"

She sighed. "It would make me feel better, him knowing and me not keeping secrets. But...I don't know. Sometimes I just want to lie in bed all day and forget any of it ever existed, like I'm a commoner who's free to do whatever I want and go anywhere I desire—someone who my parents always wanted me to be."

"What's stopping you from being that person?"

"Besides the looming aftermath if we succeed?" She sighed again and buried her face in her hands. "Myself."

He gently pulled her hands away. "Your parents loved you. Why wouldn't they want you to be who you are?"

"I just...I want to make them proud." The rest of her sentiment she didn't dare speak aloud: that if she went through with this rebellion, if she took another life, no matter whose it was, she feared she wouldn't come back from who that person might become.

As if he could sense what she was feeling, Caspian squeezed her fingers. "You—"

"What's going on?"

Adresia sprang back as far as she could without slamming into the wall and whirled toward Cota, who watched them from the doorway. "I can explain," she blurted. She begged her racing heart to calm as if it would translate something she didn't want to be known if heard.

"You weren't in your chambers when I got back from my meeting," he said, shifting on his feet. "I got worried. Gillian told me you were here."

"I was attacked."

Her best friend's fingers twitched at his sides, as if he would go for the blades that usually hung there. "Gillian said as much." He stepped further into the room, his expression displeased and confused and worried all at the same time. "But you don't look hurt."

"It was Brazen."

Any hint of distrust disappeared. "*What?*" She quickly explained what had happened, and Cota looked at Caspian when she finished, swallowing as if it was hard to get the words out. "You...you saved her?" Caspian nodded, but Cota added, "That still doesn't explain why you've been spending so much time together before this."

She almost wondered why it bothered him. But then it hit her: he was worried about her safety; he was worried about her involvement with the Hand of the Queen.

"She's been meeting me at my request," Caspian lied.

"To do what?"

"Go over her lessons, brief her about her role, review—"

"No," she said. It was too much for Caspian to lie for her. She couldn't keep the truth hidden forever. Not like this. "That's not what's been going on." Caspian glanced at her. "We've been meeting because..."

Her best friend raised his brows in concern. "Because?"

"Because we're working to dethrone Narissa."

He took a step back, his lips parting in disbelief. "You—*what?*"

She quickly explained *that*, omitting the details of her magic. He was quiet when she finished, gazing at the floor in mute shock. Caspian's hand brushed hers. She stood, wrapping her arms around herself in silent anticipation.

"Why didn't you tell me before?" Cota asked at last.

"You didn't trust Caspian," she answered.

"I don't know if I still do."

The Hand rose. "I've risked my life more than enough times to prove I'm on your side." He didn't sound annoyed, thank the Goddess—at her reaction to his touch nor at Cota's statement.

Her best friend just stared at Caspian the same way he had in the Sight Woods all those weeks ago. Stared and stared and stared until he sighed and said, "Okay. I believe you."

"You do?"

"I saw how you tried to spare that rebel in the Throne Room. And while I've had my doubts...I can't deny what's right in front of my face."

Both her and Caspian relaxed. She didn't know why she'd been so afraid. Him knowing this was better than not knowing anything at all. He was her best friend. Why had she been so hesitant to trust him?

Cota rubbed his neck and looked at the Hand again. "So I guess this means we have to be friends now?"

Caspian just laughed.

✧

"Narissa is going to attack the kingdom." Seated on the sofa in the Hand's study, the small banter between Caspian and Cota slipped into hollow silence. They twisted toward Adresia, who stood looking out of the glass wall. She'd debated when to bring the realization up. It was little more than a speculative conclusion from her readings, but it made too much sense to ignore and she doubted either of them would want her to pass it off as an unrealistic assertion. "I realized before my first mission when I was searching in the library," she added, crossing the room and sitting opposite them. Two days after telling Cota the truth, the sight of them together still sent a shock through her.

"And how did you come to this conclusion?" Cota asked, intrigued but wary. She knew he was trying to support this path that she'd involuntarily and inexplicably chosen for herself, even if he looked more tense and uncomfortable than she'd ever seen him before.

"I overheard the Queen's Warden say something during Brazen's ascension. A word: *draygonians*. I only remembered because Narissa was livid the instant she heard it."

"Why would she be mad?"

"Clearly it was sensitive information."

Her thoughts drifted to her and Caspian's discussion the other night. A secret militia, possibly supported by a handful of nobles from the Queen's Council. It would explain why the Warden felt comfortable sharing the information with her surrounding companions—and why the Queen hadn't wanted the information shared so publicly amongst the rest of the Court.

"It's what Narissa's been doing," Caspian realized.

"What is?" Cota asked.

Adresia sighed. There was still so much he didn't know. "Narissa has been raising her own personal infantry. It's why we hear about acts of terror across the kingdom with no one to blame—because it's not the Shield. Also, the Warden was gone for six months doing something that no one seems to know anything about. I assume it has to do with the infantry."

Cota just nodded, mutely taking in the information.

"What did you find in the library?" Caspian asked.

"A man named Roslyn Mendalium tamed the first draygonians on the continent," she said. "The beasts were conduits of chaos in the Fallen War. Somehow, he stopped them."

"And you now think Narissa is going to use them?"

"What better way to test such weapons than against a rebellion?"

Caspian just sat back in stunned disbelief.

A few minutes of burdening silence passed. "Any idea what draygonians are?" Adresia quipped.

Cota balked. "You didn't find out?"

"I'm sorry I couldn't read a language that was written *centuries* ago," she countered.

Cota looked at Caspian, who shook his head. "I've never heard of them either."

"You don't know anyone who knows anything?" she asked.

The Hand caught her meaning, but shook his head. "No. Not about this."

"There wasn't anything else?" Cota asked.

"There *are* more journals," she said, "but they're all written in that same language. Once we decipher them, we can figure out how he stopped the draygonians."

"You make it sound so easy," Caspian said lightly.

"Trust me, it's not. Which is why—" Adresia went into his bedroom, grabbed a stack of books from atop his dresser, and returned to the study— "I got some help."

"Where did you *get* those? And when?"

"From the library while you were sleeping." There was a loud thump as she set the tomes atop the table. They all coughed, swatting away the dusty air. "I grabbed anything that looked particularly helpful."

"I like reading," Cota muttered as he picked up a thick volume, "but *not* this." Caspian did the same with an agreeing smile as Adresia opened a random book.

They read for what felt like hours. Their studying was only interrupted by declarations of their findings in short, thwarted bursts, but, in the end, they weren't able to translate the journals, which meant they had no renderings of what the draygonians actually were, let alone why they were used in the Fallen War. Why would the Warden mention such destructive methods? What did they look like? What did they even *do*?

Cota had one hand propped under his chin, the other tapping the aged parchment before him. As if it would spark a significant memory or recover some forgotten recollection, he repeated under his breath, "Draygonians...draygonians...*draygonians...*"

Adresia's eyes had grown heavy and the words had began to blur on the old pages, so she closed her book. It shut harder than she intended, and, from Caspian's small jump, she swore he'd been sleeping even though he now peered at his page with wide eyes.

"I figured it out."

They whipped their heads toward Cota, who stared astoundedly at the mess of papers atop the table. He hastily rummaged through them, and when he found the ones he was looking for, he pushed them toward Adresia like they held the answer to everything. "Dragons," he said breathlessly. "Draygonians are the ancient translation of the word *dragons*." She believed him enough that she didn't really read the words on the parchment, instead listening as he went on, "When you match the timelines of his entries with the research of the beasts during that age, they point to the same thing: Roslyn tamed *dragons*."

"You believe those are real?" Caspian asked skeptically.

"You don't?" Adresia asked.

A shrug. "I've heard stories, I just never considered the validity of them before. I mean...they're just stories."

"So are evil Queens," she asserted with a wry smile.

He looked at her pointedly. "Aren't they extinct?"

"Obviously not."

A knock sounded at the door. Caspian mouthed, "My servant," before Adresia and Cota relaxed. They dove back into hushed conversation as a young man entered.

"Let's assume she has one," Adresia whispered. "More than one. What do we do then?"

"Our only chance at stopping them is figuring out how Roslyn did," Cota said.

"That relies on us translating his journals." Which they hadn't done.

"We'll look harder. We train, we prepare, we learn more about this rebellion, and when the time comes...we have to be ready to face whatever horrors Narissa has waiting."

"Unfortunately," Caspian announced as the door to his study clicked shut, "those plans will have to wait." They looked at him. "We're leaving in three days."

Chapter 25

The tavern wasn't as busy as Adresia had expected it to be, given the conditions outside. It'd snowed during their journey just as she'd suspected, blanketing the settlement in an undisturbed white by the time they'd arrived yesterday. The sight of Tauroben had made her pause in awe. Once they'd beheld the cramped yet boisterous village that stretched all the way to the northern coast like a fantastic city, she'd instantly forgotten about their dull ten day journey.

Tauroben was a main port to northern Morolyn and Lithelle. According to Caspian, a recent spike in demand had forced the settlement to employ every able-bodied individual to complete their weekly shipments, which had resulted in a multitude of riots. And while Tauroben was magnificent, a closer inspection revealed precisely why the citizens were displeased: the dwellings were piteous and miserable and hardly more than boxes with four barely-standing walls. But, whether the people were being compensated unfairly or not, Adresia couldn't interfere. She was meant to defuse the conflict as Ambassador and nothing more—including consolation. No matter her beliefs, if she provided any sign that they should indeed be rioting, Narissa wouldn't react as kindly as she had the last time Adresia had returned from a mission and done what she thought was right. The woman wasn't aware of how she'd aided Nikohlas, but if she helped the largest village in the kingdom...she doubted the Queen wouldn't notice *that*. So, without any idea of how to handle the conflict, Adresia had gone exploring.

At least, that's what she'd suggested to her cohort of men before she'd escaped from their sight that afternoon.

If Narissa wanted Adresia to go on a mission, Adresia would go on a mission.

She'd first gone to the docks to observe the shipment lines that Tauroben was famed for. When she'd arrived, she'd noticed the crates—or, rather, the *lack* of crates. There simply hadn't been enough goods to export to all of Tauroben's destinations. There hadn't even been enough for one ship. It was possible the village simply had a shortage that week, but with the amount of work they claimed they were exerting, she seriously doubted they had nothing to prove their efforts. They had to be shipping something. There was only one conceivable excuse. It was one of the only discussions she'd had with Caspian on their entire journey here. They *weren't* shipping goods.

They were shipping rebels.

Tauroben was expanding; it would only make sense *because* of the influx of people. It was the origin of Morolyn's common-folk, so why not the rebellion, too? It used the shipping industry to smuggle rebels, drop them off at the ports across the northern coast, and use the Findara Forest as a cover to sneak into Dazelle. And if rebels were here, why not the leader?

A few coins had the Countess easily acquiring the name of a shipping overseer. It surprised her to discover the name belonged to a woman, but she supposed the lower class had less of a reason to implement such strict divisions between men and women. If Tauroben proved anything, it was how commoners stuck together. She'd spent the evening tracking the name she'd acquired at the docks to a private dwelling, and a casual flirtation had the neighbor spilling the overseer's whereabouts: the woman could always be found at the Twilight. Adresia had entered an hour ago without anyone noticing.

Sat in a dim corner, she now discreetly monitored the gathered group: seven men and women. The wooden door creaked open and closed, lively chatter infiltrating from the salty-aired streets. Adresia didn't have to turn her head to hear; only an empty table separated them. She sipped from her cup, grimacing as she forced the watery alcohol down, and continued listening.

"Our claims were true," someone said. "We haven't lied."

"Yes, but deception on the other hand..."

"What we did was right," another stated. "For us and for the kingdom."

A voice Adresia hadn't yet heard sounded. "If you hold any shame in our actions, you can leave now." The man had spoken in a way that had the group quieting in deference; even Adresia noticed the wisdom and age in that tone. She gripped her mug, clinging to his every word. "We *have* been overworked by the Queen," he continued. "There are folks who can barely provide for their families, let alone themselves, after these last months. It isn't fair." A chorus of agreement. "We can do little while the rest of Felbourne continues to fear her. And for what? What could she possibly possess that coerces the kings to withdraw with their tails between their legs? They are *kings*—the most powerful individuals on the continent. What makes our ruler so formidable? Why is *she* the greatest of them all?"

A brash laugh. "Worrying isn't in your nature, Morphaeous." The table groaned under some strained weight. "If our efforts succeed, our Queen won't remain all-powerful for much longer." With a sidelong look, Adresia found a scrawny man with stringy hair and an eager glint in his brown eyes leaning over the table. "Soon, Morolyn will be nothing more than chaos and turmoil, and when our Queen can no longer control her citizens, the kings will have no choice but to suspend her rule."

Adresia choked on her drink. These *were* rebels.

A woman with long, black hair gave a responsive smile. Whatever authority she possessed echoed in the way she touched the man's shoulder and he instantly fell back into his seat. "Indeed, Torstein, we pray that the gods will allow peace to pass in our land. But before that can happen, we've had to take the first step. And we have quite successfully. Deploying our persistent complaints was a sensible excuse to mobilize her nobles. And now that they have arrived, it is our *duty* to show Narissa how clueless she is. She won't know what hit her when we send their bodies back to Dazelle."

The floor swayed beneath Adresia's feet. *They* were the nobles: Caspian and Cota and her. They'd been lured here to die.

She put a hand to her mouth, desperately wishing she could forget about this and let someone else handle it. They'd probably do a lot better job than she would anyway. She was tired of thinking about her problems. The kingdom's problems. The continent's. But still...she couldn't sit here and let the rebels take out the only weapon capable of destroying what they were fighting against.

She didn't know how they would react; if they would cause a scene or try to hurt her or even convict *her* of treason. Worse than that, she had no idea who was a part of the rebellion. If the group's fearless chatter meant anything, it was that everyone in the tavern was probably an ally. One wrong word from her and there wouldn't be anyone to help if they decided she was a threat. So much could go wrong. And yet, Caspian relied on her. Morolyn relied on her. She had to do *something*.

So, with a readying exhale and without giving herself the time to consider anything else, Adresia rose from her table, grabbed a chair, and positioned herself in an open space between two of them. "Your plan is going to fail." It sounded harsher than she intended, but she'd already started; she wouldn't back down now. "You can't kill those nobles."

The scrawny man—Torstein—looked like he'd been slapped. "Why not?"

"Because I'm one of them."

Brown eyes widened. "Knowing our intentions, then, does approaching us make you stupid or naive?"

Adresia bit back her scowl. "Neither. I'm trying to help you."

"Because you're surrendering your life without a fight?"

Her heart raced as she tried to remember what she had planned to say. The words were a jumbled mess in her mind. "Because I want this rebellion to succeed too."

Murmurs of confusion were shared around the table. The black-haired woman asked, "How do you serve the Queen?"

Adresia was already knee-deep in treason. It wasn't like her situation could get worse by revealing that sliver of truth. "I'm the Queen's Ambassador."

Several eyes widened. "*You're* the Queen's new Ambassador?" The woman looked the Countess up and down. "And why would you betray Her Majesty after such a promotion?"

Gods help her. "The Queen murdered my parents five years ago without explanation or reason. Three months ago, I was summoned to Dazelle. I went because I believed I could find answers about my parents death. That's it. The Queen named me Ambassador without my choice or consent. I didn't choose this. I wouldn't trust her after what she did to me. I do not enjoy my role, but it was life or death."

"I would have chosen death," Torstein muttered contemptuously.

"Keep quiet, Torstein," the woman sniped. She looked back at Adresia. "You chose the right path. Death is a shortcut for cowards. So what is it you think you'll find by supporting this rebellion? A new life?"

"A better world."

The murmuring rebels went silent.

"I've been at the castle," Adresia continued. "I've seen things. No matter the trials you've been through...you don't know what the

Queen is truly capable of. Only a fool would underestimate her. *That* is why she is so powerful. Whatever you plan to do to me, to my friends, it won't work. And it *isn't* worth it. Harming us will only inflict more pain upon you and this kingdom." Torstein mumbled a sentiment of aversion under his breath. "I don't care whether you like me or not. I don't care if you trust me or believe or want to kill me. If you go through with this, the Queen *will* annihilate you and your families. Your name will be wiped from the land. This rebellion has given me a chance I thought was lost forever. I *won't* waste it. Don't say I didn't warn you."

The woman tilted her head. "What is your name?"

"Adresia Bellum."

Confusion and surprise flickered on the woman's face for half a moment before she straightened. "You clearly know of our cause; what our plans are. If your story is to be believed, you've witnessed the Queen's atrocities as many of us have—which is rare for someone of your status. Even more so for someone at Dazelle."

"She is a *high born*," Torstein hissed. "She can't be trusted."

The woman didn't counter the claim, but instead seemed to consider his words.

"I'm not lying," Adresia sputtered. "I could have slipped out of here, escaped with my friends, and reported my findings to the Queen. You would have never known. I have no reason to tell you that I overheard your conversation or to warn you."

They just watched her; weighed her truth. It was that hesitation that convinced Adresia. Without a second thought, without pausing to decide whether it was worth it or not, she splayed her hands on the table before her. Frost coated her fingertips. "I am a mage," she quietly declared. "A Bane." The rebels paled. "I am the *only* person who can stop what our Queen has planned. Killing me would be the biggest mistake of your lives." She twisted in her chair and pulled down the top of her dress, revealing the chilling scars that receded down her back. "I received these the day my parents were killed—when the Queen's men tried to kill *me*."

A rugged man with graying hair and skin weathered from decades of work cleared his throat. Adresia pulled her cloak back over her shoulders and faced them as he said, "I don't think she would conjure up such extravagant accounts." She recognized his voice; Morphaeous. "Nor can we deny her magic, Elettra."

Adresia froze. The black-haired woman was Elettra—the leader of the rebellion.

With another glance at the Countess's hands, the woman stated, "I believe you." Whatever she realized Adresia had meant from revealing her magic—that Narissa was a Bane too, or that the Queen had something just as powerful—she evidently understood the mistake she'd be making in killing the Countess. Elettra cocked her head. "I'd like you to work with us."

Adresia's lips parted in surprise. She'd simply desired to stop them from killing her. That was it. What she'd agreed to do with her friends was one thing. But *this*...this was entirely different. This would secure her role in this war. And they didn't know who she was; hardly anyone did. As irritating as Torstein was, he was right. She couldn't be trusted. So why did they?

"Let's untangle a potential snag in this agreement," Elettra went on. "We can't kill the Queen. For whatever reason, that honor lies in your hands. But the goal has been and will continue to be dethronement."

"Why?" She knew Caspian's answer, but she wanted Elettra's.

"We need the continental excuse to rally our people against her. Only the kings can help us reinstate another ruler. If she dies now, Morolyn will descend into chaos. Kings are powerful, but not every revolution turns into peace. If we want Morolyn to have a future after we succeed, dethronement comes first. Can you agree to that?"

Adresia's mouth opened, then closed. She'd given the rebels every reason to want to join them, to officially be on their side. But she still had Caspian and Corvina and Cota to think about. They would want to hear what she'd discovered; what she'd stopped.

Elettra raised her brows at the hesitation. "Have I misunderstood your intentions?"

"No," Adresia began. "I share your burdens, but…I'm not alone. I have partners. I'd like to discuss it with them before I decide."

"You understand we are asking *you*, correct? Not your friends."

She'd have to convince them otherwise. "Yes." She stood, concealing her trembling hands behind her cloak. What had she gotten herself into? "I won't be leaving for a few more days. How should I contact you?"

"We meet at the Twilight every three days. I'll be expecting you then." Elettra eyed the Countess thoughtfully before adding, "I hope you choose correctly, Lady Bellum." Her name was said with a hint of humor, but Adresia didn't fail to notice the underlying threat: the show of power the woman indicated she possessed; the control she held over the lives of her and her noble friends.

Which was why Adresia felt nothing but satisfaction as she replied, "And you as well, Elettra Joahan." The humor vanished from the group. Even Torstein had the nerve to look unsettled. "Some advice? Use a false name to conduct your covert operations—unless you want every troop in Tauroben to be on the lookout for the figurehead of this rebellion." With an intimidating smile, the Countess finished, "I'll see you in three days."

✧

Adresia tiredly sauntered through the empty streets. Maybe it'd been a mistake to speak to the rebels. She *should* have just left when she had the chance and simply got her friends out before they were attacked. Now, she had to worry about the rebellion—about joining it.

She'd barely consented to working with Caspian and Corvina. The thought of being in the castle whilst trying to maintain contact with the leader of this treasonous plot... And she hadn't been prepared to risk her friends' lives, either, but here she was, willingly putting them into danger. She hadn't been prepared for any of this. Everyday was just an ever-worsening battle. She just wanted to sleep. Caspian would no doubt be waking her at sunrise to train anyway, so she needed as much rest as she could manage—at least before she had to relay how she'd managed to find the rebels *and* stop their plot. Gods. The thought only deepened her exhaustion. She hoped there was still food left in the kitchen. With all those men at the townhouse, it wasn't likely.

It began sleeting when she was only a few blocks away, the frigid drops like needles against her skin. And talking was the last thing she felt like doing, but, with a heavy sigh, she spun and waited for the knight to approach her at last. "Why are you trying to secretly follow me?"

Fox emerged from the shadows. "How did you know it was me?"

"You didn't answer my question."

"I wanted to make sure you got to the house safely. You don't look in the mood for company." He stopped in front of her. "You didn't answer *my* question."

"Your boots. They sound different from the others. Lighter; more worn in."

"I was at least twenty feet behind you." She stilled. She'd revealed her heightened hearing and hadn't even realized. Thankfully, Fox didn't seem to give it a second thought as he added, "I saw you at the tavern."

"So you *were* following me."

"I was keeping an eye on you."

"Did you hear anything?"

"No. But…I saw your back."

She exhaled heavily, irritably. Despite the friendship they'd begun to form, this was not what she felt like doing right now.

"What happened?" he asked.

"I'd rather not talk about it."

"I thought we trusted each other."

"I said we should trust each other, not that we do."

"And why don't you trust me?"

Why was he trying to have these conversations with her all of a sudden? "If you trusted *me*," she retorted, "you wouldn't have been watching me like a creep in the corner of the tavern."

"Now it's my fault that you were conversing with a random group of commoners and I decided to look out for you?"

"I didn't say that."

"Now *your* mood swings are giving me whiplash. You used to get upset that I wasn't doing my job, and now that I am, you're blaming me for ruining your evening."

She curled her prickling fingers. "I'm not blaming you for anything. I would just appreciate it if you don't follow me when I don't ask you to."

"What were you doing?"

"I'd like to see you guess."

"I'm sure I could."

She scoffed. "You don't know anything about me, Fox."

"I know more than you think."

She turned away again, ready to be done with this night.

"Why are you mad?" he asked.

"I'm not," she bit.

"You said that angrily."

"No, I didn't."

"Yes, you did."

Her snow-drenched hair swung around her face as she whirled. She barely registered the frigid air, her garments sticking to her skin. "Fine. I *am* mad."

"*Why?*"

Because she didn't want to be a part of this rebellion. She didn't want to be a savior. She didn't want to risk the lives of everyone she'd come to care about because of her mistakes. She wasn't just mad. She was *furious;* furious at the world for throwing everything at her all at once. And because she didn't know who else to blame and she was too tired to think about any of it right now, she snapped, "Stop trying to figure my life out when you can't even handle your own."

He frowned. "Because *yours* is much better? Don't pretend like you aren't in love with the only two people who can bear to be around you."

Embarrassment and exhaustion blurred together. She didn't even know what she was saying. "Don't pretend like you wouldn't love to retire from being my guard the second you got the chance. Maybe then you'd finally be seen as a *real* knight."

"Anything to evade the torturous remarks of a child."

"Torturous remarks," she repeated derisively. "You don't know what torture *is*."

"Look around!" he barked. "People are suffering more than your own selfish dramas!"

"I've suffered in ways you wouldn't even *know* how to comprehend!" she shouted.

"That doesn't make you special, Adresia! It makes you *human!*"

She was so angry that her eyes swam with tears. "At least I don't believe that being a knight gives you more privileges than the rest of us! You're still just doing wasteless tasks around a castle that doesn't need you unless there's a brawl to contain!"

"At least I don't sit around blabbing about my sorrows to anyone who'll give me the time of day!"

"At least I'm not a selfish prick!"

"You don't know how to *function* without thinking of yourself!"

"Why do you think I was talking with those people? Because I *wasn't* thinking about myself. I was trying to stop them from making a mistake!" She unfastened her frozen cloak, threw it to the ground, and furiously pointed at her neck. "*This* is what I get for caring about anyone other than myself. Someone tried to *kill* me because I didn't want to work with them and be the person I've spent my *entire* life avoiding."

His face was strained and flushed. "Maybe that's the *problem*. You try to help but you only make things worse. That's why you've been an *orphan* for five yea—"

She backhanded him so hard that his head twisted to the side. And suddenly—she stopped. She lowered her hand, fingers stinging from the contact. Boiling rage still simmered within her, but also guilt and remorse. She didn't know what to say, what to do. "I'm sorry," she breathed.

He hadn't moved, and he still didn't as he said softly, "You don't have anything to be sorry for." Adresia opened her mouth to correct him, but he continued, "I should have been there when you were attacked." She stilled. She didn't think he'd known. "You were *my* responsibility; *my* duty. And when I saw Caspian carry you in...I knew I'd failed. I'd chosen to attend a meeting about *guard rotations* instead of being at your side where I was supposed to be. If I hadn't been so self-absorbed with my ridiculous reputation, I could have been there for you. I could have *saved* you."

"You didn't know that was going to happen," she said. "Don't blame yourself."

He nodded unconvincingly. She wondered how long he'd felt convicted of it so far; how much he'd beaten himself up over something she hadn't even thought of. It bothered her more than she cared to admit.

He picked up her cloak. "We should get back."

She took the sodden, heavy garment, and when he took two steps forward, she said, "You heard what I said at the tavern." He halted. "If you didn't, you wouldn't have followed me." The fact that he wasn't denying it only proved it was true. "Why aren't you turning me in for treason?"

When he turned around, he found her gaze through the rain and held it. "Because I've been trying to kill the Queen for six years."

She stared at him. Her voice seemed to have left her body.

"I joined the Shield because I believed I could make a difference," he said. "I was raised with the perception that being a knight was one of the highest honors in the kingdom. But the Shield means nothing to the Queen. We're pawns; useless pieces that she can use however she sees fit and discard when we don't comply. The day I started swinging that sword and obeying orders that went against everything I believed in, my entire life was forfeited as a lie." Those amber eyes flickered in the lantern-light with more emotion than Adresia had ever seen from him. "I've done such atrocious, horrible things in the name of the crown. And I knew it was wrong, but I did it without hesitation. Why would I question it when we were the *Mighty Shield of Morolyn*?

"Six years ago, I was dispatched to a small village on the outskirts of Euwryst to deal with a traitor to the crown. I'd seen things like this before; done things like this before. I killed him without hesitation. It was only after, as his body turned cold and his pleas still rang in my ears, that I happened to see the things on his desk." There was a strangled, heart-wrenching exhale. "He'd been publicly advocating for Morolyn's support in the war—to help Gantrick and Lithelle fight the South whether the Queen planned to or not. He'd prepared areas for volunteers to assemble and learn how to fight, gathered aid from multiple villages who promised to provide supply lines, and had even acquired effective battle strategies and tactics from a few retired Generals. And as those plans sat on that desk, destined for dust, my entire life flickered before me: countless hopes and dreams and desires—buried beneath the bodies of the lives I've taken.

"In that moment, I decided I was never going to kill for Narissa again. I set out on a mission of my own: find out why I'd been forced to annihilate insignificant threats to the crown, and get retribution for what she turned me into. And if she was gone...maybe I would be seen as more than the useless man I am today. Maybe the world would be a better place; somewhere where children who look at knights and wish to protect the ones they love can be that person instead of being the ones who take their lives.

"A year after I was sent to that village, we were told that an important family would be coming to the castle. It wasn't unusual; Narissa had been arbitrarily summoning nobles since the day I entered her service. But I've watched her long enough to know that she wasn't just bothered by this family. She was tense. Worried. A few weeks later, that family didn't arrive."

Something frigid and dark bloomed in Adresia's core. She'd always been told her parents' deaths had been a result of treason. And she'd never stopped to consider the truth of the claims; she'd *refused* to believe them—until now. Because Narissa had been scared of her parents. Enough so that she'd wanted them dead. Immediately.

What did they *do*?

"What'd been written in the reports..." The knight shuddered. "I didn't know who would do those things. I didn't know why. Narissa had *never* ordered something like that before; never the obliteration of an entire family. And when they said the daughter had survived, I saw the fear in her eyes. Not because a potential loose end had been left, but because she was threatened—by a *child*."

That dreadful chill in Adresia's fingertips grew.

"And then, three months ago, you arrived: the girl who had survived; the only person I had *ever* seen the Queen fear. I didn't know what to think. But I saw you that first night, dancing and drinking and bathing in your nobility...and I assumed you'd succumbed to it. I thought you believed the lie she was feeding you. And I didn't want to be your friend because you—the person I'd prayed would finally have answers, the person I'd waited *years* for—had been so foolishly caught in the Queen's trap. I lost hope. I resorted to simply warning you, hoping it would unsettle you enough to make you aware of the mistake you were making, praying you would see the truth. But I didn't believe you would. I became distant and bitter. It was only when you called me out that I realized you'd hadn't just fooled me or the Queen. You'd fooled *everyone* into believing you were the person they thought you were. And when I saw you tonight, when I heard what you told those rebels..." There was such light in his eyes. "I have never felt such joy as I did when I realized I had reason to hope again."

She wasn't sure she was breathing. First Caspian and Corvina, then the rebellion, and now this—another person who blindly believed in her, even when she barely believed in herself. What was she supposed to *say*?

"You are totally freaking out," he said.

"No. I'm not. I'm just..." She considered his words. "I might be freaking out."

"I'd planned to tell you differently." A smile. "Less...intensely."

"Well, I hadn't planned to slap you either, but when do plans ever really work, anyway?"

He laughed, taking her response as the light-hearted break she'd intended it to be. It relieved her enough that she laughed too. "Care to join the rebellion, Fox?"

◇

It was a cloudless day. Snow-lined roofs twinkled in the sunlight. An aroma of spices poured over Adresia as she skipped into the townhouse at midday, a basket dangling from her forearm full of fresh breads and a pouch of new jewelry that had been too tempting not to purchase. The guards were spread across the long, wooden table, eating as always, and when she found who she was looking for, she casually sat beside the knight, startling a few men as she plopped her basket atop the table.

With Fox's hair pulled back, everyone could see his cheek, still dark and purple. It'd been a shock to wake up to his bruised face this morning. She'd apologized profusely, and he claimed he deserved it, but, still...it looked unbearably painful. The knight slid a full plate toward her and mumbled, "You do realize all of us were sent on this mission for the sole purpose of protecting you."

"And?" she asked before digging into a steaming meat pie.

"The men have been complaining about you leaving without warning."

"How unfortunate it is that I can take care of myself."

He smirked. It was so refreshing to see him express something other than brooding apathy. He was actually handsome, those amber eyes constantly alight.

They chatted through bites of their meal until they were interrupted by raucous snickering down the table. One of the men whistled at them. "Atlas—how'd you score that mark?"

"Must've been a nasty brawl," one guard quipped.

Another nodded toward her. "I bet it was from getting *that* lass out of trouble."

They continued their jesting, the remarks mixed with hardly suppressed laughter.

"They're just having fun," Fox muttered, although his smile had disappeared and he wouldn't look at the men. He'd stopped eating too.

"Maybe he got kicked by a mare sneaking around. It's not like he hasn't done *that* before."

"Maybe he got it when he was found in bed with one of those harlots we were eyeing up the first night." Laughter erupted around the table.

Adresia tried to finish her plate, she really did. But another added, "No, he wouldn't with that blonde-headed servant wrapped around his finger. She sure must be good if he refused one of *these* lasses."

Adresia faced them. "Why don't you close your mouths before I hit *you* next?" The laughter died. A few gaped at her words. "And the next time you insult my servant, you'll wish I let Sir Atlas handle you instead."

There was tense silence before the men mumbled their apologies, and, with a forced cough, resigned from the table and filed outside.

"They didn't know you did this," Fox quietly explained. "Now they're scared of you."

"They needed to be put in their place."

He returned to his meal. After a bite, he said, "Yes. They did."

She gave him a long look. "Are *you* scared of me, Fox?"

He downed half of his water before answering. "What do you think?"

Knowing what she was, who wouldn't be somewhat afraid of her? He'd taken *that* conversation better than she'd expected him to last night, thank the Goddess. "Maybe I can turn them into something." She knew it wasn't possible, but it was funny enough to think about. "Would a pig work?"

He choked on his water the same moment the front door swung open. When Caspian and Cota entered, she immediately stood, her expression turning sober. "I need to talk to you two." She glanced at Fox, who was still recovering from her joke. "We both do." Before anyone could protest, she grabbed Fox's arm and pulled him up and from the room. Caspian and Cota mutely shuffled after. When they entered her room on the third floor, she made sure to check down the hall before closing the door.

The men had found seats on the tarnished arm-chairs, rubbing their hands before the dwindling hearth. Adresia watched them for a moment, preparing herself for what she would say and the uncertainty of how they would react before marching in front of the flames. "Fox knows," she stated.

Cota's mouth parted in shock. Caspian grinned. "I've been waiting."

Fox returned the smile.

"We can trust him," Adresia told Cota.

He showed her his palms. "I didn't say we couldn't." He looked at Caspian. "You're sure?"

"I've known him practically my entire life," the Hand replied. "He would have joined me long before had I not had to keep the treasonous sentiments to myself."

With a nod, Cota faced her again. "If Caspian trusts him, then so do I."

It was Adresia's turn to balk in surprise. She never thought she'd see the day when Caspian and Cota *weren't* silently striving for dominance.

Fox leaned back in his seat. "Are you going to tell them how this alliance occurred, or are you waiting for me to spill the secret?"

The others raised their brows. She said, if not with slight hesitancy, "I found the rebels."

"She *met* the rebels," Fox corrected.

"You *what?*" Caspian blurted.

She gave the knight an unsubtle glare. "I might have...spoken to them."

"To their leader," Fox clarified under his breath.

Their eyes widened. "And?" Caspian pressed.

"And I found out that they lured us here to kill us," she said.

Cota was on his feet in an instant. "Are you *serious*, Res?"

"It's fine! They asked me to join them."

"By the gods, how did you convince them to change their minds to *that*?"

As if she could hide from her discomfort, she crossed her arms and mumbled, "I told them the truth." Caspian met her gaze, and she nodded at his unspoken question. They knew about her magic. "I showed them my scars." Cota sat back down, his throat bobbing. He knew what it meant for her to do that willingly.

"What was your answer?" Caspian asked.

"I told them I'd consider once I'd spoken to my partners."

"And why is this a bad thing?"

Her brows lowered. "Because it's dangerous."

"Like you care about danger," Cota muttered.

"I care about my friends not losing their lives," she countered sharply. "Being united on our own is *entirely* different from actually associating with these people. We'll have to communicate with them whilst *inside* the castle; we'll have to sneak around more, watch who we speak to, and lie and steal and cheat just to survive. It won't just be about us losing our lives if things go wrong. We'll be reliable for hundreds—*thousands*—of rebels."

They grew silent enough that she knew they were embracing the weight of that truth. Eventually, Cota met her gaze, flames blazing in his emerald eyes. She knew he'd come to a decision. "What would our parents do?" he asked.

She exhaled heavily, slowly. She only expected his answer because he wasn't aware of the pressure already weighing her down day by day; because he didn't know the truth—the *full* truth—of how the fate of their kingdom quite literally rested on her shoulders.

"They would fight," he continued. "They would do whatever it takes to free our people from the Queen's blood-stained grasp."

He was right. So much so that it hurt to accept.

She met Caspian's stare. *Your choice*, those stark-blue eyes seemed to say. Of course they did.

"So...how are we going to convince the rebels to work with us all?" she asked.

Fox sat forward with a mischievous smile. "I might have an idea."

Chapter 26

Bursts of pink and purple lined the horizon as a dark cobalt sky settled over Tauroben. Cota hadn't approached Adresia since he'd found her sitting on the stone ledge and gazing out the open window several minutes ago. Her unbound hair gently billowed in a salty breeze. She looked so content; so contrary to the tense concentration he'd seen her fall into these past weeks.

He was just about to leave her in the tranquil silence when she turned her head and spotted him. She patted the space beside her. Glad that she didn't mind his presence, he took the seat. She peered at the community over her shoulder and said, "It amazes me how much you can see at twilight," she said. Her feet swung back and forth, heels tapping the stone. "The sun is completely gone, yet it's still bright, like it's trying to prove how much light can remain amidst the darkness." He marveled at her imaginative, beautiful mind. She looked at him. "Are you ready for tonight?"

"Are you?"

"I don't know. I don't want things to go bad if they deny our offer."

"I'm not worried. You have Caspian, me, *and* Fox watching your back; we'll be fine." He bumped her shoulder with his own. The corners of her lips rose. "Besides, it's too good an offer to pass up. The rebels are better off with us on their side." She nodded, but grew quiet again. "Do you remember when our parents found us slipping out of our bedroom windows to see each other after they'd grounded us from skipping lessons?"

"They had us doing laundry for a month," she recalled with a smirk.

"More like two," he affirmed with a roguish grin.

"They were always getting onto us!"

"Only because we were rebellious children."

"Do you remember that time we hid a *dozen* sparrows in Miss Juerand's cabinets? You would've thought she found a body by the sound of her scream. And we had to cover each other's mouths to keep from laughing as we watched from the window!"

"Our fathers separated our punishments so we wouldn't distract each other," he said, "but you still snuck out for a week—until you got caught!"

"I spent *three months* shoveling the stables!" she said with a laugh. Her stormy eyes shone in exhilaration, and her smile didn't leave as a comfortable silence settled over them.

Not wanting to spoil the calm but wanting to hear her voice again, he asked softly, "What are you thinking about?"

She looked at her lap, huffing a soft breath through her nose. "Our lives before this." She stood. "Everything that seems like a distant dream in comparison to what is now our reality." He slid from the ledge too, and despite what he'd been warned against, despite what the Queen had threatened, he couldn't resist the urge to grab her hand. Now. He should tell her now. Their eyes met, and he swore she knew what he was thinking as she started, "Cota—"

Adresia wrenched her hand back as a guard marched past the alcove. Either ignorant or unaware of their presence, he disappeared down the hall a heartbeat later. When Cota found her still watching the hall with wide eyes, his momentary courage vanished—because maybe she *had* known what he was going to say. Because maybe she didn't want that. Maybe he would've crossed a line that she didn't want crossed.

He cleared his throat and stepped back. "I'll be downstairs."

Chapter 27

Moonlight glittered on the icy stones outside the Twilight as Adresia entered. The three hooded men following her lingered by the dim entrance as she strode to where Elettra and her group sat in the far corner. When the Countess arrived at the table, she said by way of greeting, hoping her nervousness wasn't as distinguishable as it felt, "I don't know why you think this is the safest—or cleanest—place to do anything."

Elettra clasped her fingers together across the table. "When everyone maintains the belief that I'm a careless drunk wasting my life away, it leaves no room for accusations."

Adresia gave a commendable nod, shrugged off her cloak, and slid into her awaiting seat, noting the group's watchful gazes, no doubt taking in every aspect of her being: her clothes, her movements, her attitude. But this was as much a test for them as it was for her.

"I assume you haven't rejected my offer if you're here," Elettra said.

A glance around the table told Adresia the group was expectant, if not vigilant. They all knew the risks of this engagement. Which was why, when she said, "My answer is yes," it didn't surprise her that the group relaxed as one. "But I have conditions."

"Conditions?" Elettra asked.

Adresia shoved her shaking fingers under her thighs. "The deal is off unless my partners are allowed in."

"And who might your partners be?"

With a quick glance over her shoulder, the men stalked from the entrance of the tavern, mutely grabbed three chairs, and sat beside the Countess. Elettra's gaze darted between the four of them. They'd prepared for hesitancy, for understandable wariness. But the woman crossed her arms and stated, "There will be no further discussion until they reveal their identities."

The Countess frowned. "How do I know you don't have men waiting outside right now, ready to seize and use us for your own vile motives? It was your plan to kill us after all."

The woman's mouth slipped into an unsettling smile. "It was."

A hand gripped Adresia's curled fingers under the table. She didn't outwardly acknowledge it, nor did she look at Caspian, but it was comforting enough that she forgot her momentary concern. His hand slipped away as she exhaled. "If my partners feel comfortable enough to show you who they are, they can do so. But the fact that they *do* risk revealing so much should speak volumes to their commitment to this cause." Adresia only believed the woman wanted to know who they were for alliance purposes—not because she was still trying to decide whether they were worthy enough to join the rebellion.

The hood to her right fell first. "Cota Bowyer," her best friend said, his green eyes twinkling with allure. "Lord of Darbania."

The second hood fell two seats to her left. Even in the dim lighting, Fox's scar gave a wicked impression. "Sir Fox Atlas," the knight stated, crossing his arms. The group shifted uncomfortably in their seats, taking the gesture as Adresia had hoped.

The last hood fell to her right. "Lord Hand Caspian Harvryd."

Torstein nearly jumped out of his seat. "You brought the Hand of the Queen here? Are you *stupid—*"

Elettra silenced him by raising her hand. The action was just as impressive as the other night. The woman waited for him to sit before calmly saying, "A spy of mine was in the Throne Room the day Obryn Drumwell was ruthlessly stabbed and executed." She met Caspian's unyielding gaze. "You tried to give him a chance, despite the consequences or your reputation." The woman tilted her head, observing the four of them. "I accept your conditions."

Adresia tried not to react. That easily, the danger of their lives had been confirmed. By the frozen calmness of her friends, they had realized the same thing. "What does this alliance request of us?" Caspian asked.

"Any and all information you can gather that benefits this cause," Elettra began, "you deliver to me—coded, of course. Trading routes, military distributions, messages with those in close contact with the Queen...things you're familiar with."

"And if we get caught?" Fox asked.

"I think you're clever enough to not let that happen."

Whatever answer the knight was looking for, it seemed to satisfy him. Adresia said, "You sparked protests to get us here. We were sent to end them. We can't return if they haven't ceased."

"That won't be an issue," Elettra replied. "By the time you arrive back at Dazelle, the complaints will be no more."

Well...that was easy. They rose. Adresia grabbed her cloak and accepted Elettra's outstretched hand. "I'm looking forward to working together," the woman said. "Your variations in nobility and position are extremely advantageous." The Countess nodded, meaning to let go of the handshake, but, with an odd glance, Elettra twisted Adresia's arm. "What is that?" Her gaze was pinned on Adresia's tattoo.

"My family crest," the Countess slowly replied.

The hesitation that followed made Adresia *very* interested in why Elettra had noticed it. "Pretty," the woman said, releasing her grip.

The entrance of the tavern slammed open. "It's happened again!" someone bellowed. "The Queen has struck barely a day's ride from Niamth Bay!" People shot from their seats, frantically following the messenger. In half a minute, a dreadful silence filled the empty tavern.

The Countess faced the rebels. Every single one of them had paled. "What is he talking about?" Adresia asked.

Torstein overcame his shock enough to glare at Caspian. "I'm surprised you didn't ask your *friend*."

She looked at Caspian. "I'm just as confused as you," he said.

"The Queen," Morphaeous voiced, "has taken it upon herself to destroy the villages of those suspected to be affiliating with the rebellion. Fire is her preferred method."

The word clanged through Adresia.

Fire.

"There are never bodies," Morphaeous said, "but the extent at which she incinerates the area, how could there be? All that ever remains is charred ground, as if the gods themselves had declared their wrath directly from the heavens."

That was what Obryn had told Narissa: *You. Will. Burn—just like the rest of them.* Adresia's head roared at the familiarity, at the horrific, disgusting thought, and it became hard to breathe—

A hand gently touched her back. She met Cota's gaze and tried to relax, even as her heart continued racing, even as she wondered why he hadn't yet spoken to her since they'd been alone in the alcove all those hours ago.

"Where?" Caspian asked, the only one of them that seemed to be able to speak.

"The eastern plains," Morphaeous answered. "They're becoming more frequent and worse with every assault. I won't be surprised if the Queen moves on to the rest of the kingdom soon."

This was what Adresia had discovered a month ago: Narissa's pursuit toward a kingdom-wide destruction. Because if she couldn't *control* her people...she would end them.

"I must go," Elettra began hollowly. Brown eyes glowed in the candlelight, and, from an angle, she almost resembled the Queen. Especially as the sliver of weakness the woman had shown vanished and she predatorily cocked her head. Adresia instinctively pressed closer to her best friend. "You now have my trust," Elettra declared. "Do not break it."

Chapter 28

Absolutely nothing remained of the village. It was as if it had never existed.

But that was the point, wasn't it?

Two hundred soldiers carefully stepped over the field of embers and ash and scanned the darkened earth. Save for the scalding terrain crunching beneath their boots, the area was unearthly silent, as if the gods themselves had abandoned it.

Perhaps they had abandoned them all.

After the Liberating, their only order was to check for signs of existence. They never found any, but if they did, there was only one rule.

Destroy it.

A brisk wind rushed by, cooling their perpetually warm skin. It didn't feel like winter. It never did. The scent of smoke and burnt wood clogged their nostrils, filling their lungs. After so many recurrences, it was familiar. Welcome. *You will learn to enjoy it*, they were told. *You will desire it.*

They did.

The soldiers approached the white-haired male and dropped to their knees. They remained that way, in the profound silence of His presence, arched over the ashen soil, until their necks grew tight and strained and their legs wobbled beneath them. They were not afraid. He knew if they were. And those plagued by fear...they were changed when they returned. Different. Brutal.

"Rise."

They met His piercing stare as they stood, and they did not back down.

He grinned. "You've been trained marvelously."

Their report rang through the silence. "There are none left, sire."

White hair glinted in the sunlight as He observed the charred field around them. "It is not enough."

The soldiers shared uneasy glances. Not once had He ever shared such distaste. It disappointed them, but they would work harder. They would Liberate more, destroy more.

They would do anything to satisfy Him.

"She's growing too fast," He continued. "Too much. I can feel her as if she's with me every moment of every day and they won't get out of my *head*." He pressed His palms to His temples and clenched His eyes shut. "It's so familiar to what flows through my veins. But I fear what it is within her is far greater than this world has ever known. Like mine, but...more."

"What will you do, sire?"

His hands dropped to His sides as He lifted His gaze. And at the sight of the army hidden in the redwoods beyond the field, readily awaiting His orders...His wicked smile returned. "Nothing." He passed the men, a dark mist shadowing His movements. "She will come to me."

Chapter 29

"Does he *ever* leave?" Harkin Sallow asked at Adresia's side. She'd been chatting with the soldier for quite some time now, exchanging their experiences during each other's absence as they strolled the castle halls. She'd been immensely shocked—and delighted—to find him still here after her month away. The Lithellian soldiers were content with staying in Dazelle for as long as they were allowed, supposedly, and Harkin had remained with his men.

She glanced over her shoulder. Fox was far enough away that he wasn't intruding in their conversation, but close enough to keep an eye on her. He hadn't left her side since they'd returned from Tauroben. With a faint smile, she answered Harkin, "At night. It's the only time I can't get myself into trouble. At least, that's what he tells himself."

The Lord grinned. "And where's Lord Bowyer? You used to see him quite often, if I recall."

A shrug. "We've both been busy." Cota was brimming with work after the Queen decided it was time for him to establish an actual Lordly influence in the city. And after their success in Tauroben, Narissa had been pleased enough that she'd sent Adresia on another mission the *day* they'd returned. The Countess had endured half a week of painstakingly boring discussions with an aggravatingly unpleasant Lord who'd had trouble with his servants abandoning their servitude and, in turn, hadn't been able to control his estate. Harkin was the first person she'd spoken to when she'd returned late last night.

She realized she'd grown quiet as she found the Lord's watchful gaze. "You miss him," he said, more of a fact than a question. "What about Tauroben?"

A sidelong glance. "What about it?"

"Lord Bowyer went with you and...nothing happened?" When her cheeks warmed, his face lit up. "Something *did* happen—"

"Nothing happened," she said, quieting his excitement. "I mean, something *almost* happened, but..." She shook her head. It felt like nothing had happened. Cota hadn't provided a single sign on the ride back that he'd noticed what had occurred between them that night. It would be foolish to hope it meant something anyway. "I don't know if you've noticed, but intimate relationships aren't exactly encouraged here."

"It's hard *not* to notice."

"It's complicated for us to be together anyway."

"Love never comes easy."

She looked at him. "What?"

Harkin patted her arm, looped around his. "I've seen love, Adresia, and trust me...the way you two look at each other is precisely that."

Don't pretend like you aren't in love, Fox had said. Perhaps it was more obvious than she realized. And maybe the answers to the questions she'd been avoiding asking herself were true too.

"I didn't have friends before I came here," she said. "Not besides Cota. But you...you've been so welcoming. You've never treated me like I'm just another noble who's making a massive mistake in being here and following orders I have to in order to survive."

"We've all had to do things in order to survive, Adresia." That was exactly what she'd told Caspian in the Sight Woods three months ago. With a confusing wince, Harkin added, "I'm totally going to ruin this moment." Stopping at the intersection of two corridors, he released her arm and faced her. "You are the kindest Morolynian I have ever met. And after sharing all that we have, I've been waiting for the right moment to tell you, but I don't think there'll be one."

A freezing slosh of trepidation cracked open in her core. "Tell me what?"

"Can you just promise, as my friend, to be...open-minded?"

A slow nod.

"I didn't tell you the entire truth about myself when we met."

"The *entire* truth?" she repeated.

He took a steadying breath. "I'm not just a Lithellian soldier."

She waited for him to go on, but when he didn't, she said, "That really clears things up, thanks." Her attempt at humor vanished when he shifted on his feet—because the Harkin she knew was *never* nervous. But maybe the Harkin she knew wasn't the real one at all.

Especially not as his accent disappeared.

"The real reason I'm here is because King Bevon—"

She slammed a hand over his mouth and pulled him into an alcove. His eyes were wide as she said in a voice he had never heard, "Do not say anything that will forfeit your life, do not say anything that you want overheard, and do *not* say anything that you do not trust me with."

When she released him, he blinked in surprise before replying, "I won't."

"We only have a few minutes before Sir Atlas realizes I'm gone," she added. Fox had been conversing with a guard down the hall.

Harkin straightened, an aura of authority dawning on him. "Something is happening in Morolyn. Something dangerous. King Bevon sent me here to investigate Queen Narissa's connection to it. We know her distaste of Gantrick and Tethoris. We won't risk Lithelle being next."

This was...unbelievable. This was ridiculous. This was completely *insane*.

"I know it's a lot to take in—"

"What's your plan if you find something worth reporting?" she asked. She hated the harshness in her voice, but as much as she knew he could handle his own—the fact that he'd remained undetected in the time that he'd been here proved just that—he *couldn't* figure out what Narissa was doing; that she was plotting destruction and that she was a mage and that there was a rebellion. Because if he did, he would stay. And if the Queen caught him spying...he would never see Lithelle again.

His brows lowered in confusion. "You're not surprised?"

"This is my kingdom, after all."

A soft smile. "You know, you're not at all what everyone believes you to be. That's a good thing, if my suspicions are correct."

She ignored whatever those might be and repeated, "Your plan?"

"I'll send a private messenger to Lithelle."

"And what have you uncovered?" He opened his mouth, but she continued, "Nothing, I take it. Am I wrong?"

"No," he answered slowly. "You're not."

"Her own people have been trying to expose her cruelty for *years* without success. What makes you think you can?"

He stared at her, confused.

"It isn't my intention to insult you or your king," she said. "I just...I care too much about you to see you make the wrong mistake and never be able to return home."

"And I care too much about *you* to let you suffer under this tyranny any longer," he countered.

She huffed in frustration. All she wanted was for him to flee while he had the chance. But she couldn't say that. Not without risking her knowledge of the truth or explaining *herself*. She couldn't force him to abandon his King's orders, just like he couldn't stop her from abandoning her efforts. And there was his unrelenting kindness that she'd cherished from the moment they met; his startling compassion for her given they'd only been friends for such a brief time. It made everything so difficult. She just prayed the soldiers would return to Lithelle before her fears could become reality. "Promise me you'll be careful," she said.

"I will."

"Don't do anything I would do."

He smirked. "Well then I'd get caught, wouldn't I?"

She shook her head, but couldn't help her smile. "You would do anything for your people, wouldn't you?"

He nodded, a grateful glimmer in those caramel eyes. "Thank you for understanding. You don't know how good it feels to have someone else know; to not have to bear this burden by myself."

"I'm glad I can help," she said, even as she despised herself. He'd not only risked his own life, but his king's and his kingdom's in sharing his truth with her. Now she was taking that bravery and stomping on it. She wasn't lying, but she wasn't telling him *her* truth—a truth that could help his king and people. But if not sharing meant keeping him from more danger than he already was, she would keep doing so.

She wouldn't visit another grave.

The nobles surrounding the Queen were quieter than usual, although, in Adresia's opinion, not any less haughty. It was probably because the Queen's Warden had withdrawn from any noteworthy discussions this Council meeting. The woman had healed since the ascension: the vicious new scar on her collarbone seen past the low-dip in her rose gown was on display for everyone to see. She claimed to have earned it during hand-to-hand combat with a guard, which was believable, as she was seen occasionally training with the Shield, but the Countess had enough scars to know the difference between an accidental strike and intentionally placed blade. What had happened to the Warden had been no mistake.

When contributing her perspective during her first Council meeting, Adresia had received more than a few unsubtle glares from the Dukes. This time, she'd refrained from talking at all. She only wanted to speak to Narissa anyway. The Countess let the morning pass with more or less intriguing banter amidst discussions about the Shield, upcoming castle events, and obligations to the Priests in Euwryst as she searched for the right moment to voice her own concerns. Nothing was interesting enough to take note of save for the extended stay of the Lithellian soldiers. The Dukes agreed Morolyn's hospitality would benefit from it. While it was nice when the castle was bustling, Adresia doubted Narissa's motive of allowing the soldiers to stay were purely out of the kindness of her heart. And if they were remaining indefinitely, the last thing Adresia wanted was more time for Harkin to risk exposing himself. He needed to leave. She just didn't know how to convince him to yet.

Adresia eyed Caspian's empty chair down the table. He was in a meeting with several local Lords who had unexpectedly arrived at the castle. She hadn't seen him in days. But his absence meant he wouldn't be here to warn her about the dangers of questioning the Queen yet again and convince her to remain quiet. She blamed him for whatever happened. The Lords could have waited.

When the Queen's attention diverted from the noble at her side, Adresia took her chance before she could talk herself out of it. "I have a question, Your Majesty."

Narissa peered down the table.

"When I was in Tauroben," Adresia began, "I came across some commoners who said there were villages being burned in the eastern plains under your orders—that people were dying because of the fires."

The Council's indistinct murmuring stopped short around the table. The silence almost made the Countess regret her prodding. Almost...but not entirely. Not as Narissa said, "Yes. Such activities are happening under my orders." There was a composure in her voice: either dangerous rage or unsettling calm. Adresia couldn't distinguish which one it was before the woman continued, "The land has been underused and ravaged by drought longer than I have been Queen. If you understand anything about land cultivation or agricultural productivity, then you will know that burning it is a reasonable tactic to combat its unfavorable condition. As for the villages, I am aware there are citizens who reside there, and I have been clear in my instruction to relocate such communities before commencing such activities. My reports have led me to believe everyone is gone beforehand, but sometimes people stay. It is no one's fault besides their own if they choose to forfeit their lives."

Adresia had thought it'd been smart to question the Queen. But now, as the weight of Narissa's words settled in Adresia like a stone, she felt like she'd played right into the woman's hand. And while the rest of the Council blindly accepted the explanation as truth, nodding with indifferent understanding before diving back into their previous conversations, Adresia didn't. She didn't know the real reason yet, but she knew the Queen was lying.

The Countess didn't talk for the rest of the meeting, instead pushing her food around her plate and refraining from meeting anyone's stare. When the meeting ended an hour later, Adresia didn't leave until the nobles disappeared out the doors and the servants politely but firmly asked her to move from the table so they could clean.

When she turned down the covered walkway, her stomach dropped. The Queen stood at one of the arched openings, her raven hair fluttering in a frigid breeze. She watched as Adresia stopped and curtsied. "Your Majesty."

Violet eyes glowed in the winter sunlight. "You seemed upset after our discussion. Were you offended by something I said?"

At this point, honesty was better than false, pleasing sentiments. The woman always seemed to know when Adresia was lying anyway. "I wish I would have known."

"And what is it you think you know?" the Queen asked.

Annoyance curled in Adresia's gut. "There were several accounts of entire villages being burned—with *all* the citizens present. So either the stories are false or your men are lying."

"Are you saying you trust mere commoners over your Queen?"

The challenge was there for the taking—and Adresia was so *sick* of giving in and backing down that she took it. "As someone who has endured unspeakable atrocities and strives to keep others from enduring a similar fate...yes, I'm more inclined to believe people who've actually witnessed such events rather than someone who institutes intimidating measures without having any way of knowing what's really being conducted in their absence."

"And would you have reconsidered your position as Ambassador if you had known what you do now?"

Adresia raised her chin. "No." It was the truth. She was using this position just as much as Narissa was using her. She wouldn't throw that opportunity away.

There was a long pause before then the Queen stepped aside. "Enjoy your night, Lady Bellum."

The Countess hesitantly stepped forward, and, seeing Fox approaching from the foyer, she sped toward him. When they met, she looped an arm through his and pulled him back to the front doors. "What are you doing?" he asked.

"Getting out of sight," she muttered.

They marched through the front doors and across the courtyard. The occasional drifts of frigid wind Adresia had experienced before they'd left for Tauroben were now consistently blowing. And while it rejuvenated her, Fox was shivering by the time they stopped at the northeastern gate. "What happened?" he asked, using the stone arch to block the wind.

"I asked her about the village burnings," Adresia said.

"Of course you did."

"I didn't know she would confront me afterwards!"

He straightened. "What did she say?"

"She tried to scope out my loyalty by asking irritating questions."

"And did you give her the answers she wanted?"

She crossed her arms. "Probably not."

He frowned, but after her pointed look—confusion and irritation and desperation all mixed in one—his mouth lifted at the corner. "You're in deep, aren't you?"

"You have no idea."

He sighed. "Go ahead." She raised a brow. "You like it out here. Take a walk. I can wait."

She excitedly rose on her toes before following the gravel path into the Outer Gardens. A sort of peace settled over her as she ran her fingers along the waist-high bushes and a light snow drifted from the cloudy sky above. This was the winter she'd been told about: cold that filled up her, calmed her, numbed her. It was the only thing her mother had missed from the northwestern kingdom that had been her childhood home after moving to Westholt.

A pebble suddenly rolled to Adresia's feet. She looked around the bushes, but no one was there. A glance back told her Fox was still at the gate. She turned back around the same time another pebble appeared. She followed its path, peering ahead. A blur of something flashed around the corner of the hedge before there was a third one.

She swiftly marched to the corner before stopping dead in her tracks. She didn't know why it surprised her; after all, her own existence was the strangest thing she could have conjured up. But she wasn't expecting to see another magical creature after half a century of them being practically extinct.

It was chestnut colored and no taller than a goblet, and its head almost didn't fit with the rest of its tiny body. Its hands, no bigger than her pinkie nail, pulled overly-large ears over round, sparkling eyes as it timidly watched her. And perhaps it was because she was just as strikingly unusual, but something told her it was harmless. At least, harmless toward her. She crouched and gingerly held out her hand. "Hello there."

As if sensing she wasn't a threat, it released its ears and let out a silvery hum. It walked to the side of her hand and tapped the middle of her palm before humming again, taking a step back, and waiting.

She wished it *could* talk. She had no idea what it wanted. She put a pebble in her hand, but the creature shook its head, instead watching in transfixed awe as a snowflake drifted to the ground. And as the falling snow at last abated, it looked at Adresia expectantly.

An idea arose. She opened her palm, closed her eyes, and focused on her breathing. Over and over she thought of her power, willing it to surface. Eventually that familiar tingling arose. When she opened her eyes, a single snowflake floated above her palm. A surprised laugh escaped her lips. The creature hummed in delight. Adresia held out her hand. It gladly accepted the gift, which was half the size of its body.

Had it known she possessed such power? And how had she controlled her magic so well? Did the creature have anything to do with it? Perhaps it was her wintry surroundings that gave her control.

A series of squeaks and hums sounded nearby. The creature turned toward them and called loudly back. It approached her still open hand and patted her finger twice with a smile that almost looked encouraging before disappearing around the hedge. She tried following it around a few more corners, barely catching sight of its floppy ears. When she finally got near, it dove into a bush and vanished completely.

Well then.

She rose with sudden clarity. The Obissean Lake stretched ahead as far as she could see, its dark waters rippling under a thinly frozen surface. She stared in awe, transfixed by its otherness as much as that creature had been by the snow. When she was out here, it was like her problems didn't matter. Whatever hardships she was enduring, whatever trial awaited her inside that castle...it was a distant thought in the catacombs of her mind. Out here, she could be herself. Out here, she could be free.

When she stepped closer, a sort of pressure swept through her body. It was like her powers had flickered in response. She instinctively took another step—and then a startled shout ripped from her throat as she was shoved from behind. She slammed into the ice so hard she felt like she'd been thrown across the lake.

With a groan, she carefully sat upright. She *was* far from shore, but...no one was there. And then a sharp noise sounded beneath her, like a screeching clap of thunder. With no small amount of horror, Adresia looked down. Cracks webbed under her weight. She put her hands down as if it would somehow help. The ice splintered worse. "Please," she whispered, "don't—"

Adresia plunged into the freezing depths below. The cold was like needles against her skin, so consuming that she could barely think straight, but she forced herself to calm, to accept the brutal chill and swim.

She broke through the surface with a ragged inhale—and then fear like she'd never felt before exploded as she was wrenched back under with a scream.

Chapter 30

Cota Bowyer had been traversing the grounds all day, accompanying Caspian in too many tedious tasks to leave any normal man sane. They were currently finishing fortification inspections. The Shield did routine check-ups, but there hadn't been one in months with so many noble events. "The Queen loves her festivities," Caspian had sardonically explained. Cota had to agree; the amount of balls and dinners he'd witnessed since arriving at the castle were far more than he was comfortable with. Did some of the nobles even *have* lives outside the castle?

After discussing their observations with one of the guards on duty, Cota followed Caspian down the stairs of the barracks, through the pitiful looking accommodation, and then out and across the courtyard. "I should have been more specific when I asked what needed to be done today," the Hand muttered, pulling his cloak tighter around his shoulders.

Cota rubbed his chilled hands together. "At this point, meetings are more bearable."

Caspian huffed a laugh. "I'm just glad Hadrian is on patrol. Conversations with *him*?" A shake of his head. "I despise those days."

"He doesn't respect you because you have the position he perceives is his?" Cota guessed.

A sidelong glance. "Did you hear someone say that?"

"I can see it in the way he glares at you every time he passes you in the corridor."

Caspian actually laughed, then. "Well, since I wasn't born a *real* noble, his grievances aren't the only ones I have to deal with. Most of the Council disapproves of my position."

"Why do you stay if you know people don't respect you?"

"Respect is a privilege that most dream of obtaining their entire lives without success. Even our Queen is feared rather than revered. I was made Hand for a reason and I'm going to utilize it to the best of my ability. I don't have to be respected to be listened to." His lips tugged up. "Not that I'm even listened to all that—"

A shout rang out, distant and broken. Any amusement Cota felt shriveled in his stomach.

"Was that from the Outer Gardens?" Caspian asked, voicing the Count's exact thought.

Adresia and Fox went that direction not long ago.

Both of them marched toward the northeastern gate. Cota prayed it wasn't them; prayed that they'd gone inside already and everything was fine. But when they walked under the stone arch and another haunting scream sounded, neither of them hesitated. They barreled into the gardens, searching with panicked steps before reeling to a stop where the hedges met the Obissean Lake. Because on his knees at the edge of the frost covered shore was Fox, staring at the frozen surface in front of him.

At the hole in the ice.

"*What happened?*" Caspian demanded.

"She—she must have fell in," Fox sputtered, "and then I heard her scream, but she hasn't—"

Cota heard the words...and dismissed them. It was like his senses had iced over, the truth of this reality numbing him. His cloak slipped to the ground as he took a step forward. The only reason he stopped was the stark tone of the Second of the Shield. "You'll only be killing yourself if you go down there."

The Count's body begged him to react, to move, but he forced himself to stop and look at Caspian. "She hasn't come up."

"I know."

"Why?"

"Because there's something down there," Fox answered ominously. "Something...*else*."

The three of them beheld the eerily still lake. A freezing wind whipped through the air and slashed Cota's uncovered skin. And then the icy surface thumped like it was vibrating from the force of something below.

Holy gods.

"She's alive," Caspian said. "She has to be."

He reached for Cota's shoulder, but the Count dismissed the gesture—the sliver of a sign that maybe after the madness they'd experienced together in the last month, he and Caspian were perhaps more than just allies compelled to cooperate under the same goal—and whirled to the knight, who was already on his feet. Blood pounded in Cota's ears, blocking out any and all reason. There was a panicked rage in him, thrashing to get out, angered at the restraint that was forcing him to remain at shore. The instinct inside of him to protect and defend...it'd turned into an uncontrollable desire to strike.

As if sensing what was boiling under Cota's skin, Fox raised his hands. "Just—just wait. I don't know what happened. I'm sorry—"

"Being sorry won't save her," Cota snarled.

"You don't get to blame me for something out of my control."

"You're supposed to protect her."

There was half a second in which devastation wracked the knight's face before the expression twisted back into that intimidating, unyielding glower. "You don't get to tell me what I—"

Cota tackled him. And Caspian was shouting to stop, to *calm down*, but there was something lupine in the Count, biting and snapping and clawing to be let out. He and the knight crashed into the frost-covered shore the same moment Cota swung.

Fox didn't fight back. He just laid still, taking the pain and blame and the ravenous anger with every punch. And when Cota went to deliver a blow that would surely do more damage than what was mendable...he halted. His fist was inches above a mangled face and swollen eyes clenched shut in anticipation. The knight had been ready to take it all. Ready to die, if need be.

But this didn't matter. *Fox* didn't matter.

Dizzy with fury and fear, Cota backed from the battered man and dropped to his knees at the shore. His bloody fingers throbbed as he watched the lake in a daze. There was something otherworldly down there with Adresia; something real and true and petrifying. And while he knew her skill, while he trusted her strength, this was different. This was magic. And before Cota could even digest the magnitude of that truth, a sharp inhale sounded behind him.

The shattered circle in the ice began to freeze over.

He'd barely risen back to his feet by the time a deep thrumming and crack sounded. The hole was just...*gone*. It'd sealed as quickly as water spilled across a table. And when he lifted his gaze higher, horror washed over him as he beheld what had happened: it wasn't just the hole that was now a thick layer of dark, clear ice.

It was the entire lake.

Caspian began, "Did that just—"

Another noise.

"That was *below* the surface," Fox rasped.

And then a hand slammed into the ice from the freezing depths barely thirty feet from shore.

Cota scrambled forward, not caring what happened as he landed above Adresia and bellowed her name. He could barely think, could barely breathe, and the pain didn't register as he punched the ice. But she was suddenly yanked down, fear-lit eyes disappearing back into darkness, and he blocked out whatever Caspian was saying as something wolfish awakened inside him. He struck wildly, recklessly, again and again and *again*, and the ice cracked and he sucked in a breath, preparing to dive below and after her as soon as the surface broke—

Caspian grabbed his arm and said, "If you do it again, you're going to break your hand."

The sudden stillness shocked Cota enough that everything became nauseatingly clear. He beheld the mess that his hand had become with a ragged exhale before looking at Caspian again and opening his mouth to say that he didn't care—but the Hand's eyes suddenly widened. Cota spun back around.

Adresia was below them.

Alive.

Chapter 31

Something had hold of Adresia's ankle, tugging her deeper and deeper into the never-ending dark of the Obissean Lake. Her ears popped as she descended, and the light of the surface faded faster than she would have thought possible. But she wasn't going down without a fight. Certainly not into the horrifying abyss that was this expanse of frigid water.

Adresia slammed her heel into the finger-like-things around her ankle. The instant they pulled back, she rocketed toward the surface. It took everything in her not to panic, to save her breath and energy and strength. Whatever this thing was, she could feel it behind her, around her. When her hand crashed into flesh so slimy that it made her want to gag and a deafening growl followed, she was glad she couldn't see past the darkness.

This beast *lived* here, knowing how to move through water as easily as she knew how to run on land. She'd barely had the chance to practice swimming regularly in Westholt. Down here, her movements were slowed, all training useless. She didn't know what to dodge or where it was coming from. Especially not as something sliced her leg.

She instinctively cried out before forcing herself to contain her air and *keep swimming*. But her gown, torn and free-floating, tangled around her legs, disrupting her movements. She frantically kicked it away before continuing up, trying not to panic as the strain in her lungs became harder to dismiss. The hole she'd fallen through was close enough that she would have sobbed if she wasn't underwater.

And then she was pulled back down.

It was more forceful this time, the beast grabbing both ankles. Her thigh seared in pain as she thrashed and threw her arms out in a desperate, futile attempt to grasp something. But there was nothing except endless, open, freezing water, and she was useless and helpless and powerless—

She stopped.

The cold. The *cold* enhanced her control—and she was in the coldest place she'd ever been.

Exhaustion coated her limbs, but she mustered as much energy as she could and prayed her theory was correct. Every feeling and thought and sense chanted the words, over and over, willing the truth into her soul: *you are strong and you are powerful and you will not die.*

She felt it before it happened. It wasn't a tingling in her hands, but lightning throughout her entire being. Its thunderous effect roared in her head, then out into the lake as ice lurched from her palms. And the build that she'd experienced every time before, the suspense that she feared would explode into catastrophe—it faded with every passing second that her magic left her fingers. She didn't know if she'd even aimed correctly until the grips on her ankles loosened. She shot for the surface again, swimming as fast as she could to escape the darkness leaking into her vision. The water became brighter as she approached that glorious air...and then ran straight into a frozen surface.

Oh gods. *Oh gods.*

Fear curdled every ounce of power she'd felt moments before. With a raging scream, she slapped the ice, the cursed aftermath of using her magic. She'd trapped herself down here. She hadn't practiced enough to know the effects of *Hiermsall*, of what she was capable of, of what happened when she lashed out. It was *her* fault, not the creature or whatever had pushed her. And then dark figures appeared above, but Adresia knew the lake-creature had survived half a second before it wrenched her down again. She'd been ready, though. A sharp sickle of ice appeared in her hand, and when the beast dove to wherever lifeless depth it would devour her...she dove too.

It paused in confusion, and she blindly shoved the weapon toward what she hoped was something vital. There was a muffled quelch that made disgust and nausea shoot up her throat and a responding screech pierced her ears so loudly that she could barely think. But those slimy fingers went taut a third time and she raced back up, praying the creature was completely immobilized, if not dead.

She launched herself at the frozen surface, desperately hitting it over and over, forcing everything she had left into breaking it, even as her knuckles began to bleed and splinter in pain. And then the ice cracked, and she shook her head, *willing* herself to keep fighting. But that thing in her, alive and breathing and pleading to survive—it felt so distant. Like it was falling deeper and deeper into the depths of her drowning soul. Her strikes slowed, each one later than the last. She struggled to keep her blurring gaze sharp. And the urge to open her mouth and quell the fire in her lungs, the desire to keep that sweet darkness from consuming her vision, it sounded...easy.

Freeing.

This wintry abyss wasn't so bad. It felt like where her mother had grown up; like the battlefields her father had trained in. She swore she could hear their voices: her mother's sweet song radiating through the frigid expanse around her and her father's warm laughter soothing her frozen fears.

The mountains, they rise, so we get to climb,
o'er the hills in search of less crime.

MARANDA BAUTSCH

The rivers, they run, and our people survive,
with the life under water so we can then thrive.

They were here, weren't they? They would greet her, if she just let go. That perfect place, without violence and fear, with an abundance of provisions and joy—it was hers for the taking. She just needed to accept it. She just needed to follow those voices.

Tell our people to no longer hide;
We came here first, although some have since died.
There will be war, brutal death, and strife,
but it is all worth this exuberant life.
Let me stay in the kingdom of...

Yes, she had experienced those things: death and war and terror and strife. But those things wouldn't last forever. They were not the end. They were not her destiny. There was something better. She was at the beginning of that exuberant life, if she wanted it. And she did. Desperately.

So, surrounded by sunlight shining into these eternally dark depths and clinging to nothing except for the hope of what she was entering into, Adresia stopped fighting.

And then the surface broke.

Chapter 32

Adresia wasn't dead. She knew because the medicinal tonics and herbal teas in the air, a silken dress on her skin, and the faded pain in her leg and body was not what was promised in the afterlife.

She'd survived.

Fighting past the exhaustion that dulled every sense, Adresia opened her eyes. There was painful brightness. She shifted her head until a figure blocked the blazing hearth and she could observe herself. There were no less than three blankets thrown atop her, adding to the already unpleasant warmth of the room. But when she recognized the golden hair inches from her face, her discomfort disappeared.

Cota was asleep, sitting with his back against her low-lying sofa. Her arm was draped over his shoulder, their fingers interlaced like he hadn't wanted to let go while she'd slept. She watched the steady rise and fall of his chest, content with the peace it brought her, so stark to the events that had brought her here.

Until she noticed the blood.

She tried to sit up, but hissed as pain shot through her thigh, and instead rose on her elbows to peer at his front. Not only were there dark splotches on his tunic, but past the dried crimson on his hands, his knuckles were bruised and split. "Cota?" she rasped.

Their fingers untangled as he awoke and twisted from the fireplace in concern. "Are you okay?"

She nodded, and he exhaled in relief. "What happened to you?" she asked.

He followed her gaze and flexed his fingers with a wince. "I hit the ice."

So *he'd* been the figure she'd seen above her.

"I also punched Fox," he quietly added.

"You *punched* him?"

"Multiple times," he said timidly. Then, at her raised brows, he explained, "He made an oath to protect you, Res, and that was the second time he'd failed to do so. I just...I lost control of myself."

She shook her head. "Don't blame him. I snuck out of his view. I got...distracted."

"By what?" He held up a fresh, white cloth and gestured to her leg—silently requesting if he could change the bandage.

She chucked off the blankets in answer, and it took everything in her not to pull them back. Her nightgown was barely long enough to drop to her thigh—*whilst sitting*. And yes, her and Cota had seen enough of each other's bodies over the past five years not to be bothered by an extremely short dress, but they hadn't seen *everything*. By Cota's brief glance at her face followed by his unmoving stare as he began unwrapping her bandage, she knew he felt the same. This was different. Gillian and Kasya were behind this, Adresia knew. She would throttle them the next time she could walk. "Some sort of creature," she answered once she was sure her voice wouldn't reflect her racing heartbeat. "It kept throwing stones at me."

"A creature?"

"Yes. But it wasn't anything we heard about as childr..." Words failed her as Cota removed the bandage. Halfway down her thigh to the top of her knee was an appalling stitched gash. That *thing* in the lake had done this to her? How was she not dead?

Cota met her gaze for half a moment before gently bandaging her leg. Her stomach fluttered at his touch. "I was so scared," he said as he finished, placing the remaining bandages on the table and sitting beside her bent knees.

It was then that she remembered how little they'd recently spoken—and how easily it'd been for her to forget him in those final, frozen moments. "I'm so sorry," she whispered.

Concern and confusion flickered across his features. "Why are you sorry?"

"Because I wanted to stop fighting."

A heavy pause. "Do you..." His throat bobbed. "Do you still want to?"

"No." It'd been so easy to give in, to surrender to the lies that told her she was weak. But she wasn't weak. She wouldn't be again.

He squeezed her hands. "I'm sorry that I didn't help you see there's something worth fighting for."

She shook her head. "There *is* something. I just..." She almost didn't say the words. "I didn't believe it until now."

Because maybe Harkin was right. Maybe Cota's distance after Tauroben hadn't been out of unshared feelings, but fear. Fear of being rejected and ruining what they had spent twenty years building together. She hadn't wanted to give this up or leave him. Down there, she'd just been so tired.

"What is it?" he asked. Those emerald eyes were barely inches from her face.

She opened her mouth to explain, to at last submit to the recklessness that had been ushering her toward that one irreversible outcome, when there was a sudden knock at the door.

Cota remained so still she swore he was going to ignore it. And she wanted to tell him to, to make him stay so she could answer, but he took a deep breath and strode to the door behind her. She despised the chill that replaced his warmth. A moment later, Caspian's voice drifted into the room. "Is she awake?"

"Awake and better than ever," she answered as loud as she could.

The door creaked open, then closed, and approaching footsteps sounded. Caspian's eyes were attentive and observant as he rounded the sofa. Cota returned to his place beside her the same time the Hand sat atop the table directly in front of her.

"Don't trust my word?" she asked wryly.

Caspian crossed his arms. "I do, but you had one foot in the grave when I saw you yesterday, so I had to check for myself."

After what had happened, she could only imagine what she'd looked like. Of course it'd scared them. "I'm sorry," she blurted.

"It's not your fault."

She swallowed. "Well...thank you for saving me. Again."

"You saved yourself."

"What?"

The men shared a look before Cota explained, "I tried to punch through the ice—" He raised his pitiful fingers, then nodded at Caspian— "But he stopped me before I could do any more damage. We thought you were gone. The surface had completely frozen over. But *you* broke through. We dragged you out as soon as we saw your hand."

Adresia looked down. Her knuckles were pink and tender, scars already forming where her skin had been ripped and scraped. She remembered hitting the surface and pleading for her life, but the instant she'd decided to stop...the memory went fuzzy. Blank.

She glanced at Caspian, who answered her unuttered question with a subtle nod. Her stomach dropped in both apprehension and excitement. Not only had her magic defended her against that beast, but it had kept her alive. It'd saved her.

Gods above, how powerful *was* she?

Chapter 33

Unmoving and silent, Adresia stared at the shore of the Obissean Lake as she had all morning. It'd been two days since she'd been trapped under that ice, believing she was dead. And perhaps she was a fool to return so soon, but she didn't want to be afraid of the truth. Not of what lurked below the surface, nor what flowed through her veins. Not anymore.

In addition to finding it difficult to walk, her leg still throbbed relentlessly. Her magic was healing her faster than a human, but it would still take time. And despite the inconvenience it caused, all the Countess had wanted was to leave her boiling, gods-awful chamber, if only for a few minutes. So she had.

Hair unbound and blowing in the wind, she stood in the tranquil hush until a presence arrived at her side. Cota hadn't left her until he'd been called away that morning. "You're leaving," she said. He and Caspian had been ordered to a village near Euwryst, a three-day ride away, in her place. Narissa hadn't been pleased to hear that her Ambassador wasn't well enough to travel, but Caspian had insisted—excluding the details of nearly-drowning-in-the-lake-to-a-magical-beast.

"Yes," he answered.

"For how long?"

"Twelve days, including travel."

Her stomach twisted. They'd be apart for nearly a fortnight, the longest they'd ever gone without seeing each other. She faced him. Snow fell atop his traveling outfit, and his hands were finally bandaged despite his protests that he was fine. She didn't realize she hadn't moved until he embraced her. His warmth soaked into her skin, and she pressed her nose in the crook of his neck, intent on never letting go.

Something had happened yesterday. The confusion that she'd always had, the voice that had always worried if he felt the same...it was gone. She finally felt safe enough to push that limit. But he was leaving, and she didn't want to start anything she would have to wait to finish. So she simply said, "Come back to me."

Her best friend pulled away with a gentle smile. "I'll always come back to you, Res."

◆

Despite being occupied over the next five days, Adresia's attention couldn't have been farther away from the castle. Unwelcome trepidation filled the gaps between her activities. She couldn't help but wonder whether her best friend was safe or not and if he'd ben able to meet Elettra. That'd been the reason they'd gone: to meet with the rebels. Their plan was on the brim of being ready, so the woman had found a way to lure them from the castle. And Adresia was nervous because the scholars and teachers within Euwryst—a province nearly as pompous as Dazelle—would do anything to retain the Queen's blessings, including turning in traitors. Cota and Caspian *couldn't* get caught.

As a distraction, Adresia had pored over an endless pile of books with Corvina. They'd discussed everything that there was, from the history of mages and their powers and cultures to Morolyn and the rebellion to the war in the South. It made Adresia realize how detrimental it was that this kingdom have a future free from turmoil and darkness.

When Adresia wasn't with the Princess, she was training with Fox. He was still healing from Cota's assault, but, thankfully, there wouldn't be any long-term damage. Her best friend had tried apologizing multiple times before he'd left, but Fox was persistent in his acceptance, claiming Cota had nothing to be sorry for. That grieved Adresia more than seeing the knight in pain. His injuries didn't stop him from pushing her to her limit, though. Most days, she was so exhausted that she tumbled into bed without dreams.

When she wasn't doing either of those things, she was visited by Harkin. He had yet to relay any progress he may have had with his spying, and she wasn't going to mention it unless she found a reasonable excuse to convince him to leave. Instead, he continued to share stories about what he remembered from Lithelle. She asked about his times in the Southern Continent, too, but he claimed there wasn't anything worth recalling; he spent most of his time in war tents with dull Lords and stern Commanding Officers. She'd stopped asking when she realized how impolite it was to force him to constantly relive his times of war. That wouldn't be something she would want to relive, either.

One night, Adresia and Corvina were lounging in one of the farthest alcoves of the library when the Countess stopped one of her anxious-filled spirals and attempted to focus on what her and the Princess were doing. "I keep wondering why Narissa summoned me," Adresia quipped.

Corvina didn't look up from the book she was reading—something about ancient cultures and the history of the gods—and asked, "Do you?"

"It's because she wants to kill me."

The woman's head snapped up. "Why do you think that?"

"She intended to five years ago. Now she has the chance to finish it."

A thoughtful pause. "She's threatened by you, yes. But she can't kill you."

"What do you mean 'She can't'?"

The Princess closed her book, a finger wedged between the pages. "My sister needs you to trust her, to feel safe. But you're not."

Adresia knew that already. "If she suspects what I am, then it's a risk to keep me alive." A shrug. "It's not like many people would rage over my death anyway."

A small smile. "The fact that you don't see how important you are is astonishing." Adresia's brows furrowed. The Princess explained, "The rebels have waited *years* for this chance. If Narissa kills you now, she'll hang you from the castle wall as a show of power. Elettra would undoubtedly respond, finally unleashing the might of the rebellion, and, as much as my sister doesn't want to admit it, she's wary of what they can do. And now that Elettra knows the truth about your magic, she knows the truth about this rebellion—about how vital you are in all of this. Your death would be enough to set off a war for more than just a few acquaintances. People would fight for you. Cota would. *I* would. And you bring out a side of Caspian that I've spent years trying to lure from his guarded walls. Because more than just being a weapon...you're a really nice friend."

The Countess didn't know what to say. "Oh."

"Yes, *oh*."

Trying not to think too much about her significance to so many people, she asked, "How are they keeping my powers a secret from Cota?"

"I've already informed Elettra to not say anything."

"You're in communication?" Elettra had said they would exchange coded letters, but Adresia didn't know they'd already been getting them.

The Princess smiled. "Be treated as an inferior for long enough and eventually you'll become one of them—and inherit their methods of discretion."

"So you know which servants are rebels?"

"A few."

"Why didn't anyone tell me we were getting letters?"

A wry smile. "You were preoccupied trying not to die, if I recall."

Adresia let out an amused huff. Right.

"You're not unimportant just because you didn't know," the Princess added. "Just...sometimes, not everyone needs to know everything all of the time."

Like Cota, Adresia thought. "Well, thank you. I know it's difficult to work around my secrets."

The Princess continued reading. "There are worse things than keeping secrets, Adresia."

The Countess wasn't too sure. She looked back down at the note concealed in her book, rereading it like she had for the past hour, another one of her unshared secrets.

Your power is your own. Trust no one with it. Not yet.

She'd found the parchment wedged between two tomes, the edge sloppily jutting out as if it'd been hastily tucked away. Her mouth had gone dry at the words, knowing without a doubt that it was meant for her. She'd quickly grabbed a random book and found Corvina in their alcove, and while asking the Princess about it wouldn't have hurt, Adresia hadn't, and, for the last hour, she'd kept it hidden.

But it was driving her insane.

She hadn't searched the shelves around them. Someone knew about her powers; they may very well still be watching them. And while her leg had healed enough that she could run around with ease, she didn't feel like going on a chase. Not here. There might be something other than a human lurking within these dark depths.

"What are you so interested in?" Corvina asked. "That book is useless."

Adresia hoped the mage couldn't hear her heart skip a beat. "I'm just trying to figure out the mixed dialect."

"There's only one chapter in there of note—about a poison that suppresses our powers and hinders our healing."

"There's a poison that can do that?"

"Infirma. It's rare to make and even harder to find the ingredients for, but it was used, once, when the Elders banished Banes. They used to coat their weapons in it so that after a mere slice, Banes became weak enough to kill." Corvina tossed her book aside, unbothered by the information. "Let's try your powers now."

Adresia's stomach twisted. "*Now*?"

"Yes. You need to practice."

The Countess swallowed hard, setting her book down. 'I don't know..."

"You can't let fear control you. That's how my sister wins. If you refuse to practice anything, it doesn't matter that you have power strong enough to oppose her. You'll die."

A wave of courage suddenly pressed in, and remembering how she'd felt all those days ago at the edge of the lake, how she'd promised herself that she wouldn't back down from her power, that *she* controlled it, she took a deep breath. "What do I do?"

"Close your eyes." Adresia did. "Imagine your power within you. It can be physical or just a feeling, but I visualize a well. Sometimes your power overflows. That itchy feeling you get, like you need to let something out? That's it overflowing."

The Countess pictured that well inside of her, full of icy magic, glittering and deadly. "How do you stop it?"

"You can't." Adresia tensed, but Corvina continued, "You can expel it, though; take out the excess in the well."

"How? Unless we want iced-over floors, it's not like I can release it in the halls whenever I want."

There was a smile in the Princess's voice. "Of course not. Mage's powers aren't entirely physical. While Banes can manipulate theirs into something—in your case, *Hiermsall*—most of the time, it can be released like an invisible wave that spreads through the air. Smaller emissions, like filling up a room, usually aren't felt by others. It simply fades into nothing as it stretches out around you. But larger waves that are built up over long periods of time, especially from stronger mages, can be felt by other beings. I've only felt my sister do so once, and it went on for miles."

Holy gods. *Miles.*

"Your magic could probably incite a storm if built up enough," Corvina mused, "but most mages aren't strong enough to contain their power for too long. If they do, they tend to feel reckless, irritable, paranoid. It can drive mages insane."

Of course it could.

"Try to release some of it now," the Princess said. "Focus on your breathing. Picture the excess of that well rising into a soft wave. Let it fill you up and then pass through. Once it's out, it's gone; it'll dissipate on its own."

The Countess let that familiar tingling rise, and she tried to imagine what Corvina had suggested—she really did. But her thoughts drifted. How much power would she let out? What if Narissa felt it? What if she couldn't control it?

"Focus, Adresia."

What if this was what Narissa has been waiting for? What if the Queen went after her friends? What if everyone she cared for was killed—because of *her*?

"Breathe. You can do this."

Adresia shuddered against the pressure in her veins, willing it to obey. She would not let Narissa win. Not after Brazen or the lake or the disaster that her life had so far been. She wasn't afraid. She was in control. She could trust herself.

That wave swelled and swelled, rising and cresting—and then a frigid wind blew around the space, fluttering parchments and rustling her gown as her power washed over her. It was more relieving than anything she'd ever felt before. As it dissipated, it was like she could hear clearer, perceive sharper. She hadn't realized how much she'd been holding in. Even her blast a week ago hadn't been enough to drain that well inside of her. When she opened her eyes, Corvina was smiling.

"With practice," the woman said, "that will get easier. But you did the hardest part. A mage overwhelmed by their magic is the most dangerous mage of all."

"I still can't manipulate it," Adresia said. She'd failed to mention the snowflake from the gardens, what she'd done in the lake, and her frost at Tauroben, and she didn't want to now, knowing what would happen anyway.

"Open your hands," Corvina said. The Countess obeyed. "Make something."

"I can't just *make* something."

"Because you need...what?"

Through everything the Princess had taught Adresia, the history of mages and their powers and cultures, this was one of the few things she hadn't forgotten. "Emotion," she answered.

A nod. "You used fear and anger to manipulate your power just now. Negative emotions are strong, but so are positive ones. Search for something that makes you happy. Stronger emotions, whatever they might be, will aid you."

Adresia took a deep breath. "Happy," she mumbled. "Think of something happy."

She thought of Cota. The way they'd looked at each other, the way his touch made her feel. It was so new, yet felt so familiar; like home. And his scent: oak and vanilla and *warmth*. She let the thought of him fill her up and surround her senses. When that tingle in her fingers appeared, her heart skipped a beat—but it didn't do anything more. She flexed her hand, willing her magic to act, to move, but the spark she'd felt vanished. She exhaled sharply. "It didn't work."

"We'll try again."

"Later," the Countess said, suddenly exhausted.

"It wears you down," Corvina said. "You'll get stronger over time. It's like training with weapons: no one is good at first, and you're tired and sore for what feels like forever. But one day, you'll wake up, and swinging that sword becomes the easiest thing in the world—like it's always been a part of you. That's what your magic will do."

Adresia smiled. "I'll be waiting."

⋄

The next few days were dull. Adresia practiced her magic to a fruitless end, and while Corvina remained optimistic, the Countess couldn't get past her frustration. Why wouldn't it just *work*?

Eight days after Cota and Caspian had left, the evening turned out to be just as unsuccessful as every other. She *had* discovered that the small creature in the gardens was a Willowboe. Centuries ago, they had been servants of mankind. They were tortured and beaten, their families ripped apart and sold across the continent. They varied in size and appearance, but the most favorable were males. They were wildly ferocious and some rose as tall as humans. The trade of their people continued this way for decades until the Willow Folk revolted, having used their captivity to learn the ways of man. Some still wanted revenge for their enslavement, but their rulers decided long ago that peace was better for their survival. The numbers had been astonishing. Even after the mass killings and savage slaughterings, Willowboes outnumbered humans a hundred to one. They could start and end a war in the same day.

And yet, they were nowhere to be found.

That was all she uncovered. There wasn't a whisper about the Obissean Lake, nor anything that even *resembled* the dialect of Roslyn's journals. There weren't any books about Morolyn either, strangely enough. They must be in a larger, older library somewhere else.

She'd found enough about what she'd come here for, for now. But there was more. More about Dazelle and the kingdom and the

Queen and her parents, even if Adresia had no idea what to look for, if these books held the answers at all.

Her gaze snagged on a flickering lantern, the candle inside almost completely gone. Had she really been here all night? She stretched her stiff legs, but when she glanced down the aisle again, her eyes widened. A parchment had appeared—one that hadn't been there moments before. The Countess staggered around the chairs and tables and marched to the aisle, snatching the lantern from its hook before swiping the paper from the shelf and opening it.

I want to help you.

She lifted the lantern in the darkness. "Who are you?" she asked. A thud sounded nearby. She darted around the corner before her foot hit something: a book. With a defeated sigh, she turned back around—then sucked in a breath as she came face to face with someone. She involuntarily took a step back as she observed the young man and breathed with a nervous chuckle, "By the Goddess, you scared me." He simply tilted his head, black hair spilling over dark eyes. "You're the one who has been leaving these notes," she said. He glanced at the paper in her hand, then back to her face, as if it was answer enough. "Who are you?" she asked again. He just turned around and began walking down the aisle.

She didn't know who he was, but she had a feeling if she didn't follow, she wouldn't see him again. So she kept a few steps behind, her lantern lighting the shelves around her and nothing more. She couldn't tell where they were among the aisles, but he continued ahead without halting, as if he'd wandered this darkness hundreds of times and knew exactly where to go.

The minutes merged together, and when Adresia began to feel like she might have overestimated her trust in this stranger, they stopped. "What are we doing?" she asked. He just pointed ahead, into the inky shadows. She cautiously walked where he'd indicated. It was a matter of seconds before she ran into another book. She bent down, peering at the markings on the open page. One line had been vigorously circled several times over.

The questions not dared to ask will be answered once everything has been forgotten.

"Why have you shown me this?" she asked, picking up the book. "I don't know what it means." Another question was already on her lips as she turned.

But he was gone.

Chapter 34

After being at this village for five days already, Cota Bowyer had spent far too much time in the dark corners of bustling taverns and shaded back alleys. Currently pressed beside Caspian against the shadowy side of an inn, Cota's tolerance grew thin as the elongated eave of the roof did little to block the snowfall.

Honestly, it'd been too easy to get here. A coded letter from Elettra had told them how they were to meet: she would intentionally spark protests, causing enough disturbances to become a nuisance to the crown and require a noble solution. A few days later, they weren't surprised when reports of unrest arrived along with several exaggerated complaints and the Queen sent them almost immediately to deal with it. Caspian even managed to convince her to let the two of them handle it themselves, no extra guards needed. "It's less intimidating for the commoners," Caspian had claimed. Narissa had taken the bait, and now, here they were: three days from the castle in an underdeveloped village that was little more than wooden shelters weathered by years of hard labor and poor improvements.

The final workings of their plan were to be discussed this evening in one last meeting with Elettra and a few trusted others permanently stationed at the village. The realization had stumped Cota when he'd arrived: that there were rebels everywhere, across the whole of Morolyn; that this idea of freedom had been established long before the rebellion had officially appeared all those weeks

THE BANE

ago. How many rebels had they known in Westholt? How many had they walked by and talked to day after day?

Cota leaned his head against the stone wall, a gust of frigid snow drenching their already stiff limbs. They hadn't stayed more than one night at the same place in order to stay as anonymous as possible, and thanks to their previous meeting running later than planned, by the time they reached the next inn, it was full. In fact, all of the inns were. *That* was thanks to the storm.

"Well," Caspian mumbled, his breath curling in front of him, "this is fantastic."

Thunder rumbled in the distance. "I bet Adresia's enjoying herself," Cota remarked. They were headed back to Dazelle tomorrow. He hadn't let himself acknowledge how much he missed his best friend; it wouldn't do any good. Not until he returned.

"A gold coin says she'll do something rash before we get back."

"Two says she doesn't get caught."

Caspian grinned. "Deal."

Despite the roaring wind being loud enough to muffle their words to any listening ears, Cota still lowered his voice. "Do you think it'll work?" Honestly...Elettra's plan had shocked him. She was an eager leader, and the rebels had certainly waited long enough, but he hadn't expected such a monumental course of action. Not yet.

"I was young when I arrived at the castle," Caspian said, "but not young enough to forget what life was like before I knew the burden of Court and everything I loved was taken from me."

Cota stilled. He had never considered Caspian's life before—that the Hand had even *had* a life before; that he'd been anything more than what his position makes him out to be, than what it'd shaped him into.

The Hand said, "I know what it's like for these people to blindly follow the orders of a ruler who knows no limits. That's what I've been raised with. I was given a warm bed and food and someone to look after me and I'm expected to obey or all of that will be stripped away. So for everyone outside to say they have it harder..." A shake of his head. "*They're* the lucky ones. *They* have a choice. People run away everyday and start a new life somewhere else. But I can't. Even if I just slipped out of the castle one fateful night and never looked back...there are promises that I have to keep. Narissa has ways of destroying my life long after I forget what the inside of those walls look like."

Cota swore the glimmer in Caspian's eyes wasn't from reflecting snow. He was one of the most powerful individuals in the kingdom, and, yet, he hadn't wanted to move against Narissa until he was sure of the rebellion—until he had a monumental force on his side. What did the Queen have that instilled so much fear in him?

"Narissa has *always* been one step ahead," Caspian continued. "She can kick your legs out from under you and crush them until you don't stand a chance of ever rising again. But this rebellion...it's ten steps ahead. We've managed to slip between the cracks in that castle and bury ourselves so deep that she stands no chance of surviving when it crumbles around her." He looked at Cota. "So yes, I think it will work. It has to."

And it was the determination in the Hand's eyes—the same determination Cota had felt when he'd been ready to dive into a frozen lake to save his best friend—that the Count realized maybe it wasn't *what* Narissa had...but who.

Shouting suddenly emitted down the road, startling Cota and Caspian into defensive positions. A flow of people hastily surged past the alley. Those weren't the scared, alerted voices he'd heard during the village's regular outbursts. These were outraged. Plaintive and outraged.

A shared glance between him and Caspian had them following. They didn't have to walk far; the crowd lining the market square was so dense it seemed the entire village was present. It was as if Cota could smell the peoples' anger, the scent shoving up his nostrils so fiercely that his head throbbed. He copied Caspian and flipped up his hood. As they wove through the crowd, Cota craned his neck to see the center of the square.

A memory flickered in the back of his mind at the blood, a bright scarlet atop the white snow. It was everywhere: dripping from the wooden block, pooling onto the stones, sliding down the discarded axe.

They'd heard the executions since they arrived, but they hadn't yet witnessed one.

"His name is Zadkiel." Their heads snapped sideways to the woman beside them. "He's the last one tonight." The snow dampened her red hair, deepening it shades darker, so similar to the blood that lay thirty feet away. "He was a Holy Apprentice."

Holy Apprentices were warm, gentle people who worked toward Priesthood. Cota's mother once told him he'd be fit to be one, with all the reading he did. They'd even visited a temple, and while the library was magnificent enough to keep him from leaving too quickly, when a soft-spoken Priestess approached him while he was out of the sight of his mother and told him that the gods had other plans for his life, he wasn't too eager to return. Holy Apprentices, Priests, and Priestesses—they did no wrong. The thorough investigations and trials arranged during their training were a testament to the brutal measures meant to extract those entirely and completely fit for the position. Only those chosen by the gods passed, as everyone believed—as he believed.

Cota looked around. These people…they weren't disgusted by Zadkiel. They were here to shun the crown and the injustice of what Narissa had ordered. All of them—for just one man.

Caspian voiced Cota's exact thought. "What did he do?"

"They say he was helping smuggle rebels to safety," the woman answered. "They claim he killed a royal guard too." She shook her head. "But he didn't do it. *He didn't.*" And she said it not in disbelief that someone she trusted could have done something so terrible...but like she knew who had.

A silence as terrible and unsettling as the wild glint in the crowd's eyes fell when three dozen guards entered the square. But instead of that familiar silver armor and billowing capes, these men wore all black and had an intimidating sword strapped to their backs and two lethal curved blades hanging at their hips. Caspian tensed beside Cota, realizing the same thing he had. These weren't guards.

These were soldiers.

The clank of chains echoing against the worn stones was frighteningly stark against the hush that was only interrupted by gusts of frozen wind. Two soldiers flanked Zadkiel. The executioner—a broad-shouldered, burly man with a wicked gleam in his eye—was steps behind. As they passed, muffled cries and angry murmurs broke out. Zadkiel's robes were tattered and ripped, and his face brutalized, but the apprentice held his head high. He hadn't been broken.

When they stopped in the middle of the square, he was brutally shoved to his knees at the wooden block. Even from where Cota stood, he heard the crack. But the young man didn't cry out. He simply pressed his lips together, eyes glistening with unshed tears.

"You have been found guilty of treason and murder," one soldier bellowed. "Do you have anything you wish to voice before your sentence?"

Zadkiel's gaze flicked to the crowd, but he didn't answer.

The soldier grunted. "Very well. The punishment for your crimes is death." He waved a hand to the executioner, who grabbed the massive axe, and as the soldiers forced Zadkiel's head onto the block—that was when he spoke.

"May the gods save me."

Someone began weeping.

"Let me enter their embrace, without fear, without pain."

The crowd bristled closer to the unyielding line of soldiers, and silver glinted in the corner of the Cota's eye as a blade slipped from someone's sleeve. When he looked around, he realized what was happening. "We need to leave," he muttered to Caspian. *"Right now."*

The Hand remained unmoving, and when Zadkiel spoke again, a chill went down Cota's spine. The entire square was chanting the prayer. "Let me not fall to darkness, but return to the Land of Light."

"*Caspian*," Cota urged. The man met his gaze with shining eyes, and as the next line was uttered, they slipped from the crowd.

"Hold me close, my kith and kin."

Cota glanced back to see the executioner raise his axe and Zadkiel peer into the crowd, looking into the eyes of his friends—into *Cota's* eyes.

"This is not the end," the apprentice said as the executioner swung.

Even the wind silenced as the axe met its mark. And in that moment, as Zadkiel's head rolled across the stones, red darkening the fresh snow, no one breathed. No one moved. No one spoke. For that split-second, life halted altogether. And then it was over.

But they weren't done.

"This is the beginning," the crowd finished.

The soldiers glanced at one another in eager desire.

That's when chaos erupted.

Chapter 35

There was fighting all around Caspian. Dozens of bodies littered snowy, stained stones; the weak and impoverished villagers were powerless against the ruthlessly trained soldiers. Arrows and weapons ricocheted off of the black armor as if it'd been made of something impenetrable. It wasn't like the soldiers needed the protection; their colossal blades already sliced through flesh like stocks of wheat.

The Hand had read the recurring riot reports: the villagers wouldn't stop. They'd keep fighting until they were all dead; until they were martyred, just as that apprentice was; until the echo of this tragedy was felt across the entirety of the kingdom. And looking at those soldiers…Caspian knew they wouldn't stop either.

He could barely hear himself over the commotion as he told Cota, "We have to leave, now!"

The Count stepped close. "This wasn't part of the plan."

Anger lined his words. "Elettra and I will have a little talk the next time I see her."

Cota held up a dagger. "We're a part of this rebellion too, you know."

Caspian shook his head. "Not like that." He doubted Cota had ever taken a life, but the Count looked between the uproar and his blade like it was everything in him to not walk over to those soldiers and spill their blood on the stones. And for what had happened to him, to Adresia…he deserved that retribution. But Caspian knew what came after, and it wasn't pretty. He wouldn't

THE BANE

be the reason that part of Cota scarred forever. "You'll have your time," Caspian affirmed. He grabbed Cota's arm, pushing the dagger down, away from prying eyes and temptation. "But not today."

Cota tucked the blade in his belt and nodded, but Caspian heard it before it hit him.

Something exploded at his back, a roaring *boom* that shook the ground and shattered in his ears, and he slammed into the ground so hard that it all went black.

⟡

Everything hurt.

Rubble fell from Caspian's clothes as he sat up with a grunt. His head pounded, and he coughed harshly when he inhaled, the air thick with dust instead of snow. A horrified sorrow settled in his chest as he looked around. Half of the people had been wiped out, both soldiers and villagers, but countless others still remained. Had the explosion been a part of this sacrificial riot too?

Caspian put a hand down to stand up and hissed at his stinging right arm. It'd been cut. Deeply. Ripping a piece of cloth from his cloak, he swiftly bounded the bloody wound, shoving down his cry of pain before rising. As much as he wanted to keep helping...this wasn't his fight. He didn't plan on dying today. It was time to go. Besides, they couldn't attend Elettra's final meeting anymore when the village would no doubt be crawling with guards from Euwryst. They couldn't be seen anywhere near here. They had to leave, now. Caspian took a step forward before halting.

Cota. Where was Cota?

Caspian darted through whirls of snow and dust, hurdling over mounds of rubble and scorched limbs, eyes burning as he stared into clusters of fighting and frantically searched for his friend. Somewhere. He was *somewhere*—

There. Outside of what was once a fabric shop, Cota was raising his hands as a wild looking soldier neared him, blade in hand. The Count was saying something urgent and rushed, and when his gaze landed on Caspian, his face lit up in relief—until the soldier shoved the blade into Cota's front.

Chapter 36

They were being hunted.

Frozen air slid down Caspian's throat as he readjusted his grip under Cota's shoulders. He was running as fast as he could, but practically carrying the Count's entire weight was one of the hardest things he'd ever done. Hours ago, they'd only stopped long enough for him to check on Cota's wound, and without anything to stitch it with, Caspian had been left with straps from his cloak to stop the bleeding. It'd worked, temporarily, and he'd let Cota rest for an hour until those familiar, demanding voices sounded nearby. The soldiers who Caspian had angered in his effort to save Cota and flee the village.

After sending out a prayer for Cota's recovery, Caspian had quietly lifted his groaning friend and took off before those shouts could get too close. Now, as moonlight shone above them, panic settled in Caspian's gut. They had no food or water, and Cota's condition was becoming increasingly concerning: face wan, skin balmy, breathing labored. There was no indication of the road that they'd traveled on during their initial ride to the village, but it should've been close. At least, that was what Caspian had thought before he reeled to a stop, panting as he beheld the woods before him.

The Sight Woods.

He'd been going in the wrong direction—for *hours*.

Cota's eyelids fluttered. "Need...to...get back..."

"We will," Caspian rasped. "We just—"

There was something in the trees ahead. Something so monstrous and dark that, as it moved closer, untamable fear exploded throughout the Hand's entire being. He twisted as quickly as he could and practically dragged Cota back across the plains, praying whatever he'd seen would stay in the trees. But then Caspian tripped over a rock protruding from the soil and Cota gripped his core with a pained groan as they strained to stay upright. The Hand's apology was cut short as a hair-raising clacking echoed around them—even though it wasn't possible, even though there wasn't anything *to* echo against.

The soldiers weren't just after them.

The creature was too.

Caspian cried out, a terrified, frustrated, exhausted sound, but when he regained his balance and lifted his gaze to a flickering light in the distance, he nearly sobbed in relief. Cota didn't protest as Caspian began sloppily darting toward the village, not slowing until they stumbled onto the dimly lit main road. Cota mumbled something about how Caspian couldn't just knock on a random door.

"I have to do *something*—"

"Psst."

Caspian halted.

"Over here," someone whispered. It'd come from the alley.

And maybe he was seriously an idiot for even considering it...but they were running out of options.

With a dagger half-unsheathed at his side and an arm still wrapped around Cota, Caspian neared the alley between two inns. He nearly shouted in alarm when a young woman stepped into the faint lamplight. "You came from Todsmorren?" she asked.

Caspian nodded carefully. "Yes."

She looked them up and down, gaze snagging on their bloody, torn clothing. "And who did you fight with?"

"We didn't fight," he admitted. "My friend was stabbed, though." Cota gave a pained, groggy smile. "Now we're being followed."

She just watched them, her dark brown eyes like rich, fertile soil. And then: "If you want your friend to live, follow me." She turned on her heel.

Caspian shared a look with Cota, who breathed, "Go." The Hand sheathed his blade and followed. After crossing another road and weaving around a few buildings, they arrived at a small house. Warmth embraced Caspian like a blanket as they entered, and he prayed that whatever creature was out there didn't know how to open doors as the woman shut it and blocked out the wintry wind. "You can lay him down here," she said, gesturing to the blankets layered before the fire.

To Caspian's astonishment, the house was actually one large room. As he pulled Cota's arm from around his sore neck, he asked the woman, who couldn't be much older than Corvina, "What's your name?"

"Streya."

Caspian watched Cota slip into an exhausted slumber before turning around and meeting a blade angled at his throat. He didn't move. He simply returned Streya's unyeilding stare and asked, "Why are you helping us?"

"Why were you at the riot?" she countered.

Any other time, the stubbornness would have intrigued him. But he was more than drained, and any moment those soldiers could find them. So he waited.

She pressed closer. "If I told you my brother went to Todsmorren and I received news today that he'd died, would you believe me?"

"From the belongings in this room, I'd wager there are two of you." He'd already gathered enough information to know exactly how to escape, what to use if she attacked him, and who she was—if this was even her house. "Whether the other is dead or alive remains to be seen."

She eyed him closely before pulling her blade away and sliding it into a slit along her belt that hid all but the end of the handle. When she passed him, he didn't let her leave his sight. "My brother believed the rebellion could offer us something more," she said. "He'd been planning to join for months, so I finally let him go. I didn't know there would be a riot or that he would die, but that's how things work, I suppose." Streya knelt at Cota's side, lifting his bloody tunic. She made a face before gathering supplies around the room. "I believed in my brother. And if he believed in this rebellion, I do too. *That's* why I'm helping you."

"Even though you know who we are?"

"You're nobles. What does that matter?"

"I'm not just a noble."

"Higher up then." She twisted around with a bundle of things in her arms. "It doesn't make a difference. If you wanted to harm me, you would've already."

She had a point.

"There's fresh water in a pot by the back door," she added before kneeling beside Cota again.

Deciding she wasn't a present threat, Caspian marched to the pot, grabbed two cups, and scooped as much water as he could without spilling it. "Can you help him?" he asked when he'd crouched opposite her again, gently shaking Cota awake. Their cups were empty by the time she replied.

"He'll live. The wound needs to be stitched and I can make a tonic to prevent a fever, but he needs rest. You can stay here for a few days."

"We can't wait a few days."

A shrug. "If you want to risk tearing the stitches then that's on you." She glanced at Caspian's poorly bandaged arm. "I'll stitch that for you."

"Thank you," he said.

Too tired to even open his eyes, Cota breathed, "She'll be wondering where we are."

"I know," Caspian said.

"She'll come after us if we don't come back."

A sigh. "I know." Which was why they had to leave as soon as possible. Adresia was skilled and powerful, but if Narissa was at last sending out her personal infantry to control the kingdom...Morolyn was more dangerous than it had ever been.

Over the next two days, Streya stitched Cota's wound, cared for him with impressive quality, and even went so far as to offer him some of her brother's old clothes. The knowledge and mannerisms had prompted Caspian to inquire about her familiarity, and she'd revealed that her mother had been a healer. Her and her brother, Hollis, learned everything that their mother had gathered from her travels across the continents. When their parents died, the two of them had moved here. They'd dreamt of traveling too, but, overtime, the desire to make a large impact in the small area had convinced Streya to become the village's healer. *Sometimes*, Streya had said, *people need you to remain more than your dreams want you to go.*

Caspian spent most of this time peering through the small window beside the front door and monitoring the streets. It was more useful than watching his friend's slow recovery. The village was quiet, and every movement made him tense in anticipation. With the storm, everyone had fled indoors until the snowfall abated. It made it easier to spot approaching strangers, if anything. He hoped the soldiers' delayed arrival had meant they'd intercepted whatever creature had left the comfort of the Sight Woods and hadn't survived.

"You should get some sleep," Streya quipped from across the room. "If you plan to leave soon, you'll need it." He opened his mouth to object, but she said, "I'll take watch, Caspian."

With a grateful smile, he slid from the windowsill and sauntered to the bulge of blankets that was their bed. When he rested his head on a makeshift pillow, Cota lifted his head beside him. "How long has it been?"

"Only an hour since you last asked," Caspian replied. It'd been a relief to witness the color return to Cota's face. He still rested most of the day, but every time he awoke, he would ask for an update as if anything could change without him recovering first.

It was silent long enough that the Hand thought Cota had fallen back asleep, but the Count's voice flittered over the crackling hearth again. "I promised her I would come back."

From the corner of Caspian's eye, he saw Streya turn her head toward them. "We will," the Hand promised.

"The last time we were apart for this long, it didn't end well."

It took everything in Caspian to keep his face calm. "Nothing is going to happen, Cota—to either of you."

"I think the gods have something against her."

"Why would you say that?"

"She deserves more than this life she's been given."

Caspian swallowed. "Yes, she does."

"I don't want to be someone else she loses." Cota's eyes clenched shut as if he could block out the thought. "I don't want to be the one to break her."

"You won't."

Cota looked at Caspian. "How do you know?"

"Because if she breaks...she would use the pieces to build something else. Something better. Something unbreakable. That's just who she is."

"If I don't make it—"

"Stop. You don't have a fever; you'll be fine." He didn't mean to sound harsh, but the words had scared him enough that he'd responded before thinking. He added softly, "We'll get back, Cota. Get some rest." The Count inhaled deeply, nodded, then turned back toward the fire. Within a few minutes, his chest rose and fell deeply. Caspian ran his fingers through his hair with a hard exhale.

"Who's the girl?" Streya asked.

Caspian rose on his elbows. "Adresia."

She looked between him and Cota. "Does she know you're both in love with her?" Caspian's eyes widened, and he whirled to make sure Cota *was* actually asleep before facing Streya again. Her brows had risen. "*He* doesn't know that you...?" She huffed a laugh. "Oh, that's one complicated situation."

Caspian shook his head. "I don't know what I feel."

"Does she love you?"

"No."

"How do you know?"

"I just do."

"But—"

"The only advice I need is how to help my friend—*not* my relationships."

Her lips thinned, and she turned back to the window.

He sighed. She'd struck a nerve, but he *must* be tired if he'd snapped back. Their conversations so far had been nothing but pleasant. "I'm sorry," he said. "Things are too confusing to attempt unraveling whatever is going on. And it doesn't even matter what she feels if they choose each other."

Streya released the curtain and looked at him. "I'd choose you."

"You don't even know me."

"I know you risked your life to help your friend get back to the woman he loves. I know you're willing to give her up even though *you* want her, because that's what she wants. I know you're not a bad person."

"I'm not all good."

"No one is."

He watched her with heavy eyes, his lack of sleep over the past two days finally catching up to him. "I'm sorry your brother died."

"I'm sorry about a lot of things. But if he didn't die, then you wouldn't have come here, and we wouldn't have met."

With a small smile, Caspian rested his head back on the pillow and closed his eyes. "I'm glad I met you too, Streya."

Chapter 37

Adresia jolted awake, gripping her sheets so hard her fingers turned white. She scanned the room, but, as always, found nothing. She rubbed her face. Another nightmare. It'd been such a relief these last two weeks to sleep long and undisturbed. But they always returned. And more nightmares meant more uncontrolled magic.

Like a wasteland that had been frozen for a thousand years, the chamber was covered in a thin layer of frost. It didn't surprise her anymore. Freezing temperatures, frost covered surfaces, barriers of ice, and doors frozen shut—something always happened. The first time had terrified her. If Gillian or Kasya had walked in or a guard had noticed the chill leaking into the hallway...she hadn't let herself think that far. While her magic lashed out on its own, she'd been able to stifle whatever strange thing occurred before someone discovered it.

Adresia drearily staggered through the room, absorbing the blanket of ice with each step on the cold, marble floor. She barely registered where she was going, only her instincts leading her toward that place of comfort and safety as she slipped into the hallway. A moment later she passed through another door. It was warm in here, and her unease disappeared as she crawled atop the mattress and tugged the thick covers around her, the scent lulling her to a peaceful darkness where even her nightmares couldn't disrupt her.

Chapter 38

"Caspian."

He mumbled a tired excuse, waving his hand in dismissal.

"*Caspian.*"

His eyes shot open.

Streya was crouched beside him, a blade in her hand. "They're here."

He was on his feet in an instant, pulling the bag full of food and supplies she'd packed for them over his shoulder. "Where?"

"The other side of the village. It's already on fire. They'll be here any minute." His stomach lurched, but she added, "Don't think about it." He wondered what horrors had left her so unfazed at the destruction of her home. "Take the backdoor. There's a trail into the woods that will give you better cover than the main roads. It ends early on, but if you keep going in that direction, you'll reach the castle in two days."

Caspian shook Cota awake and explained what they needed to do before putting an arm under the Count's shoulder. Cota could walk on his own, but it still pained him. The Hand didn't think about what might happen if they needed to run.

Streya raised her weapon at the front door, and when daunting shouts sounded down the road, Caspian said the words before he could stop himself. "Come with us." She twisted to look at him. "I can get you a well-paying position at the castle. You can work with us—with the rebellion."

"I can't, Caspian. Take Cota and go."

"Please."

Her mouth tugged into a sad smile. "I died the minute my brother did. You aren't saving anyone by waiting."

The shouting grew closer.

"Streya—"

"*Go*, Caspian. I won't say it again."

"Just—thank you. For everything. And if you get out...meet me in Dazelle."

She twisted back around. "With a blade at my throat in greeting, no doubt."

Despite the approaching chaos, he couldn't help but smile.

When he opened the back door, he almost mistook the flames jutting over the top of the house as the morning sun. This was the result of a rebellion. This was what happened when a kingdom was ruled by a tyrant. Deliverance demanded destruction. He closed the door the same time the soldiers entered from the other side. He heard Streya's useless attempts at stopping them. He heard clashing and banging and enraged shrieks.

He didn't wait to hear the silence that was sure to follow.

He tightened his grip around Cota and swiftly entered the snowy woods. Dawn was approaching, but it was still dark. Too dark. "I can't see anything," Caspian grunted, already struggling with the familiar weight.

"I can," Cota breathed.

"What?"

"Just—go through those trees."

Caspian heeded Cota's guidance through the forest. The trail ended after a few hours like Streya said it would, and before they could get lost, the morning sun rose and they were able to maintain a straight course. They checked behind them every so often, but it didn't seem like they were being followed.

After a day, Cota offered to walk on his own. He hissed and winced as he slowly attempted to keep up, but Caspian didn't mind the pace. He was just grateful they weren't in the Sight Woods. They took turns sleeping, comforted by the fact that there weren't horrid creatures watching them in the dark—even if their cloaks did little to keep the snow from seeping through and numbing their already chilled limbs.

Halfway through their second day they found a stream. With bright eyes, they hobbled closer, and Caspian gave Cota a second skin to fill up at the edge of the frost-lined bank. When they'd quenched their dry throats with the frigid water, they split a piece of cheese and ate two apples before falling onto their backs. The chaos of the past few days seemed so far away compared to the serenity of these woods; to the white treetops, to the flowing water, to the icy leaves, shifting in the frozen wind.

"Caspian?"

"Hmm?"

"Why did you save me?"

Caspian looked at Cota. "What?"

"You could have left me and been at the castle already, reporting the news of that tragedy."

A beat of tense, unsure silence. "Why would you think I want that?"

"I know how everyone looks at her."

It took a moment for Caspian to understand what the Count meant; to grasp the unspoken addition: *so why wouldn't you be the same?* The Hand inhaled deeply, steadily. "I didn't save you because Adresia needs you, Cota. I didn't save you because she doesn't deserve another loss after what she's been through. I saved you because *you* don't deserve that. Because you're my friend."

There was a surprised smile on Cota's lips. "I'm in love with her."

"I know."

Cota looked at him. "What?"

"Of course you are."

"It's...obvious?"

"More than you two think."

Emerald eyes widened. "You mean—"

"That she's in love with you? I'm surprised you haven't realized. As much as you both show it, neither of you ever notice the other."

"Huh," Cota said, stunned. And then: "I'm sure this wasn't how you intended to spend your nameday."

"How do you know about that?"

"Corvina told me."

Caspian shook his head with a disbelieving smile. "Of course she did."

"Have you ever celebrated it?"

"Sometimes we sneak into the cellar and steal one of the most expensive wines, but...it's not something I care to publicly share."

"Bad experience?"

"Something like that." A shrug. "Twenty-six isn't anything special."

"Adresia pushed me into a pile of mud when I turned twelve," Cota recalled. "She said she 'wanted to keep things interesting.' It's been a tradition to find the strangest ways to celebrate our namedays since."

"So those cakes a few months ago...?" Adresia had invited the most renowned bakers in Dazelle to the castle and forced Cota to try every flavor of cake imaginable.

The Count grinned. "It was more of a joke than anything. I don't care what we do, as long as it's with her."

"We're all better with her by our sides."

"Don't let her hear you say that. She already thinks she's *extravagant*."

"How much are you willing to bet she had a more exciting week than us?"

"A dull time alone isn't in her nature," Cota said. "But I'd like to see her beat this."

"Is that how she's always been?"

The Count raised a brow. "How?"

"Wild and untamed."

"Yes." A dramatic sigh. "It's gotten worse with age, though."

They broke into laughter, the sounds bouncing off the trees around them. But as Cota was pulled from the ground with a deadly blade pressed against his neck, their amusement vanished.

Chapter 39

There were three soldiers. One grasped Cota in a deadly hold as two others surrounded Caspian. They looked like they hadn't seen civilization in weeks, a sadistic gleam in their red-lined eyes. "We don't have to fight," Cota said in a futile attempt to distract them. "Just let us pass."

"You're already dead," the soldier holding him snarled.

"The Queen doesn't want us," Caspian refuted.

"Maybe not," another quipped. "But we do."

Cota met Caspian's gaze. They both knew how this was going to end.

It was a good thing they hadn't noticed the blade in Cota's hand.

It took one nod from Caspian before the Count moved. He sliced the soldier's free arm the same time he grabbed the hand against his throat and twisted. The man growled in pain before Cota released his grip, already winded. He barely avoided the sharp blade that suddenly swiped through the air and elbowed the man in the back, but when the soldier just hissed and raised his head with an icy glare, Cota's stomach dropped.

Faster than Cota could anticipate, the man lunged. They crashed into the ground so hard the Count wheezed, unable to stop as he was struck. Then there was a pause before a dagger appeared above him, angled toward his chest.

Cota pushed past the dizzying pain and shoved up with all his might. He let out a frustrated cry when he managed to direct the soldier's aim away and the blade pierced the grass inches from his head. Cota reacted as fast as he could and *kicked*—but the man didn't move. Instead, a devious smirk found the soldier's mouth half a second before hands wrapped around Cota's throat. The air in his lungs vanished. He desperately searched for something around him, and when his fingers wrapped around a rock, he slammed it against the man's head. The soldier went limp. Cota frantically wrestled out from underneath the body, panting and clutching his core, and stumbled toward the stream. When he glanced behind, the soldier was no longer there, but as soon as he turned back around, the soldier crashed into him. They tumbled backward, the frozen soil scraping and scratching his arms. And then they rolled into the stream and Cota was under the frigid water, pinned to the bottom with unearthly strength. He thrashed and bucked and scratched and clawed, trying with all his desperate efforts to remove the hands keeping him down, but he couldn't, and he swore the figure above him was laughing, laughing, laughing, and he was going to *die*—

It was as if the thought awakened that thing inside of him. A fury took over, so blindly and consuming that he barely registered what was happening. He lurched from the water and flung the soldier against the bank with staggering strength. Terror flickered across the man's face and he hastily scrambled back, raising a hand as if it would stop Cota. But it didn't. It couldn't. There was nothing but that dominating, seizing, controlling instinct to defend; to fight; to survive. And as he struck, that familiar pain returned to his knuckle; groans and a piercing red stained his senses. He was stronger. Better. *Deadlier*.

And then he stopped, realizing he hadn't yet breathed, and as if a veil was lifted from his face, he suddenly heard and saw everything around him with shocking clarity: his throbbing, broken hand and the rushing stream and the soldier.

The ground swayed beneath him. The soldier who wasn't moving. Because he was—

Cota whirled toward a muffled cry. Beside another lifeless body lay Caspian, weakly fending off the man strangling him.

Cota was there in an instant, tackling the soldier trying to kill his friend. Fingers dug into arms as they rolled, and a kick to Cota's core had the Count crying out in pain. Caspian appeared in his view, but a flick of the soldier's hand had a blade slicing through the air. Cota glimpsed Caspian on the ground, gripping a bleeding arm, before a fist crashed into his mouth. He slammed face-first into the dirt as an all-too-sudden weariness swept through his body. The soldier flipped Cota and pinned his arms to his side, striking brutally, savagely, endlessly. The Count couldn't breathe, couldn't *think*, each blow a torment of crimson pain. But when the soldier paused to take a breath and the immovable hold on him loosened, Cota summoned whatever strength remained in him to snatch the stray dagger laying beside them and shove it into the man's chest.

The soldier's eyes went round. Cota ripped out the blade and red spilled down his arms, his face, his neck. The man uselessly grabbed at his chest, toppling backward and crashing onto his back. The gurgling ended by the time Cota wiped his face with a blood-soaked sleeve.

It wasn't until he got to his feet that he realized the stain down his front wasn't entirely the soldier's. And there was that sharp, tight pain in his core and the lightheadedness he had grown all too familiar to. He stuck out an arm to balance his quaking knees, but the ground came all too fast. The last thing he saw was Caspian racing toward him.

Chapter 40

It was morning. Adresia could feel the warmth of the delicate, golden rays leaking through the window even though she hadn't opened her eyes. But not the sunlight nor her untroubled sleep could overshadow her racing thoughts.

Cota and Caspian were meant to be back by now.

Maybe they *were* back. Maybe she would open her eyes to find Cota in the armchair across the room, his golden hair falling over his eyes as he slept. She would wake him with a toss of the pillow and he would complain about her being in his bed, but they would laugh and take a walk through the gardens, and he would tell her all about his time away. So she opened her eyes.

But the room was empty.

She loosed a panicked exhale and paused on the edge of the bed to calm herself, feet dangling above the floor. Not wanting to return to the library just yet, she'd trained all evening yesterday, and she'd been so exhausted afterwards that she hadn't even realized what day it was before tumbling into bed, nor when she'd wandered into his chamber last night.

A day. They were an entire *day* late.

The room grew cold, and not because of the dying fire. Her fingers turned into fists. It was fine. They were *fine*. They could be delayed for a number of reasons. She was just overreacting. Still, she spent the next few hours looking at the door, rummaging through Cota's things, mindlessly scanning the few volumes he'd selected from the library, and observing what garments his servants had made for him. None of it distracted her enough. By midday, she was restless. She couldn't go after them; she didn't know where they were or how to reach them. It'd be stupid to leave only to miss their return. So she decided to wander the corridors in the hopes to catch their return instead.

After an hour of fruitlessly searching the underused common folk quarters, her anxiety began to creep back in. The corridor was just as empty as the rest, and while she hadn't expected them to be back here, a part of her had hoped...

Screw waiting. She would find them herself.

As she took a step toward the Suites, voices filtered down the hallway. Male—but none she recognized. She quieted her steps and neared the corner to listen.

"We could execute this plan flawlessly. We just need your approval—"

"You haven't given me a substantive proposal yet, Connolly." The voice was female.

Boots crinkled, like someone shifting their weight. "My men and I will explain it simply, Your Grace."

Your Grace. A Duchess?

"We've already eliminated the threats that any pre-existing settlements have posed," Connolly said. "It's time to eliminate further suspected forces."

"Removing these civilians to snuff out a *possible* threat is a fine line," the woman countered. "How will you remedy alienating the kingdom after killing a third of it based on speculation?"

"It's not speculation, Your Grace. We do not get to question. Whether there are or are not innocents holds little significance. Our orders are to proceed with this course of action, and with your advisement, if possible."

A moment of silence. Then: "Convince me."

"The settlements priorly incinerated are all within a few miles of one another. We've been ordered to continue with this system of extermination before the threat proliferates any further."

The village burnings. That's what this was about.

"How will you handle Tauroben?" the woman asked. "If this is about potential threats, that community is most pressing. Do you believe it to be the stronghold for the rebellion too?"

"Our sources have confirmed Tauroben's affiliation with the rebellion. The eastern expanse being cleared is proportionate to that of the labor camp introduced three years ago—four times larger than that village. We can put them into this camp, solve this kingdom's plague of lies, and teach them a lesson about defying their Queen." A chorus of agreement echoed down the hall.

Gods above. They *were* killing everyone in the east. And they were going to imprison Tauroben—

"I approve this proposal," the woman stated. "Initiate preparations before the next Council meeting. Do not pester me until then."

Five days. Adresia had *five days* to warn Elettra, to get the people out before they were made slaves and this kingdom dug itself deeper into the grave it was already in.

The voices grew louder. Adresia darted down the corridor, her heart racing, because if they caught her, if they suspected her of hearing *anything*... She turned down the intersection.

And then reeled to a stop as she came face to face with Captain Hadrian Aeron.

He stared at her as if he was trying to figure out what was happening. She tried as best she could to calm her breathing and appear unbothered and just as confused as him. But then he drawled, "You really should be more careful wandering around the castle. You get lost, you run into people you don't want to see...it's a dangerous place." He knew. Somehow, he knew where she'd just come from and he knew she'd just trapped herself.

Adresia looked at the men behind him. "Am I supposed to be scared of the six of you?"

"Your words do nothing to hide your fear, Lady Bellum."

She itched to grab the concealed weapon in her pocket, but what would she do with it—attack the Captain of the Shield? "How's Brazen?" she asked distractingly. "After I escaped, he scurried off with his tail between his legs."

A small smile. "You think you escaped?"

She stilled.

"Captain."

Adresia's stomach dropped a second time as they both turned and met the menacing stare of the Queen's Warden. A dozen men in dark armor stood behind her. *She* was a duchess?

"You're looking well, Jadice," the Captain said, lowering his chin a fraction of an inch.

"Flattery doesn't suit you, Hadrian."

He tensed. Adresia had the impression she should be more afraid of Jadice than she was. Especially as the Warden's dominating gaze fell upon her.

"What about this one?" the woman asked.

This one. As if Adresia wasn't worthy of being an actual person.

"We'll dispose of her accordingly," the Captain replied.

"I haven't done anything wrong," Adresia protested.

With a wave of his hand, two men grabbed her. "You've been caught, Lady Bellum."

A sort of fearful lightheadedness overcame her as she wrestled against their grips. They were as strong as Brazen.

"It's best if you confess now," Jadice added before turning away, her cohort of men following. "We already know you were hiding."

Adresia's defense faltered for half a second before she blurted, "What will the Queen do when she finds out you've falsely charged her Ambassador?"

Jadice looked over her shoulder. And without saying a word, any hope Adresia had came crashing down as the Warden smiled.

The knights practically dragged her across the castle. She didn't think about what they would do to her if she didn't get away now. She didn't think about how she would soon know what the feared dungeons of Morolyn looked like. "Let me go," she said, tugging against them again. They were halfway down the lesson hall. "You hold no evidence I've committed a crime."

"Worded *so* deftly," the Captain replied. His eyes were bright, as if he found her scramble for justification amusing.

She looked around for something to aid her, but the hall was bare and useless. *She* was useless. Even if she could get free, what could she do? She had nowhere to go and no one to go to. She barely had control of her magic; one wrong move and this castle could crumble around with her. She couldn't—*wouldn't*—risk the lives of innocent people.

They turned down the covered walkway. Servants and nobles, both familiar and foreign, gawked as they passed. Great. Now she'd be the castle gossip. Not that it mattered; she'll be too busy rotting in a cell to notice. As soon as the thought processed, the magnitude of it echoed inexhaustibly in her mind. Her insides ignited with unprompted pressure, and she pushed against the men as if it would push back her power. "Don't do this," she pleaded.

The Captain didn't look at her. "Scared of something, Adresia?"

She hated him. She hated the laughter in his voice and the sound of her name on his lips and his *stupid*, hideous face and the fact that she felt everything so frustratingly easily. "Everyone is afraid of something."

"Tell me yours and maybe I'll let you go."

"Tell me why you're such a bastard and I just might."

The men holding her didn't let her recede as the Captain whirled. And at the deadly glint in his eyes, at the hand that had so swiftly and undetectably gripped her face...she realized why he commanded the greatest force in the kingdom. "You believe you know everything, but you *don't*," he snapped. "You think you're so clever befriending that foreign Lord and gaining Caspian's trust. Just wait until the Queen finds out how close you two *really* are." She angrily wrenched her face from his fingers. "I've noticed you sneaking from his chambers. Knowing Her Majesty's view on the subject, I'd say the two of you would have a slim chance of keeping your heads. I bet she'd even convict your dear friend, Lord Bowyer, too, with a little persuasion."

She lunged forward, but the men mercilessly yanked her back, so hard that she cried out at the pain in her arms. "You *would* murder innocent people," she snarled.

"You're not innocent," he said, resuming their pace down the main staircase.

"I didn't do anything!" she shouted as they descended the last step and turned. When the dungeon entrance came into view past the covered walkway, she shoved her heels against the floor. "Stop." She was going to get her and her friends killed, all because she hadn't minded her business. "Please," she breathed, "you can't—"

"There you are!"

The men turned around in confusion and surprise.

At the sight of Fox, Adresia could have sobbed. "Where have you *been*?" he asked. A trio of maids gave him alarmed glances as they ascended the stairs. "You requested my assistance after you missed your lesson yesterday and *this* is how you repay my generosity? I've been waiting for an hour!" The knight barely contained his exasperation, a vein jutting out in his neck.

She had to give him credit; his acting was so good that *she* almost believed him. Caspian had ended her lessons weeks ago, convincing the Queen that he would teach her when she wasn't gone on missions. It was true, but also the perfect excuse for their frequent, otherwise treasonous discussions. As if realizing what he was looking at for the first time, puzzlement contorted Fox's features and he stepped closer. The hands on her arms tightened. "Is everything alright?" he asked.

She blurted the first excuse that came to mind. "I went to the library where you told me to meet you, but you weren't there, so I went looking in the common folk quarters."

The Captain arrived at her side. "What's going on?"

Fox crossed his arms, the most defiant looking she'd ever seen him. "I was waiting to meet Lady Bellum in the library, but she never showed. She said she was searching for me in the common folk quarters..." He met her gaze. "Which was exactly where *I* went looking."

The Captain narrowed his eyes at them, looking back and forth as if trying to solve a puzzle. Finally, he settled on her. "Why wouldn't you first search somewhere guards are frequently found—like the barracks?"

"It's not my fault my knight's behavior is unpredictable."

A confused pause. "So you didn't hear...?"

"Hear what, Captain?"

The Captain's mouth clamped shut. "Nothing." But after another thoughtful moment, he inhaled, seeming to come to some realization. Then the front door was thrown open with a booming echo, and Caspian stumbled in holding an unconscious Cota. Both of them were covered in blood.

Chapter 41

Panic.

That was what Cota sensed. His head was pounding and he was too exhausted to open his eyes, but he heard the voices. Frantic, worried, troubled; they bounced through the room.

"It happened so fast. I barely had time to react."

"They were executing a Holy Apprentice?"

"Yes. And then the people started praying, but it wasn't a prayer, it was—"

"A calling of arms."

A beat of silence, then shuffling feet.

"We were about to flee when something exploded, and when I woke up, I watched it happen."

A terrified exhale. "If anything happens to him..."

"He'll be okay, Res."

The panic grew.

Darkness swept in.

Chapter 42

"They caught me."

Cota could taste the fear on his tongue.

"They *caught* me, and they would've taken me to the dungeons and done *who-knows-what* if you hadn't arrived when you did."

"Glad I could be of use."

"It's not funny."

A sigh. "I know. Why didn't you just tell them the truth?"

"Would you have believed me if I said I was searching for friends who weren't even at the castle?"

"Probably not."

"Exactly."

"Well, I convinced Hadrian to forget about it, at least until you do something else. Don't think they aren't watching."

"They're going to enslave the kingdom, Caspian—*our people*."

"It's not all on you, you know. You're not their Queen."

"It *is* on me and you know it. I won't let Morolyn be destroyed." Someone moved. "But if they're worried about overpopulation, that means numbers. That's an advantage."

"What villages did they mention?"

"I didn't hear."

A pause. "That's helpful."

Cota heard Adresia's scowl, but it was draining to stay awake. Sleep pulled him under.

Chapter 43

"How do we know it will work?"

The voices were softer now. Not panicked, but...tense. Uneasy.

"That's exactly what Cota asked me."

A chair groaned. Steps tip-tapped on the floor—pacing. "A hundred things could go wrong."

"Or nothing at all."

"Narissa knows something's coming."

"That's why we wait."

The chair whined as weight sank back into it. "I hate waiting."

Chapter 44

"I didn't think we were going to make it. I didn't have time to breathe before we were running again and I was praying he would stay alive."

It was different than before; starkly different. Tranquility floated in the air.

"I'm glad you're alive, Caspian."

"Well, I knew you wouldn't be particularly thrilled if I'd returned alone."

"I wouldn't have been too thrilled if *he'd* returned alone either."

"Are you sure about that?"

Her reply was instantaneous. "Yes."

Cota wanted to keep listening, wanted the warm relief that accompanied the sound of her voice, wanted to know what she had meant by her answer...but he was so tired. He didn't hear what they said after that.

Chapter 45

Three days passed. Three unbearably long, anxious days in which Adresia sat and paced and waited for her best friend to awaken. He'd groaned and thrashed when the healers had held him to the bed and re-stitched his wound, treated the fever that had begun to wrack his body, and forced him to swallow a dark, bitter-smelling liquid. And then they'd told her to wait.

"Until what?" she'd asked.

"Not *until* anything," one healer had refuted. "To see if he wakes up."

"He may not wake up?"

"From what the Lord Hand told us, he's lost a copious amount of blood and has severely strained his body. Tonics help break fevers and combat infections, but only *his* body can overcome the effects of whatever it is he's experienced. I'm sorry," he'd added, "but all you can do is wait."

Caspian had stopped by the first two days, explaining what had occurred at the village and asking for an explanation to what *she'd* been doing when he'd arrived. They'd both recalled their tales, but neither had been distraction enough. His attempt at consolation resulted in them sharing a dark moment in which she considered the possibility of a future without Cota.

And then the moment passed, Caspian's visits along with it.

Now, sat on the edge of the mattress, Adresia gripped Cota's hands, rubbing her thumbs over his scarred knuckles. "I can't do this without you," she whispered. Too much—they'd endured this too much, both of them thinking they would finally lose each other for good. They were never given a chance to breathe before something else happened and they had to fight to survive. She'd *forced* herself to wait, to not say anything about what she felt, to express what had been buried in her heart for so long because she had so foolishly believed that they had time; that he would return and everything would be okay. And although she'd managed to stay strong for Caspian...she couldn't anymore. Her sobs came out in great, heaping waves. "You are *not* going to die. You are going to wake up and come back, *just like you promised*."

It was then that the rise and fall of Cota's chest that'd she spent hours watching, praying to continue, begging to never end deepened for the briefest of moments, so quick that she thought she'd imagined it. Her breath hitched in her throat and she blinked back her tears.

"The last time we were in this situation," Cota mumbled, "you were the one bedridden and in need of considerable care."

"You're—You—"

"Look terrible, I imagine."

A surprised laugh tangled with a sob escaped her lips, and she threw her arms around his neck. He hugged her back like his life depended on it. "I didn't know if you would wake up," she said.

"I told you I would," he said, pulling back. He tenderly brushed the tears from her cheeks. "I couldn't stop thinking about you."

She smirked. "Of course you couldn't."

His chuckle twisted into a wince. She pulled away the gray duvet to reveal the line of stitches across his muscled midriff. "That's going to leave a scar," he mused.

"You were so jealous of mine that you just *had* to get your own."

"Caspian told you what happened, then?"

She nodded, but her eyes welled again. She shut them and took several calming breaths, listening to Cota's heartbeat. It was no longer a faint pulse, but a steady, relaxed rhythm. Minutes passed in warm silence.

"I killed someone." Cota was staring at his hands when she opened her eyes.

The right reply clogged in her throat. Caspian had told her as much. "I'm sorry you had to do that," she said.

He lifted his gaze to hers. "I would do it again, to get back to you."

Her stomach fluttered at the dominance in his voice and at the oath he'd uttered—and at the realization that they had somehow managed to lean within inches of each other without realizing it. There was a dreamy twinkle in his emerald eyes as his fingers wrapped around her nape and pulled her closer. Her heart was beating louder than it ever had. And nothing had happened yet, but it felt like the world had caught fire. This was it. This was what she'd been waiting for.

Until the door creaked open.

Adresia was across the room by the time the healer entered. Remnants of Cota's warmth was still on her neck, her face. Just like Tauroben, it was like her body had reacted before her mind had. She didn't know why she was afraid. She didn't know what she was afraid *of*. She just knew as the healer set a plate of food at Cota's bedside and began questioning how he was feeling, Adresia was glad to have the excuse to leave. She caught him looking at her as she swept out the door, longing and confusion etched across his features.

Bitter air bit Adresia's skin as she prowled through the library with unnatural stillness. She wasn't sure what she was looking for, but something had tugged at her that morning. Perhaps the gods were trying to tell her something. Or perhaps she was just delusional. Lack of sleep would do that to a person. She hadn't visited

Cota again, too embarrassed and nervous to confront him, but had spent every night of the past four days awake, asking healers and servants to check on him, praying he didn't die from some unexplained, fatal infection.

She paused. Maybe she *was* delusional.

Trekking down the next aisle, she shook her head in silent amusement. Cota was fine; he was healing and safe and she had nothing to worry about. Although, from what Caspian claimed, he'd grown quiet. If it was because him taking a life was finally setting in, she hadn't asked. Processing it on his own was expected. And if it was because of what had almost happened... Well, she was waiting for that conversation. Too many things had been left unsaid. Too many things left undone.

The glowing light of her lantern illuminated the aisle as she held it higher. It had taken everything in her not to search every inch of the vast space to see if that stranger was still here, ready and willing to give her the answers she so desperately desired. She wasn't sure she wanted to find him. He might tell her something she wasn't ready to hear. The gods loved interrupting the brief periods of mundane normalcy in her life.

"Adresia?"

Her lantern teetered as she spun. "Harkin?"

The Lord's hand unsubtly slipped behind his back. "I didn't know you were in here."

Her brows furrowed at his pitiful concealment. "What are you doing?"

"I—" He hastily scanned the shelves around him. "I was scouring manuscripts of Morolyn's history."

She stared at him. "Did you find anything?"

"A few annotations about the royal line."

"That's interesting."

"How so?"

"Because there are no books about Morolyn's history in this library."

He just stared at her.

"That's a letter to King Bevon, isn't it?" she asked.

"No."

"Then you wouldn't mind showing it to me."

With a defeated exhale, he brought his hand to his side. "How did you know?"

"Hardly anyone cares for leisurely reading."

"*You* do."

"What were you doing with it?"

"What else do you do with a letter besides deliver it?"

She crossed her arms. "How were you going to send it? Being a foreign noble doesn't grant you the freedom to send undisclosed information *anywhere*, let alone another kingdom."

He opened his mouth, stopped, and then closed it.

"You were meeting someone," she said slowly. He'd mentioned a private messenger the last time they'd talked. She only just realized he'd probably meant someone *already* in the castle.

"And if I was?"

She stepped closer. "What does the letter say, Harkin?"

"Nothing."

"Because you haven't found anything?"

He frowned. "You told me I wouldn't."

A wave of relief washed over her. She didn't want to stop him from helping his people or kingdom, but after Jadice, after uncovering Narissa's intentions to *enslave* her own people, she couldn't let him find out. She couldn't let him fall prey to such atrocities. "You need to leave Morolyn."

"I already told you—"

"I thought you had time," she stated. "I thought you would be fine meddling and snooping, but would come up empty handed and would return to your King. But you can't *be* here, Harkin. Not anymore."

He straightened. "Why not?"

"The soldiers are returning to Lithelle at the end of the month." The men had finally come to the conclusion that they preferred their island kingdom to this one. "You can return with them."

"*Why*, Adresia?"

"You just have to trust—"

"How am I supposed to trust you when you're keeping secrets?"

"I'm trying to protect you."

"Are you?"

Her hands dropped to her sides, but her voice remained steady. "Yes."

"If I don't send back *something*, Adresia, I'm letting down my King."

"I'm sorry."

"Is this because *you* don't trust *me*? I've risked everything in telling you who I am—"

"That's not it, Harkin."

"Then what is so dangerous that knowing would put me at more risk than I'm already in?"

She just shook her head.

"I'm not leaving until you tell me," he stated.

"Then you'd better find a comfortable place to rot with the rest of these books."

He crossed his arms. "I'm just as capable of handling myself as you."

"That doesn't mean anything here."

"Why not?"

She turned away. "Just forget I said anything."

"No—Adresia!" He darted in front of her, caramel eyes shining with urgency and concern. "If you care *anything* about my kingdom, about a free people who want to live without fear of oppression, then please, *please* tell me."

Her brows lowered. "That's harsh, even for you." She cared more than he would ever know. It was *her* kingdom under an oppressive ruler, after all.

She began walking away again, but he suddenly said behind her, "You aren't keeping secrets for my *protection*. You're doing it because you're a—"

She twisted. "A what?"

His mouth slammed shut.

"What am I, Harkin?"

He read the quiet threat in her voice, unsettling enough that his hand inched toward the sword at his side. Because maybe he realized he *was* in a foreign court and he didn't know her as well as he'd thought. Whatever the reason, it didn't stop him from answering. "A coward."

She'd known what he was going to say. She'd *expected* it. And she even realized in his posture that he felt bad saying it. But hearing it still hurt. Worse than hurt. "You don't know what you're talking about."

"Because you spend *so* much time dallying in the issues of commoners—"

"Because I risk my life everyday trying to dethrone the Queen!"

Harkin's face contorted in shock and disbelief, and he took a step back, his throat bobbing as if he was afraid.

He should be.

"You're trying to dethrone the Queen of Morolyn," he restated, emphasizing each word like it would help him grasp the weight of it.

"Feel free to tell your King you've received the information you've so desperately been searching for."

"I never intended to put you at risk, Adresia."

She knew that. His efforts proved that he was someone to be trusted, someone who didn't betray or deceive. But too many people had already died and many more still would. She wouldn't let him be a part of that count. "Now that you know I'm already working toward the same goal as you, you don't have to continue to risk your life."

"I won't give up on my kingdom," he stated.

"I'm not asking you to."

"Then why ask me to leave? To return to my home where my King is expecting information that will change the course of *history*?"

"Have you not been listening? I don't want you to *die*, you idiot!"

"Why do you think I'm going to die?"

"Because it's dangerous, Harkin."

Caramel eyes searched hers. "What else do you know?"

"Nothing."

"Why do you want to dethrone her?"

"Because she killed my parents."

He shook his head, unconvinced. "You don't have to do this alone. I can help you. We can stop her *together*."

"No."

A defiant look appeared on that handsome, regal face. "I'm staying. Your Queen needs to be removed before history repeats itself. She'll annihilate the Kings of this continent just like she did with Morolyn's last."

"Harkin—"

"I understand, Adresia: you don't know my King, you hold no loyalty to him, and you don't care about the future of my kingdom. But I have responsibilities and I won't let my people down." She stepped back. She was ready to be done with this; ready to figure out how to keep her companions from being found out, too, thanks to her untamed tongue. But he added, "You can't be mad at me for trying to save my kingdom when that's *exactly* what you're doing."

Anger surged up her throat. "That's the problem. You're thinking of *your* kingdom—not mine."

"If I didn't care about your kingdom, I wouldn't *be* here!"

"You're only here *because* you're thinking of yours! You said yourself that Lithelle is afraid of a tyrannical ruler overtaking it. If you weren't, would your King have given a second thought toward the injustice in Morolyn? Would *you*?"

He blinked. And she knew they both knew she was right, but his gaze still hardened. "I'm going to prove you wrong."

She ignored the lick of worry up her spine. "I'd like to see you try."

In two movements, he opened the lantern and caught his sealed letter on fire. When it was nothing more than dust on the stone floor, he met her gaze once more. "Then watch me."

She waited long enough for him to be back at his chambers before she stomped toward the entrance. If he wanted to risk his life knowing there was more at stake than just uncovering a scandal about the Queen, then he could go right ahead. She was tired of thinking about it. She was tired of worrying about everyone else.

When she emerged from the shelves and beheld the individual stood upon the library steps, she gave a thin-lipped smile, her annoyance barely contained. "Tell me, Brazen: why are you blocking the door?"

The leather pauldron strapped across his chest squeaked as he crossed his arms. Her hand itched to put one of his blades to his throat. "Hello Adresia."

"What do you want?"

"Did anything...*interesting* happen on your casual stroll through the depths of this aged chamber?"

A dramatic exhale. "Just the usual: a hidden door behind a painting, an ancient book telling me my future—"

"You didn't happen to see your close companion Lord Sallow?"

She tried to casually step around the knight, but he kept himself in front of her. "I must have missed him."

"Oh?"

"You know, I'm not too sure anymore. All those cobwebs..." She ascended the stairs, forcing him backward. "The depths of this *aged chamber* must truly be affecting my memory."

He raised his brows and looked her up and down. "You've healed pretty well, all things considered."

"Did you come to finish what you started?"

"I *was* rudely interrupted, but no. I have more important proceedings to attend. And you're far too valuable to ruin just yet."

She scowled as she mounted the top step and stalked to the entrance. Brazen followed. When she opened the door, she faced him. "The next time you sneak up on me, *I'll* finish what you started, and you *won't* end up as pretty as me."

Heinous delight shimmered in those crystal-blue eyes. "Next time, don't lie so much. It makes you look ugly."

She slammed the door in his face.

By the time she returned to her chambers—having kept one eye behind her the entire trek—Gillian and Kasya had brought lunch before the fire. Adresia ambled to their sides and plopped in front of the food with a loud sigh.

"Is everything alright?" Gillian asked.

"I don't want to talk about it until I've eaten at least half of this," the Countess replied.

The woman smiled. "I'd be disappointed if you didn't."

Adresia consumed as much as she could, and when just looking at the food made her nauseous, she forced them to finish the rest. There was no way the meal was going to waste when she knew both of them hadn't eaten yet. They'd told her about their schedules, treatments, and leisure time; it bothered her just how much she'd lived better than them the past five years, despite being as penniless as the poorest citizens of Westholt. It bothered her how normal it was to them.

When they finally cleared their plates and Kasya returned to her sewing, Adresia cleared her throat. Based off the looks they kept giving her, they were still waiting for an answer to Gillian's question. She couldn't tell them the truth, but she *did* have a question. "I was discussing the Queen's rule with someone and they said something about how the Queen annihilated Morolyn's last ruler. Who was he—the previous King? No one ever talks about him." Now that she realized it, she'd never even heard his name.

For some reason, Kasya's hands went still. Gillian set her mug down with a startled expression.

"Do you not know?" Adresia asked.

The servants didn't reply.

The Countess loosed an exasperated sigh. "Then I'll just ask—"

"No!" Gillian blurted, instantly slapping a hand over her mouth. Kasya looked like she'd just witnessed as murder.

"No?"

"You can't ask anyone."

A surprised, confused exhale. "There isn't a *single* person in this castle that would tell me anything? Just a name?"

Again, no answer.

"Fine. I'll look in the library."

"Those books were burned fifty years ago," Kasya countered.

That would explain why there wasn't any information about Morolyn in the library. "Then I'll go to the city," Adresia said.

"They won't tell you either."

"Why not?"

Kasya shook her head with pleading eyes. She didn't want to answer.

"An entire *province* doesn't speak his name?" the Countess asked.

"It's not just Dazelle," Gillian said.

Adresia's stomach twisted. "The kingdom?"

They nodded fearfully.

Holy gods.

"He was tyrannical," Kasya quietly explained. "He committed such abhorring, vile acts that it was the easiest deposition in centuries. Morolyn *rejoiced* the day he was executed."

Not dethroned.

Executed.

Who *was* he?

"That's all we'll say," Gillian declared. "Just mentioning it could have our heads."

They were protecting themselves, as they should. And Adresia was in no positions to risk their lives. They'd been here far longer than she had, and servants would always know more; see more. Sometimes the most dangerous people were the ones invisible to everyone else. But with more knowledge came more risk, and that didn't always mean sharing it. She just wanted a straight answer for once. She walked to her window and said, "I won't let that happen."

"If the Queen wants us dead," Gillian said, "then we already are."

Adresia agreed there was little she could control; little any of them could. They were mere pawns in the grand scheme of this Court, able to be used as seen fit and discarded when deemed no longer beneficial. But that didn't mean they had to sit here and not fight back. That didn't mean things couldn't change.

She watched the snow fall outside until the sound of Kasya's creativity resumed and Gillian began clearing dinner from the table. "Lord Bowyer is in the gardens," Adresia announced. "If someone asks where to locate me, do let them know they can find me *anywhere* else."

To her relief, the women smiled.

Chapter 46

Even from the second story window, Caspian could see Adresia beaming at Cota as he limped through the gardens. After Todsmorren, after what Cota had professed, Caspian thought they would disregard Narissa's rule entirely. But if their proximity proved anything, it was that they hadn't yet crossed that line. They stood closer than friends...but not close enough. Sometimes Caspian had no idea what was going on between them.

Adresia laughed at something her best friend said and lightly shoved his arm. Beguiled, she took no note of Cota's captivated stare. At least the Count had broken from his unusual reticence. The brooding silence had done little to comfort anyone.

"Have you spoken to your sister lately?" Caspian asked, peeling his gaze from the glass to the Princess at his side. Her golden hair hung down the cloudy blue gown he'd gifted her for her twenty-ninth nameday earlier that week.

"I've talked to her as much as I talk with everyone else," she said. So she didn't know, then. "Why?"

He gestured outside. "She's frustrated by them. And it's...worrying," he quietly added.

"Is this about her dispute with dear old romantic nobility?"

"It's not a dispute." He glanced down the hall to make sure no one was listening. "It's a one-sided hatred of anyone being romantically involved with anyone: *the greatest distraction that impedes on noble duties*. She'll do anything to stop their attention from being preoccupied."

Corvina shook her head sorrowfully. "The last time something like this happened, with the betrothal of that poor couple..." He tensed. "They barely witnessed the fruits of their marriage before they were beheaded."

He tried swallowing. Twice. "I remember."

Corvina turned, eyeing him carefully.

Cota had become a good friend. And Adresia...he didn't know what she was. But there was no way he would let either of them die. Not because of this. Not when they were all breakers of that unuttered decree.

"Cota's healing fast," he quipped. Only a week had passed since they'd returned half-alive and, already, the Count was up and walking, if not pausing every few feet. It was a miracle. "Are you sure he's not a mage?"

The Princess gazed back out the window. "He's not a mage."

It had been a joke, but the way she'd responded, agreeing with him yet insinuating more... "But he's human—right?"

"Yes. He's human." There was astonishment and awe on her face. "It's so familiar," she said, almost a whisper to herself. "But it can't be." She shook her head. "It can't be."

He opened his mouth the same instant one of his servants appeared at his side. "The Queen requests your presence, Lord Hand."

"Thank you, Nyka. I'll be right there."

Corvina didn't look at him as he departed. He wanted to say something; to ask what had so suddenly caught her attention. But he didn't have the time, and he wouldn't ever truly understand. Not this. So he left the Princess staring out the window, lost in the thoughts of her magical world he would never be part of.

Chapter 47

The shining sun glittered upon the Outer Garden's white bushes, snow layered the trodden paths, and icicles dangled from the castle exteriors. Adresia inhaled the crisp winter air, stopping to admire a wild flower that had somehow managed to resist its inevitable icy demise. Saturated, violet petals drooped wearily. The little thing, surviving even now, when everything commanded it not to.

Fox peered over her shoulder. "You're more fascinated with the scenery than anyone I've ever seen on these grounds—and Sir Talene knows every leaf on every tree."

She ran her fingers over the soft blossom once more before they resumed their stroll. "My mother was born in Gantrick," she explained. "All she knew was cold fingers and snowy grounds, but she loved it with all her heart. She used to tell me stories about her adventures: traversing through winter storms, celebrating in frozen wastelands, finding light in the dark months where being numb to the bone was normal. It was a life I dreamt of as a child; the one place I could imagine that didn't have an imprint of nobility; the only world in which selfishness couldn't exist. I guess it's why I love winter so much."

"Winter seems to like you, too."

She smiled. "When I used to feel that first frigid breeze plow through the land, drifting into the heart of Morolyn, I found a comfort I couldn't find anywhere else. Those winds were the only winter I ever knew growing up in the sweat and heat of Westholt.

But *this*..." She gestured to her winter surroundings. "It's better than anything I've ever imagined."

Fox was watching her in the familiar way he did—head slightly tilted and eyes narrowed. As they passed back through the gate, he said, "I'm glad your dream came true."

"Res!"

Caspian and Cota waved at her from the other side of the courtyard. It'd only been a fortnight since Todsmorren, and every time she beheld Cota walk without that pained expression, it still made her heart jump. How he'd managed to heal so quickly was a myst—

Something cold and wet smashed into her shoulder. Laughter traveled across the expanse as she stared in shock, the remnants of the snowball slipping to the ground. "Did that just happen?" she asked.

"I think it did," Fox said.

They shared a look, the knight's face just as equally expressionless...and then she sank to the ground, shoveling snow as fast as she could. When they realized what was happening, Cota barely had time to dart behind Caspian before her snowball crashed into the Hand's chest. He actually *giggled* before twisting away and shoving Cota toward her.

Her wicked grin promised nothing but mayhem.

Between stopping for breath from both running and laughing so hard her lungs hurt, the three of them had launched into a full-out snow war. A hit to the limb was desired, but they all knew they were aiming for the face.

Launching himself sideways to avoid her throw, Caspian chucked his snowball midair. It hit Cota in the back of the head the same time Caspian landed in the snow, and when the Hand rose and ran toward her, she squealed and raced toward her best friend for cover. He ushered her closer, but she glanced back the same time Caspian's snowball hit her back. Defeated, she faced Cota—and a snowball smashed into her face.

Bent on getting revenge and ensuring he didn't win, she sprinted after him. Caspian delivered no aid as Adresia tackled her best friend. When Cota rolled onto his back, gripping his core with a grimace, her laughter faltered. "Are you okay?"

His feigned discomfort vanished as he grinned. "Never better."

She calmed her racing heart before pulling him upright. "That *wasn't* funny."

"Yes, it was."

"Fine," she admitted with a smile. "It *was*. But you still deserve this." She smashed her snowball in his face.

Caspian was still grinning when they stood. Fox was standing at the edge of the snowy patch, arms crossed despite his prevailing effort to not smile. Always so serious. At least until a snowball hit him in the side of his head. He was so shocked that he didn't move, gaze darting between the three of them and their wide, guilty eyes.

And then he burst out laughing.

"We haven't heard from Elettra in over two weeks."

Adresia turned, wincing at her sore shoulders. It'd been a long day of training with both the Shield and Corvina, but there was always more to do. The rebellion would wait for no one.

Cota dropped a stray parchment onto Caspian's desk and finished, "What is she *doing*?"

"I sent her three more letters after the first, too," Caspian muttered beside Adresia. He'd warned Elettra about the labor camp as soon as he could, but the five days had come and gone, and then ten, and now sixteen. They had no idea if the rebels had received their warning. They had no idea if Jadice's plan had already begun. Adresia knew Elettra was busy; she was the leader of the rebellion, by the Goddess. But she'd kept them informed before. She'd *never* ignored a letter. And now...there hadn't been so much as an informative glance within these walls. The few Corvina knew were gone. Even if there were any left, they were doing a great job of remaining undetected. It only made it harder for them. There were too many servants; too many risks of asking the wrong person. Without Elettra, they were left waiting, alone and oblivious.

"Do you think the letters were intercepted?" the Countess asked.

"If they were," Caspian said, "we wouldn't be sitting here. Although, castle patrols have increased more than I've seen in years. Even if Narissa doesn't suspect us, she knows something's happening."

"What do we do in the meantime?" Cota quipped, sinking into the armchair beside them.

"What we've been doing," Caspian stated.

"And if Elettra decides to act without us?" Cota pressed.

"Then we move too."

Right. The plan. Adresia had barely thought about it since Caspian had told her. After the riot had interrupted their final meeting in Todsmorren, they'd assumed the plan was still as they'd discussed it the day before—which was *insane*, to say the least. Like her companions, she'd expected something; after all, it was their goal to dethrone the Queen of Morolyn.

But she hadn't anticipated this.

The door unexpectedly opened. Adresia heard the swish of the beaded fabric before she saw who it was. When Corvina closed the door behind her and faced them, Cota instantly rose, face contorting into surprise and confusion. Adresia hadn't told him yet. She'd completely forgotten.

Noticing their silence, Cota straightened. "Did I miss something?"

Adresia strolled to the Princess, looped arms, and walked to the sofas. "Cota, meet Corvina. Corvina, the best friend you've heard all about."

The woman's honey eyes were bright. "It's nice to finally meet you, Cota. I hope I didn't startle you too much."

Cota gave Adresia a look that said, *Is this real?*

She just grinned.

He looked at the Princess again. "It's nice to meet you too...Corvina. You've been working with us the entire time, then?"

"No one expects me to hate my own sister, do they?"

Cota's chuckle was half-nervous, half-relieved. "No. They don't."

After returning to their seats, Caspian updated the Princess with Elettra's lack of response, and they discussed the dull happenings of the castle before falling quiet. Adresia stirred her cup of tea with a spoon, watching it swirl around and around and around and—

"What..." Caspian began hesitantly, "what were your parents accused of, Adresia?"

The tea suddenly became very uninteresting. "Treason," she replied slowly.

"Did anyone in Westholt know it was the Queen's men who were sent to handle it?"

She didn't know what he was getting at. "No. That information was never revealed. Their deaths were horrific enough."

Corvina sat up in interest. "It wasn't a public execution?"

Adresia's stomach dropped. "It was a midnight assassination."

Caspian shared a look with the Princess, and Adresia was about to ask what was so interesting when he muttered, "Obviously she didn't want people knowing about it. She only does that when..." He put a hand over his mouth.

"When what?" Cota asked, just as confused as Adresia.

"When she's trying to keep something hidden," Corvina said.

"Like what?"

"Something not recorded in the reports."

Adresia had never believed for a moment her parents had done anything to deserve their fate. But the words tugged at that dangerous thought she hadn't let herself ponder; the thought she was slowly realizing might be the answer she'd been looking for all along. She looked at Caspian. "You said you knew about the rebellion long before the rest of us did. When did you find out?"

There was a long, dreadful pause before Caspian met Adresia's gaze. "Five years ago."

Oh gods.

"Why?" Corvina asked.

Adresia stared at her hands as if she could somehow find the answers to everything written in the lines of her palms. She didn't want to believe it. She didn't want to *think* about it. But everything aligned too well, too perfectly: the way Elettra had responded to her name and how her parents had been murdered. To hide Narissa's involvement, yes...but to also deal with the threat her parents had supported. A threat that the Queen knew would have grown more significant than she could have ever handled if left unchecked.

She hadn't suspected it. Cota's parents must have. They came charging in that night, seeming to know exactly why those guards had come; seeming to know exactly what they were dying for. But despite her parents' warnings of the crown and their disdain for Court, even knowing that they'd risked abandoning their former lives in search of a new one—a *better* one—Adresia hadn't imagined this for a second.

She looked at her friends. "My parents were a part of the rebellion."

✧

There had been chatter in the castle all day. Gantrick had won a sea skirmish against a Southern fleet in the Sarinthian Sea, and while no one knew if it meant an end to the war, there was excitement nonetheless. From where Adresia stood near the gate in the courtyard, she swore if she listened hard enough she could hear the city rejoicing. It wasn't their war, but her own delight proved that Morolyn was desperate for something to celebrate. Something good.

Escaping the wind that nipped at her cheeks, the Countess strolled back indoors. She was observing the strikingly bare Inner Gardens when she rounded a corner and slammed into someone. "Harkin!" she said as they reeled back. She watched him straighten his tunic before saying, "I haven't seen you in a few weeks. I was beginning to think you'd left." It *had* been a while: his clean-shaven jaw now possessed a light scruff that stripped away any indication of his youth.

"That's what you want, isn't it?" he asked.

She frowned. "You make it sound like I don't like you."

He turned away.

"You don't have anything to say to me?" she asked, trailing him.

"No. I don't."

"Why are you acting like that?"

"Like what?"

"Like a *prick*."

He faced her.

"I don't know why you're upset," she continued. "*You* insulted *me* last time we spoke."

He crossed his arms. "You made it quite clear you didn't want to...mingle."

"That's not what I said, nor what I meant. We can still be friends."

"It's too *dangerous*, remember?"

"It doesn't have to be like this."

"Like what? All it seems to me is a bunch of lies."

"I'm not—"

"You *are* a liar, Adresia. And unless you tell me why it's not safe or what you *really* know, I won't consider you anything else."

He disappeared around the corner a moment later. And she debated going after him, but...he was right. All she wanted was to convey the severity of his spying; she *wouldn't* tell him anything else. Still, if he refused to listen to her warnings, she wouldn't bother anymore. With a frustrated groan, she continued down the corridor. By the time she arrived at her chambers and slumped atop her bed, sheets warmed thanks to her wonderful servants, she'd brushed off the encounter. But the word still echoed in her head.

Liar.

Her parents had lied to her. At least, if what she thought was true—if they *had* been a part of the rebellion—her entire life had been a lie. They hadn't moved to Westholt for her safety or to keep her from Court, but for their own agendas; to aid in the most dangerous plot in the kingdom. And even when they had every day to tell her, even in the spare moments when those guards had been outside, her parents had *still* chosen to withhold the truth. Why?

The Countess sat up when a knock sounded at the door. "Come in."

Caspian entered with raised brows. "Not the person you wanted to see?"

A sigh. "I don't really know who I was expecting."

He wrapped a hand around the wooden column of her bed. "Why aren't you in the city? I know how much you love dancing."

She rolled her eyes, already planning to join the celebrations at some point. "I remember how much you enjoyed my welcoming ball—or was that just for show?"

A crooked smile. "Actually, in the weeks before I was named Hand, I practically lived in the city. I would sleep during the day just so I could stay up all night with everyone else."

"*You?*"

A laugh. "Doesn't sound like me, does it?"

She shook her head. "I thought you were perfectly mannered from the moment you could walk. But no one is ever as they seem. Even the Hand of the Queen."

He gave an agreeing nod before she grew quiet again, her shoulders slumping with that familiar weight. He sat beside her. "What's wrong?"

"Everything."

"Obviously. But what specifically—what right now?"

She exhaled. "My parents; the inevitability of opposing the Queen; the fact that Elettra won't respond. All eyes are on me and I can't even control my powers yet. What am I supposed to do if we have to act and I'm not ready? I can't let down our people. I *can't* fail this kingdom."

Caspian grabbed her hands, sapphire eyes shimmering like the cobalt coasts of an ocean she'd never seen. "You can do this, Res. I know you can."

A soft smile. "Thank you." She looked at their fingers, and noting the way her skin sparked at his touch, an idea suddenly tugged at her. She placed one of his hands between hers.

"What are you...?" he started, but, seeming to realize her intention, he fell silent.

She concentrated on nothing except controlling that roiling wave inside her. The faintest of pain feathered in her head, but before it could bloom into something bigger, something dangerous...it happened. Like a soft ripple of water lapping against the shore, a drop of power surged from her, sweeping up and through her arm and down her fingers.

When she lifted her hand, a delicate, frozen deer lay in Caspian's palm. The tiniest of snowflakes had shaped its eyes and different icy patterns resembled fur. She let out a soft, surprised laugh, meeting Caspian's own awe-struck gaze.

She hadn't let herself think about it: the moments with him when she felt like the world had suddenly disappeared; when she didn't have to be anyone but herself and he gladly accepted that truth. Fox had said Caspian was in love with her. Is that what this was?

But when he leaned ever so slightly closer and something sparked throughout her body, Fox's claim suddenly seemed all too real. Too frightening. They were a hands breadth apart when she whispered, "I'll be in town if you need me." She didn't let him pull away, but slid from the mattress first. And even after she'd changed into a more flexible dress, swiped a pack of coins, and grabbed her cloak, Caspian still remained on the bed, staring at her spot like he was trying to find a ghost.

✧

Over the next four days, Adresia found herself at one tavern or another. She thought of nothing except the delightful tunes in her ears and the faces of the companions that joined her, clapping and twirling and dancing, cloaks and jackets forsaken somewhere. She tucked those moments in the deepest part of her soul, where there was nothing but pure bliss, where no one and nothing mattered, where they were just broken people in a broken world, temporarily healed by the joint fissure that was their rejoicing. And while she knew it wouldn't last forever, she hadn't expected it to end so soon.

At a table laden with kegs of ale, scraps of crusty bread and meat, and a foul-smelling liquid she didn't dare get too close to, Adresia was sipping from a goblet of water when someone said at her side, "You've been enjoying yourself."

She met Cota's emerald eyes amidst the pulsing candlelight and fluctuating shadows. "Why sulk in my chambers when I can utilize the excessive earnings the Queen pays me?" she asked. She greeted Caspian with a nod before her gaze drifted to the bar, where a large group of commoners gathered excitedly. "How did you find me?"

"Who else would've *accidentally* let slip that Her Majesty was paying for a tab that hasn't closed after three days?" the Hand asked.

She grinned.

"A certain knight has also been keeping an eye on you," Cota added.

"Oh?"

"Unlike you," the knight said, arriving at her side, "some of us have actual occupations that keep us from revelries like this."

She cocked her head. "I wasn't the only one having fun." She'd seen him enter that first night and claim a seat in the darkest, most unnoticeable corner. But if his current appearance reflected anything, it was that he'd broken his observing to join said revelry. The top of his tunic was unbuttoned, his eyes were bright and hair slightly disheveled, and glancing at his now-abandoned seat, Adresia spotted a few empty mugs.

"As much as we'd love to join," Caspian interjected, "your absence hasn't been received lightly." Sapphire eyes roved the cramped room. "Your swift return has been requested."

Adresia's brows furrowed. "Why?" She'd spent plenty of time in the city, thanks to her missions. What did Narissa suddenly find so odd about it?

"I advise we take this conversation elsewhere," Fox muttered.

She narrowed her eyes. Did he know something she didn't? He'd been here just as long. The knight grabbed their discarded items and the four of them exited the tavern, a cool night wind instantly kissing her skin. She let out a long breath. How good it was to feel the winter air again!

As Adresia followed her friends through the streets, she hummed the merry tunes that repeated in her head, not yet wanting to forget the feeling that had overtaken her the past four days. But when they rounded another corner and the shops and inns she'd memorized on the road to the castle turned into unfamiliar streets lined with attractive, cozy townhomes, she stopped. They weren't headed toward the castle. "It's not the Queen who wants me," she realized aloud.

The men faced her. "No," Caspian admitted.

She folded her arms across her chest. "I was having *fun*." The instant the words came out, she dropped her arms in shock. Since when did she *whine*? Whatever explanation her friends had was cut short as she shoved through them and shouted, "Harkin!" There was only the faint torchlight of the gated houses to light the darkened road, but she was sure she recognized the Lord. The man froze before turning. It *was* him. She began walking, her friends silently following. Once they were close, she said, "I'm surprised you're not celebrating."

Harkin's gaze traveled to the three men behind her. "I've been busy."

"With a *woman*, by chance?"

Catching her tone, Harkin looked directly at her. "I'm meeting someone now, actually."

"Who?"

"Someone from the castle."

"*Who*."

He crossed his arms. "Jadice Wren. The Queen's Warden."

Adresia's mouth went dry. It was a trap. It had to be. Brazen had overheard them and told Narissa, and Jadice had been sent to converse with Harkin—to *deal* with him. "Don't go," she blurted. As much as she didn't want her friends knowing, as much as she wanted to handle it on her own and get Harkin out of Morolyn and just *resolve* this, she couldn't just let him leave knowing full well it might be the last time she ever saw him alive.

"Why?" he asked.

"She's dangerous." She prayed he could see how she was silently begging him, see that she was *sorry* and that she cared too much to let him make a fatal mistake.

But he just said, "You say that a lot," and turned on his heel, continuing toward a narrow alley.

"Wait—"

"Thanks for the warning."

"Harkin, just—"

"I can take care of myself, Adresia."

Panic swelled in her throat. Think. *Think*. She frantically looked around, and she didn't know whether it was the lingering fervor from the past few days or purely her own untamed emotions, but she didn't stop to reconsider. She grabbed the blade from Fox's waist, faced Harkin, and *hurled*.

The dagger thudded in the wall directly beside the Lord's head. He tried to speak as he turned, but she was already there. "Listen to me. It has been *weeks*. You haven't found any valuable information besides what you know from *me*, and I guarantee that this little meeting you're going to—you won't walk out alive." His throat bobbed. "You have *no* idea what Narissa is capable of. You have no idea what *I'm* capable of." Her next words stalled in her mouth, and she glanced behind her, not knowing what her friends had yet guessed. If they hadn't interrupted this far... "I'll tell you," she said. "I'll tell you what I know, but only so you can see how *blind* you are and that you don't know what you're up against."

Harkin blinked. Twice. And then, in a surprisingly steady voice, said, "I know a safe place to go."

Sat around the small kitchen table, Harkin's knee bounced beside Adresia. They were in a quaint apartment in a quiet part of the city. Supposedly he'd rented when he first arrived so he didn't have to stay in the castle all the time, but judging from the dust on the shelves, it hadn't been used. "So you're working to overthrow the Queen of Morolyn with the help of a *rebellion* that has been going on for five years," Harkin reiterated, "and the four of you are part of it."

"And Corvina," Adresia reminded him.

Caspian, Cota, and Fox silently watched the Lord rub his face. They'd piped in when necessary and had asked for an explanation in return, but they hadn't been upset. Their unwavering trust unnerved her more than the relief from their easy acceptance consoled her.

"Did you think she was keeping secrets because she wanted to?" Cota asked. "One wrong word and she would have been worse than dead."

Harkin swallowed. "I knew it was more serious than she was letting on; than *anyone* was. But, again—" He looked at her— "I never intended to put you at risk."

"I know," she said. He was doing what he could for his kingdom, as she was for hers. "And now that you're aware of our *very* detailed plan to eradicate the threat, you can leave."

He frowned. "I'm not going anywhere. I can *help*; I know how to listen, how to talk to servants and soldiers. And I've probably remained undetected far longer than you have."

"The more of us there are in the castle, the more at risk we are," she argued. "I won't risk exposure *or* put another life in unnecessary danger."

He crossed his arms. "It's a good thing it isn't and has never been your choice what I do."

Caspian disguised his surprised laugh with a cough, and Cota tried suppressing his smile, but both were so blatantly obvious that she glared at them.

"*If* we work together," Fox started, "King Bevon might provide us with enough resources to get what we want sooner than expected."

He was right, but wasn't helping her argument. She glared at him too before falling into a long, thoughtful pause. Her eventual exhale must have been telling though, because Harkin was smiling before she even spoke. "The *instant* your life is at more of a risk than necessary, you're going back to Lithelle."

"Deal," the Lord said.

"Well, here's your first update as a rebel," Caspian declared. He'd been abnormally quiet so far. She had a sneaking suspicion she knew why. "Elettra replied."

"She did?" Adresia blurted.

A nod. "They managed to clear out every village at risk of the Warden's expansions."

Which was why they hadn't answered the letters. They'd been occupied resolving the issue they'd been warned about. And to think the woman might have betrayed them…

"Why do I feel like this isn't the news you're wanting to tell us?" she asked.

"Because it isn't." Caspian shared an unreadable look with Fox and Cota and huffed a loud breath. "Several shipments of poison-pearl just arrived in Dazelle."

Adresia's eyes went round. "Why is there *poison-pearl* in Dazelle?"

Harkin's look of horror only magnified the terror that slithered along her bones as he breathed, "Poisonblades."

Her father had mentioned them once. A century ago, when Felbourne had fought against the Eastern Continent, poisonblades had been vital to the East's success. They were made by extracting toxins found in poison-pearl—an ore found exclusively in the frozen depths off the East's northern shores—and then fused into dangerous blades that could cut through flesh like water.

"We have to tell Elettra," Adresia said. "Before it's too late."

Because if Narissa supplied her personal infantry with the most lethal weapons in the world, she would wipe any chance the rebellion had of defeating her from existence.

Chapter 48

Adresia was utterly terrified of this gathering. Not because of the roaring headache that had surfaced the moment she'd entered the Throne Room, and not because both Hadrian *and* Brazen flanked the Queen's side, a trio she had never witnessed before.

She was scared because Caspian, Cota, and Corvina were nowhere to be seen.

After dinner, she'd spent the subsequent hours monitoring Narissa as they had all agreed they would. A silent force waiting to rupture, the woman hadn't moved from her throne, but instead mutely watched the nobles mill about, too absorbed in the ramblings of their own lives to be concerned with their daunting ruler. Currently lingering against the far back wall, Adresia was hidden behind the crowd. She wrung her fingers together, every sudden movement making her jump. Whether Narissa could feel her power or not, Adresia could feel the Queen's. It was like darkness and despair; chilling, deadly.

Harkin appeared at her side. "Guards at every door and window. They wouldn't let me leave."

That wasn't good.

Adresia shifted closer to the Lord as Narissa at last stood. Her voice rang throughout the vast chamber. "For weeks, I have been hard at work, determined to put an end to the treasonous efforts that plague this great kingdom. I had reason to believe we were on the path to extinguishing the rebellion once and for all—until three weeks ago, when several villages in the southeastern plains were suddenly vacated." Adresia stilled. "It appears the residents of those villages had obtained false information warning them against ill intentions set forth by the crown. In doing so, the people willingly fled after being seduced to follow the wretched and pretensive lies that the rebel movement in this kingdom has adopted as their motive. All of those people, now rebels, are traitors to the crown. And as this intel was only revealed to very few confidants...it appears there is also a traitor among us."

Adresia stopped breathing. Brazen and Hadrian had disappeared from their posts.

They didn't—*couldn't* know. As close as she'd been to bursting when Hadrian had dragged her toward the dungeons, she hadn't revealed that she knew anything. And Caspian had convinced the Captain that, without proof, she was innocent. It could have easily been Fox or anyone else who had overheard them.

"But while so many villagers forfeited their rights as citizens of Morolyn," Narissa continued, "not *all* were able to flee."

Startled whispers erupted as Brazen and Hadrian emerged from the shadows behind the throne, each holding a chained, gagged individual: a man and woman. Their clothing was ragged and torn, and their skin was covered in a mixture of blood, silt, and bruises. The chains suddenly loosened, and the pair desperately stumbled toward each other, but the moment they got close enough for their fingertips to brush, they were brutally yanked apart. There was half a second in which Adresia noted the shining silver that glinted on both of their left hands: wedding rings.

Oh gods.

Adresia covered her mouth. It wasn't them, she reminded herself. *It wasn't them.* But even that truth couldn't block the fear that closed up her throat as the couple was shoved onto their knees before the steps. Tears streaked down their cheeks. Adresia's fingertips prickled. Not now. *Not now.*

Narissa took a long, sharp blade from a nearby guard. "Let this be a reminder to you all: no one defies this kingdom and succeeds."

The man began weeping, his muffled cries haunting the silent room. He desperately reached for his sobbing wife.

"No," Adresia whispered. She stepped back as if she could avoid what she knew was going to happen. Harkin glanced at her.

It was her fault. These people were innocent, but because of *her* actions, she'd delivered them directly to the Queen to be tortured and to suffer and to die in a way so much worse than they would have if she hadn't done anything at all. There was nothing to ease the pain in her chest, the stain on her soul. Nothing to keep her power from thundering and her breaths from quickening. She couldn't watch this again. It was too much, too similar, and they looked just like them, and Narissa *knew*—

There was a thump.

A pause.

A scream.

And then people were pushing and running—*fleeing*—as exclamations of magic spread throughout the room. Panic turned into a raging havoc when men in dark armor burst from servant's entrances and attempted to reinstate order. It was no use: the doors opened and the Court flooded out. But Adresia hadn't moved. Because through the turmoil of the fearful crowd...she'd seen them.

She almost convinced herself that they were asleep; that the blue tips of their fingers and the whirls of white etched into their skin that horrifyingly resembled the frost on the windows was just her imagination. But the Queen was there too, staring and staring and staring at the bodies at her feet as those black-armored men searched for a culprit—*a mage*, she'd heard someone say.

Harkin was pulling her. "We have to get out of here," he said.

She didn't remember if she nodded or not, but he tightened his grip on her hand and surged through the swelling crowd. They managed to escape just before those strange men began forcibly detaining those in the room. When Harkin split from the group around them and pulled the Countess down the corridor, she had to remind herself to breathe. She hadn't meant to. She hadn't *wanted* to. She'd only ever taken a life to defend herself. Never intentionally. Never an innocent. Her power had lashed out for a split-second, too fast for her to counter.

She'd killed them.

Something like a whimper sounded in her throat. Footsteps sounded nearby, and Harkin stopped so abruptly that Adresia crashed into him. He pulled her into an alcove, covering her mouth with his hand as he stared into her glimmering, gray eyes. "If you cry now, they'll hear us and they'll find you." His voice was quiet, but not soft. "I know you're scared, but you *have* to calm down until we're somewhere safe. You have to trust me. Can you do that?"

She nodded and he slowly pulled his hand away. They waited for several tense seconds that felt like an eternity as those armored men passed, running too quickly to notice them. Harkin peered back into the corridor, and, deeming it safe, took her hand again. But as he led her down the hallway as quickly and quietly as a mouse, she didn't register the halls. Just one word, over and over; her never-ending song.

Murderer.

Chapter 49

"Why does everything keep getting worse?" Caspian asked.

That was the question: why? Why had they been notified only now? Why, when they had just barely gotten used to the idea of lethal weapons not seen since times of magic being inside Morolyn's borders? Cota didn't have an answer. Instead, he looked at the Princess, who tapped her crossed arms with a manicured finger. "You haven't said anything, Corvina."

He'd been headed to the ball when the Hand had found him. Without saying a word, Cota had known something had happened. He'd immediately followed Caspian through a servant's passage and into a room in the abandoned wing. Corvina had arrived moments later. And when Caspian had told them what the ball tonight was *really* about...well, Cota understood precisely why it took the Princess this long to speak.

"We need to stay wary," she said. "Caution our movements. Refrain from communicating with Elettra unless absolutely necessary."

"Communication doesn't matter if Narissa already knows about us," Caspian quipped.

"That's not what we need to worry about," Cota stated. "She caught two people fleeing from those villages."

Like the braided crown of hair atop her head, the Princess's mouth twisted in thought. "If they're rebels, they would have already spilled what they know and we wouldn't be here right now."

"You have a lot of faith in this rebellion," Cota said satirically.

"Corvina's right," Caspian said. "You don't know what horrors await those who are captured. I don't go to the dungeons unless..." He didn't finished as a dark look crossed his face.

"They could be villagers," Cota suggested. "They might not know anything."

"My sister would use that exact thinking to trick us," Corvina countered.

Caspian rubbed his temples. "Confidential information has slipped. Narissa knows someone inside divulged the information; that's how Elettra arrived at the villages on time. Jadice, Hadrian, and a multitude of others can put Adresia under suspicion for hearing that conversation. I wouldn't be surprised if Narissa already knows."

"I thought Fox was there too," Cota said. The knight, currently on patrol at the southern gate into the city, was missing quite a significant night. "Why don't they suspect him?"

"Fox doesn't have a reason to be allied with us; he's just a blindly loyal servant in the crown's eyes. Besides, *he* wasn't the one caught running from the scene."

The blood drained from Cota's face. "Narissa's going to make a spectacle of those villagers tonight."

Caspian and Cota locked gazes half a second before a scream sounded somewhere in the castle.

Shuffling and marching sounded outside, accompanied by aggravated shouts.

Cota raced toward the door, and as slowly and quietly as he could, he cracked it open, praying it didn't make a noise. His stomach plummeted as he beheld a dozen men swarming the corridor, clad in dark armor—just like the soldiers from Todsmorren. Many had their helmets off, revealing hair streaked with light gray and white. A putrid tang leeched up his nose.

Ash. That was ash in their hair.

He immediately closed the door. Locked it. Braced a chair against it. Corvina and Caspian were gaping when he faced them. "There's soldiers out there," he whispered. "Troops from the east; the ones who burned the villages." He swallowed his unease. "And there's ash in their hair. They reek of smoke and...burnt things."

Corvina blanched.

"It's the infantry," Caspian muttered.

"We have to go," Cota said. "Now."

"If we do, we'll get caught—and if we get caught, we die."

"We're safe in here," Corvina agreed. "Until they leave."

Cota blinked, the only sign of his surprise. "You're suggesting to *wait*?"

"Do you have a better idea?"

"If these soldiers are here, that means Narissa plans on using them. We can't leave Adresia alone and unaware—"

"We *can't* go," Caspian stated. "Narissa won't do anything to her unless we're there." But even as he said it, the Count knew none of them believed it. "So for now...we wait." He huffed an anxious sigh and fell into a dusty armchair.

One minute turned into ten, and ten into thirty, and all the while they remained in that abandoned room, silent and tense. It was like Cota could smell his friends' anticipation as he paced the room. Back and forth, he thought and calculated, praying that Adresia was safe, that they could get out of this gods-awful room already, that they hadn't been foolish enough to fall into the Queen's trap.

Cota checked every nook and cranny twice, hoping there was some secret door that they could escape from instead of the hall. There wasn't. When he went to check a third time, Caspian muttered, "Nothing's changed since the last time you looked."

The glittering moon and stars eventually replaced the descending sun. Cota impatiently tapped his fingers on an old jewelry box he'd found. Thank the gods it was broken; Caspian and Corvina had nearly fallen out of their seats to stop him when they'd seen him trying to open it earlier. It didn't *look* like a jewelry box, let alone one that played—

His head perked, but not at a sound. At the silence.

He tossed the chair aside and wrenched open the door. At the sight of the empty hallway, he rocketed from the room, taking the servants stairwell two steps at a time and sprinting across the quiet, empty castle, ignoring the faint soreness in his core that still occasionally bothered him.

Caspian and Corvina weren't far behind, but he didn't wait. Not as he turned down the corridor, begging that she was here. He'd broken his promise to always be there, and if something had happened to her…

He barreled into her chamber before reeling to a stop. Harkin met Cota's gaze from the sofa. Adresia was sitting at the Lord's feet, her knees pulled to her chest. He brushed her long, chestnut hair like he'd been doing it for a while.

Caspian and Corvina entered behind him, halting with ragged breaths. As Cota crossed the chamber and knelt in front of Adresia, Harkin placed the brush on the table and strode to their side. "Res?" Cota asked, gently pushing back a strand of fallen hair from her face.

She hugged her knees tighter.

"There was a mage at the ball tonight," Harkin announced.

"What?" Cota breathed.

"A mage," the Lord repeated, looking at Corvina and Caspian. "Two villagers were caught, and this person…" He searched for the right word, and Cota wondered why Harkin didn't just say *kill* when he instead finished, "ended their lives, before they could suffer any further. Even the Queen couldn't seem to process what had happened. The Court descended into further chaos when these *soldiers* came bursting in."

"Magic isn't gone?" Cota asked.

"No."

"And there's a *mage* inside the castle." Beings that hadn't been seen in decades. Beings that, if his memory served him correctly, were the true targets of poisonblades. All of his books had burned with his childhood home, but he'd never forgotten the few things he'd learned about magic. It was as if he had always expected, someday, it would return.

"Yes."

Caspian was right. Everything *was* getting worse. Because if the Queen knew there was magic... What she would do if she got her hands on a mage was so much worse than any threat the rebellion could ever face.

Remembering Adresia had witnessed the whole thing, Cota grabbed her hands. "I'm sorry I wasn't there. I tried, but I—I couldn't get to you." He wanted to explain more, but she stroked the back of his hand and peered at him with those beautiful, gray eyes.

"You can tell me tomorrow," she said.

"Are you really okay?"

"Yes. I'm just...tired."

"What about the magic?"

He swore he heard her heartbeat quicken. "We can use it to our advantage," she said.

The corner of his mouth lifted. She was always calculating and planning. Anyone else would have been scared out of their minds. "A mage *would* be good for the rebellion," he agreed lightly.

"Maybe we'll find who they are before Narissa does and get them to ally with us."

He squeezed her hands. "Maybe."

Or maybe the mage had been a part of Narissa's plan, too. Maybe the mage was already on the Queen's side and hadn't intended to kill the villagers—but someone else. No, Cota realized, the last thing he wanted to do was find that mage.

Chapter 50

A part of Adresia had broken today. A part of her she had thought wholly shattered when her parents died. But it hadn't. Not even close.

Grief didn't have a limit, an end.

Harkin had sat with her while she'd alternated between periods of weeping and staring at nothing. In a way, she was grateful for what had happened; she'd saved those villagers from a death far worse than what they'd received. But her own excuses weren't the only reason she wasn't completely falling apart.

"You should be afraid of me," she'd told Harkin.
"Why?"
"I could have hurt you."
"You didn't."
"Do you know what I am?"
"Not all Banes are bad, Adresia."
"It's my fault they're dead."
"It's your fault those villages were saved."

Adresia hadn't asked him how he knew. He had his own sources, and, as far as she was concerned, had seen things much more inconceivable in war than magic.

She didn't feel like thinking about anything. She was exhausted from crying; from wallowing in her guilt; from the expense in which she had used her powers mere hours before. But it was now, half an hour since her friends' voices in the hallway had faded, in the frigid loneliness of her bedchamber and in the afterthoughts of Harkin's unexplainable belief in her, that the memory returned.

"*Res! Where are you, my love?*"

Adresia had hidden from her father on many occasions. His rumble of laughter echoed in her ears, and when his boots creaked the floorboards inches in front of her, adrenaline surged through her veins. She was under the dining table, the linen tablecloth draping over the sides: the perfect hiding spot. Or so she thought.

A squeal escaped her lips as massive hands pulled her out and set her on her feet. "*I thought I'd done well that time!*" *she exclaimed.*

Her father gave a warm, crooked smile and plopped a kiss atop her head. "*You did, Res.*"

They'd been playing this game since she was a little girl, and when he'd started training her all those years ago, it had turned into an exercise. But no matter how good she got—even after five years with Kovare—her father always found her. It was probably because she'd used the limited number of hiding places in their quaint house tenfold.

A wooden table sat directly in the center of the room, and her mother and father brewed dinner beyond that; to her left was the front door, flanked by wooden walls and stained windows; to her right was a counter with shelves that held so many things she knew not where anything was nor went; and behind her were two doors that led to their too-small bedrooms. She couldn't wait to move into the manor. It wasn't that she wasn't content with her home, but to have space to run and feel free...

Her father's whisper to her mother was anything but quiet. "*She's getting better, Sadira. I barely heard her this time.*"

Adresia beamed with delight, but not pride. If her father said she was improving, she was glad. But it was just a game, after all.

"*The stew smells delicious,*" *her father said, looping an arm around her mother's waist. Sadira let out a surprised laugh before gazing at her husband. Adresia hoped to find someone who looked at her like that one* day, with an everlasting love that outshined even the darkest parts of each other's souls.

Adresia had always been told she'd obtained her mother's beauty and her father's liveliness. But if her secrets proved anything, it was that she had never been the daughter they deserved. Her mother's compassion had been replaced by an easily-rifled anger and her father's humility with a swallowing impulsivity. She'd spent her entire life being convicted by the struggling desire to make her parents proud. And while they probably were, she couldn't help feeling like she always failed in the end.

"It would be done faster, Rik, if you helped." Sadira poked him in the chest, but he grabbed her hands and pulled her into a kiss.

Adresia scrunched her nose. "Mother, how can you kiss him? He hasn't trimmed his beard in weeks!" The girl tugged on a strand before her father swatted her away with a laugh.

"Because I love your father, and his looks—even the scruffy ones—are just a part of that." Adresia tilted her head in contemplation. Her mother added, "I think you'll end up loving someone very similar to your father. I bet he'll even have a beard."

Adresia shook her head. "I don't think so."

"Hasn't anyone caught your attention? You're fifteen now; you should be looking for a husband in the coming years."

Her stomach fluttered at the thought, but she didn't have to answer as her father asserted, "You and I both know those silly traditions don't matter, Sadira. Marriage isn't about money or power, but love. Adresia will marry someone perfect for her."

"Like Cota Bowyer?" her mother teased.

Adresia's face bloomed pink, and her parents laughed. "That's not nice!" she complained. "He's just my friend!"

"Mhmm," her father hummed. "Will the Bowyer's be joining us tonight, Sadira?"

"Always, Rik."

Adresia hadn't seen Cota since he'd gone to visit a Morolynian temple out west. It was the longest they'd ever been apart. The past six days had been dreadful.

Adresia opened her mouth, prepared to ramble in excitement, but when voices sounded outside, she frowned. That wasn't the Bowyers. Then there was a knock at the door. Three little taps that, for some reason, made her parents flinch. And when her father faced her with wide, fear-lit eyes, she stilled. He feared nothing. But whoever was outside...

They scared him.

"We're here under the orders of Morolyn's sovereign ruler, Arrikus," a daunting voice said.

Adresia's confusion only grew as her father doused the fire, shoved her mother away from the door, and silently approached his daughter, the slowest she'd ever seen him move. His engulfing hands gripped hers, and she forced herself to focus on the safety and warmth that radiated from them—not the fact that they had never been involved with the crown their entire lives; not the fact that her parents had never shared why they had deserted their fortunes and positions in favor of Westholt; and not the fact that they had always told Adresia the Queen couldn't be trusted.

She strained to hear her father's quiet voice even though he stood right in front of her. "We're going to play a game, Res, like we always do." He glanced at the door. "There are dangerous people out there, and they're probably going to come inside soon." Adresia swallowed, wondering why royal guards would be dangerous. "When they come in, they'll most likely leave the door open and unguarded. The moment you get the chance, you run as fast as the wind can carry you. Run to the Traderious Woodland and stay there—hidden. Do not, under any circumstances, *come out. Wait for the Bowyers to find you. Wait for Cota. You cannot trust* anyone. *Do you understand?" She gulped, her response stuck in her throat. "Do you understand, Adresia?" She nodded even though she really didn't understand, and her father pointed to his chest, to the tattoo peeking out under the open collar of his tunic, to the sacred symbol she'd been forced to draw and learn and memorize the moment she knew how. "Do not forget this,"* her father ordered. *"Do not forget what your family means and what you are willing to do for them. Swear it."*

"I won't forget," she breathed.

"I love you, my daughter." She swore his voice broke in the slightest. *"We will always love you."*

And as if the words weren't simply a declaration, but a promise, her father returned to her mother's side. He glanced at his colossal sword hanging above the fire. It was a sword she had never once seen him use, not in the fifteen years since he'd stopped fighting. He grabbed it and unsheathed it the same time her mother covertly reached behind her and grabbed a large, sharp knife.

Adresia flinched when the man outside spoke again, breaking the thick silence. *"Let us in and we can do this the easy way, Rik. We can talk."*

"There is no easy way," her father said, lifting his blade higher. A brave, courageous look had appeared on his face. It made Adresia stand a bit taller.

"Then I'm sorry it had to come to this."

She heard the displeasure; the lie. The man wasn't sorry at all. But her father didn't reply, and when her parents looked at her, there was only one thing written in their eyes: run.

Havoc exploded as the door flew open and men poured in. Adresia just watched as her father took down five men, his movements as fluid as water. She shouted a warning half a moment before a needle-like blade slashed his side, but her mother was there in an instant, swinging. Adresia had never seen her move so fast, had never seen such hatred and wrath and trepidation in her eyes. Adresia never knew her father had taught his wife how to fight.

The girl hastily scanned the scene before she found an opening. A path to the door had been left undefended. She stepped forward before a man appeared in front of her, spinning a dagger in his hand. His body was covered in strange, indecipherable tattoos. When he stepped closer, she reeled back, putting more distance between her and the door. *"So you're the one He wants."*

"Why are you doing this?" she asked, shoving down her panic to no avail. "We've done nothing wrong."

"Wrong? Your parents are guilty of the highest crimes in Morolyn, girl. Treasonous bastards they are. And you—"

Chaos escalated as the Bowyers appeared in the doorway. Cota met Adresia's gaze as his parents went for their friends, and while the man turned his head, Adresia took her chance. She struck his stomach and ducked around him, but before she could reach Cota, a hand snatched her hair and brutally yanked her back. She cried out and tried pulling away, but the grip was too solid. Instead, she kicked the man in the shin. He growled and struck her so hard she crashed into the floor, stars dotting her vision.

Cota's cry of fury echoed in her ears. She got to her feet with a groan, rubbing her stinging scalp, and she shrieked as the man struck Cota so hard her best friend's head whipped to the side. Cota was pinned under strangling fingers before Adresia could register what was happening. A sudden wave of courage swept over her. She grabbed a shard of a broken plate and sliced the man's arm. His angered howl made her skin crawl, but the instant he released Cota, her best friend kicked the man in the chest, sending him crashing into the back wall. Blood dribbled from Cota's lip as he grabbed her and scrambled to the still undefended door. But then Adresia glimpsed the crimson room.

Where the kitchen table used to be, the Bowyers stared lifelessly at the ceiling. Half a dozen bodies were strewn across the floor amongst broken furniture. Adresia's father held a bloodied hand to his side as her mother shoved the last guard into his awaiting blade. For some reason, Adresia couldn't move. Cota's pleas for her to keep going interlaced with her parents' as they noticed her. They begged her to go, to get out of there.

And then a blade jutted through both of their chests, straight through the symbol her father had desperately begged her to remember.

Adresia lunged forward with a scream, but Cota wrapped his arms around her, his grip crushing and impenetrable as the blade was ripped back. Her parents uselessly clutched their chests, mouths widening in a *futile effort to speak. And when they fell to their knees, the impact vibrating through the floor and settling into her bones...a part of Adresia broke, something so permanent and deep she knew there would be no mending.*

As long as she was alive, she would never forget that sound.

The tattooed man was standing behind her parents, twin swords gleaming red. "The Mighty Warrior and his wife," he declared, "on their knees for the first time in their lives." With a simple touch of his foot, the man kicked her dying parents to the crimson floor.

Adresia slumped in Cota's arms, her blubbering apology barely decipherable past her weeping.

Run, they had told her. Run.

She didn't hesitate. She grabbed Cota's hand and sprinted out the door. Tears blurred her vision as they raced into the forest, surrounded by the dark of night. And as they hastily squeezed into a hollow oak, it wasn't a furious cry of outrage that sounded behind them, but a silence—a silence that seemed to fill the cracks of their tree as they realized what was happening. They heard it, smelled it, felt it.

Their homes were on fire.

Splintering wood and crackling flames dominated Adresia's silent sobs. Cota clung to her as light flickered against the darkened forest past them. Because just barely above the roaring destruction of their lives was a haunting, terrifying noise: the whistling of their parents' murderer as he waited for them to come out.

For an hour, they didn't move.

For an hour, the fire grew.

For an hour, they waited to die.

"We have to leave," Cota finally whispered.

Adresia wiped her eyes. "We have to fight."

"Res, we can't—*"*

"We can*, Cota. My father trained us both." A wicked, dangerous feeling bloomed inside of her. "I'm not letting him get away unscathed," she added darkly.*

Cota shut his eyes as if her words were as scarring as the horror they had just witnessed and took a deep, steadying breath. "Okay."

She clenched her eyes shut too, resisting the fear and grief that overwhelmed her, infinite and relentless. "One," she whispered. Cota laced their fingers together. "Two." The hair on her neck stood up, but it was only until she inhaled again to finish counting that she realized why.

"Three."

Pure terror hindered Adresia's movements as she and Cota were ripped out of the tree. They thrashed against too-strong grips, their arms twisting behind their backs as their burning houses came into view. Her temper blazed like the scorching flames a hundred feet from their faces. "Let us go, you monster!*"*

With a hum that skidded along her bones, that strange man said, "You're the last part of my mission, Adresia—and I won't fail Him."

"Don't you touch her," Cota snarled.

One of the men laughed. "He's threatening you, *Romliss."*

Romliss pointed his dagger at Cota. "Do you really think you'll survive this?"

It wasn't a burning fire in her, Adresia realized. It was a dark, lifeless, cold. Cold this man would soon know. Even if she killed herself in the process.

"Do you really think you *will?" she asked him.*

The grips on her arms tightened as Romliss turned. His sandy brown eyes were bright against the dark blood on his shirt. "What I think *is that you mean nothing. You* are *nothing. No one will remember your parents, and no one will remember you." The edge of his blade was at her neck before she could blink, and, with a grin that made something frozen splinter in her core, he stated, "Let's have some fun."*

With brutal force, the men whirled her around and ripped open the back of her top. Cota's voice was sharp with terror. "No, don't—"

A scream tore from Adresia's throat as pain worse than anything she'd ever felt raked through her body. Romliss was digging into her back, cutting her open, killing her so unbearably slowly. She couldn't think past it. It could have been an hour or minutes later when the guards kicked her legs from beneath her, sending her collapsing to the ground. She watched her blood seep into the soil, too exhausted to move. There was nothing she could do. Nothing that didn't result in excruciating agony. Nothing—

Nothing except what she'd always trained for.

She weakly lifted her head. Cota had been beaten, but was still conscious; enough so that she caught his eye, silently communicating through their gazes as they always did. Romliss wasn't here. Now was their chance to escape.

She'd never taken a life before. Her father had told her about the stains it left on the soul, of the aftermath that came with killing. But she didn't care. In half a breath, she grabbed the discarded blade Romliss had used on her. Hot, sharp pain lashed through her back as she rose, but she clenched her teeth and bit down the agony. The men who had held her were on the ground before the others realized what was happening. Cota merely knocked his men out. Even after what they'd done, he was still too good to become a killer.

She wasn't. She made sure they didn't rise again.

Branches snapped behind them the same moment the final body collapsed to the ground. Her vision swayed as she turned, and Cota grabbed her, careful not to touch her ravaged back. She leaned against him, forcing her eyes to stay open.

Romliss was at the edge of the forest, his hands dangling emptily to his side. "And you call me the monster?" he asked. She shook her dizziness away with an irritated groan, but he noticed her struggle. "You've lost a lot of blood, little Adresia. Are you sure you can finish what you've started?"

"You are going to die for what you've done," she breathed.

"You won't kill me. Not tonight."

"You can't run forever."

Something flickered in his eyes, something she couldn't entirely comprehend in her half-conscious state, before he replied darkly, "I don't intend on it."

Adresia never saw Romliss again. But he was out there, somewhere. Waiting for her to fulfill her promise.

A flurry of snow pooled above her open palm before turning into a frozen butterfly, its icy wings as clear as glass. It fluttered and flapped an inch above her hand. Life—that's what she could create. Things that could provide hope to those who didn't know that surviving wasn't the only option. Despite what she'd done that terrible night, how she had sullied her soul, Adresia had saved those people today. Because of her, the rebellion had grown by hundreds. Something inside of her had broken, yes, but something had also mended. And while her magic still terrified her, while she wasn't perfect and didn't know if she would ever have as much control as Corvina did, she could feel the command in her. *She was master of her power, not the other way around.* She brushed a thumb over the symbol on her arm, remembering what each mark meant; the promises and stories and songs etched into her heart; the people and faces she'd associated with each line, both old and new.

She would never stop protecting her family.

Chapter 51

Someone was in the castle.

After remaining in her chambers for four days, heeding Caspian's advice to remain inconspicuous and not attract attention after the ball, Adresia had grown restless—and hungry. If the Queen wanted her, the woman would find her; hiding in her room wouldn't change that. So the Countess had decided to risk retrieving a sweet snack that night.

It was on her way back that she heard footsteps that weren't hers.

There was no telling what kind of strange activities occurred in the dark corridors at this time nor who they hosted, and she didn't plan on finding out. She dove behind a thick pillar without glancing down the intersecting hallway. The footsteps grew louder, and when they were close enough that she heard the swish of their cloak, she'd held her breath. *Not this way.*

When the person didn't pass her, she peeked around the pillar. The individual walked down the opposite corridor. By the size and build, it was a man. But there was something oddly familiar about the cloak...

Adresia realized who it was at the same moment someone else appeared.

She pressed herself into the wall half a breath before they could see her. After a few moments, another glance around the pillar told her the second person—undoubtedly male, although slightly less muscular and cloaked as well—trailed Harkin like a shadow. And when the Lord turned right and the man did the same, Adresia knew it wasn't by accident.

Alerting Harkin would only result in two possibilities: the man harming him or fleeing. She wasn't going to let the tracker escape without obtaining an explanation, and there was no way she was going to leave Harkin unaware. So she waited until they turned the next corner before she straggled behind, her slippers near silent against the marble floor. In the minutes that she followed, she sorted through the questions in her head. Had Harkin been followed from wherever he'd come from? Where would he have even *been* at this time? Had he finally been caught spying and the man had been sent to deal with him as Adresia had anticipated all along?

The second man halted at the edge of an intersection. Adresia counted her breaths from where she stood one corner behind, never looking away, and after ten, he disappeared. She darted after, and watched him enter a chamber down the hall. As silent as a snake, she sprinted after him and slipped through the door before it could close.

Harkin was sat before his vanity, unfastening his doublet and oblivious to the stranger approaching him. Adresia's blood went cold when a blade slipped from the man's sleeve. With a glance in the mirror, Harkin's eyes went wide. His seat toppled over as he stood.

The man barely made it another step before Adresia swung out her leg and swept him off of his feet. He landed with a thud and grunt before scrambling back, allowing Adresia to put herself between him and Harkin. "What do you want?" she demanded.

He stood and glanced at Harkin. "I have business to do."

"You'll have to leave unfinished."

"Get out of my way or you'll be next."

"Leave now and maybe you'll live."

The man looked at her. His eyes narrowed. And then he lunged.

Adresia sidestepped him and slammed her elbow into his back. He hissed and spun, swinging with both blade and fist. She ducked half a moment too late, and an angry cry left her lips as he sliced her upper arm. But when her magic knitted the skin back together in a matter of moments and a newfound excitement coursed through her body like lightning...she suddenly realized exactly why Banes had been feared. It almost made her feel bad for him. At least until he snarled, "Your friend won't be getting a clean end anymore."

She grabbed his face in her hands. His pained cry rang through the room. She released him, breathing hard, and he stumbled back. He'd been burned—burned with ice so cold it was like the heat of a fire. Where her fingers had been, frost had permanently seeped into his skin.

He lunged for her legs. She dove over him, rolling before she grabbed the discarded sword resting at the edge of the bed. She had it pointed at his throat by the time he fully rose. The man glared at her, but didn't resist. Not as Harkin pressed the tip of *his* sword into the man's back. The Lord's shock had been replaced with puzzlement and irritation. The face of a soldier. He'd be fit to lead, if he ever had the chance.

"Who sent you?" Adresia asked.

"Like I'm going to tell you," the man retorted.

She jutted her chin toward Harkin. "Why kill him?"

"He's a threat."

"To whom?"

"He sees and knows too much."

"*To whom?*"

Despite the blades, the man cocked his head. "Do you really think you can stand against what's coming?"

"And what would that be?"

He ignored her. "No matter how many people join the rebellion, it won't be enough. No matter how many lives are spared or villages are saved, *it will never be enough.*"

Rage and confusion twisted in her stomach. "Those marks look pretty painful," she said. "I'd hate to make them worse."

The confidence in his eyes vanished. "You are going to die," he breathed. But not as a threat. Like a fact.

She watched him carefully. And then she said, "You get one chance to live." Both men gaped in surprise. "But you will not return to whoever hired you. You are going to leave this castle and *run.*" Her fingers wiggled at her side, and the man's eyes widened at the spark of magic. "You are going to run as far as you possibly can, and then farther. Do not come back to Dazelle, do not come back to this castle, and do not come back to Morolyn. You are going to do *exactly* that, because if I ever see you again..." He flinched when she raised her hand. "I won't kill you with a blade."

The man nodded and edged to the door, completely and utterly aware of the weapon that was one flick away from opening his throat. The instant the door clicked shut, Adresia set into motion, grabbing the satchel hanging on the wall and pulling open Harkin's drawers. The Lord lowered his sword, metal tapping heavily against stone. "Who was that?"

She tossed his things into the bag. "An assassin."

"Why did you let him go?"

"Because killing him would've been a mess."

"He can come after you now."

"He won't."

"How do you know?"

"Because Narissa already tried. It didn't work."

A pause. "What does this mean?"

She shoved the satchel into his arms. "It means you're going back to your King."

He put the bag atop the dresser. "No, I'm not."

"We made a deal."

"I don't care."

With a deep, calming inhale, she continued searching every compartment of the room, dumping his belongings in another bag. "Narissa can't kill me, Harkin. But you're a foreign noble. It's easier to chalk up your death as a tragic accident. Narissa *won't* hesitate to try again, and next time, I might not be there."

His brows lowered. "I'll be more careful."

"Words won't save your life."

He pulled her to a stop. *"I'll be more careful."*

"We're not arguing. You're leaving."

"No, I'm not."

"Yes, you are."

"I have obligations here."

"Not anymore."

"You—you can't just tell me what to—"

She threw her hands down. "My parents were murdered by Narissa's assassins!" His face fell, and whether he suddenly realized why the ball last week had affected her so deeply or not, he didn't say. "I couldn't save them. I won't let that happen again. So please, *please*, return to Lithelle where you're safe. You can help from there. Convince King Bevon to aid us."

They stared at each other until his hard, determined expression softened and he huffed a breath from his nose. "Fine."

"You'll go?" she asked.

He gripped her hands. "Not for this rebellion. Not for this kingdom. For *you*. For someone who can do something great; for someone who can make a better world."

Her throat burned, and he squeezed her fingers once more before grabbing his bags and swords. The corridors were quiet as she led him through the castle and down an abandoned hallway. "Caspian uses this door to get into and out of the castle unseen," she explained. "The guard rotation leaves a three minute gap, but this part of the wall isn't checked very often anyway. You can steal a horse on the outskirts of the city and ride until you reach Sheavania. Get on a ship there and *get home*."

He finished strapping his swords to his belt. "You pay a *lot* of attention."

"I thought you were the soldier." He hummed a laugh, and she added, "Thank you."

"For what?"

"For never giving up. For showing me there are people out there who believe in what I'm fighting for. For being my friend."

It surprised her when he pulled her into a hug. "Don't die while I'm gone, okay? I have to show you Lithelle one day."

Despite her best efforts, despite her laugh, a tear slipped free. "I'll try not to."

He pulled away and wiped her cheek, that familiar light in his caramel eyes glowing. "Narissa might be able to bear the weight of the crown, but she can't win against what you're fighting for." A winter breeze blew his dark curls as he cracked the door open. "She can't win against hope."

Chapter 52

Harkin Sallow was tired of secrets. Tired of lying, too. But there were too many plans at play, too many people involved, and too many things to do. He looked at the Hand of the Queen. "This is bigger than what anyone thought. It will make the war against the South look like child's-play."

"It's what we've prepared for," the Hand replied. "It's what we're training her against."

"Her parents were right," the Princess quipped. "The prophecy is true." The woman had been an unexpected ally. He'd known there were nobles who despised the Queen enough to join the rebellion, but her own sister? It'd been more than enough evidence.

"Do you think she's ready?" He didn't know why he asked; he'd been there when she'd killed those villagers. Adresia truly had no idea just how much power she had—how much of a threat she really stood against the Queen. Once she stopped being so terrified of herself, she would be powerful beyond measure. Lithelle could use a friend like her.

"She will be," the Hand promised.

With a glance at the darkened sky, he realized how late it was. He had too many letters to answer and not enough time. He rose and fastened his cloak around his shoulders. "My people will be waiting."

"Your Majesty," the Hand started, "why don't you tell her who you really are?"

Grabbing the handle of the door, the King of Lithelle smiled. "I want to surprise her when I return."

Chapter 53

Cota Bowyer strolled down the main corridor of the Suites. The castle had been different since the ball. The halls were eerily empty, as if everyone had fled to their chambers. The Shield was more scarce than ever, and even the servants scurried quickly from one place to another in hushed pairs. Perhaps it was to escape the frigid weather outside. Or perhaps it was to escape the mage the Queen had yet to identify.

Thankfully, his never-ending amount of meetings had been postponed; many of the Lords hadn't arrived at the castle just yet. It'd given him an excuse to see Adresia more, and he'd gladly kept her company, especially since Harkin had disappeared a week ago and left her with entirely too much time to plot and train.

Things were different between them. Her behavior had undoubtedly changed since they left Westholt, but he hadn't been sure until after Todsmorren, until he realized that his far-fetched, unrealistic dreams weren't that at all. They were real. They were exactly what he had hoped was happening. And they hadn't talked about it, but he knew they both thought about the day he'd awoken. About what had almost happened. He could tell it in the way they shared glances during dinners; how they coincidentally seemed to always find each other during the Queen's events; when they would brush fingers on their strolls in the gardens. Wherever they went, they were drawn together.

Cota stalled in front of the slim glass panes, overlooking the Inner Gardens that were blanketed in white. Wind whistled outside the walls. Rain and snow slammed into windows. And he was so distracted by the sight that he didn't notice the other reflection in the window until hands wrapped around his mouth and pulled him backward.

He thrashed against their grips, but the men carried him with ease through the corridors, solid and silent. It wasn't until they reached the Throne Room that they halted and he shoved them away with a flustered growl. "What are you *do*—" The words died on his lips as the doors opened and he turned to face the room.

Adresia was kneeling at the foot of the Queen's dais.

"Lord Bowyer," Queen Narissa quipped from her throne. Adresia's head snapped toward him, gray eyes as dark as the storm outside. "I'm pleased you could join us so quickly."

He cautiously marched to Adresia's side, the doors shutting behind him. Men lined the walls of the empty room. Men in black armor.

Remain calm; he had to remain calm.

When he stopped at his best friend's side, Narissa uncrossed her legs, her silken dress like flowing water. "Do you remember our last conversation, Lord Bowyer, or would you like me to remind you precisely what happened?" The woman looked at Adresia as if the words weren't threatening enough.

"There's no need for a recollection," he said. "I remember perfectly."

Stay calm; composed. Everything was fine.

The Queen smiled, and that thing inside him growled as if displeased it'd been awoken, as if repulsed by the sight of her. Narissa said, "I told you to refrain from pursuing any personal endeavors with Lady Bellum and ordered you to cease your courting." Adresia didn't stir at the information. "I gave you incentive to do so, too."

"You threatened me," he snarled softly.

"And *yet*," Narissa continued, "you pressed on. Without an *inkling* of hesitation." She descended the dais with a dramatic sigh. "I should have known. After all, nothing can keep *love* apart." Her shoes clicked against the marble steps. "Unfortunately for you, I uphold my promises." She halted inches in front of Cota, and he feared she was going to do what she'd done in his chambers again...but soldiers grabbed him instead.

"What are you doing?" Adresia demanded.

"I warned you there would be a punishment if you proceeded," Narissa told him. "So a punishment there shall be."

Violet eyes settled on Adresia, and fear surged up his throat. "They were *my* actions," he said. "I disobeyed you. She had no part in it. There's no reason for her to be here."

"Ah, but there *is*," the Queen countered. "She knew exactly what she was getting into. She knew what it meant."

"Then I'll take the punishment for us both."

"No," Adresia blurted. She met Narissa's dangerous gaze with one of her own. "Do whatever you want to me. Your efforts are wasted. It won't change a thing about what I feel."

He wanted to reply, to tell her to stop being so heroic and foolish, but Narissa was silent, and, for a moment, he swore he could feel the deadly rage boiling under her skin.

And then the woman laughed, surprising him so much that he flinched.

Adresia shot to her feet, but the Queen held up a hand, and when he looked at his unresponsive best friend, his blood turned to ice.

There was such fear in Adresia's eyes. Fear and *pain* as she dropped to the floor and gripped her head in her hands.

"Res?" he asked fearfully. He wrestled against the soldiers holding him.

Narissa dropped her hand. "What you feel for each other, the *strength* you receive from being together...it is a lie. Love cannot save you from anything."

Just when Cota escaped the men's clutches, just when he thought he was free, a fist slammed into his jaw. He rocketed to the side.

Another blow knocked him to the ground before he could steady his balance. He barely took in a breath before he was being attacked, so brutally and quickly that he had no time to recover before another strike landed. He stopped moving when he could no longer breathe, wrapping a shaking hand around his core. They picked him up and slung him between their arms. Adresia was in the same place she'd been minutes before, but her cheek bloomed a dark pink as if she'd been hit and she was glaring at the Queen. "*You'll pay for that*," she seethed.

"No," Narissa said. "I won't."

Adresia fell to the ground as if an invisible, violent *something* attacked her, and a scream tore from her throat. It was the worst sound Cota had ever heard. He bucked and pulled, his limbs barking in pain, but as he realized what it was, what Narissa was doing, he stopped.

It was magic. Magic—because the *Queen* was the mage.

Chapter 54

Adresia had never felt anything more unbearable. She was being burned alive; her skull was being cut open; she was drowning in that freezing lake, over and over and over again. The pain was relentless, unforgiving, never-ending, and it became hard to breathe; to see. Her hands ached as she kept them in fists, the power she was containing burning her own fingers. She'd tried letting it out, once. She hadn't cared about revealing herself, she'd just needed the pain to stop. But it hadn't. Her power had buckled under the strength of Narissa's magic, *refusing* to come out.

The Queen crouched in front of her. "You're struggling," she said. "It wants out, but you won't let it."

That agonizing torture was still there, every bone in Adresia's body tightening like they might snap, but it'd dampened enough that she pushed herself onto her hands and knees and weakly lifted her head. "I don't know what you're talking about," she rasped.

"You won't fight back," Narissa continued, "because of me?" The woman lifted her gaze, peering at something. When she looked at Adresia again, she was grinning. "Secrets aren't secrets forever, Lady Bellum."

Magic pricked at Adresia's skull, a challenge and a taunt, and she tried to resist it, tried to beg the Queen to not say anything, but she couldn't. A strangled groan came out.

"*Let her go,*" Cota said with exhausted fury.

Narissa waved a hand. "Get him out of here."

Adresia could do nothing as they dragged her best friend away, his protests echoing against the walls even after the doors shut behind him.

"You will not see him again," Narissa ordered. "Not if you want his head to remain on his body."

Adresia said between ragged breaths, "I'm...not...scared...of you."

The Queen just smiled, and that pain returned with Adresia's screams.

✧

Two men were carrying Adresia through the corridors. Multiple footsteps told her there were more following behind. Keeping her eyes closed and breathing steady, she used her heightened senses to her advantage. It wasn't difficult to pretend to be unconscious, if not weak enough to not be able to rise; remnants of that torture was still there, still in her bones. It would take her a long while to forget how it felt. But no matter how searing or excruciating it had been, she hadn't succumbed. She'd fought every second until that sweet darkness overtook her.

Had it been minutes or hours since the Queen lashed out a second time, hoping to leave the Countess broken and cowering? Whatever the intent—to force her to expose her power, to profess her unyielding obedience—it hadn't worked. Adresia wasn't scared. She was enraged. And when the soldiers stalled outside her chambers, their grips loosening in the slightest, she made sure they knew it.

She shoved her elbow as hard as she could into the gut of the soldier on her right. He receded with a surprised grunt. She spun, twisting the other soldier's arms and kicking his feet out from under him. The other five rushed at her. Seven men—that's all Narissa had felt was necessary? It was a little insulting.

When they pulled out their blades, she tutted, "Now, that's not fair. *I* don't have a weapon."

"Get in your room," the one she'd kicked snarled. "*Now*."

She jutted out a lip. "But I'm having fun out here."

The first guard swung, and she ducked before the blade could slice her face. Assaults ensued from every direction. She managed to dodge them before three hits landed at her sides and back, and when she realized that they weren't using their blades, she grinned. Narissa *still* didn't want her dead.

The Countess sent a satisfying blow to one man's face and slammed her foot into another's gut. "You're not even trying to keep us down," one said, hardly winded.

"I need the practice," she replied sweetly, breathing hard. They *were* stronger than the guards she trained against.

"Too bad practice didn't help your lover."

Adresia's swing halted, fear distracting her focus. Her face slammed into the wall, and she spun with a growl, but not fast enough. A second strike had her rocketing sideways. There was a wicked laugh, and a kick sent her toppling backward. With an angered cry, she twisted and dug her nails into one guard's arm, but another ripped her back and threw her into an awaiting fist. The tang of metal exploded in her mouth, and before she could retaliate further, they grabbed her, shoved her through the open threshold of her chamber, and sent her crashing to the floor.

Chapter 55

The accompanying entourage of guards had become a nuisance. The Queen had immediately sent Adresia on a mission after attempting to destroy what little hope the Countess had for herself, and after four days traveling to the northern province, Adresia *was* beginning to lose hope—in her patience. She was utterly exhausted from riding, and the half a dozen sentinels surrounding her wouldn't stop giving her uncertain glances, like she might combust at any moment. But she didn't feel like drawing anymore attention by barking at them to quit, so, for now, she let the stares persist.

Five months ago, she would've hated to visit Sheavania. Anything that reminded her of her parents, she'd wanted nothing to do with. It'd been a punishment, she supposed, because since her parents would never see these places again, she shouldn't either. But she'd finally realized punishing herself wouldn't change that. She wanted peace. Desperately.

Adresia glanced over her shoulder. Cota was at the back of the group, mingling with another as he had the entire journey. She couldn't see the bruises under his clothes, but they were there; she'd seen him wince every time he moved the wrong way too quickly. His eyes swept over the company, then back to the man at his side, and she almost didn't notice; almost thought he hadn't even looked. But from the split-second that their eyes had met, in the half a heartbeat in which he'd acknowledged her, relief pooled in her gut.

"It's been half a week," Caspian murmured as he steered his horse to her side, "and you two haven't said a word to each other."

She faced forward. "You know why."

"All of the men were ordered beforehand to watch both of you."

"Obviously." She'd expected this was some sort of test; to determine whether they took the Queen's threats seriously or not. Especially since Brazen had somehow managed to squeeze himself into the group on this mission. Caspian didn't say anything else, but she felt his stare, the silent question simmering at the surface. She looked at him sideways. "What?"

"The servants saw both of you go into the Throne Room that night."

She shook her head. "I can't talk about it."

"You don't have to. But..." He inhaled sharply, as if restraining himself from saying something. His voice softened. "I'm here, if you need me."

She tried with all her might not to notice the way his hand so subtly moved closer, as if he might try and reach for her. But he didn't, and instead ran a hand through his hair. "This never gets easier."

"Being sent to do the dirty work?"

His blue eyes darkened besides being anything but. "I hate it. I *hate* meeting these people and having to pretend to be their friend until I've determined a fate that has never truly been up to me to decide. It doesn't matter whether they're innocent or not. They desire mercy—the one thing I can't provide. And so it ends the same way: me, being regarded as the undesired noble that I was sent as, and them, hating me for a decision I had no part in making."

"You don't really mean it," she said, knowing what the Queen really wanted out of this mission—what she wanted Adresia to do.

A grim smile. "They don't see that when I'm forced to ruin their lives."

"I'm sorry you have to do that."

"I'm sorry the burden is on you now."

A shrug. "If I'm given the power to do something, to make a decision...I'm going to make one whether she likes it or not."

"I thought you'd say something like that." The corners of his mouth lifted. "I'll stand by you no matter what."

"Good." She would need him to, if things went in a way Narissa didn't like. She wondered why it was different now, though; why he was willing to risk the Queen's wrath even though he had never before; if it was because he'd been protecting himself all along—or if there was a different reason else entirely.

A large, magnificent manor came into view through the parting trees. Adresia's mouth opened in awe as she beheld it: pale, orange bricks and rectangular windows and pillared corners rising into pointed turrets. It was three stories high and wide enough to be an entire wing of the castle. How many people *lived* there?

They dismounted their horses at the edge of the trimmed, green lawn and trekked to where a group of people had appeared to greet them. There *were* a lot of them, but they couldn't be servants; most were children.

At the front steps, a bearded man—the Lord—stepped forward and bowed low, the group behind him doing the same. There were eight in total. A family, Adresia realized. They all shared the same warm, brown eyes and chestnut hair as the man—except for two. With hazel eyes and black hair that curled at the ends, the eldest child was nearly identical to the woman beside the Lord. "Welcome, Lord Hand," the man said warmly. The lines around his mouth indicated a smiling nature. "It's an honor to receive you in our home."

Caspian dipped his head. "The honor is mine, Lord Havversford."

"You have a beautiful home," Adresia proclaimed, still marveling at her surroundings.

The Lord's brows furrowed in the slightest. "Thank you, Lady...?"

"Lady Adresia Bellum, Ambassador to the Queen."

"*You're* the Queen's new Ambassador?" His ears went red. "I—I meant no offense—"

A crooked smile. "I was surprised too, don't worry."

The man scratched his beard. "And you're...how old?"

"Twenty."

"Why, Aldrich, she's only a year older than Sterling!" the dark-haired woman remarked. A spark of excitement in her eyes, and she placed a hand on the round belly Adresia hadn't yet noticed.

"By the gods, I should probably introduce my family," the Lord exclaimed, wrapping an arm around the woman's waist. "This is my wife: Lady Evette, Countess of Havversford." He gestured to the young man with hazel eyes. "My eldest son and Viscount of Havversford, Sterling." Sterling stood proudly beside his parents, and although his gaze was piercing, it wasn't cruel, just...curious. "My eldest daughter, Elysia," the Lord continued, gesturing to each of the children. "My other sons, Baylor and Ruslan, and my youngest two, Avery and Jenni." The smallest, Jenni, hid behind Baylor's leg. Her head was just below his waist.

Adresia crouched down and held out her hand. "It's nice to meet you." The girl's brown eyes went round, but her lips perked up. Hesitantly, she stepped forward. "How old are you, Lady Jenni?"

The girl stuck her fingers up one by one before proudly stating, "Four!"

Adresia's smile widened. "You're very pretty."

"Thank you, Sia!"

There was a laugh behind her. Adresia rose and peered over her shoulder. Cota had appeared beside Caspian, green eyes crinkled at the corners. "I think Sia is *much* better than Res. Very clever, Lady Jenni." He winked at the girl, who giggled at his compliment before scurrying back to her brother's side.

THE BANE

"This is Lord Cota Bowyer," Caspian announced.

"I'm not as young as this one," Cota jested, jerking his thumb in Adresia's direction.

"You're barely a year older than me!" she objected with a laugh. He looked at her, but she turned before their eyes met. Sterling was watching them with a small smile.

"My sons will take your mounts to the stables," Lord Havversford said. "Shall we head inside? I'm sure you're hungry and tired."

"I could eat a horse," Adresia mumbled. A chorus of laughs sounded around them. And beholding the sparkling light of the wonderful family, the weight of the burden she was about to put on them seemed to crush her shoulders. Caspian was right. It never got easier.

✧

At the head of the oak table, beside Lady Evette and the Viscount, Lord Havversford's smile had shifted into a sobered hardness. Adresia sat at the opposite end, Caspian and Cota flanking her. She wrung her fingers together beneath the table and recited the rehearsed explanation. "The Queen has requested the remaining sums of your district's taxes. The funds you've provided in recent months are insufficiently below quota."

A muscle feathered in Lord Havversford's jaw. "Sheavania isn't as small as it was five years ago. We can barely provide for our families, let alone fulfill taxes."

The plethora of food spread across the table became suddenly unappetizing. There was no telling how many had gone without meals so they could deliver this feast.

"Winter is in its final descent," Caspian said, breaking the tense silence that had arisen. "Hopefully the snow that has just melted is the last. When do you normally resume crop preparations?"

"Two weeks ago."

Caspian blinked, the only sign of his shock. "You mean you've been unsuccessful?"

The Lord cast an uncertain glance at his wife. "We've never had this problem with the land before."

"My mother was a gardener," Cota interjected. "I don't know if it's any different from what you do, but she taught me some things. What do you grow?"

"Beets and asparagus," Sterling answered.

"Have you ever tried rotating the crops?"

"Yes. It stopped working."

"Does it rain often?"

"Enough that we don't need to water the fields ourselves."

"Was it the same time this year?"

"Same as always."

"Where do you plant the crops? Can you describe the land?"

Lord Havversford rose and grabbed a scroll from a basket in the corner before spreading it across the table. With an encouraging nod from his father, Sterling explained, "We use this western dale near the Lyssen River."

Cota's eyes darted across the parchment in thought. "I think I know what the problem is." Lord Havversford lifted his head. "If it rains as much as you say, then the dale, specifically here—" Her best friend pointed to a spot on the map— "is being flooded and drowned every time the river overflows. Water is good, yes, but too much can be detrimental. It must have been going on for so many years now that the entire land has died."

"So what do you suggest we do?" Sterling asked. Adresia looked up. The Viscount's gaze was on her.

"Unless you have enough resources to level the dale so the river stops overflowing into the cropland," Cota began, "I suggest moving the fields. Do you have any unused land?"

"There are a few acres off the coast, to the north."

Cota nodded. "Move them there. The land will receive enough water and any more will runoff into the sea. Those crops grow better in coastal regions anyway."

Lady Evette huffed a surprised, but delighted breath and grabbed her husband's hand.

"I'm afraid you must still acquire your taxes," Caspian stated. "The Queen desires the full amount by the time we leave."

Adresia's heart stumbled at the devastation in their eyes.

"We're remaining in town for a few days to give you time to come up with the funds," Caspian added. They all knew those days were useless. It wasn't enough time to prepare the new land, grow crops, or sell anything at all. The Queen had sent them on an impossible mission.

As they stood, Adresia said, "I'm sorry. I wish I could help." Sterling met her gaze with an equally wistful expression.

Lady Evette said, "It's late. There's no need for you to go all the way to town. We have an empty wing with plenty of rooms." Adresia glanced at Caspian, but he kept his mouth shut. Her decision. "Please," the woman urged. "We have more room than we could ever need."

Adresia smiled. "That would be wonderful. Thank you."

Lord Havversford and the Viscount led them to their chambers. Caspian swiftly informed the rest of the men of their accommodations, who boisterously voiced their gratitude whilst eyeing Adresia as if it had been her choice to originally make the trek into town at this hour.

There were six rooms down a single hall, three on each side. Adresia, Cota, and Caspian each took one on the right, and the guards split into the ones on the left. Fox lingered outside her door while the Havversfords made sure they had everything they needed. When they at last disappeared around the corner, Adresia approached her door. Fox uncrossed his arms and handed her her bag. "Good news or bad?"

She gave him a hard stare as she took her things.

"Bad news," he concluded. She rubbed her tired eyes. "Someone will be posted out here eventually," he said. "I'll see you in the morning."

She waved a farewell and entered her quiet, unlit chambers.

"You have no servants either, I see."

A blade was in her hand before the sentence had been fully spoken, but recognizing Caspian's figure in a chair beside her bed—illuminated by the bright moonlight outside—she took a deep, calming breath. "You know," she said once she sheathed her blade and placed her dropped bag behind the dressing screen, "one day I'm going to mistake you for an actual intruder." He laughed unspiritedly, no more than a huff of air through his nose. "How did you get in here?"

He gestured to the door beside him. "Joined rooms." She tossed a few logs into the hearth from the stack nearby before grabbing the scraps of flint and steel from the edge of the ashes. It took four strikes before a flame burst forth. She strolled behind the dressing screen, changed in a nightgown, and was halfway through brushing her hair atop her bed when Caspian spoke again. "You did good today."

"You did most of the talking," she countered.

"I've done this enough times to know the right responses."

She noted his tone. "It's not entirely lost. They have a solution."

"They *hope* for a solution. It doesn't change the fact that they won't have the funds by the time we leave."

She lowered her brush. "What happened to standing by me no matter what? If I haven't given up then you can't either."

He smiled, and she didn't realize his lack of emotion had been bothering her until something in her chest eased at the sight of it. He rose and approached her bed. "Fine. I won't give up until you say so." There was a humored light to his eyes, but something else, too. Something darker. It was worrying enough that she grabbed his hand. He peered at their tangled fingers. But a noise outside her window made her pull away, and heat immediately rushed up her neck.

Caspian didn't look at her. He just loosed a loud sigh before walking into his room.

◆

Adresia spent the next day bored out of her mind. Lord Havversford had gone to the fields to start the relocation, and while she'd requested to be of some sort of use—especially since she'd found out it hadn't just been her and Caspian without servants, but the entire estate—she hadn't been offered any opportunities. It was understandable: she wouldn't trust a strange noble in her house, either. But her sanity was on the verge of collapse that evening as she turned down a corner followed by four of the Queen's men and ran into the same trio—one of which was Brazen—the third time that hour. "Don't any of you have anything better to do than following me around?" she snapped.

Brazen stepped so close she could see her reflection in his armor and grabbed her arm. "Like putting you in your place?"

"Let go of me," she warned.

"I don't think I will." She recoiled as he pulled her closer, his stale breath spoiling the air between them. "We've been depleted of certain pleasures in accompanying you here. And seeing as you're so readily available...it's almost as if Her Majesty knew what a dozen men would need after such a dull journey."

The men laughed, and panic surged up Adresia's throat.

"That's enough, Voss," said another voice, authoritative and demanding. Adresia practically shook with relief as Fox appeared at her side, his amber eyes settling on Brazen. "I can take care of the Countess quite well on my own. Why don't you busy yourselves in the gaming room? I heard our hosts are supplying a few rounds of cards and ale each night until we leave."

Brazen looked between them with a snarl, but, seeming to realize a brawl was not the wisest decision, he squeezed her arm before practically shoving her into Fox. The men strode down the hall after him, grumbling as they went.

"Are you okay?" Fox asked her.

"I'm fine," she breathed, her trembling turning into a ferocious rage. "They're going to try that again—and you can't protect me every moment of the day."

"Good thing you can." She huffed a surprised, yet still irritated laugh before Fox jerked his chin to follow. She raised her brows in silent inquiry. "Caspian's orders," the knight said.

Fifteen minutes later and joined by Cota, they followed Caspian down the narrow gravel road that led into town. The evening sunlight accompanied a crisp breeze, but Adresia's rifled mood hadn't yet abated, and, after tripping on a rock for the third time, she snapped, "Where are we going, Caspian?"

"A tavern," he answered puckishly.

She shared a look with Fox. This wasn't the time or place for festivities. "The men will notice we're gone."

"They're distracted by beer and billiards," Cota quietly claimed beside her.

She met his gaze for the briefest of moments before looking away. They were silent as they entered town, weaving around commoners and children. And when they actually *did* enter a lively tavern, Adresia demanded again, "What, in the Goddess's name, are we doing?"

Caspian glanced at her over his shoulder, but remained silent. They followed him to the back of the tavern and through a dim hallway before they stopped at the single door at the end. He tapped on it twice before asking, "You don't have any weapons, do you?"

"No." She'd left her dagger at the manor, but now she regretted not bringing it. "Why would I...?" But as the door opened, she found her answer. A group of rebels were seated at a small, round table. Some faces were familiar, some not.

Elettra was at the door.

The Countess heard her name being called in tune with startled gasps as she pinned the woman against the wall, her forearm pressed against the leader's throat with relentless, magical strength. "If you *ever* pull a stunt like the one in Todsmorren again," Adresia snarled, not needing to raise her voice to express her rage, "*I will kill you.*" The room went so silent they could hear the strings of the instruments and stomping boots in the main room.

Despite her struggle to breathe, Elettra said, "Your friends are alive and well."

"That's probably not the right response," someone muttered from the table. Morphaeous.

"You planned that riot, made innocent people die, and almost got my friends killed," Adresia seethed. "Who knows if they're suspected of aiding the rebellion when the riot coincidentally occurred just before they were supposed to depart?" The woman's face reddened as the girl pressed harder. "Do *not* keep vital information from us again."

With one final squeeze for emphasis, she released the woman. By the time Elettra found her breath again, Adresia had sat down between Caspian and Cota. The leader said, "Even if I had told you, you wouldn't have agreed. I'm willing to do what's necessary so this rebellion can continue. That riot *had* to happen. Do you know why? Because people *die* in rebellions, Adresia. They sacrifice their lives so the rest of us can finish what they started. *That's* how it works. And if the Queen suspected you," she added sharply, "you'd already be rotting in the ground." The woman was right, but it still didn't make Adresia any less angry.

Elettra began by reminding them all why they were there before recounting the plan that they'd established in Todsmorren. Caspian had explained it, but hearing it now...it was more detailed than she'd expected. More brutal. And so much bigger than an individual assault, than Adresia against Narissa. If the Queen didn't surrender...she was insane.

Half an hour later, Elettra acknowledged them again. "After your *persistent* letters, I informed you that we postponed this plan to retrieve the villagers immediately at risk of the labor camp. We've accomplished that. Now you've informed me we need to move as soon as possible. Why?"

"The Queen has poison-pearl," Adresia declared. Elettra paled, to her satisfaction. "We have to stop her before she can make poison blades."

The woman regained her composure unsettlingly fast. "And when do you propose we make our move?"

"The night of the Moon Festival." It was Dazelle's most anticipated festivity of the year. The entire Court was invited to celebrate spring's first full moon where they would pray for good fortune in the upcoming season and celebrate the joy that blooms after every winter. "We'll be back at the castle the day before it begins. Narissa won't be expecting an attack. That should give you enough time to gather the rebels and hide throughout the city like we talked about. We'll send a messenger when it's time."

Elettra narrowed her eyes. "Will you be ready then?"

A hesitant pause. "Yes." She had to be.

"This rebellion can't afford to run on false promises."

"*I will be.*"

"Prove it."

Everyone in the room froze. It took everything in Adresia to not look at Cota, to keep her stare locked with the black-haired leader who was watching her like a hawk. "I don't have to prove anything to you," Adresia snarled quietly. "Either believe me or not. We're going through with this plan, and you'll play your part as I'll play mine."

"You know, your friends are a lot easier to work with. *They* remember who's leading them."

"You're not my queen."

"And you're not as important as you think you are."

"Without me, this plan would have *no* hope of succeeding."

Elettra rose, the table groaning under her palms. "This rebellion didn't start the day you decided to join. You've helped things proceed a lot easier than it would've been without you, and your information has been more than beneficial, but don't think for a *second—*" Cups rattled as she slapped the table— "that I'm not using you for what you are: a resource. *That's it.* I could care less about the opinions of an inexperienced Countess who knows nothing about what I've sacrificed."

"I know more about sacrifice than you ever will," Adresia spat. Caspian subtly grabbed her hand under the table, and she suddenly realized how cold her fingers were; how cold everything was.

Somehow, Elettra noticed the movement, her brows rising in the slightest. But she didn't acknowledge it, instead saying as Caspian released his grip, "I'm not going to waste any more time arguing with a child. We'll be in Dazelle by the Moon Festival."

There was more to it—more to why Elettra didn't want Adresia risking herself. They all knew what she had to do and how she was the only one who could do it. But in her angered reaction, Elettra hadn't been able to hide the fear in her brown eyes. For whatever reason, she feared for Adresia.

"Admit it," the Countess said.

Elettra met Adresia's gaze. "Admit what?"

"That you need me."

"I don't."

"Then why are you scared?"

A pause. Then: "You're asking questions to things you don't understand."

"Like what?"

The woman just shook her head.

"*Elettra.*"

Silence.

Adresia slammed her fist on the table so hard everyone flinched. "Stop keeping things from me and tell me the truth!"

"Because you don't need to die like your parents did!" the woman shouted back.

It felt like the air had been sucked from the room.

Elettra's eyes were glassy and wild. "Arrikus and Sadira Bellum were two of the bravest, most active opposers of Narissa's rule. They gave *everything* so this rebellion wouldn't fall into the sullied embrace of this appalling kingdom. And they were my *friends.*"

Adresia felt like her heart was caving in.

"You wonder why I don't want or need anything more from you?" Elettra asked.

"Because they died?"

"No, Adresia. Their deaths were tragic and setback a lot of plans, but Arrikus and Sadira were more than just martyrs."

The Countess didn't want to ask, didn't want to confirm the truth she'd suspected for a long, long time, but the question tumbled out before she could stop it, no more than a shaky huff of air. "What did they do?"

Elettra stood taller, prouder. "We're here because your parents decided to stand and fight. Because they *loved* you. Because they were the sole founders of this rebellion."

Chapter 56

Adresia didn't remember walking back to the manor. She didn't remember responding to her friends' hushed discussion or entering through a side door so they wouldn't be seen. She didn't remember Caspian silently asking her to meet him in his chambers or Cota's comforting squeeze on her shoulder as they parted. She just wandered the corridors, thinking about everything all at once and nothing at all.

Had her father known these people? He'd traveled when she was a babe. She thought it'd been to conclude relations with his home province so they wouldn't come looking or to simply finalize his retirement as a General, but perhaps she'd been wrong all along. Perhaps he'd come for the rebellion.

She wasn't upset. Her parents had kept the truth from her to keep her safe, to protect her. She knew that in her soul. But how many others had her parents requested secrecy from? Elettra had remained silent until Adresia was ready—at least, that's what the Countess had been told before she'd left that evening. And despite the leader's claim, her parents hadn't just started a kingdom-wide revolt for their daughter. No, there was something else. Something they knew. Something they believed in. It'd been important enough that they'd *died* for it.

But what?

Adresia turned a corner. All she saw was a flash of dark hair before she slammed into the Viscount. She muttered, "Gods, not again," the same moment he exclaimed, "Lady Bellum!"

He stepped back with a soft laugh. "I guess running into people is a common tendency of yours?"

It took her a moment to process his question. She felt like she'd been startled back into reality. "It happens more than you think," she replied.

"Where were you headed?"

She wanted to say nowhere, that she just wanted space and to be alone, but...there was a faint smile on his lips and an intriguing curiosity glimmering in those hazel eyes. "To my chambers."

"Care if I walk with you?" He offered his arm, and a memory flashed in her mind: a specific Lord escorting her through the corridors with that same, roguish charm. "What's wrong?" Sterling asked.

"Oh, nothing." She took his arm. "You just reminded me of a friend."

"An intimate friend?"

She smiled despite knowing why he asked. "No. Far from it."

"Where is this friend of yours, Lady Bellum?"

"Somewhere safe, I hope."

They began walking. Intricate rugs and furnishings decorated the corridors and spare rooms. Large windows allowed the last bit of sunlight to warm the floors. It was cozy despite the large space, like generations of Havversfords had worn the walls with their love and laughter.

"Adresia," she suddenly stated. The Viscount looked at her sideways. "You can call me Adresia. I don't like the titles."

"Sterling," he replied.

"I expected you to be in the fields with your father."

A sigh. "I grew up in the fields, so I think making me remain here is just his way of helping me obtain experience in everything. Although, I wasn't expecting province-wide expenditures and mounds of traveling requests." A shrug. "I guess those are just the tedious roles of an Earl."

"It's boring, isn't it?"

A look that told her *boring* didn't cover it.

Her smile fell as male voices suddenly drifted down the hallway ahead, including Brazen's spirited yet slurred words. Sterling must have recognized her panic, because he said, "In here," and pulled her into an empty closet. The door clicked shut just as the group rounded the corner. Adresia tried not to breathe until the men had completely passed, their voices fading with every passing heartbeat. Sterling opened the door, and, after a steadying exhale, she began walking. "Are you okay?" he asked once they were down the hall.

She dragged a hand through her hair. "I have to be."

"Is that what it's like working for the Queen? Hiding from and avoiding people you don't want to be seen by?"

"Sometimes."

"What else do you do?"

She didn't know what to tell him. He was intelligent, but just how much experience did he have? "I'm given various tasks to conclude on Her Majesty's behalf. Sometimes it's dull. Sometimes it's anything but. At this point, I prefer the dull days."

They turned down her hall. "Are you forced to...do things?"

Perhaps he wasn't as callow as she thought. "You'll have to be more specific than that."

"Have you ever killed someone?"

"Not because the Queen told me to."

"Have you ever seduced someone?"

"Not because the Queen told me to."

"Have you ever—"

"These are dangerous questions, Sterling." They arrived at her door. "Why are you asking them?" But as she faced him and heard the rapid pace of his heart, she found her answer. He was protecting his family—from *her*. Out of fear that the Queen had ordered her to interfere in the Havversford's diligent but content life, and that she would obey because she had to, as she had before. "I'm not going to let anything bad happen to your family, Sterling, let alone be the cause of it. That might be why the Queen sent me...but it's not who I am."

His shoulders relaxed, and she almost warned him that she could have just lied and he'd so easily fallen for it, but he said, "I'm sorry if I offended you."

"You didn't." He looked at her the same way he had when they'd first met, and it intrigued her enough that she asked, "What do you see when you look at me?"

That familiar light returned to his eyes. "I'm not sure yet."

"Is that a good thing?"

A soft laugh. "I hope so."

✧

Over the next few days, it became easy for Adresia to feel like the last five months had never happened. No one mentioned Elettra or the meeting again despite the conclusion they'd come to—that when they returned to the castle, it was finally time for the rebellion to make their move—and while Caspian occupied Adresia's mornings and evenings with training, he didn't so much as hint at practicing her magic.

Sterling made an effort to meet her in between helping his father and exercising his many household duties. They bonded over their shared experiences—or rather, her lack of it the past five years—and after her pestering requests to be of some sort of use until she returned to Dazelle, Sterling had relented. She'd helped with nearly every meal by chopping potatoes, stirring stews, and seasoning meat pies. She'd even attempted baking an apple tart, which ended up blackened and tasting suspiciously salty.

She'd also been kept entertained by the children while she'd helped Lady Evette do the laundry, tidy up rooms, maintain the garden and courtyard, and groom the horses in the stables. Sterling eventually asked why she was content with such tedious, repetitive work, and why she had a smile on her face every time they gave out extra food to the passing villagers.

"I like being here," she answered.

"This is where your father lived, isn't it?" he asked.

"He was born here," she answered, diving into another one of the stories she'd had recited as a child. "In the early days of the war, a southern fleet sailed into Niamth Bay. The South wanted to stop Lithelle from providing troops, so they targeted Sheavania as an outpost. My father and his closest friends fought alongside a Lithellian fleet to defend their home, and he found enough purpose in it that he joined the ranks a year later. He was hardly more than a common soldier when he fell in love with a certain General's daughter."

"Your mother."

She grinned. "My father clawed his way to the top just to prove he was worthy enough to marry her—and to help his people in the best way he could. He fought for this place so that the children in this house and the people in this province could have a life. I want to do the same."

Sterling gave her that look he always did. "I hope you will."

Five nights after arriving at the Havversfords, reality set back in. After being conveniently and pleasantly absent, Brazen at last crossed her path, although without any of his irritating companions. He stopped in front of her. "Finally ready to give in?"

She crossed her arms. "Honestly, you took longer than I expected."

"I was busy discussing with the rest of the men how we would take turns with you."

Her stomach twisted. "You're disgusting."

"And you're—"

An excited squeal echoed through the corridor, followed by a blur of lavender and a head of chestnut hair. Adresia didn't see Jenni until she was gripping the Countess's hand. "Sia, I have a surprise!" the girl chirped.

Brazen's suggestive grin was sickening enough that Adresia stepped protectively in front of the girl. "Don't even think about it," she warned.

His expression didn't fade, but he raised his hands in feigned defeat and gave a wide berth. Jenni barely spared him another glance before pulling Adresia down the corridor. The Countess didn't ask where they were going; she was just thankful the girl had arrived when she did. When they at last stopped in front of a wooden door that Adresia hadn't given a second thought about, she asked, "What are we doing, Jenni?"

"We always dance before bed!" the girl said. She pushed open the door with a struggle. Ruslan was playing a piano in the corner with glorious skill. A glittering chandelier hung from the ceiling, under which Elysia was dancing with Baylor in a synchronized waltz. Avery jumped excitedly around them.

Jenni held up a wad of fabric almost as big as herself, and Adresia raised it in front of her. The gown was a beautiful forest green with embroidery that winded around the loose, flowy bottom like vines and flowers.

"It was Mora's," a voice said beside her. Adresia turned. Elysia had an admiring, yet somber twinkle in her eye. "Our sister."

"Where is she?" Adresia asked.

Lifting the skirts of her little gown, Jenni swayed back and forth. "She got sick. Papa said she had to leave so she could be happy again." The girl gazed dreamily across the room. "I pretend I'm dancing with her sometimes. I hope she dances too."

Adresia's throat tightened. She looked back at Elysia, who said, "The dress will fit you better than any of us if you want to wear it."

"Why?"

Elysia smiled. "I saw my mother laugh for the first time in months yesterday when she was with you in the gardens. My father hasn't stopped raving about the new cropland because he's so excited. And Sterling finally found the time to continue reading books with me after breakfast every morning like we used to." They watched Jenni dart toward Baylor's open arms. Instead of running into his embrace, though, she stepped on his toes. They both tumbled to the floor, cackling as Baylor clutched his foot in exaggerated distress. "I finally feel like a family again," Elysia continued, "because of you."

"I was sent here to be a burden," Adresia quietly admitted.

Elysia smiled again, as if she knew something the Countess didn't. "You can't burden a people who've already burdened themselves." Brown eyes flicked to the gown in Adresia's arms. "So dance with us and then tell me how you feel afterwards."

When Adresia opened the door from where she'd changed, Jenni was already there, tugging her into the middle of the space. "Play something fun, Ruslan!" she demanded. With a laugh, her brother obliged. The song was so passionate Adresia swore he would have been content to do this forever. Baylor and Elysia grabbed each other's hands and spun in circles, and with another excited laugh, Jenni, Avery, and Adresia abandoned their shoes by the door and bounded onto the floor with the others.

The five of them didn't stop except to switch partners between songs. Despite their parched throats, the children talked in half-shouts, enthusiastically relaying anything and everything they could to Adresia: their wildest dreams, current friendships—or romantic efforts, in Baylor and Elysia's case—and what they were learning in their lessons. They would occasionally break into fits of laughter when they either ran into each other, tripped over each other's feet because none of them were moving in any particular pattern, or simply looked at each other a certain way.

It had taken five years for Adresia to finally remember what it was like to have a family.

A particularly exciting song was playing when Baylor gave her a nod, signaling they were about to switch partners again. He released her hand as they turned, letting her continue twisting until she reached Avery and Jenni. But Adresia spun into Cota's arms instead, and the undiluted joy that'd been building in her chest burst forth in another unrestrained laugh, even as the hand at her back sent sparks up her spine. "How long have you been here?" she asked.

His mouth was pulled into an unwavering beam. "Not long."

When Ruslan switched to a lovely, slow melody, Adresia couldn't help but think it'd been intentional on his part. Especially as Cota stepped closer. There was such wild, unrelenting emotion in his eyes: admiration and awe and tenderness; so foreign to the way he'd looked the last week. It surprised and scared her so much that she pulled out of his grasp.

His brows furrowed in confusion, but instead of explaining, she simply turned and sped out of the room, catching sight of the children still dancing before the door shut. Adresia shook out her hands, thinking about the floor under her toes, cool and soothing and distracting. Her nerves only swelled when guards sounded distantly down the hall. She darted into a large, open room, moonlight spilling across the furniture. In a shadowed corner, she rested on the arm of one of the sofas, rubbing her chest as if it would somehow alleviate the dissaray of the questions swirling in her head: why hadn't Cota talked to her the past week? What had happened for him to show up tonight looking as unburdened as her?

As if the gods themselves ordained it, Cota tumbled into the room, ducking behind the door. He waited as the mens' voices outside grew louder and then faded before raising his flushed face. That was when he noticed her. He shoved from the door, each step in tune with her beating heart. And when he stopped in front of her, she tried to step around him, but he grabbed her dress. "Wait." His words were barely more than a whisper. "Don't run away. Please." Her responding intake of breath was nothing but shaky. "Talk to me, Res."

She looked at him. "Why aren't you mad?"

"Why would I be mad?"

"Because..." Her throat bobbed. "It's my fault you were beaten."

He released his hold on her dress. "In the Throne Room?"

She nodded.

"Is that why you haven't spoken to me?"

"Yes," she said timidly.

"You can't keep blaming yourself for things that that woman does," he said. "*She's* the one who lies and keeps secrets. *She* did that. Not you."

Her heart thundered in her chest. "I'm scared."

"Of what?" he asked.

"Of losing you."

"Why would you lose me?"

The words stuck in her throat, but as if knowing her answer, he said, "Our plan is going to work." His fingers gently gripped her waist. "And you won't ruin this."

She met his emerald gaze. "Ruin what?"

Something jolted down her spine when he stepped closer and his legs brushed her knees. "Us."

Her breath seemed to have slipped from her lungs. "Is there an us?"

He leaned closer, his scent lacing the air around them. "What do you think we've been doing for months?"

Her fear of the future melted away as he wrapped his fingers around the back of her neck, and when the silent question appeared in his eyes, she nodded.

So he kissed her.

There was nothing better than this, than the feel of his fingers on her skin, than the fire that replaced that frigid pit inside her. Sparks shot through her body so profoundly she wondered if she'd ever been truly alive before this. They parted long enough for his tunic to slip to the floor, and then he pressed his lips back to hers, fully, desperately, as his hands roamed her body through the thin material of her gown, saying everything they'd been too afraid to voice before.

What had she been so afraid of? The threat of the Queen seemed so small in comparison. Adresia's secrets faded into the catacombs of her mind. He wanted her, despite everything that had happened. He wanted her even though she did nothing except put them into danger. He didn't blame her or despise her for pushing him away again and again. There was just this, a fusion of two souls, a choice to love in spite of everything else.

Adresia's sleeve slipped down her shoulder. He kissed her neck, and she dug her nails into his back, pulling him closer, wanting more, *needing* more.

"Now *what* would I do if I were one of our escorts?"

They whirled toward the entrance. Caspian held up a lantern, an unfamiliar distaste glinting in his narrowed eyes. Cota remained pressed to Adresia's side, but save for the heat that now stained her neck and ears and face, the warmth she'd felt moments before was gone.

"Caspian—" Cota started.

"Get dressed and go back to your chambers," Caspian ordered. "*Separate* chambers." After a long look, he stepped back into the hall.

Cota retrieved his tunic before kissing Adresia on the cheek and slipping out the doors. And as Adresia pulled her sleeve back over her shoulder, she suddenly became all too aware of how vulnerable she was in this dress, in this house. Brazen could have so easily done what he'd been wanting to do. Anyone could have walked in, and the parts they'd agreed to play upon their return to Dazelle would have failed. In a single, fleeting moment, so much could have been ruined.

She left the room to find Caspian gazing out the corridor's arched, rectangular window. "I thought you weren't together," he drawled, his head bobbing in the slightest.

She wrapped her arms around herself. "It just...happened."

The light of the lantern on the window ledge flickered against his features. His blue eyes were almost...distraught. "It was reckless, Res."

Her brows lowered. "I don't need a lecture."

"No, but I'm still disappointed."

Her arms fell to her side. "How can you even say that?"

Caspian looked at her sideways. "You *know* why."

"Why would you...?" She stopped. "Are you—" She sniffed. "You're drunk!"

"I'm not *drunk*—"

"You've had enough that I can smell it on you." He went to reply, but toppled forward, and she caught him the same time he found his balance by grabbing her shoulder. "What were you *doing*?"

He drew back enough to peer at her. "Wallowing in my grief from all the times you've denied my affections." She stilled. "Or maybe I just had a *little* too much fun playing cards earlier." A shrug. "Could be anything."

"You don't even know what you're saying."

"I know *exactly* what I'm saying; I've just drank enough to numb the fear of voicing it without feeling sorry for myself."

She clenched her jaw. "So I can't risk my life with him, but you want me to risk it with someone else? With *you*? Do you hear how ridiculous that sounds?"

"Is it? Is the thought of us together buried *so* deep in your mind?" His voice lowered as he stepped closer. "I know you've thought about it."

She receded a step. His grip on her shoulder slipped away. "That's not fair."

"Why not?"

"Because I *need* you in my life, Caspian. But I can't—I *won't*—if you choose to blind yourself by a—a fantasy that will never happen. So *decide*, Caspian: do you want to be my friend, or nothing at all?"

Silence filled the space as his eyes searched hers. For what, she didn't know. But when they dropped to the ground, she knew he'd found his answer. She just hoped he didn't want to lose her as much as she didn't want to lose him.

"I want to be your friend," he whispered.

She calmed her roaring emotions enough to reply, "Good choice. Now go back to *your* chambers." She turned on her heel and strode down the hall, and when she rounded the corner, she halted, trying as best she could to calm her frantic heart.

She wanted Cota. But, despite his drunkenness, what Caspian felt for her, whatever was between them…she couldn't get it out of her head either. Gods, she couldn't be near him without her mind drifting to dangerous places. It drove her insane.

When Adresia at last returned to her chambers, exhausted in every way possible, she tumbled into bed. But she didn't sleep.

Chapter 57

Adresia couldn't stop yawning during breakfast. Caspian had purposefully sat at the head of the table, forcing her beside Sterling instead of her best friend. The Viscount and her conversed as they razed the tray of fruits, pastries, and tarts displayed before them, but whatever Caspian had hoped would come out of it, Cota still placed himself across from Adresia and spent the entirety of the meal exchanging silent glances with her.

"Have you found our home to your liking, Lord Hand?" Lady Evette inquired. Baylor threw a berry at Avery, but Ruslan snatched it mid-air and ate it, sending the rest of the siblings into a fit of laughter.

"Very much," Caspian answered. "The men have had no complaints, and my bed here might be more comfortable than the one back in Dazelle."

Lady Evette smiled. "You're too kind."

The Hand looked at Adresia with knowing eyes. "Didn't you say it was—what was the word? *Memorable?*"

She downed her juice to hide the pink that bloomed in her cheeks.

Lord Havversford raised his brows, a hint of a smile on his lips. "Is that so, Lady Bellum?"

Adresia quickly swallowed. "Oh, yes. I especially love what you've done with the drawing room." Caspian choked on his water. She returned his knowing look. "Isn't that what I told you?"

He kicked her shin. Hard. She sucked in a breath to disguise her grimace. She was debating the best time to throttle him when he took note of the knife she'd squeezed beside her plate and smoothly changed the conversation. Smart move.

When their plates were nothing but crumbs, Adresia at last rose. "Thank you for breakfast," she said, "but unless there's something you require of me, I think I'll—"

"Actually," Sterling interjected, "I was hoping we could walk through the gardens."

And just because Caspian was watching so closely, his brows annoyingly raised in expectation, her lips tugged into a warm smile. "That would be delightful." She caught the Hand's confused, suspicious look as the Viscount led her outside.

After fifteen minutes of small talk about the flowers and foliage that had begun to bloom and all the paperwork Sterling had to do, the Countess grew bored. Her attempt at perplexing Caspian hadn't been thought out nor at all worth it. At least, it *hadn't* been—until they stopped behind a bush that rose far above their heads and Sterling stated, "I didn't come out here to talk to you about plants, Adresia."

Her ears perked. "Then what?"

"You told me you aren't who the Queen wants you to be. Someone who—and correct me if I'm wrong—cares about my family."

"I do." She had a feeling she knew what he was going to say. "Very much."

"Then you know the direness of our situation."

"Yes."

"Help us. Please."

Her heart strained. "Sterling...there's so much you don't understand."

"I understand more than you think."

She eyed him carefully. There was a facet in his posture—a courageous allure and defiant bravery—that she hadn't yet noticed before. Or that he hadn't yet been willing to reveal. "Your father keeps a third of the tax as Earl," she said. "What about that money? I can convince the Queen to accept a portion of your debt now, and—"

He shook his head. "My father doesn't keep that money, Adresia. Haven't you noticed how few decorations we possess? How my younger sisters wear the same three dresses and how we have no servants?"

She'd noticed. "What does he do with it?"

"You could probably guess."

"He gives it away?"

Sterling nodded. "My father refuses to let anyone else struggle while he lives comfortably in this manor. He is with this community from dawn to dusk *everyday*, helping them plant and hunt and fish and survive. He won't leave them to starve, even if it means his family has to face some of those consequences."

"That's why you haven't been able to pay the debt," she said quietly.

"We can't give the Queen what she wants. But you...I can see you want to help."

She grabbed his hand. "I *do*. But there's only so much my position can offer—"

"Then don't do it as Ambassador." He squeezed her fingers. "Do it as my friend."

She could. She knew she could. She'd been fully prepared to disregard Narissa's wishes the moment she'd met the Havversfords; when she'd danced in that room with them and she'd seen the Lord surrender the solace of being an Earl and she'd witnessed Lady Evette give away most of their food to—

Adresia froze.

People were being given meals and clothes. People who, somehow, were *all* in poverty, without food and money. And she'd gone into town; she'd noted the full inns as they'd walked by, people piling out the doors because there were no vacancies left, because they had no home to live in.

Sheavania isn't as small as it was five years ago.

I wasn't expecting province-wide expenditures and mounds of traveling requests.

You can't burden a people who've already burdened themselves.

The Havversfords had been hinting at it for a week, subtly conveying and disguising their loyalty this whole time.

They were supplying rebels.

Adresia's stunned silence must've been telling enough, because when she met Sterling's keen gaze, he stated, "I won't apologize for doing what's right."

A soft, unexpected laugh fluttered past her lips.

"Why are you laughing?" he asked warily.

"Thank the *Goddess*," she exclaimed.

He straightened. "You aren't going to report us?"

"Not when I have every reason to be beheaded too."

His mouth opened and closed in an effort to state his astonishment. "You're—I mean, I'd hoped in my wildest dreams—but...how?"

"My parents *started* the rebellion, Sterling." His hazel eyes went round, and she added, "I'm going to finish it."

He blew out a long breath. "That sounds big."

"It is."

"When?"

"Soon."

Seeming to get past his shock, he sheepishly rubbed his neck. "We couldn't tell you outright."

Her lips lifted at the corners. "Believe me, I understand."

"I believed in you from the moment you arrived."

As always, the words brought with it a confusion both unexpected and predicted; encouraging yet burdening. She hid it with a smile and said, "I'm sorry for what you've had to give up."

"I'm not. If I hadn't, I wouldn't have met you."

"You're very kind."

"And you're very beautiful."

Her blush wasn't entirely feigned, but when he leaned forward, she stopped him with a hand to his chest. "Sterling..."

He pulled back. "Did I do something wrong?"

"No."

"Then why did you stop me?"

Her smile was barely more than a wince. "I'm...already vouched for."

He glanced toward the manor, then her. "By Lord Bowyer."

"Yes."

"I've seen the way you two look at each other, but I thought..." He chuckled. "It was worth a try."

She looped her arm through his. "It's always worth a try."

When they entered the manor gain, they parted with relieved, knowing smiles. She approached Cota, who was leaning against the wall outside the dining room. "How did it go?" he asked.

"Careful, Lord Bowyer," she drawled, "or you might lose me to the Viscount."

His brows rose. "So he *did* try to kiss you."

"How did you know he was going to kiss me?"

He pushed from the wall. "Who could resist?"

Her laugh skittered down the corridor, but she noticed Caspian out of the corner of her eye and her smile fell. When he stopped before them, she sketched a dramatic bow. "What is it you require, milord?"

His brows twitched together with the faintest amusement, but he merely stated, "Time to train."

Hundreds of unbloomed flowers littered the forest floor and birdsong echoed through bare trees as Adresia and Caspian trekked through the woods by the manor. It was a balmy enough day that she abandoned her cloak by the time they stopped in the clearing they'd used the past week.

Adresia blamed Caspian for her unrelenting exhaustion. If he'd simply minded his own business last night, she might have gotten a *few* hours of sleep. But he hadn't, and here she was, unrested and irritated. The fact that he wanted to train knowing full well her opinion of him this morning was not in his favor...she glared at him at he rolled up his sleeves. Maybe she'd turn him into ice. It'd solve a few problems of hers. Sort of. "Gods, it's early," she groaned.

The Hand rubbed his temples. "Don't remind me."

"Rough night?"

He frowned and unsheathed two short swords. "Something like that." He tossed her one. "I think both of us need this."

"Definitely," she agreed with a yawn.

They started with a warm up, tapping blades and circling each other. When her arms and shoulders felt loose enough, she pulled a hand behind her back. Caspian did the same, and when his brows rose, a silent request to begin, she didn't reply before reacting. A challenge glinted in those sapphire eyes as he blocked the blow, and when she pressed on, he was ready. It was a simple strength exercise; a drill she'd easily executed a few weeks ago. But when she switched her sword to her opposite hand and *swung*, her blade flew from her grasp. The tip of his sword was instantly at her throat.

"Tired?" he sniped.

Oh, he *definitely* remembered last night.

"Something like that," she retorted, shaking out her aching hand before retrieving her weapon. When she approached him again, she proposed, "How about a duel? No drills. Just you—" She dipped her sword— "Against me."

"Sounds easy enough," he said.

Flipping her sword around her hand, she planted her feet in the soil and bent her knees. Then, as quick as a rabbit, he struck. She lost herself in the flow of the duel, gritting her teeth as the clang of their weapons reverberated through her arm. She swung; he parried. She whirled; he dodged. A waltz; that's all this was. Iron sharpening iron.

When he raised his blade just a moment too late, she threw all of her might into her swing. The tip of his sword drove into the ground. She clenched her jaw as she pushed against his strength, keeping him down. He grabbed the handle with both hands, trying to pull up. "Why don't you try harder?" he asked, breathing hard. But their eyes locked—and that was all it took.

Her strength faltered long enough for him to yank his weapon free and fling her sword up. She regripped her handle, but he was already swinging. She jumped over his blade, still gaping at him when he rocketed toward her again. But he was moving too fast and she had a stable stance, so when he swiped, it took one step for her to get behind him. She shoved him from behind and he went crashing into the soil. With an exasperated exhale, he stood. They began circling each other again. She hummed a laugh, taking a step forward—

"Wait." He held out a hand. Sweat lined his neck. "I'm sorry about last night. I drank too much, and when I found you two..."

"You were jealous," she said quietly.

He met her gaze almost hesitantly. "Yes."

"You can't control my decisions or feelings, Caspian." He opened his mouth. "*Just* like I can't control yours." His mouth slammed shut. "And you were right." She almost bit back the words, but if she didn't say them now, she might never. "I *do* feel something for you. But I can't. I *can't*—do you understand? I choose *him*. I won't ruin what little happiness I've found after feeling like I would never get it again."

There was a long pause. And then he said softly, "You deserve to be happy, Res...with whoever you want."

She didn't feel like smiling, but did anyway. "Thank you."

He exhaled loudly. "Well, as fun as this was, I didn't bring you out here so you can beat me to a pulp with your sword skills."

She raised a brow. "Then why?"

He grabbed both of their swords and chucked them aside. "To test your powers."

Her smile fell. "Are you serious?"

"You told Elettra you were ready."

Heat rushed up her neck, but she stated, "She needs to believe we're ready."

He stopped in front of her. "Do you?"

She huffed a sigh and asked warily, "What do you want me to do?"

"Something small." He grabbed her hand, and despite the conversation they'd just had, something bloomed in her stomach at his touch. "Try controlling the flow of your power." He tapped her palm. "Here." Her fingertips. "Here."

She knew he was aware of how bad this could go. She'd controlled it before, but it hadn't been...*this*. If she couldn't, if it overwhelmed her before she could stop...

He kept his grip firm when she tried to pull away. "Don't be afraid."

Don't be afraid. Those were the first words he'd uttered when her powers had appeared. And she'd clung to that statement, to the look he'd had: *his* lack of fear; his confidence. The same look he had now.

"*You* are in control," he said. She didn't resist as he placed her hand on his forearm. "Just breathe."

She closed her eyes. Inhale. Exhale. She could do this. She *had* to do this.

"It will try to escape without you noticing," she heard him say. "It will try to evade your inexperienced, untrained efforts to keep it locked down. That's what this is: learning how to contain and manipulate it—the first step toward mastering your magic."

It's what she'd been doing for weeks. Poorly attempting—and failing—to summon her power. To control it, master it. Could she actually do it? Could she be as powerful as she made herself out to be to the rebels?

She concentrated harder, and for several minutes, there was nothing, the same as always. Just stale, mundane nothing.

Until there wasn't.

Her magic grew so suddenly, so fast that she sucked in a breath, and her grip on his arm tightened involuntarily.

"*Breathe*, Res." Distantly, somewhere far from her body, she felt his fingers lace through her free hand. "I trust you."

She exhaled shakily and relaxed her fingers. She was in control—not her fear. She had to be ready.

Her power became a steady flow, and she focused on it, grounded herself to it. When it tried to burst forth, desperately wanting *out*, she locked her defenses in place. Like a second skin, her magic raged inside, rebounding off her invisible shields, thrashing and roaring. And then...it stopped. It snarled at the walls she'd built, but curled inside her. Waiting. Submitting.

Slowly, she summoned a thread of it from the depths of her being. When cold flooded her palm, she reeled it back, forcing herself to remain calm. Her walls were ready to shut at her command. *She was the master of this power.*

She took a deep breath as a single strand leaked from each of her fingers and onto Caspian's skin. His intake of breath told her he felt it too. The chill increased, but her power remained constant. She could stop it at any point if she wanted. Minutes passed before Caspian's breathing changed—quickened.

Her eyes flew open when he staggered back with an alarming cry. "Did I hurt you?" she asked.

For a moment, he just gripped his arm in shock. And then his eyes lit up and he grabbed her face with a rich laugh. "You did it! You actually did it!"

She laughed too. "Thanks to you." She didn't realize how close they were until his gaze lowered to her mouth.

They both stepped back, and she rubbed her flushed neck as he sat on the grass beside their swords. "We can do this," he said softly, as if knowing the nerves that hadn't left her since the meeting with Elettra. "You can."

"I know."

He looked at her. "We're going to win."

She met his gaze and smiled. "Yes, we are."

At midday, Adresia stood before the Havversfords at the bottom steps of their glorious manor. Behind her, Cota and Caspian had their horses saddled and ready to leave. Fox had somehow convinced the rest of the guards to join him by the gates—far out of earshot.

"We should get started," Adresia announced at last. Her voice echoed off the stone steps, loud and oddly intimidating.

"We have no money," Lord Havversford stated. Beside him, Lady Evette's hazel eyes were lined with silver.

"I know." The Countess took a deep breath. "But your debt won't be an issue for much longer."

Confusion and trepidation crossed the Lord's face. "Why not?"

Sterling watched her with a fixed stare. Adresia knew exactly why he was so still; why his breath was quick and heart was racing. It was why she locked eyes with him as she stated, "Because the Queen will be removed before she can make you suffer further."

Their eyes widened, and the Countess couldn't decipher the reaction—couldn't tell if they believed her or not; couldn't tell if she'd said the right thing or if they even knew what she was talking about.

Sterling stepped forward. "She's telling the truth."

"Sterling?" Lady Evette started.

"We already spoke. She knows that we're helping the rebels. If she wanted to turn us in, she would've. She cares about this family—and I believe her."

The Lord looked at Adresia. "You're serious."

She nodded. Sterling's eyes were bright as he waited for his father's response. Several beats of tense, unsure silence passed. And then the Lord's gaze softened. "We were wondering if Arrikus's daughter had followed in his footsteps."

Cota's surprised, relieved laugh matched the feeling in Adresia's chest. "You knew my father?" she breathed.

"There isn't a soul in Sheavania who doesn't know his name." The Lord descended the steps. "And there won't be a soul who forgets yours."

Adresia didn't think she was breathing. "I—I haven't done anything."

"Names have power. They can do monumental things when backed with truth. And Bellum? That is a name that will continue to change this kingdom for the better."

Lady Evette gripped Adresia's hand. "We've waited years for this rebellion to stand a chance—a *real* chance. If you can do what you say, if you can finally take the Queen off the throne...perhaps then our children will finally have the future they deserve."

Adresia nodded and blinked away the burning in her eyes.

The Lord said, "The day your father came to our doorstep and told us what he and Sadira were doing..." He shook his head as if still in disbelief. "We have never given up the hope he gave us five years ago. We've never forgotten what he did for us, for everyone in this kingdom. If you ever need help, you have a safe place here."

"And if you ever need a handsome, single, suitor," Sterling added, stepping around his father, "you know where to find me."

Adresia grinned. "Next time I visit, Sterling, be sure to have married a nice, lovely girl who is just as intrigued by your enthralling gaze as I was."

The Viscount just winked. Adresia gripped the reins of her horse and bowed her head at them, the family who had reminded her what it meant to fight for the people you loved. Before she could leave, however, the rest of the children bounded down the steps. Their squeals and laughs and words intermixed as they embraced her. "Thank you for being our sister," Jenni said softly.

The Countess crouched before the girl and squeezed her tiny hands. "Thank you for being *my* sister, Jenni." Elysia and Baylor pulled their sister away before she could hug the Countess a second time, gratitude shining in their warm, brown eyes.

She could stop the Queen. She could save this kingdom. She *would*. For her parents. For Kovare. For the Havversfords and everyone else who deserved more than the scraps they'd been given. They were returning to Dazelle where the rebellion would make its stand, and no matter what happened, she would not back down.

She would be the bane of Narissa's existence.

Chapter 58

Spring was in full bloom by the time they returned. Tulips and daffodils blanketed the castle grounds; trees hung with cherries and plums and pomegrantes. The halls were bustling with lively servants, bundles of flowers and fresh breads and sweet desserts piled in their baskets. It was all for tonight—for the Moon Festival.

The end of their Queen's reign.

Despite the dozens of accounts of the festival Cota had received beforehand, when he entered the Inner Gardens that evening, it was beyond anything he'd ever imagined. The area had been completely cleared of its hedges. The gravel path lining the grassy square was strewn with endless tables of food: venison and roast, apricots and pears, raspberry tarts and gooseberry pie. Smiling servants wove through bustling crowds, offering goblets of varying wines, the most expensive of ales, and a bubbly clear drink he'd never seen before. Banners and yarns were twisted around pillars, fabrics were ribboned across the courtyard from balcony to balcony, and flames flickered in hanging lanterns like tiny, glowing insects. Nobles lounged upon low, cushioned sofas in open tents, a gentle spring breeze fluttering the pinned curtains.

Cota's attention drifted from the extensive decorations to the balefire in the center of the green expanse that sputtered sparks into the darkening sky. He stepped to the edge of the grass. Along with the musicians, countless others danced around the golden flames. They twirled and jumped and darted around with locked hands as if lost in the inviting, orchestral melody. Gray-blue eyes and a beaming smile swept by him before being swallowed back into the group.

Cota scanned every passing person before he found Adresia again, looping around the opposite side of the fire. It was her dress, white as snow and snaking along her skin like the flames before her, that he kept track of as she sashayed across the lawn with a laugh, shoes discarded somewhere. Caspian stepped to Cota's side, sipping from one of those glasses of clear liquid. "She's having fun."

"She always does," Cota agreed.

"You haven't talked to her yet. Today, nor since we've been back."

Cota couldn't tell if it was a question or observation. "It hasn't been of demanding significance." It wasn't a lie. He and Adresia had agreed to remain distant. At Sheavania, they'd been lucky. But here, they couldn't see each other. Not until things were different. Better.

"Because of our little...problem."

"Not little," Cota said, "but yes." His gaze shifted past the enormous fire, to the *problem* that had kept him on his toes all night.

Corvina and Narissa sat at a large, oak table, cleverly positioned at the head of the garden so the Queen could keep an eye on the entire festival, he guessed. It was precisely why, in the hours since he'd arrived, he hadn't sought out Adresia; hadn't dared to look at her, until now. Just in case they were being watched.

"Not one for a drink, Lord Bowyer?"

Cota took a deep, uneven breath before meeting that familiar, ice-blue gaze. "I suggest you find somewhere else to be, Brazen." Adresia had relayed what the knight had almost done in Sheavania. The thought was enough to make the Count's fingers curl. But he couldn't satisfy that familiar rage that crept up his spine. He had to play his part. He had to wait.

Brazen held up a finger with an irking smile. "It's Sir Voss, now. *I* suggest you address me as such."

"My rank is higher than yours."

Brazen cocked his head. "Is it, though?"

Caspian quipped, "Find somewhere else to be, Voss." Cota had almost forgotten he was there.

Brazen glared at the Hand. "Where's darling Adresia?" A fake gasp. "Surely she isn't injured again? She *does* have a tendency to get herself into unfortunate situations."

"She's fine." Cota's jaw was so tight a cramp began to form. Play the part. He couldn't ruin the plan before it began.

The knight jutted out a lip. "Pity."

Cota took an involuntary step forward before a hand clamped onto his shoulder. "I said leave," Caspian told the knight. "*Now.*"

Brazen just rolled his eyes before sauntering away.

With a heavy exhale, Cota unfurled his fingers. "Sorry. Sometimes my anger gets the best of me."

"It happens to all of us," Caspian replied.

Cota didn't think so. This fearful anger and impatient discomfort...it wasn't normal. Cota tried refocusing on the fire before him, but images flashed in his mind: a blood-soaked stream; a decimated village; four bodies in that cramped kitchen; the screaming and weeping of all the memories that perpetually stained his past.

It was different this time. He couldn't stifle the heaviness he'd spent weeks struggling to stifle and ignore. It crushed his chest. He felt as if he was being pushed underwater and brought up again just when he could no longer hold on, over and over, a never-ending torture. Had Adresia felt this way? Had her father? He didn't regret what he'd done, but this...this wasn't what he'd anticipated. It wasn't what he wanted.

And he didn't know how to stop it.

A servant walked by offering a platter of drinks, and blue eyes met Cota's half a moment before the servant pushed between the men and pressed a slip of paper into Cota's hand. It was in his pocket by the time the servant was fully past.

He and Caspian casually turned from the balefire and strode to the gravel path, plucking various appetizers from the tables before strolling toward the southern wing. They halted by an iron fire stand, and Caspian nonchalantly glanced around before nodding at Cota. In one movement, the Count read the note and then tossed the note in the blazing fire. He began whistling in tune with the music as they strode back toward the balefire.

But then the hair on his arms rose. He stopped, instinctively sweeping his gaze across the courtyard, scanning for any obvious threats, for a hint of whatever was off. Caspian's voice pierced his vigilant concentration. "What is it?"

"The guards," Cota said.

"What about them?"

"There aren't any here."

"What?"

"There isn't a *single* guard save the ones at the Queen's table."

A pause, then a curse.

Cota met Caspian's bewildered stare with one of his own. "Something's wrong." And he took a step forward, but the world *lurched* as something exploded behind them.

It was the same as before.

Cota was on his back, a shrill ringing piercing his ears. The bright, round moon had at last crested over the castle. It felt like he'd been staring at it for hours. But, there—in the corner of his eye. Movement.

A flaming banner floated slowly to the ground.

And as that head-throbbing ringing finally ceased, it was replaced by something so much worse Cota had to clench his eyes for a moment to bear it.

Screaming.

The ground swayed beneath him as he strained to his feet and coughed, inhaling dust and smoke. This wasn't a part of the plan. This wasn't the rebels. It couldn't be.

As he beheld what had happened, horror washed over him like a bucket of freezing water. The lower level of the southern wing had been blown apart. Hanging fabrics were torn and burning; shattered lanterns and chipped stone littered the gravel. Dazed, injured nobles stumbled around. Others knelt before the debris, shouting and weeping for people that could no longer hear them. Caspian was already at the collapsed wall, attempting to move the boulders himself. Cota approached him and started, "Caspian—"

The Hand faced him with wild eyes. Blood slid down his temple. "*Help me.*"

He gripped the Hand's shoulder. "It's no use." Just the two of them couldn't move the massive remnants of the wall. And even if there *were* people under there...they hadn't survived.

Realizing Cota was right, Caspian loosed a distraught exhale. He took half a step away from the wall when Cota's senses shot awake again.

The screaming had stopped.

There was nothing beyond the crackle of the flames. Just an awful, unsettling silence. Cota peered at the faces around him, trying to figure out what had happened, why everyone had grown inexplicably quiet. Their attentions were fixated on something else, something behind him. He whirled toward the center of the courtyard.

A man was holding Adresia in the air, his hands wrapped around her neck.

Chapter 59

Adresia had never hated anyone more in her entire life. And the man clutching her throat—with those familiar tattoos webbed over his arms and chest and neck—knew precisely that. He knew what she remembered.

He remembered too.

Dark hair fell over sandy brown eyes as Romliss tilted his head. "It looks like Arrikus's little girl isn't so little anymore."

"*Murdering...bastard*," she gasped out.

"You haven't changed all that much, then, if you speak with that same untamed tongue. It'll get you killed one of these days."

She tried to take a breath, but the corners of her vision darkened. He was so much stronger than she remembered. She grabbed his wrists, pulling her magic up, wrapping herself around it as it awakened inside of her.

But it didn't come out.

Her shock barely registered before she was thrown to the ground. A pained cry rang out when her head slammed against the soil, and as she gasped down that sweet, night air, Romliss grabbed the back of her neck and pulled her against him. A blade was at her throat as they turned, and when she beheld Caspian and Cota—alive, with blood and dust crusting their faces—she could have sobbed in relief.

Until she saw the men.

Scattered around the courtyard were monstrous soldiers clad in leathers as black as a starless night. Lethal longswords were strapped down their backs and numerous other weapons littered the belts at their waists. Where was Elettra? What had gone wrong?

"You'll do well to listen!" Romliss bellowed. "My men and I have infiltrated the castle, relieved the royal guards of their duties, and will now proceed to take control of this Court. Unless you want to make our job that much easier by foolishly risking your lives in an attempt to flee, I suggest you follow my men into the Throne Room."

Adresia saw Cota step forward, but Caspian grabbed him half a second before Romliss spun her around and marched across the courtyard. They halted before the Queen, and she hissed as his blade pricked her neck. The only guards remaining were the four flanking the royals, valiantly raising their swords. There was a mocking smile in Romliss's voice as he spoke. "What courageous sentinels, protecting your dear Queen. How does it feel to have failed your sole duty?"

Confusion flickered across their faces half a second before two arrows landed in their chests. Corvina let out a startled gasp as they tumbled to the ground. Narissa hadn't even flinched. Why wasn't she using her magic?

"You will obey," Romliss told the Queen, "or they will not be the only additions to this graveyard."

The woman just stared at him.

Narissa wouldn't risk everyone's lives like this. She wouldn't sacrifice her Court to this monster. "Do something," Adresia said, shoving against Romliss's grip. Elettra would be here any minute. Whatever this was...they just had to wait. Narissa was one of the most powerful beings on the continent. This ridiculous effort to scare her was useless. "Give him what he wants."

"I would listen to your Ambassador," Romliss said. Then, after a thoughtful pause, he added, "Unless you want her to be the first to join the dead?"

The Countess had never believed in the Queen; had never trusted her. This world wasn't fair, and it didn't make sense, and selflessness was a trait only very few actually possessed. But when Romliss made a move to slice Adresia's throat and the Queen bristled in the slightest, a haunting, enslaving terror Adresia hadn't felt in five years bloomed in her chest. No. *No.*

Romliss paused, realizing the same thing she had. "Is that it, Your Majesty?" There was a smile in his voice. "Is Adresia's poor, miserable life worth more than your Court's?"

Narissa looked at the Countess. And as that brutal, unwavering dominance faltered in the slightest, Adresia half-begged, half-growled, *"Save them."*

But Narissa didn't listen. For whatever selfish reason, she wanted Adresia alive. And although she saw it coming, although it was entirely expected...Adresia still froze in horrified devastation as the Queen of Morolyn lowered her chin in submission.

✧

Adresia slammed onto her knees before the dais, clenching her teeth to bite back the pain. A dagger still threatened to slice her neck, but now by one of Romliss's belligerent companions. The weapons strapped onto him dug into her back. When she tried to pull away, he growled in her ear, "Move, girl, and you're dead."

These men were remorseless and unhesitant, trained to kill without so much as blinking. She saw it in the way they hovered around the surviving nobles, also forced onto their knees before the thrones. She saw it in the look on the soldier's faces: loathing and malice and a terrifying hunger. Eager to see the lives of these innocent people ended.

Everything had been planned out. Every line and crevice, every detail and step. Nothing should have gone wrong. The rebels were in the city. They should have seen any unwanted foes entering the castle. Why hadn't they stopped these men? Why weren't they here?

Caspian and Cota had been forced a ways down from the the Princess and Queen in the front row. Amongst the group, Fox was holding Kasya tightly to his side. Adresia looked at Narissa, who stared emptily at the floor. Why wasn't she *doing* anything?

Heavy footsteps penetrated the petrified silence. Romliss crossed the room and crouched in front of Narissa. "The Mighty Queen of Morolyn—on her knees for the first time in her life." The words sparked a memory Adresia reviled so much it became hard to breathe. "What do you think gives you your power? Is it your crown? Your title as Queen? Your infantry that is *nowhere* to be seen? So much for loyalty, huh?"

Narissa didn't look at him; didn't show any indication she'd heard him at all.

"He said you were stronger than the others," Romliss went on. "That you'd fight more. I guess He was wrong." He rose from the Queen.

It was then, as the word rebounded off the walls, that Adresia remembered what Romliss had said all those years ago: *We're here under the orders of Morolyn's sovereign ruler, Arrikus.*

This entire time, with every chaotic incident and unexplainable horror, Narissa had never been entirely honest. She'd never once admitted to doing what she'd been accused of—because maybe it wasn't Narissa. Maybe it was someone else entirely committing these devious acts under the crown's name.

Romliss walked by. "Why are you doing this?" Adresia asked.

He stopped, cocking his head with that infuriating arrogance. "I worked for your Queen once, although never *officially* under her command. I don't make those kinds of commitments to anyone else." So there *was* another. "We did her bidding, as you well know....but we never got our payment. A hefty price; the largest sum I've ever been offered to this day."

"You're doing this over *money*?"

Romliss approached her so quickly she made to scramble back. Instead, she tripped over her dress as the man behind her kept her from receding. Romliss snarled, "I lost fifteen men because *she*—" A finger pointed at Narissa— "wanted it done that night. Back then, my position didn't offer the privilege to ask questions or suggest a later date to prepare. You think I'm evil, but you have *no idea* how I got here. My life doesn't revolve around the comfortability and survival of anyone besides my own. I don't have that choice."

"We all have a choice," Adresia bit. "And if this is the life you chose, then you're a *coward*."

She didn't realize he'd struck her until the stars in her vision subsided, followed by a searing pain in her left cheek. His angered voice rang through the room. "Either your Queen delivers what she owes me or the dead will start to outnumber the living!"

All Narissa gave him was a glare, a spiteful look.

Panicked shouts and pleas erupted as Romliss surged into the crowd and grabbed someone. Absolute horror swept up Adresia's spine. "No," she started, "don't—"

"*Shut your mouth*," he hissed. A vicious sharpness stung Adresia's neck, but she didn't care. Not as Romliss pulled Gillian in front of the Queen, squeezing the back of the servant's neck. "Give me what I want or she dies."

Gillian was crying. Strands of the scarlet curls she had so thoughtfully woven into a beautiful plait had come loose, framing her face like a wildfire.

Adresia furiously pleaded with her magic, willing it to surface as her friend frantically begged for her life, as Kasya clutched Fox with wide eyes, as tears silently slipped down Corvina's cheeks.

But her magic wasn't working. *It wasn't working*.

"Just give it to him!" Adresia shouted in desperation.

Narissa raised her head, and everyone stilled, hanging onto every heartbeat, any sign of an answer. A grin crept onto Romliss's face as he waited.

But when the Queen spoke, her very being was void of emotion. "I will give you nothing."

Adresia didn't have time to blink before a violent crack sounded and Gillian's body hit the floor.

Kasya's wail echoed against the walls. The soldier holding Adresia gave a brutal squeeze as she slumped against him, crying. The nobles, weeping and pleading, scrambled from the soldiers pressing in on them like they could escape their fate. *Where was Elettra?*

Adresia widened her tear-stained eyes as she met Cota's gaze. He wanted to help her. Like an *idiot*, he was going to try to get to her. She silently pleaded with him, subtly shaking her head, but he lunged forward.

A shortsword was angled at his throat half a second later. "I was waiting for the first foolish attempt to be brave," Romliss said. "That makes you the next to die." Cota looked back at Adresia the same time Romliss swung.

"*NO!*" she screamed.

The blade halted an inch from Cota's heart.

Adresia let out a strangled sob and pushed against the soldiers unearthly strength to get to her feet. She barely had time to swallow her anguish before Romliss was in her face. "Is there something you want to say?" he asked. "Something you want to *do?*" She couldn't stop the tears that streamed down her cheeks. The man pulled back and observed her and Cota. His expression twisted from anger into confusion and then sick delight. "The Count's son." He gestured between them with his blade. "The one who helped you that night." Adresia held her breath, waiting for his response. "Maybe he'll prove useful." With a jerk of his chin, two men grabbed Cota, monstrously large compared to her best friend. Adresia exhaled, but the relief didn't come. Not as Romliss looked her up and down, his gaze snagging on all the wrong places. "I remember that night. I remember your skills. I wonder if they've matured as much as you?" Out of the corner of her eye, Adresia saw Caspian lean forward as if he would do something as idiotic as run for her. "Your Queen won't save her people," Romliss continued, "but would you?" Not expecting a response, he turned away.

Her answer echoed through the chamber. "*Yes*."

Romliss faced her with a devious smile.

"What do you want?" she asked.

"I know you've been wracking through the possibilities in that pretty, little head of yours," he said. "There's only one way out of this."

One way—because Elettra wasn't coming. Because Adresia was on her own, as usual. Because this was how her life had been since the day she'd been born, since her parents had started a rebellion and thrust her into a future she would have to fight to obtain: running from death only to find that she had been running toward it all along.

Romliss opened his arms wide. "Kill all of my men and you go free. But fail...and no one leaves this room alive."

She saw Caspian's eyes widen. Heard Cota breathe, "You're insane."

The corner of Romliss's mouth tugged up. "Am I?"

No. He wasn't. Because he knew what she was capable of. He *wanted* this—wanted her to fight him. She just wished her glare was enough to end him. But it wasn't. So she wiped the tears from her face and declared, "You'll die last."

"Is that agreement?"

She refused to look anywhere else but him. "Yes."

The soldier holding her released his grip, and she sucked in a breath to prepare, but was instantly shoved forward. Romliss sidestepped as she tripped over the folds of her dress and crashed before the nobles. No embarrassment came as she raised her head and met the wide-eyed gazes watching her. There was no humiliation in a fight to the death.

Adresia spun. Soldiers approached from all sides, blades singing as they were drawn. Whoever she decided to fight, another would attack from somewhere else. *And* she was weaponless. *And* in a dress. A rebel intrusion would sure be convenient right about now. She glanced at the doors wishfully, but they remained closed. No one was coming to help her.

And yet, she rose.

The first soldier swung. She ducked under the blade, but there was already another, and she only had a moment to process its meaning as she hastily twisted out of reach: these men weren't like the ones five years ago. These men were dangerous. *Unearthly* dangerous.

Another sword was already whistling through the air. She barely dodged it, her body straining at the too-quick movement, and turned, evading a stab to her ribs the same time she pulled her arm from a ruthless strike that nearly took off her fingers. The soldiers pressed in, one after another, and she swiped and blocked faster than she ever had before.

She kicked back another's advance, trying to think past her defense to somehow attack and get past their thick, black armor, but there was a swipe too fast to register. The thin slash on her forearm flared with agonizing pain, and her stomach plummeted. There was nothing she could do as the infirma mixed with her blood, instantly slowing her movements and staunching her healing process. They knew who she was—*what* she was.

And there were so many.

One man tackled her. She growled in pained frustration as they hit the ground, rolling and flipping and scratching before they were on their feet again. She grabbed his face, one of the only exposed parts of his body, and dug her nails in so hard that they drew blood. He growled in pain, but didn't retaliate—not as the white's of his eyes disappeared and he said in a voice that sounded anything but human, "*You cannot defeat us.*"

She released him and stumbled away in horror.

The soldier backed into line with the circle of men around her and grinned. "*We are your destruction.*"

Holy gods.

She wasn't fighting men.

She was fighting monsters.

Someone shouted for her, and she couldn't tell who it was before a fist to her jaw rocketed her head to the side. She stumbled into another soldier-demon who grabbed the back of her dress and pushed so hard she slammed face-first into the marble floor, teeth singing. Blood dripped from her lip. She spat before rolling, dodging the blade that stabbed where her head had just been half a second before. Her responding groan was a trembling, fearful noise. She rose again, limbs heavy and sluggish.

She raised her arm to block another attack, but pain shot through it so suddenly that she couldn't block the punch to her gut, and as her breath swept from her lungs, a dreadful thought seeped into her mind.

Maybe she wasn't strong enough.

A fist slammed into her shoulder, then again, in her back, and a cry broke from her lips.

She couldn't save this Court; she couldn't even save herself. Why had she ever thought so before? One person couldn't bear the weight for everyone else and come out unscathed.

There was another ambush from behind, sweeping her legs out from under her. Her limbs barked in agony as she slammed into the pristine marble.

Romliss was right: she was nobody; nothing.

She crawled away, her breath ragged in her throat. "Behind you!" someone shouted—Caspian. It wasn't soon enough. One of those creatures grabbed her leg and wrenched her back. Her fingers squeaked against the floor as she desperately fought for some sort of resisting hold that was nowhere to be found, but then the grip on her leg disappeared. She grabbed a dropped blade beside her and twisted the same moment a soldier bounded atop her. She plunged the dagger up and into the armor, but there was a strange scraping noise.

She pulled the blade back—the *bent* blade—in horror. Because the armor where she'd stabbed was undamaged, the metal intact and unaltered. Save for the faintest scratch, it wasn't even dented.

Whatever it was made of, the armor was impenetrable.

Understanding her horrified realization, the creature grinned and joined the others stalking around her. They eyed her like prey, taunting her before they ended it. She scrambled to her feet, even as her mind began a free fall into itself, into fear and dread. She raised her hands and whispered, "No." The word was a plea and protest.

A kick to her chest sent her slamming into the ground so forcefully her back arched. She tried to suck in a breath, but another strike to her side made her clench her core in pain. And then the men picked her up and shoved her into each other, kicking and punching and slicing, cackling and basking in her despair.

She clenched her eyes shut. She wouldn't look at the faces that she had failed, at the Court she hadn't saved. They would soon know the fear that had plagued her in her last moments. They would all die as she would, without answers, without hope.

She didn't want this. She didn't want pain. She didn't want her friends watching her die. But she had nothing left. She was broken and worthless and powerless, and no one was coming to save them.

Time slowed as a voice sounded in the back of her mind, warm and deep and comforting.

Do not fear, my daughter.

Adresia began weeping as she heard her father for the first time in five years.

There is a time for your rest, but it is not now. Not yet.

How? How could she continue when she was already in the hands of Death, already at the jaws of the lions prowling before her, ready to end her once and for all?

You are watched over. Loved. Heard. It may not feel like it, but you have someone fighting for you, with you. You have never been alone.

"I'm sorry," she cried aloud. There was a pause, a break in the beating, as if she'd confused the demons with her words. She was so used to saying the phrase; it'd become another truth she'd spoken over herself for years. But this time...it was different. She didn't have the strength to hide the guilt and shame. She couldn't bear the heartache on her own.

My love overshadows your mistakes, as it always has. It is enough.

Her father's words were so comforting, so peaceful compared to the afflictions that destroyed her with every passing second. "Don't leave me," she begged. She could feel her father's responding smile, illuminating her soul like a lamp in the darkness until she felt the promise in her bones: he had never left her; he never would. And she knew his next words were his last as he answered the final question she didn't have the energy to voice.

Keep fighting, Adresia.

This wasn't the end. She'd been made into a fighter before she'd ever discovered she was a mage. She'd been given everything she needed all those years ago, when two warriors had gifted a young girl the chance to change and protect and save the world. She didn't need Elettra. She didn't need a rebellion. *This wasn't the end.*

And it was as if the thought, the belief, was the key as that thing that she'd held back her entire life exploded.

Time resumed its pace as she was shoved forward. It was like her lungs had opened so she could breathe deeper, her vision had sharpened so she could see clearer, her body had adjusted with the air around her to move quicker, fluider. Using the momentum to her advantage, she gritted her teeth and *swung*, and when the creature in front of her toppled backward with a loud grunt, the rest of them straightened in alarm. She swept out her legs before they could fully register her renewed strength and knocked another off his feet.

Keep fighting.

There was an opening in the armor: just below the armpit, on either side above the ribs. Adresia bounded atop the fallen soldier and plunged one of his blades into the slit. He was dead before he could think to regrip his weapon.

Keep fighting.

With two blades a soldier jabbed at her. She easily deflected them, sending one down to slice his own leg. His angered response was just barely slow enough. She plunged her blade into his unprotected side and a moment later, he slumped beside the other corpse mere feet away.

Keep fighting.

Over and over, they launched themselves at her, growling and shouting with every companion that went down. She wasn't even close to being winded when the final soldier dropped to the crimson stained floor and she spun, looking for him—

Adresia's power flickered in her veins as she found Romliss holding a blade to Cota's throat. Her best friend swallowed, but beyond that, there was nothing. No hint of emotion. Because if he wasn't scared, she couldn't be either.

Tears streamed down Romliss's cheeks, and he ordered, "*Drop it.*"

Her dagger clattered to the floor and she raised her hands. "Don't."

He would do it. The look in his eyes—human, thankfully—was nothing short of maniacal. With trembling fingers, he pressed his blade harder against Cota's throat. "I told you to get *all* of us."

"Please," she breathed.

"I did *everything* I was told." His voice was hysterical. "I obeyed *every* order. And this is what I get? You...*murdering* my men yet again."

She flinched at the word before lifting her chin and stating, "You can't kill everyone here."

"Can't I? Maybe there are more soldiers outside, waiting for you to leave—just to obliterate you all anyway."

Her voice broke as she said, "You are going to *die* for what you've done."

Remembering the repeated promise, his glistening gaze met hers. "Not before I kill him." Romliss plunged the blade toward her best friend.

Adresia reached out with a desperate cry when, faster than she thought possible, Cota twisted out of the man's grasp and shoved the blade into the Romliss's own chest.

The man looked at her the same way she looked at him: disbelief that it hadn't been her, that he actually hadn't won. And then he toppled to the floor, clutching his chest, his fear cutting through the air like a knife.

The entire room watched until that pool of blood around him stopped growing, until he ceased to move, until no more sound came from his mouth and his heartbeat halted altogether, even as that wild fear still shone in his sandy eyes. But then that same look of horror flashed across Cota's face, and Adresia followed his gaze to the corpse—to the dagger embedded deep in Romliss's chest.

The dagger she'd coated in ice.

Chapter 60

Adresia was covered in the blood of those creatures. She shifted uncomfortably in the armchair, clenching and unclenching her sticky fingers, her stained dress clinging to her skin. The multiple scrapes on her limbs stitched together as the Infirma's effects finally wore off.

Cota inhaled sharply from the other side of the table, a hand over his mouth. His eyes darted back and forth as they had for the past half hour: at the dagger atop the table before them, at his feet. The dagger. His feet. The overbearing silence had long since burdened her.

The blood on the blade had dried, but the icy handle had yet to thaw, like her magic wanted her to remember the night and all the lives she hadn't been able to save. *Your fault*, it seemed to say. *Their blood is on your hands.*

Cota finally raised his head. "How long?" The bitterness in his tone wasn't fully suppressed. It struck her harder than she'd anticipated, and when she opened her mouth to explain, the words stuck in her throat. "Long enough, right?"

She blinked away the burning in her eyes. "I was shocked too."

He scoffed.

"I didn't want to keep this from you," she said.

"Then why did you?"

"Because, I—" She paused, unsure what to say. In all the weeks she'd hidden the truth, she hadn't yet prepared an answer.

"To keep me safe?" he prompted sardonically. "To protect me?" She went to say *yes*, but he was already shaking his head. "You kept this from me even though we *promised* no more secrets."

"I—I was doing what's best for you—"

"What's best for *me*?" He released the hold on his emotions as he rose. She saw it in the way his fingers anxiously wiggled at his sides, in the way his voice trembled ever so slightly. "You were only thinking of yourself. Like *always*."

"I'm sorry." She stood too. "I'm *sorry*. I wanted to tell you, but—"

"I heard what Narissa said that day in the Throne Room," he said. "That you were hiding it because of me." She went as still as death, every word a knife to her heart. "And the *lake*...you broke through the ice because of your magic, and I trusted you enough to ignore what was right in front of my face: that you were *lying* to me." He shook his head in disbelief, golden hair swaying. "All of those years of training, you *let* me beat you. I knew you were better. Stronger. But I didn't think..." A shaky exhale. "You used me. You made me believe you needed protecting, and all along, I was fooling myself."

Her words tumbled out, quick and panicked. "I saw how you reacted when you heard about the mage. It *terrified* you. And I was so afraid you would detest me for it—for being something I can't control. I thought if you knew, you would hate me."

"*Hate* you?" He breathed a laugh, full of sorrow and anger and strife. "After *everything* we've been through, you thought I would hate you? I thought you trusted me. I thought you *needed* me." She reached for him with bloody hands, but he stepped away, practically recoiling from her. "But you don't. You never have." She couldn't stop her rising agony as he backed toward the door, his gaze empty and hollow. "I don't trust you." His voice broke. "I don't *know* you."

"Cota, wait—"

"Don't follow me, Adresia."

The door rattled as it slammed shut.

Chapter 61

Caspian couldn't have known, right?

It was the only question on Cota's mind as he strode toward the Hand's room after half an hour of mindlessly wandering the corridors, intent on finding out the truth.

Blood caked the lines of his palms. He didn't care about the men. Especially not when he'd found out they weren't human. They deserved to die, and he was glad their parents' murderer was rotting outside the walls alongside them. But their deaths hadn't been what had rocked him to his core.

It'd been Adresia's magic.

And maybe he'd been too harsh, too quick to judge. Maybe he should have given her time to explain. He didn't have anything against it. It scared him, yes, but everything made sense now; their entire life, he'd known she was different. Special. He just...hadn't expected the betrayal. He never would have thought her capable of doing that to him.

He hadn't meant the things he'd said. Not entirely. He'd been confused and shocked, and after the disaster of a night they'd had, he hadn't been able to withhold whatever was brewing inside of him. Like an idiot, he'd let emotions cloud reason. Like an idiot, he'd left her alone when she probably needed him more than ever.

He was halfway through the covered walkway when footsteps sounded behind him. His stomach fluttered at the idea of trying to mend the damage of his words, but the guilt wasn't enough to keep him from apologizing, from understanding. They'd experienced too much together for this to be what pulled them apart. So he turned around.

But it wasn't Adresia.

Chapter 62

The images and sounds replayed on a loop, violent and haunting and stirring.

Romliss grinning at a broken Court.

Gillian crumpling to the floor with tear-stained cheeks.

That lethal blade plunging toward Cota's chest.

Narissa bowing her head.

It was that final image that kept Adresia marching through the castle, her stormy eyes glinting with that same ferocity those black-armored soldiers had had an hour ago before she'd ended them.

The Queen hadn't cared—hadn't even *tried*. Because she'd been afraid or surprised, Adresia didn't know. But because of it, half the Court was dead. Because of it, Gillian was gone. Because of it, Cota now despised Adresia.

She replayed the evening in her head, over and over, trying to figure out what went wrong, how two dozen intruders had gotten past the entire Shield and wreaked havoc upon the castle, why she hadn't sensed the explosion and Romliss's arrival. Elettra was in Dazelle. Rebels were *everywhere*. Someone should have seen something. Someone should have warned them.

Ash and dust and dirt stained the marbled, empty corridors. Outside, the Inner Gardens were barren and abandoned, looking like a century-old ruin with its crumbled wall. Only the still-flaming decorations indicated the destruction had recently transpired. The halls were eerie, silent. Empty.

It'd been an hour since those creatures had tried to kill her—since the Elettra hadn't come. As always, Adresia was on her own to finish the plan.

She rounded the next corner before halting. Three servants stood in the middle of the corridor. Over their tattered clothes were fighting leathers, and at their waists, weapons were strapped to their belts. They beheld the Countess's bloodied dress in fearful awe.

"Where is she?" Adresia's words bounced off the walls so suddenly, so loudly, that the rebels flinched. "Where is Elettra?"

The left one, a tall woman with auburn hair, stepped forward bravely. "Run, while you still have the chance."

"Why would I do that?"

"Because she did."

Adresia's eyes widened. "El–Elettra's gone?"

"We watched her leave the city. Watched her walk straight into the woods with someone else—a man."

The Countess let out a trembling exhale. "When?"

"Right before the explosion."

There was a heavy pause in which the words settled into Adresia's soul, ruffling her calm composure, disturbing the hopeful longing she'd clung to for the past hour. She took a slow, unbelieving step back, then another, and before she knew it, she was sprinting down the halls, panic and trepidation surging up her throat like fire.

Elettra had known. She'd known about Romliss and she hadn't warned them—warned *anyone*. Instead of staying, instead of waiting to see if Adresia survived, instead of seizing this opportunity to execute their plan smoother than they could have ever anticipated, the woman had fled. Not once had she shown doubt toward overthrowing the Queen or confronting the defensive measures of this castle. No...this was different. Something else was coming. Something big.

Something Elettra was scared of facing.

The Countess bounded down the foyer's stairs, whirled around the bottom post—and halted as she beheld the Queen five steps ahead. The woman stopped too, raven hair spilling over her shoulders. She'd changed into a dark, plum gown, so clean and unscathed compared to the crimson still staining Adresia's body, so readily able to ignore the tragedy of what had occurred that night.

Rage and grief gripped Adresia by the throat, and the demands of reality slipped away into a distant memory. The Countess couldn't do anything else besides blurt, "Why?"

"Why what?" Narissa asked.

"You know what."

There was a twitch of a smile. "I know a lot of things. You'll have to be more specific."

Adresia's fingers itched for a blade that wasn't there. "Those people were *your* people—*your* Court. Gillian was *your* servant. And you just let them die."

Narissa lifted her chin in the slightest. "A necessary sacrifice."

The words were like a slap to the face. "What?"

"Dying for one's kingdom leaves an impressive legacy."

Gray eyes widened in enraged disbelief. "Th—They weren't *martyred*. They were *murdered*." She huffed a stunned breath in realization. The reaction she had been expecting was nowhere to be found. "You don't even care, do you?"

"It cost me something to do what I did, Adresia."

"What—*kneeling*?" The woman opened her mouth, but Adresia continued in a fury, "You just *sat* there while *I* killed those men. *I* stopped Romliss. *I* saved our Court."

"Did you?"

Adresia receded a step and looked—truly *looked*—at the Queen, at her unbothered, relieved posture and the expectant twinkle in those violet eyes. Romliss had known exactly where to enter the castle undetected, how to remove the Shield without notice, when to rig the explosion in the conveniently vacant servant quarters.

Like someone had told him.

"You planned that massacre," Adresia breathed.

"*I* didn't do anything," Narissa said with a snake-like smile.

Something altered in the world as that horrifying truth arose in startling clarity. "You're working for Him, too."

"We needed you to kill those men."

The ground swayed beneath Adresia's feet. "I—I almost died because I was being *used*?"

The woman waved her hand dismissively. "Don't act so shocked. From the beginning, you were made into something for someone else. You have been born and molded to serve me, just like everyone else. I will not apologize for doing my duty as your Sovereign—"

Narissa went silent as a spear of ice appeared at her throat. Adresia said dangerously, quietly, "You are not my master. You are my rival and oppressor and *enemy*, and I will destroy you as the last of our kind: *Bane against Bane.*"

She made to step closer, but Narissa said, "You don't know how long I've been waiting for that confession." And when a wicked grin appeared on the Queen's lips and those violet eyes flickered with something wild and raw and terrifying, Adresia's courage crumbled.

No. She'd almost had it. She'd been so *close*—

Magic took hold of the Countess, paralyzing her limbs and body, controlling her movements. Her weapon slipped from her fingers as she was forced to her knees. Narissa didn't have to raise a finger. Like a shadow from her being, darkness floated from the Queen. It slithered toward Adresia as if it had a mind of its own. "This has always been the plan," the woman said. "*You* have always been the plan."

Adresia shivered as that eerie, onyx power got closer and snarled, "Let me go."

"How many rebels do you think will have to die before they realize they never stood a chance?"

Dread blanketed Adresia's senses. "No," she breathed.

"How much longer do you think they will last when He finally stands unopposed?"

"*No*," she repeated as that threatening darkness snaked around her limbs and curled up her face. But her plea did nothing. The magic drowned her senses and thoughts and mind like water so fully, so irreversibly, that a strangled whimper left her throat.

"My descent was not easy," Narissa said, "but I did it. For this—for you. I will not let that gift slip between my fingers again."

Adresia fought with everything she had to unfurl her hands, to break free from the invisible, painful chains constraining her, to resist the fear curdling every ounce of will she had left.

"Today marks the start of a new beginning," the woman continued. "My dominion will be purged of its disloyalty, its disobedience, and—as you have so kindly made clear—its only threat."

"Please," Adresia whispered, shaking her head as if she could stop the tear that slipped down her cheek, as if she could reject the inevitable fate that she had so foolishly not anticipated, that she had so naively let herself become trapped in, as if she could staunch the humiliation that came with her begging.

Violet eyes appeared an inch from Adresia's face. "Don't be afraid." Narissa's voice was strikingly soft, disorientingly tender. "Everything has worked out how it was meant to. Now, I can instill order to this fragmented land. Now, you won't have to suffer. Now, you won't have to live in pain." The woman grazed the Countess's cheek with a finger, and as gentle as a lover, smiled. "Don't worry. I'll make sure your friends know just how little their glorious Savior's pleas did to stop their heads from going on pikes."

Adresia lunged forward. It was far enough to make Narissa to step back in sudden surprise, but those shadows were too tight, too thick. She was brutally wrenched back to her knees. And as that crack sounded, as the marble floor cracked beneath her bones, Adresia made her final promise with a broken sob. "You will *never* win."

Narissa's grin had nothing human in it. "I don't have to." And then the Queen of Morolyn grabbed Adresia's face in her hands and unleashed the hold on her magic.

Chapter 63

The Queen waited an hour after the calamity in the Throne Room before ordering the Court to bury their dead, if they could find a body. It was fitting, Caspian thought, that the woman who had fought so little to save the lives of her people was now dismissing them as she cowered in her castle and hid in humiliation.

It'd been two hours since Caspian last saw Adresia. Two hours in which he hadn't rested or let himself think about the tragedy of what had happened at the festival. Two hours in which he had thought of nothing but her, of what she'd done, of her undeniable, awestriking, wondrous power.

From the window in his chambers, he watched the last of the carriages depart through the southeastern gate and into the city. The nobles that hadn't immediately fled had been ordered back to their estates until the threat of another attack was settled and defenses were restored. Servants were rarely seen, having relocated to the north wing to escape their exposed quarters that had been home to the explosion. Guards were even scarcer. Only an appalling twenty seven of the five hundred men in the Shield were left. They'd been found in the dungeons, merely incapacitated, thank the gods. A profound, anticipatory silence now inhabited the corridors.

Until the door to Caspian's study flew open and Cota stumbled in, bloodshot eyes stark against panicked green.

Adresia was in his arms, limp and unmoving.

Caspian's seat went tumbling backward, and he raced toward them, but Corvina appeared behind Cota, breathing hard. And at the horror in her golden eyes...Caspian felt a fear he hadn't allowed himself to in a long, long while. "Narissa's infantry," she said. "They're ten miles away." The Princess looked at Adresia. "They're coming for her."

"Is she—"

"Alive," Corvina stated, face pale. "But something's been done to her. Some sort of spell."

"How do we wake her?" Cota asked desperately.

"I don't know."

Caspian and the Princess shared a look before the Hand said, "I might know someone who can." He grabbed his sheathed sword beside the door and strapped it to his belt. "But we need to leave. Now. Grab what you need."

Cota lifted Adresia higher. "I already did."

Corvina pulled a small bag over her shoulder. "Me too."

Caspian nodded, and with long, deep breath, he gave himself ten seconds to look at the room, to study the things he would likely never see again, the luxuries he was about to forfeit.

When the ten seconds were up, he gestured for them to follow.

There was no one to stop them as they silently strode through the corridors, as they snatched several bags of food from the kitchens, and as they reached an obscured side door Caspian had used dozens of times throughout his life. He didn't think twice before pulling it open.

There was a sharp inhale, and Caspian heard Kasya's horrified voice before he saw her. "Adresia?" She stood with Fox beside several horses, a torch in her hand. The knight balked at the sight of them.

"There's no time to explain," Corvina said before gripping the reins of a black mare and saddling it. "We can't stay here."

Fox got over his shock enough to take Adresia in his arms. "Where is it safe?" he asked.

"Probably nowhere," Cota answered as he saddled his steed, a brown horse with white flecks. "But anywhere is better than here." The knight helped lift and strap Adresia atop the mare so she was secured against Cota's chest.

"What about the plan?" Kasya asked.

Caspian whirled toward her, and Fox sheepishly said, "I filled her in."

"It's fine," Caspian said. "The rebels didn't come. So wherever Elettra is, whatever is going on…the plan isn't happening tonight." It was only once he'd saddled his mare did he realize there weren't any more. "Why are there only three horses?"

Fox wrapped an arm around Kasya's waist and said, "We're not going."

Caspian's stomach dropped. "What?"

"You'll need someone on the inside," Kasya explained. "We can help you from here."

Caspian opened his mouth, but Fox interjected, "Don't argue. Just go."

The Hand stared at one of his oldest friends and the soft-hearted servant at his side. There were so many words he could say and yet he had no idea which ones to pick. "Don't die," he said at last.

The knight just gazed toward Adresia with glassy eyes and replied, "Tell that to her."

Corvina glanced toward the castle and asked Caspian, "Aren't you going to—"

"No time," he stated before clicking his heels against his mare. The Hand didn't look at the castle as they rode into the Findara Forest. He didn't look at Kasya and Fox entering the side door, didn't listen to the mourning city, didn't wait for the infantry that would arrive at the castle unsettlingly soon. He just plunged into the pitch black night with three of his closest companions, praying he was right, praying he would find answers.

Cota guided them through the spruce trees over the next few hours, able to see better than either Caspian or Corvina could. The full moon twinkled above like a lulling fireplace and hooves crushed mossy soil in a soothing rhythm. Despite their growing exhaustion, they didn't want to stop. But Corvina yawned a fifth time within the span of two minutes, and Cota at last halted.

The Princess started drearily, "I'm *fine*—"

Cota shushed her, turning his head in different directions as if he could hear something they couldn't.

"What is it?" Caspian whispered, stalling his mare beside the Count.

"There's people nearby," Cota whispered back. "Two individuals."

"I don't hear anyone," Corvina said.

"Where?" Caspian asked.

Cota pointed to their left. "That way."

Caspian slid from his horse and handed the reins to Corvina. "Where are you going?" she asked.

"I'll be back soon," Caspian said. Normal people—besides themselves, of course—didn't wander this forest, and someone had to make sure they weren't being followed. "Get some rest." Before his friends could protest, he pulled the dagger from his belt and strode through the trees.

He didn't know how long or far he walked. It felt like two miles, but it could've been one hour or four. Time blended as easily as the darkness in front of—

Caspian halted. The darkness ahead wasn't completely dark. Flames flickered distantly between the trees. With slow, cautious steps, he continued forward, and when he reached the individuals sitting around the fire, he sheathed his sword and said as he stepped into the firelight, "So this is why you didn't show."

Torstein paused his wooden carving and looked up in surprise. Beside him, Elettra looked Caspian up and down before answering, "It is."

"Why did you run?"

"Good leaders know when they're outmatched."

"Good leaders don't underestimate the person the kingdom calls a Savior."

Elettra's smile was thin, snakelike. "And where is the Countess now?"

Caspian didn't know why, but he had a feeling it wasn't the wisest decision to tell her the truth. Not about this. Not about Narissa's power. So he lied, "She's obtaining what we need to defeat Her Majesty once and for all."

The woman's expression slipped. "Adresia's alive?"

Caspian crossed his arms slowly, analyzing the stunned words. "You expected her to fail?"

"I expected Narissa to have a plan of contingency. And then a backup plan for that backup plan. The Countess might have magic, but, like I said, she's inexperienced."

"So the agreement we struck, the role you were going to have her play...it was all a lie?"

"It was a distraction. She needed to think she was important—that she could face Narissa."

"You were using her as bait," he realized.

"People are resources."

"Adresia *can* face Narissa."

"Can she?"

A sharp, angered inhale. "Have you ever believed we could win?"

"I never said I didn't."

"You never said you did."

Elettra just lifted her chin, that wry smile returning.

"What's your plan?" he asked. "You fled for a reason."

"You fled too." At his pointed look, she professed, "To regain our numbers."

"Our numbers are fine."

Torstein huffed a laugh. "Not for long."

"You're talking about the infantry," Caspian said.

"The *infantry*," Elettra repeated sardonically. "It's not an infantry, Lord Hand. It's an army."

Something in Caspian's chest pulsed and trembled. "What?" he breathed. An army. Narissa had an *army*.

"They'll crush everything we hold dear."

"You—you knew that and yet, you were just going to let us die in that castle?"

"Wars cost lives."

Torstein stood, flipping his wooden spike around his hand. "I'd get farther from Dazelle, if I were you."

Caspian digested their information, the chaotic reality that they had just admitted was happening, allowing it to crack and contort the sliver of peace he had known for the briefest time in his life, before schooling his features in a sharp, gallant expression. "And I'd start running, if I were you."

"Are you threatening us?"

Caspian pulled out his sword, allowing a moment of silence to pass, a moment in which the marching of the Queen's army could be heard where they had begun stalking into the Findara Forest half a minute ago. And as it dawned on Elettra and Torstein, as their excessive pride shifted into unanticipated fear, Caspian couldn't help but feel a smug satisfaction.

Elettra's brown eyes danced in the firelight between them. "What's your plan, Lord Hand?"

"To go back to Dazelle."

"When?"

"As soon as I can."

"You're quite confident for someone who's running away."

"So are you."

She cocked her head. "I would wait."

"Well, then it's a good thing I'm not you," Caspian said as he began backing up, as he prepared to race back through the trees to his friends. "I'm not afraid of what I need to do and I'm willing to do it when it needs to happen." Moonlight spilled through crevices of the treetops like rods of light around him. "I'm going back, and I'm going to finish what you failed to do. I'm going to finish what was started five years ago. I'm going to keep fighting. And one day," Caspian declared as Narissa's monsters latched their claws into the soft flesh of this vulnerable kingdom, "we will be free."

Acknowledgments

My Jesus. The Ultimate Creator. The Artist of Life. Thank you for creating me with a facet of your imagination and creativity. Thank you for giving me the tools and means to share this story. Thank you for your provision throughout this journey and for instilling in me a passion to share who you are through this story. Lord, let me love this world into being. Let your grace turn anything not of you into something that can reflect your character. Author of Stories, rest upon the pages of this book. Oh Spirit of God, breathe life!

Mallory, thank you for investing in this story. Thank you for joining me these past seven years. Thank you for being there in the valleys and on the mountaintops. Your excitement and encouragement kept me eager to make this dream a reality. I wouldn't want anyone else to know this story like you do. I wouldn't want any other person to have heard it first.

Mom, Dad, Braxton, Breah, Keith, and the rest of my family: thank you for supporting me along this journey. Thank you for pushing me to achieve my dreams even when the world is screaming at me that it won't happen. Thank you for loving me, encouraging me, and believing in me.

To all of the friends who have supported me since seventh grade: I can't express how grateful I am that so many of you showed interest in my passion for writing and have cheered me on all these years. Every one of you—and I know you by name, there are just too many to list—has played a vital role in pushing me towards this dream when I felt like it wasn't possible. One message can change someone's life.

Everyone else who has been there for me through this journey—my college friends, my church, and so many more—I cannot articulate just how much of a blessing you all have been. Without your constant encouragement, this story may not have come to fruition.

And to you, reader: you are enough. You are seen. You are loved. Keep fighting.

About the Author

Maranda Bautsch is a fantasy author from south Texas. Storytelling became her passion at the age of twelve, and her writing career was kickstarted with her debut novel The Bane. Her childhood was spent recreating plots of her favorite Disney movies with an imagination built upon original pieces such as the Harry Potter series, the Percy Jackson series, and the Chronicles of Narnia. A lover of anything fantasy, sci-fi, and dystopian, Maranda thoughtfully crafts such worlds with the hopes of bringing magic into the daily life of all who pick up her book. She currently lives in College Station, Texas where she is working towards a bachelor's degree in Business Marketing at Texas A&M University.

Printed in the USA
CPSIA information can be obtained
at www.ICGtesting.com
LVHW050314310823
756768LV00004B/22